THE LEAK

FOR THE LOVE OF TRUTH

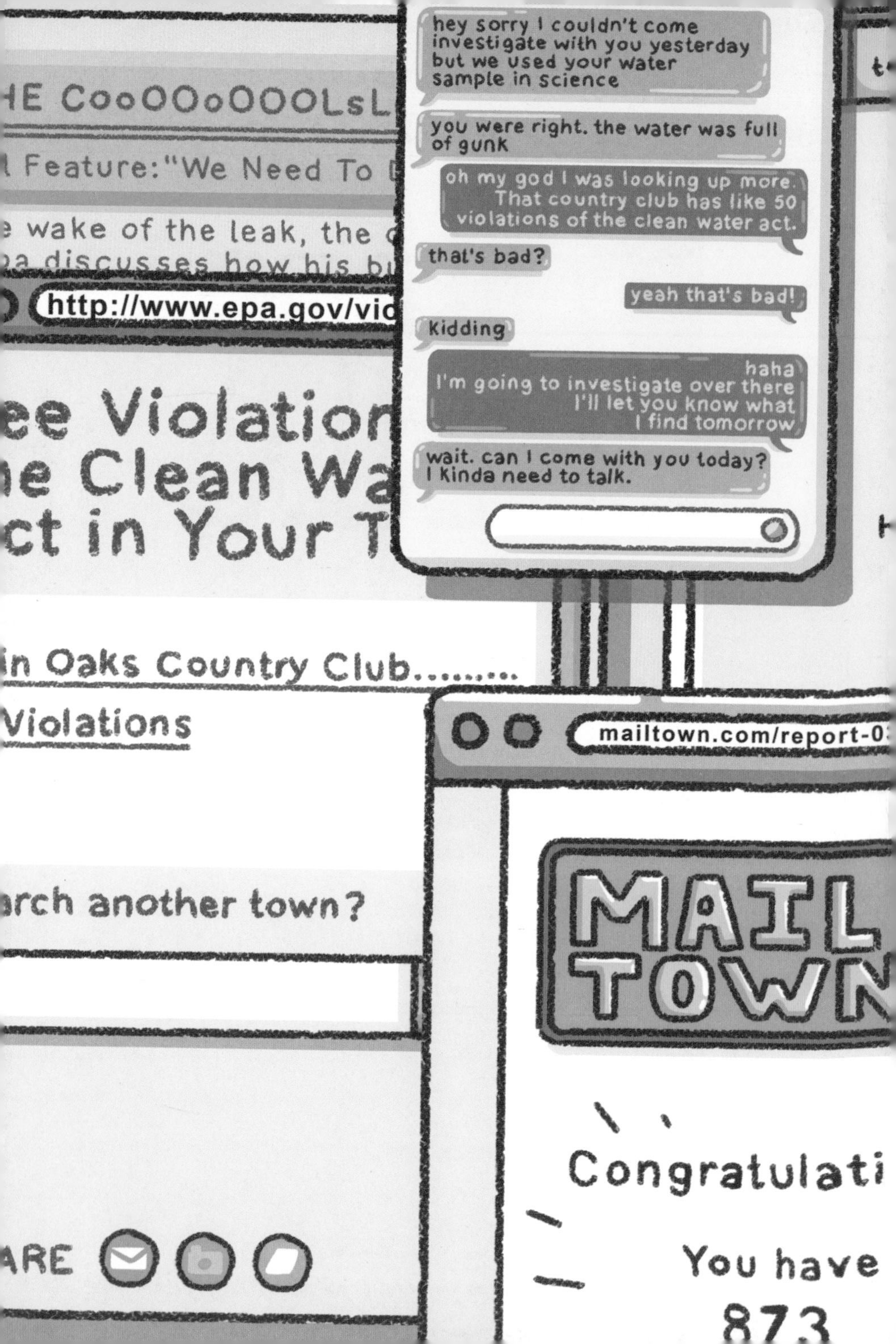
HE CooOOoOOOLsL
l Feature:"We Need To
e wake of the leak, the
http://www.epa.gov/vio
ee Violation
e Clean Wa
ct in Your T
in Oaks Country Club........
Violations
arch another town?
ARE
hey sorry I couldn't come investigate with you yesterday but we used your water sample in science
you were right. the water was full of gunk
oh my god I was looking up more. That country club has like 50 violations of the clean water act.
that's bad?
yeah that's bad!
Kidding
haha
I'm going to investigate over there
I'll let you know what
I find tomorrow
wait. can I come with you today? I kinda need to talk.
mailtown.com/report-0
MAIL
TOWN
Congratulati
You have
873

THE LEAK

FOR THE LOVE OF TRUTH

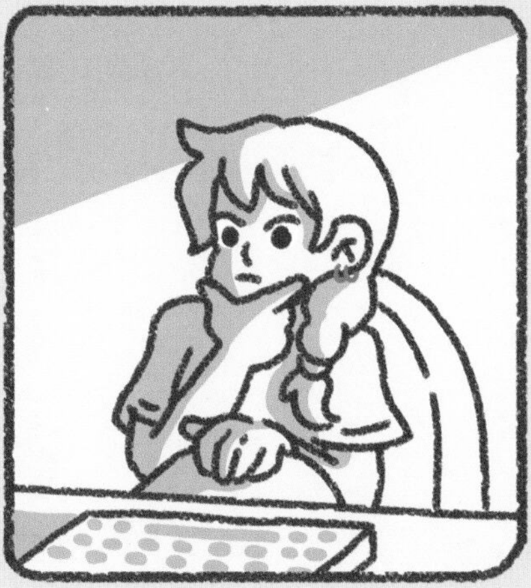

WRITTEN BY
KATE REED PETTY

ART BY
ANDREA BELL

:01
First Second
NEW YORK

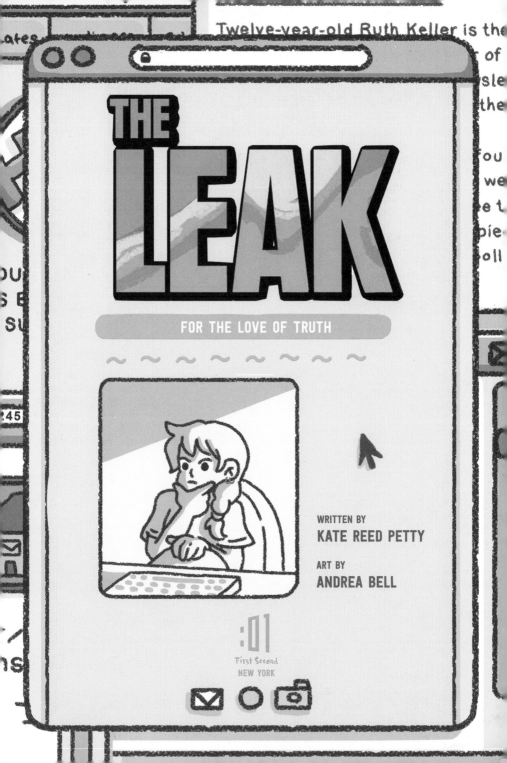

This book is for the people of Flint, Michigan

and for Susan Bell Knisely —Kate
and for Liz Bell —Andrea

First Second

Text Copyright © 2021 by Kathryn Petty

Illustration Copyright © 2021 by Andrea Bell

Published by First Second

First Second is an imprint of Roaring Brook Press, a division of Holtzbrinck Publishing Holdings Limited Partnership

120 Broadway, New York, NY 10271

Don't miss your next favorite book from First Second! For the latest updates go to firstsecondnewsletter.com and sign up for our enewsletter.

Hardback ISBN: 978-1-250-21795-0
Paperback ISBN: 978-1-250-21796-7

Our books may be purchased in bulk for promotional, educational, or business use. Please contact your local bookseller or the Macmillan Corporate and Premium Sales Department at (800) 221-7945 ext. 5442 or by email at MacmillanSpecialMarkets@macmillan.com.

First edition, 2021

FIRST EDITION

Edited by Mark Siegel and Samia Fakih
Cover design by Kirk Benshoff
Interior design by Sunny Lee
Printed in China by RR Donnelley Asia Printing Solutions Ltd., Dongguan City, Guangdong Province

Digitally inked with a soft 8B lead-type of pencil-brush and thoughtfully colored in Photoshop.

Paperback: 10 9 8 7 6 5 4 3 2 1
Hardcover: 10 9 8 7 6 5 4 3 2 1

BY ART WE LIVE

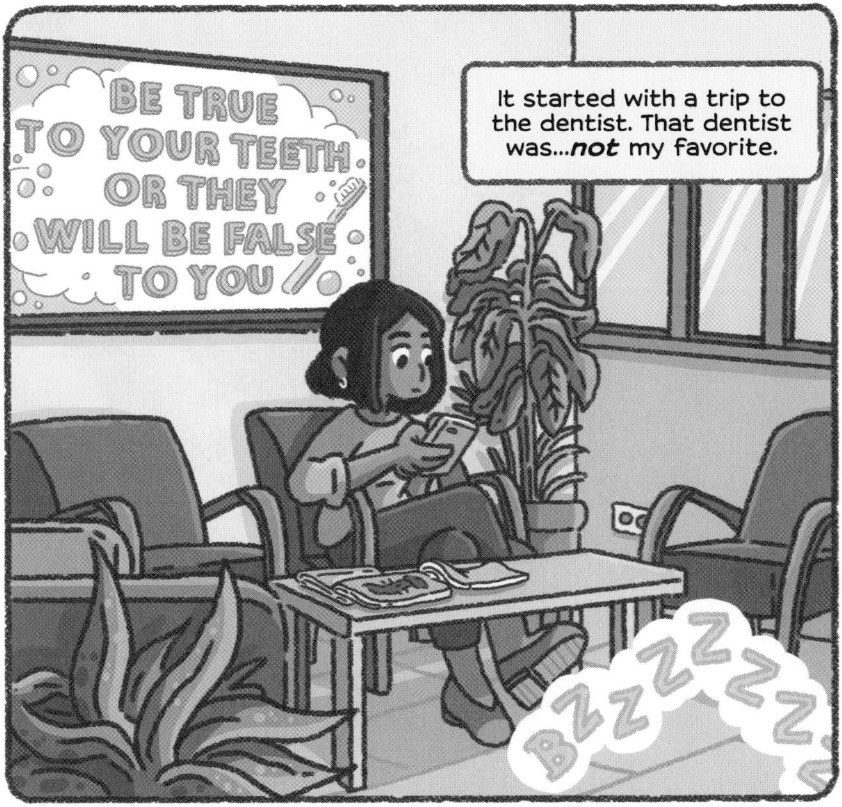
BE TRUE TO YOUR TEETH OR THEY WILL BE FALSE TO YOU
It started with a trip to the dentist. That dentist was...***not*** my favorite.
BZZZZZZZ

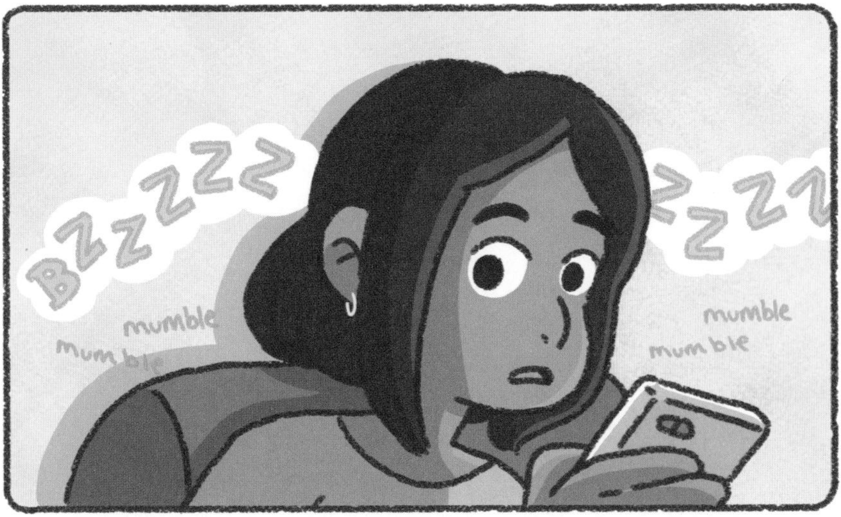
BZZZZZZ
ZZZZ
mumble
mumble
mumble
mumble

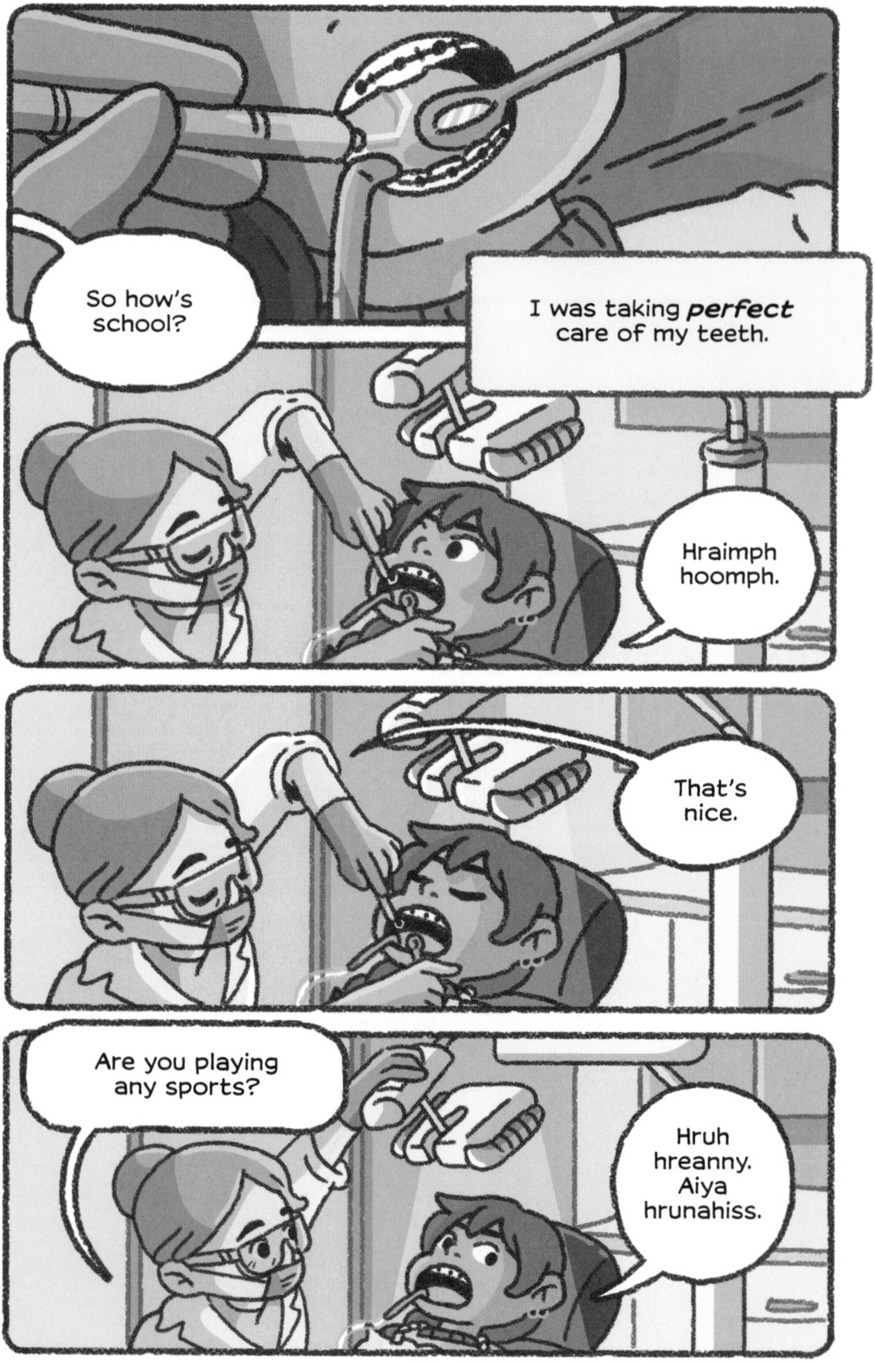
So how's school?
I was taking ***perfect*** care of my teeth.
Hraimph hoomph.
That's nice.
Are you playing any sports?
Hruh hreanny. Aiya hrunahiss.

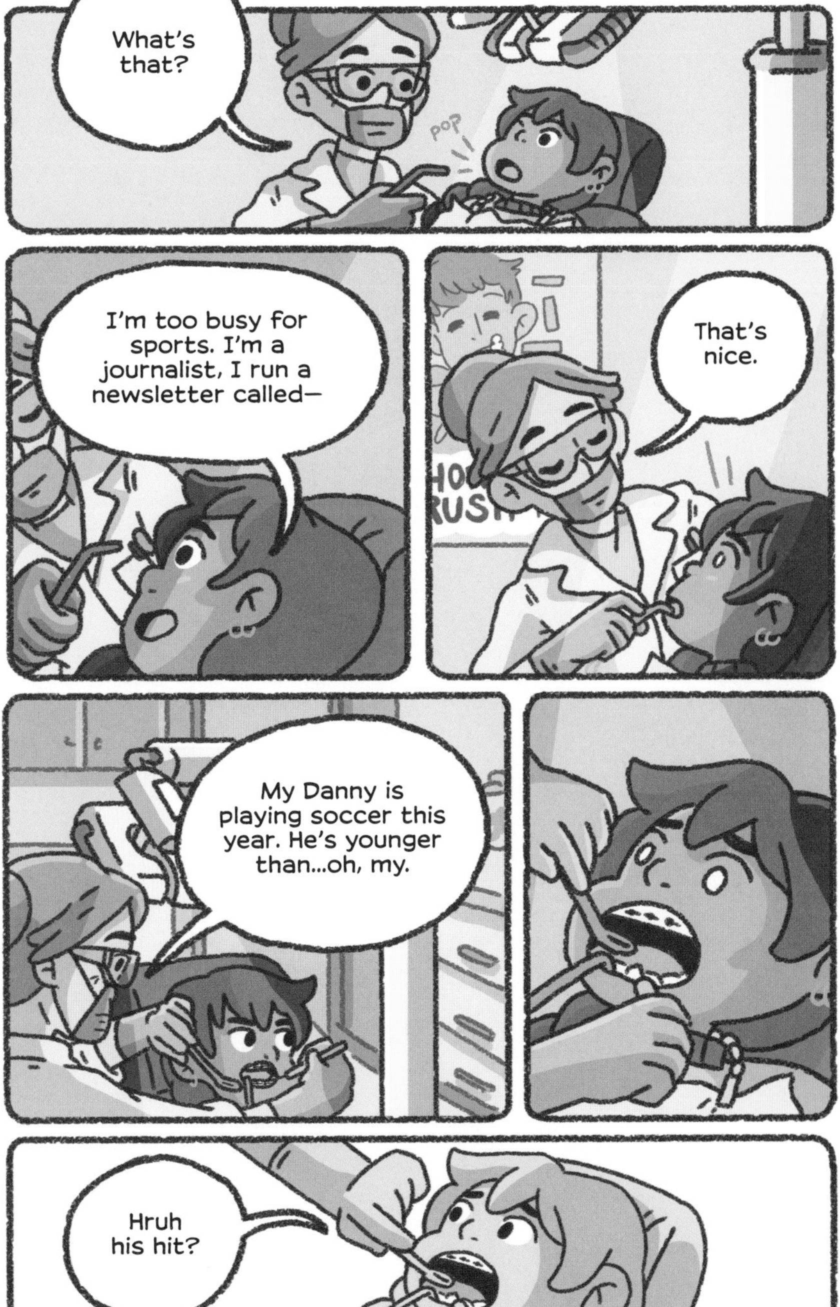
What's that?
POP
I'm too busy for sports. I'm a journalist, I run a newsletter called—
That's nice.
My Danny is playing soccer this year. He's younger than...oh, my.
Hruh his hit?

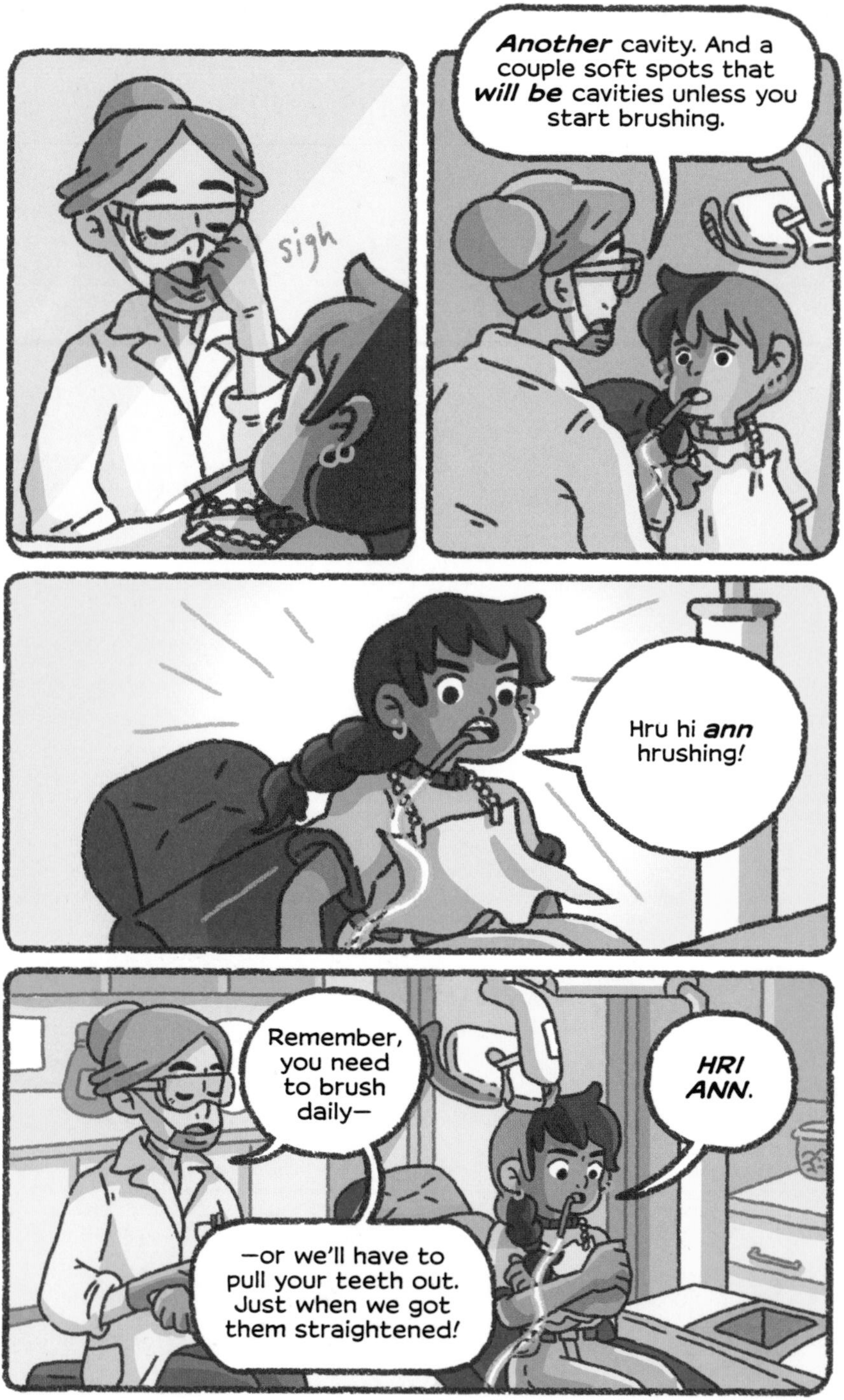
sigh
Another cavity. And a couple soft spots that ***will be*** cavities unless you start brushing.
Hru hi ***ann*** hrushing!
Remember, you need to brush daily—
—or we'll have to pull your teeth out. Just when we got them straightened!
HRI ANN.

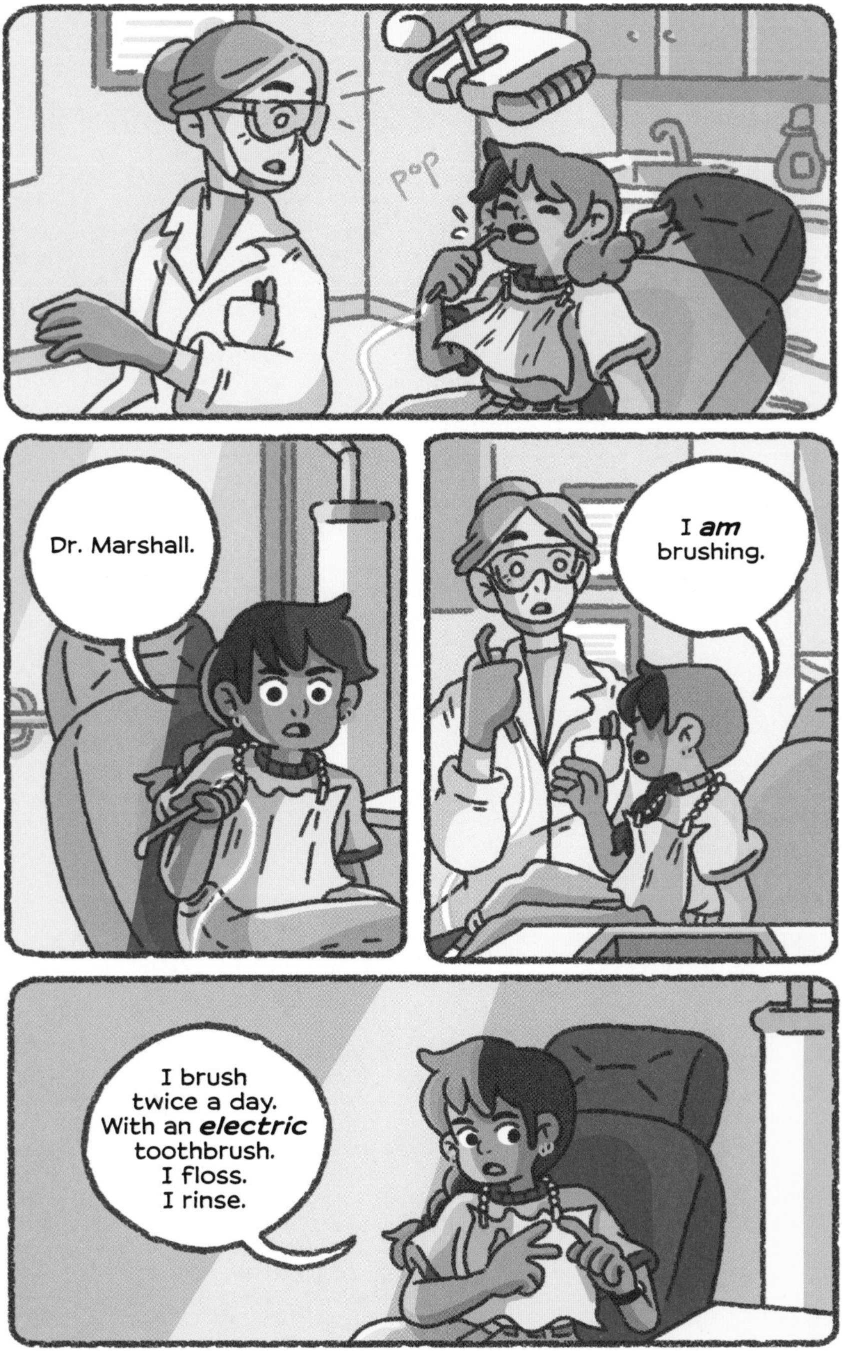
pop
Dr. Marshall.
I *am* brushing.
I brush twice a day. With an *electric* toothbrush. I floss. I rinse.

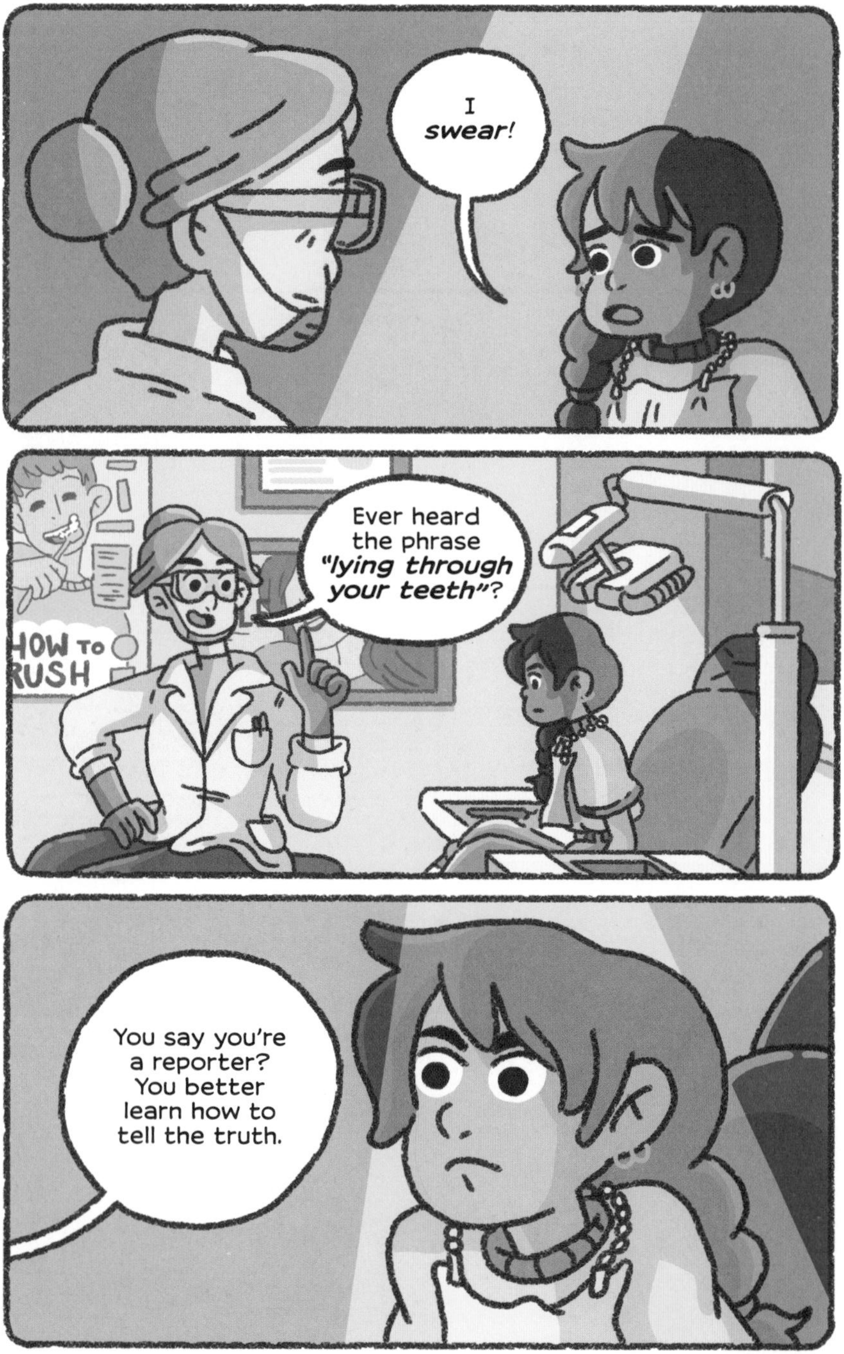
I *swear*!
Ever heard the phrase ***"lying through your teeth"***?
HOW TO
RUSH
You say you're a reporter? You better learn how to tell the truth.

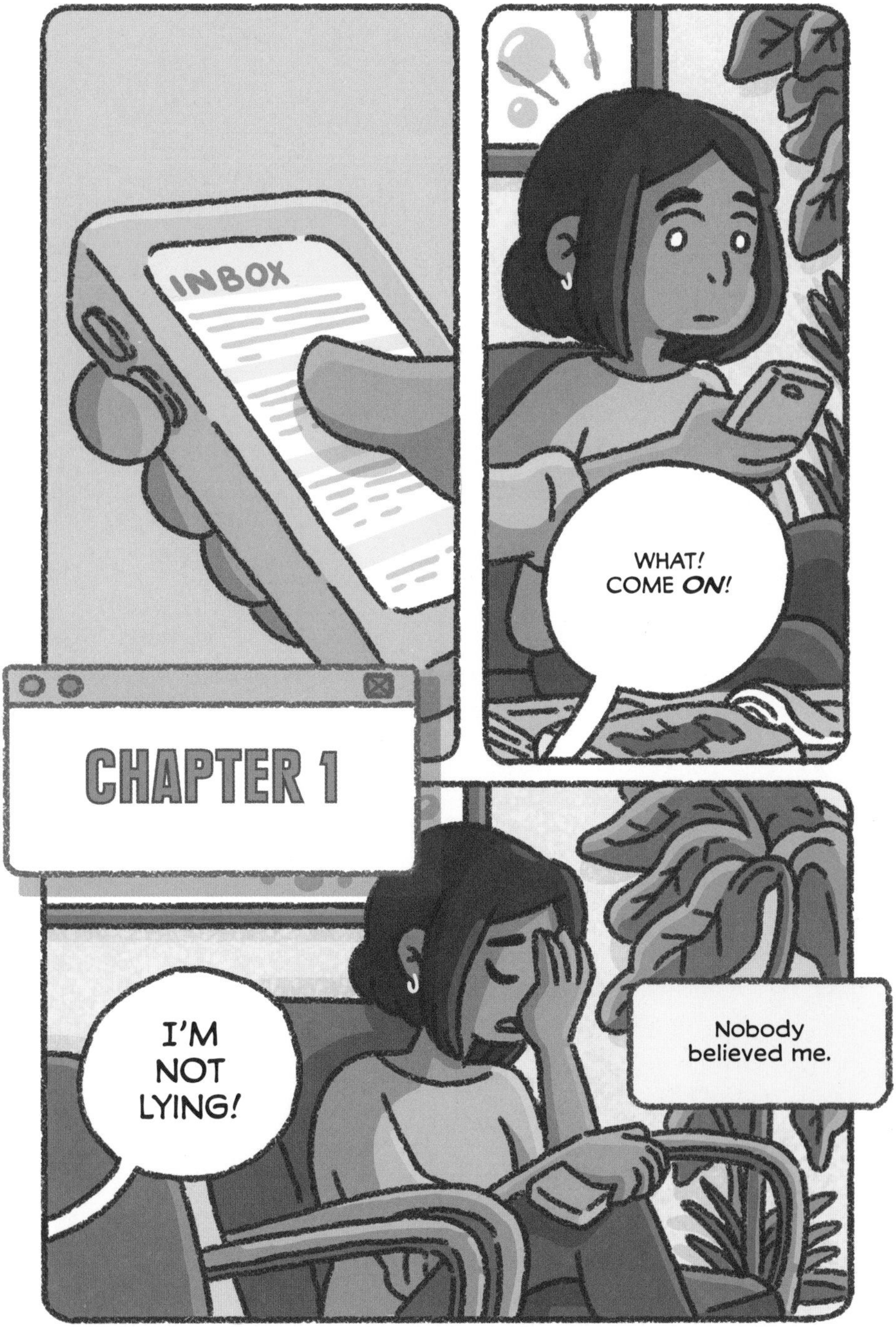
INBOX
CHAPTER 1
WHAT! COME *ON*!
I'M NOT LYING!
Nobody believed me.

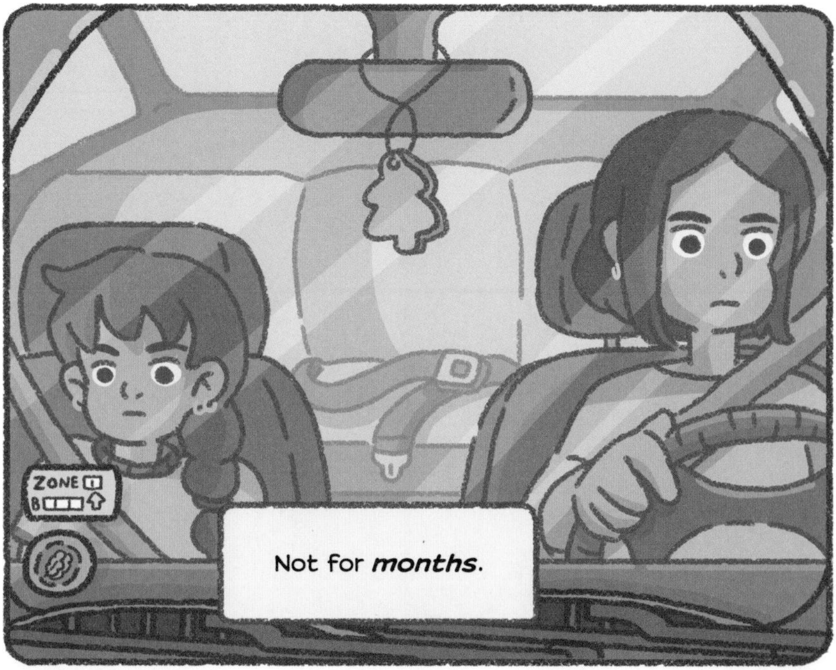
ZONE
Not for *months*.

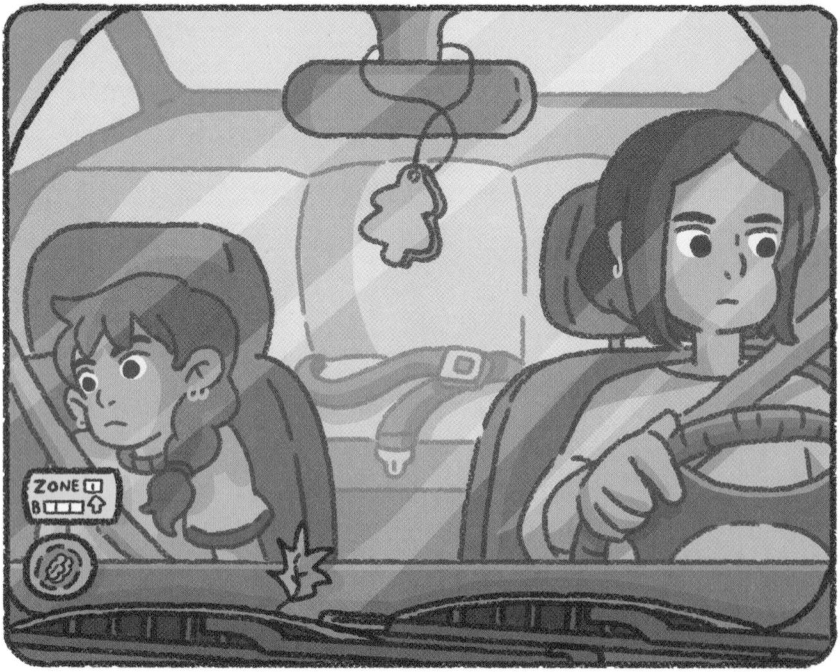
ZONE

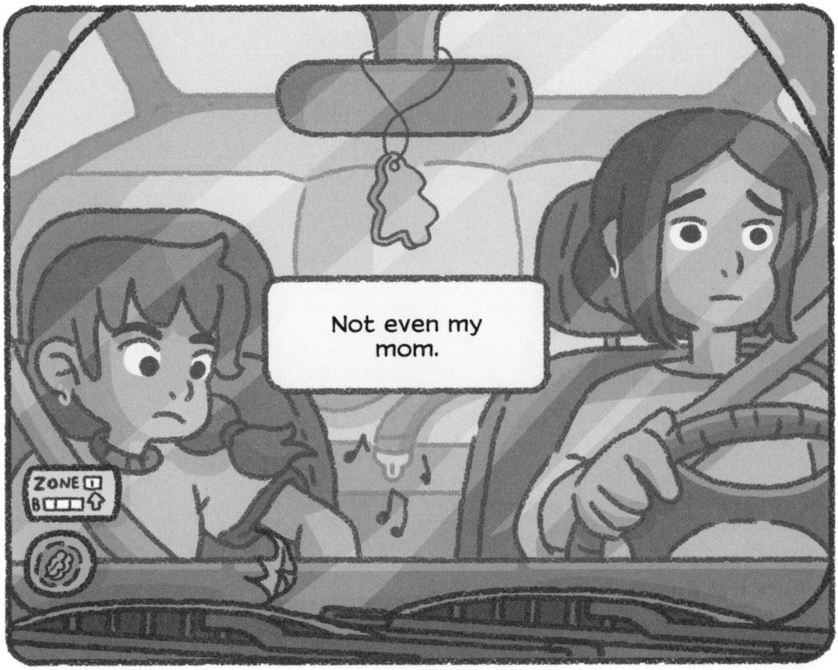
Not even my mom.

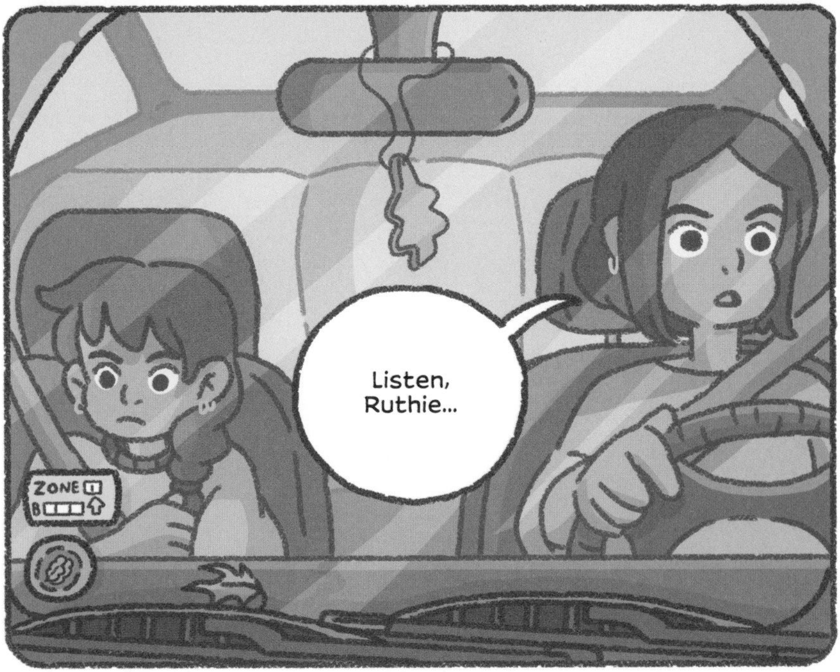
ZONE
Listen, Ruthie...

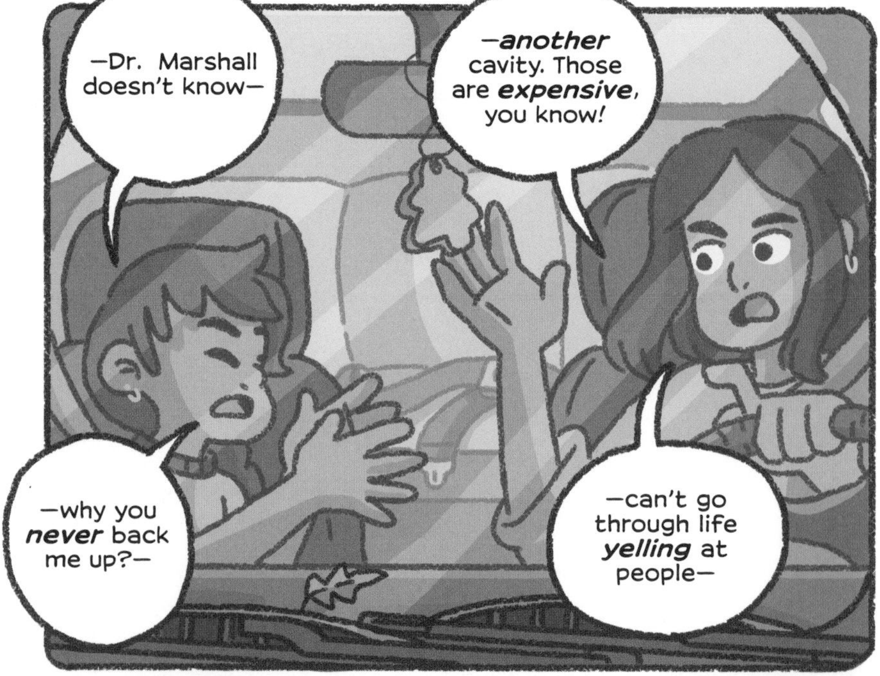
—Dr. Marshall doesn't know—
—*another* cavity. Those are *expensive*, you know!
—why you *never* back me up?—
—can't go through life *yelling* at people—

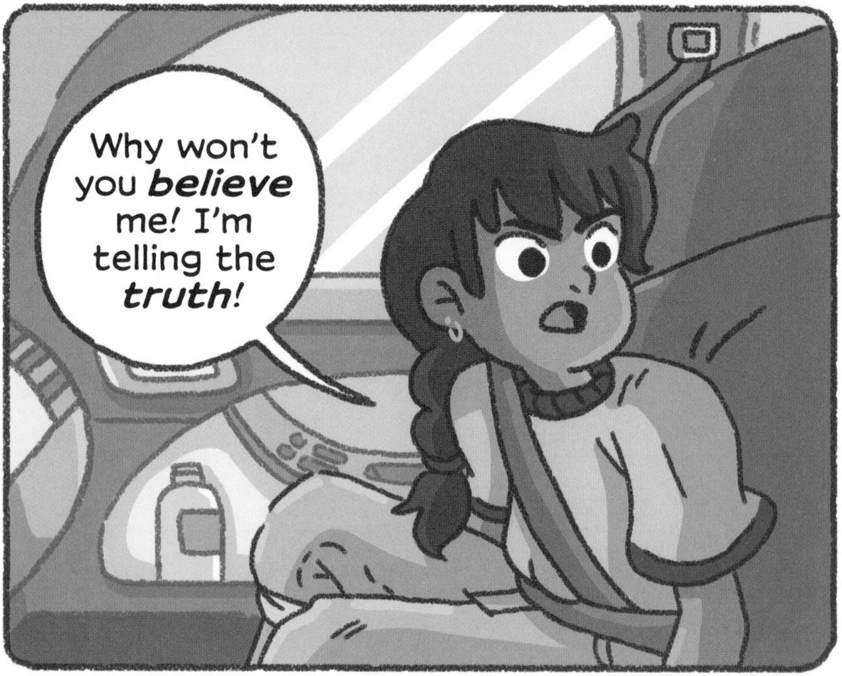
Why won't you *believe* me! I'm telling the *truth*!

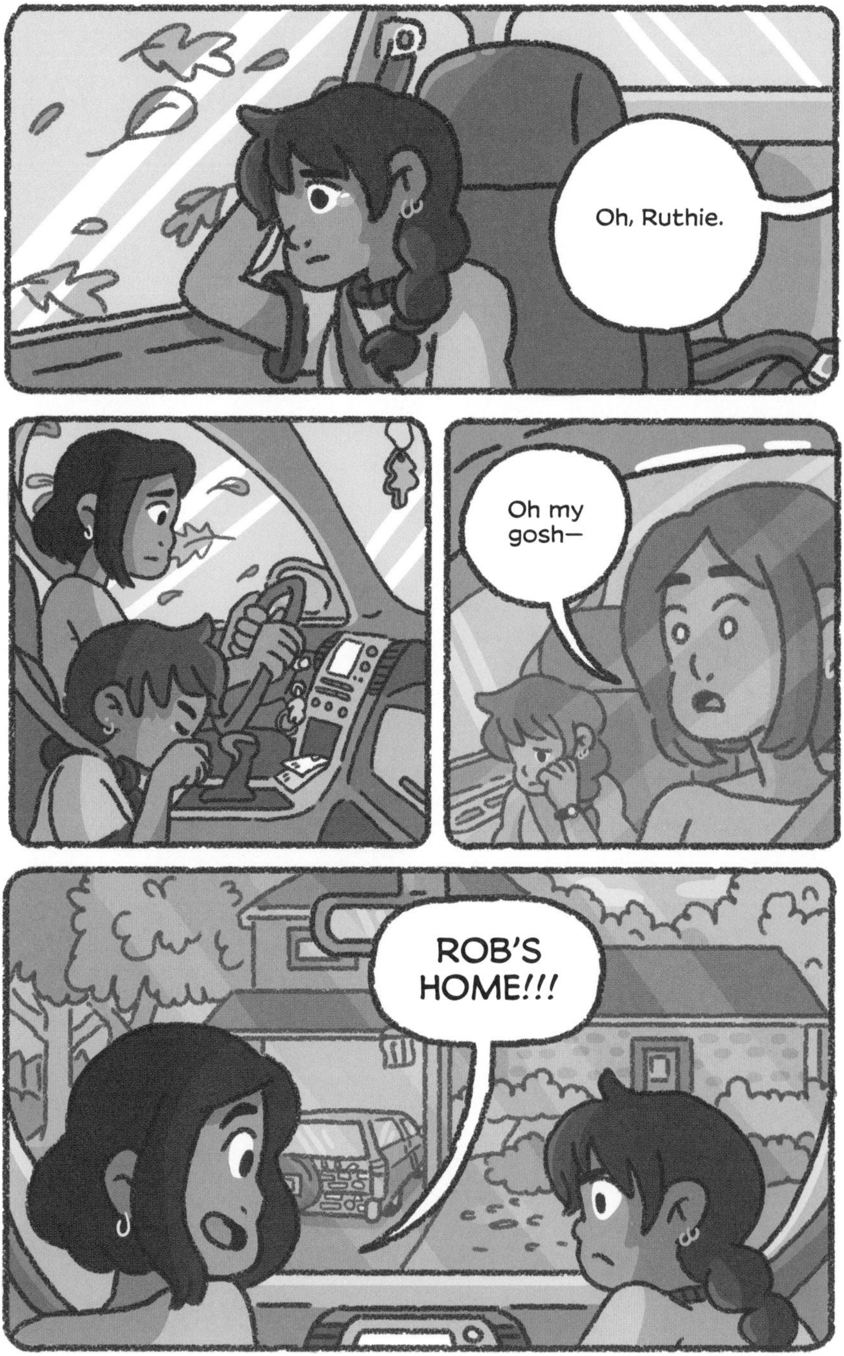
Oh, Ruthie.
Oh my gosh—
ROB'S HOME!!!

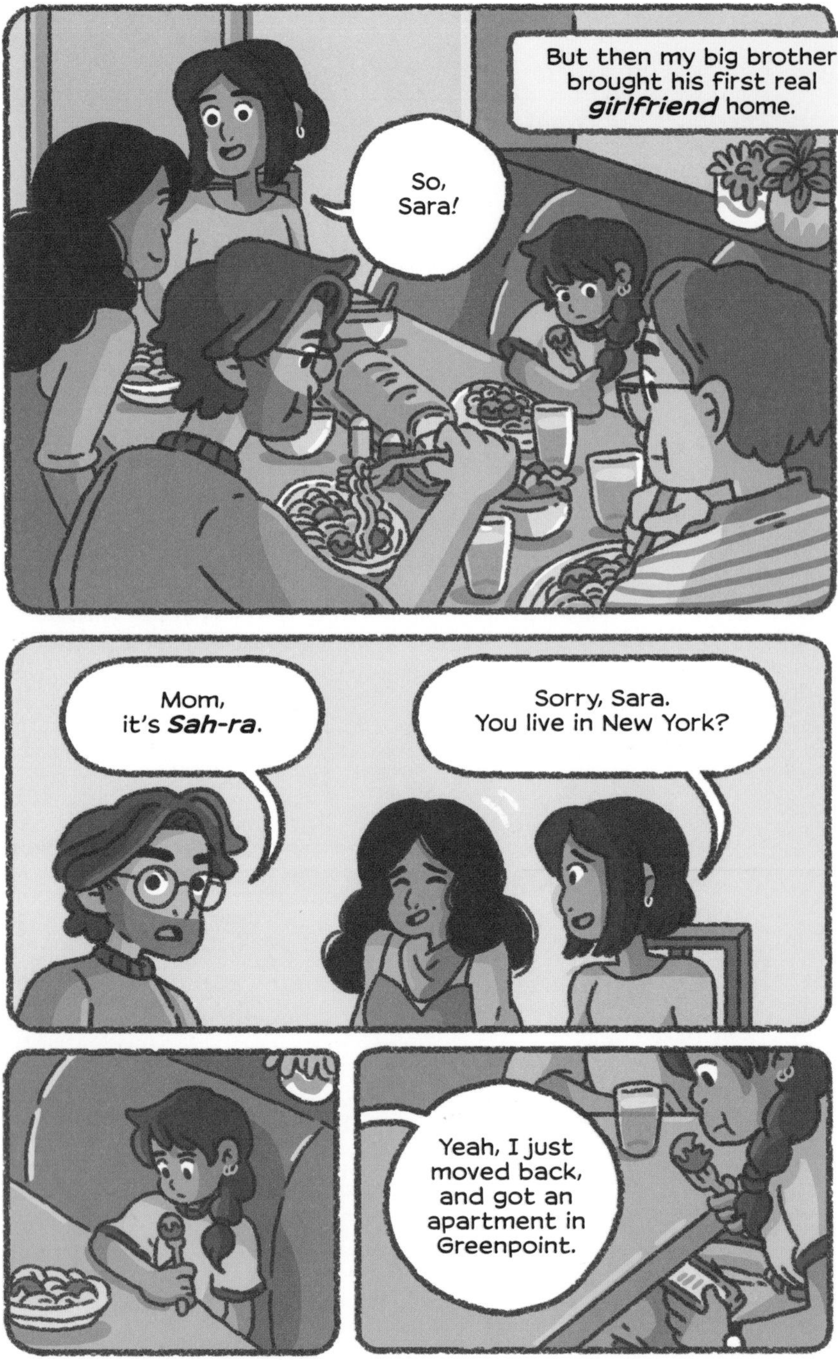
But then my big brother brought his first real ***girlfriend*** home.
So, Sara!
Mom, it's ***Sah-ra***.
Sorry, Sara. You live in New York?
Yeah, I just moved back, and got an apartment in Greenpoint.

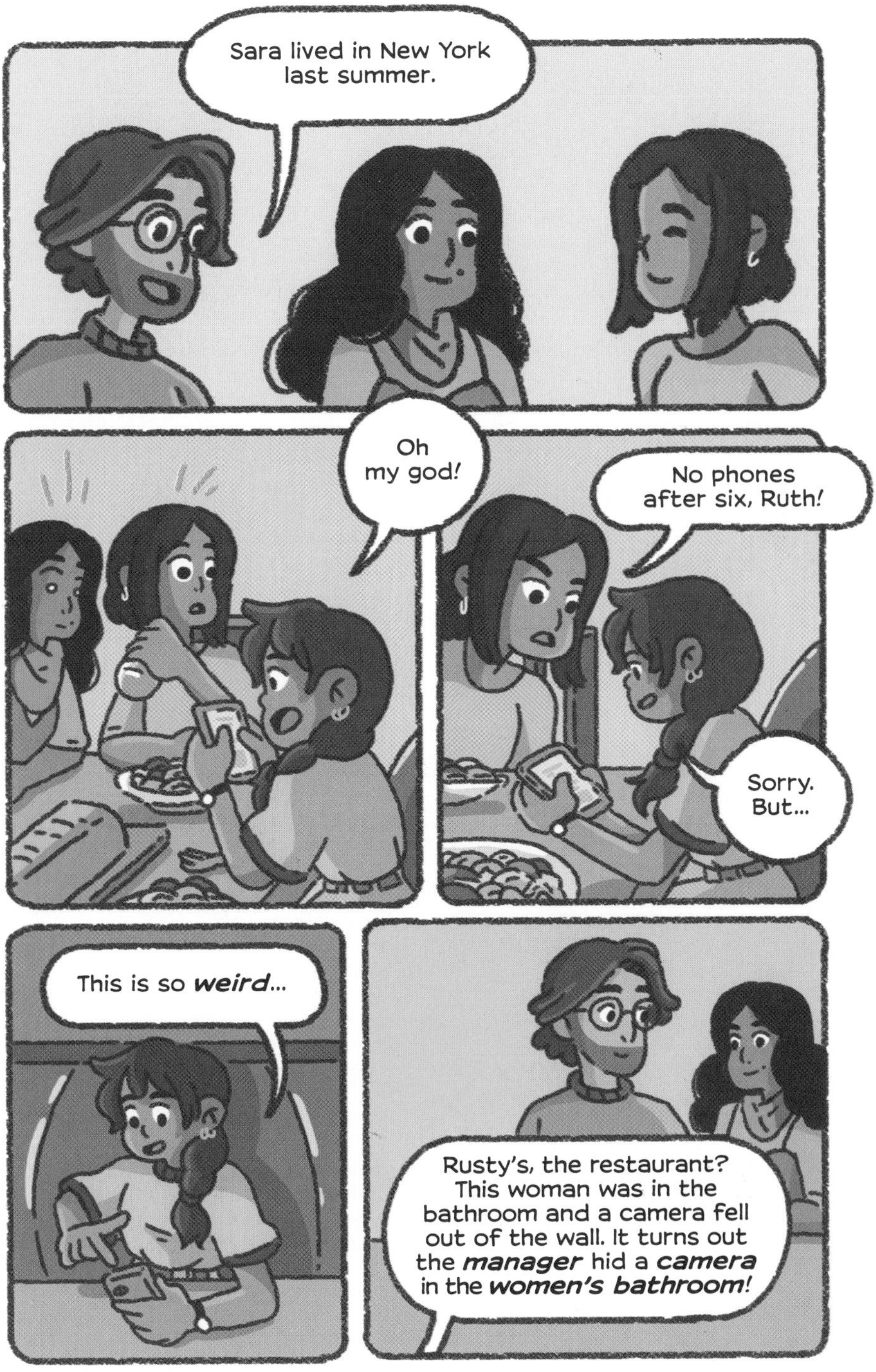
Sara lived in New York last summer.
Oh my god!
No phones after six, Ruth!
Sorry. But...
This is so ***weird***...
Rusty's, the restaurant? This woman was in the bathroom and a camera fell out of the wall. It turns out the ***manager*** hid a ***camera*** in the ***women's bathroom***!

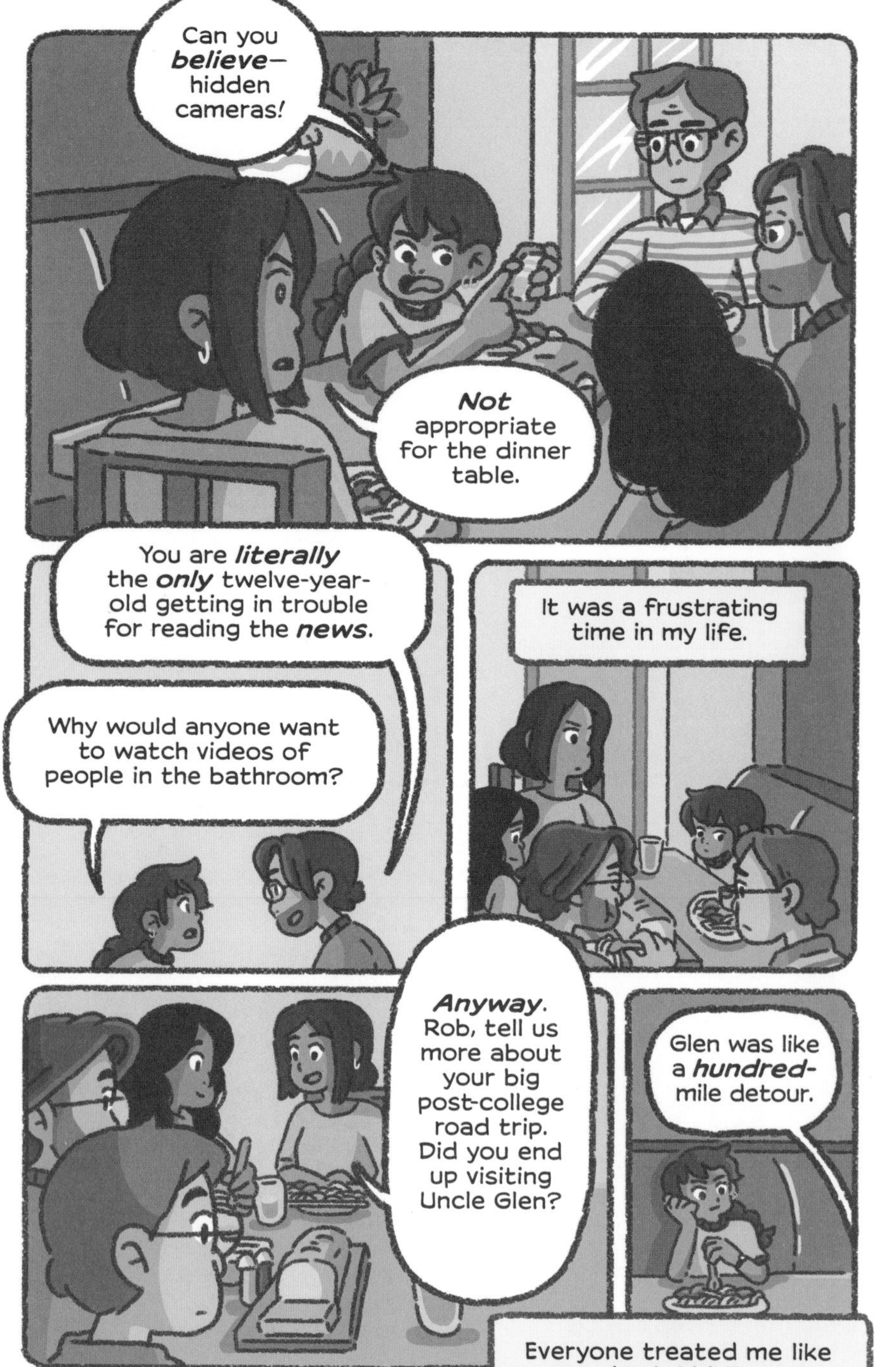

Can you *believe*—hidden cameras!
Not appropriate for the dinner table.
You are ***literally*** the ***only*** twelve-year-old getting in trouble for reading the ***news***.
Why would anyone want to watch videos of people in the bathroom?
It was a frustrating time in my life.
Anyway. Rob, tell us more about your big post-college road trip. Did you end up visiting Uncle Glen?
Glen was like a ***hundred***-mile detour.
Everyone treated me like some dumb kid. Except...

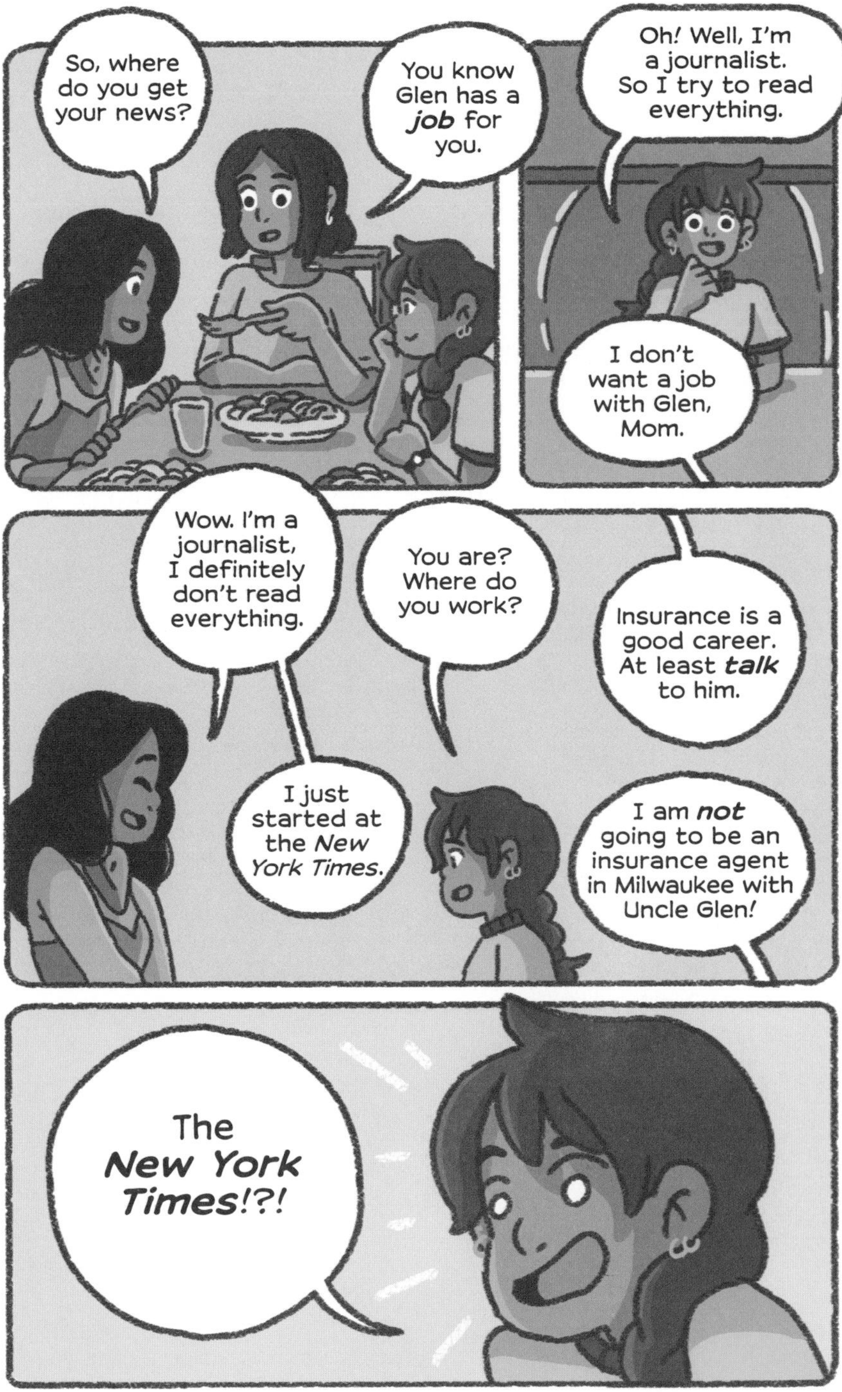
So, where do you get your news?
You know Glen has a *job* for you.
Oh! Well, I'm a journalist. So I try to read everything.
I don't want a job with Glen, Mom.
Wow. I'm a journalist, I definitely don't read everything.
You are? Where do you work?
Insurance is a good career. At least ***talk*** to him.
I just started at the *New York Times*.
I am ***not*** going to be an insurance agent in Milwaukee with Uncle Glen!
The ***New York Times***!?!

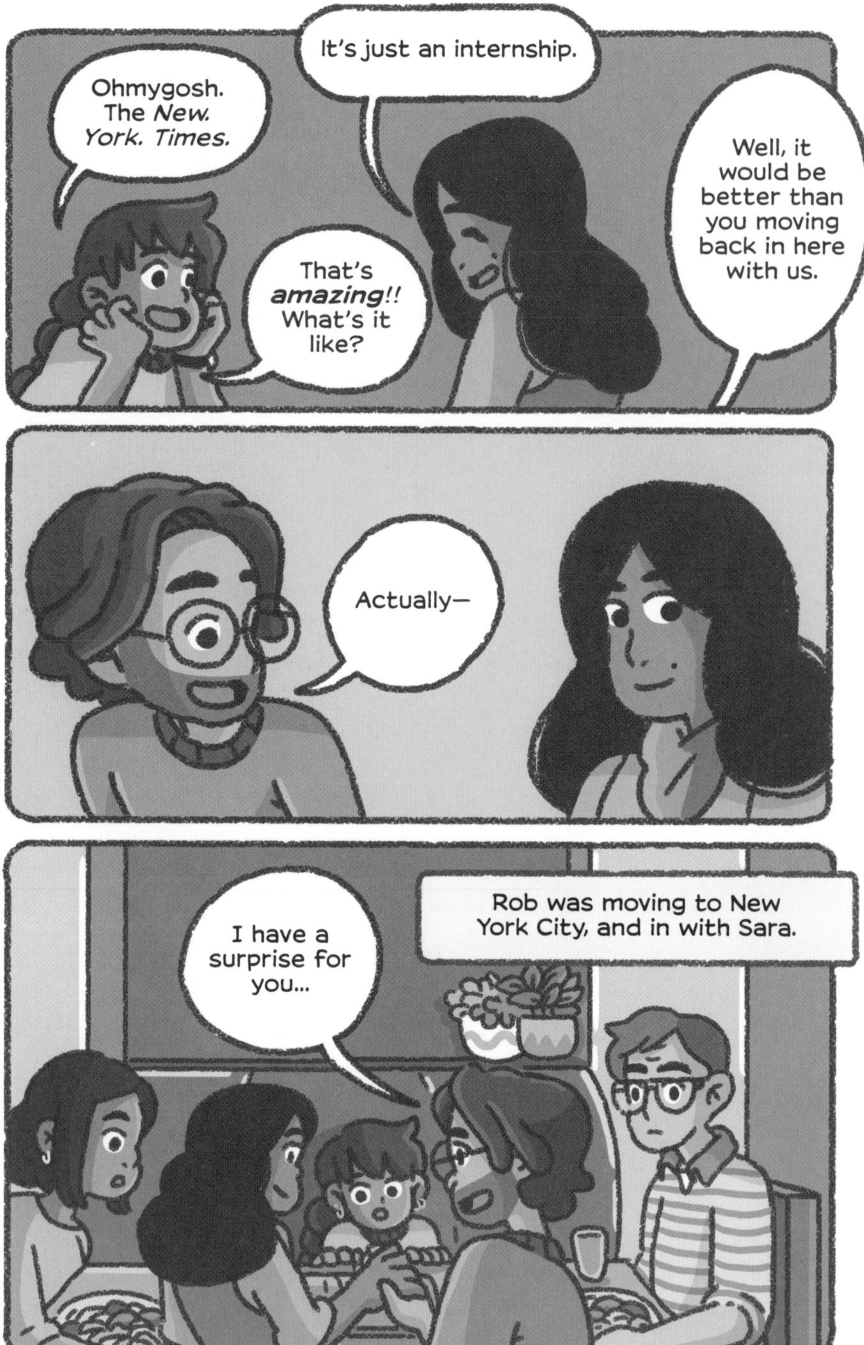
It's just an internship.
Ohmygosh. The *New. York. Times.*
That's ***amazing!!*** What's it like?
Well, it would be better than you moving back in here with us.
Actually—
Rob was moving to New York City, and in with Sara.
I have a surprise for you...

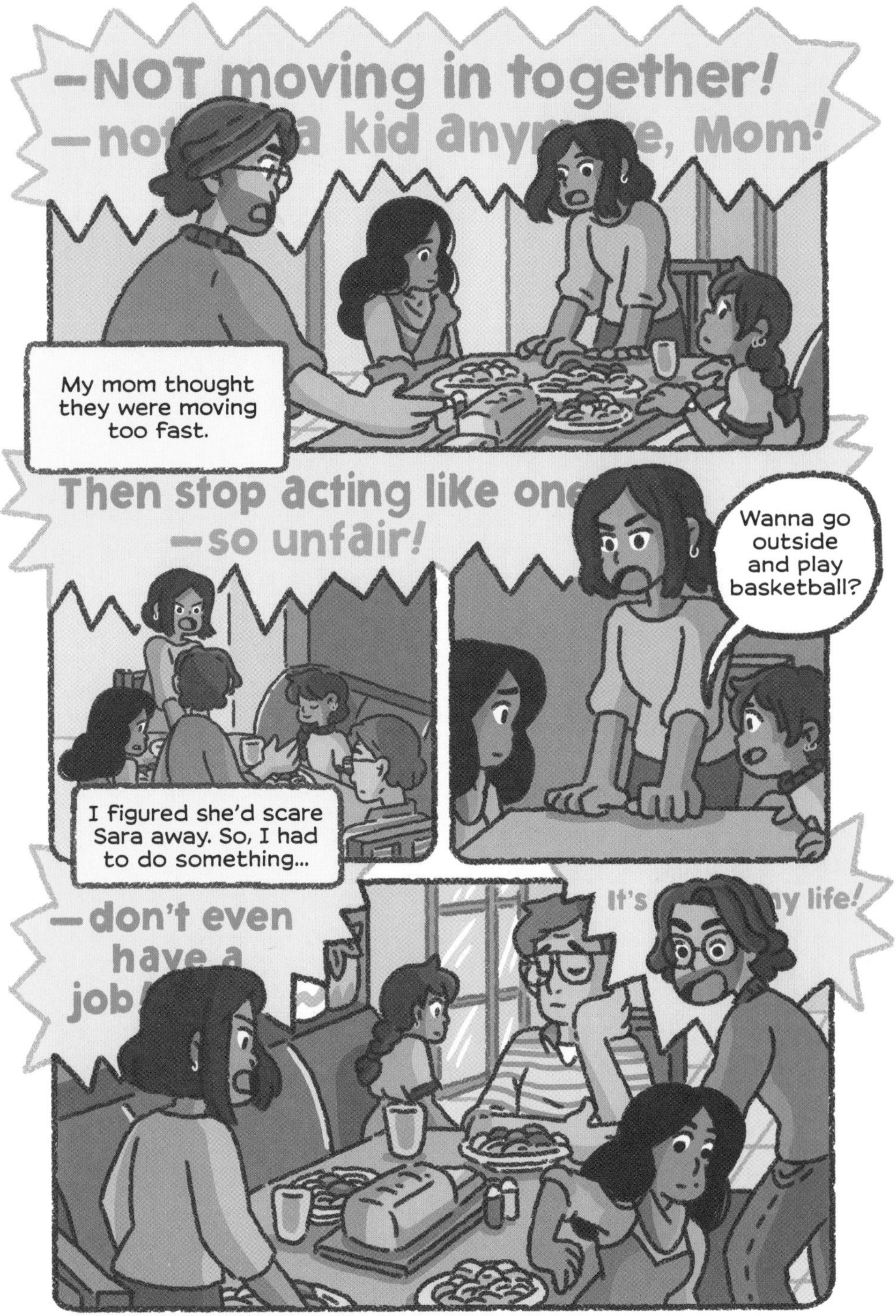
—NOT moving in together!
My mom thought they were moving too fast.
Then stop acting like one
—so unfair!
Wanna go outside and play basketball?
I figured she'd scare Sara away. So, I had to do something...

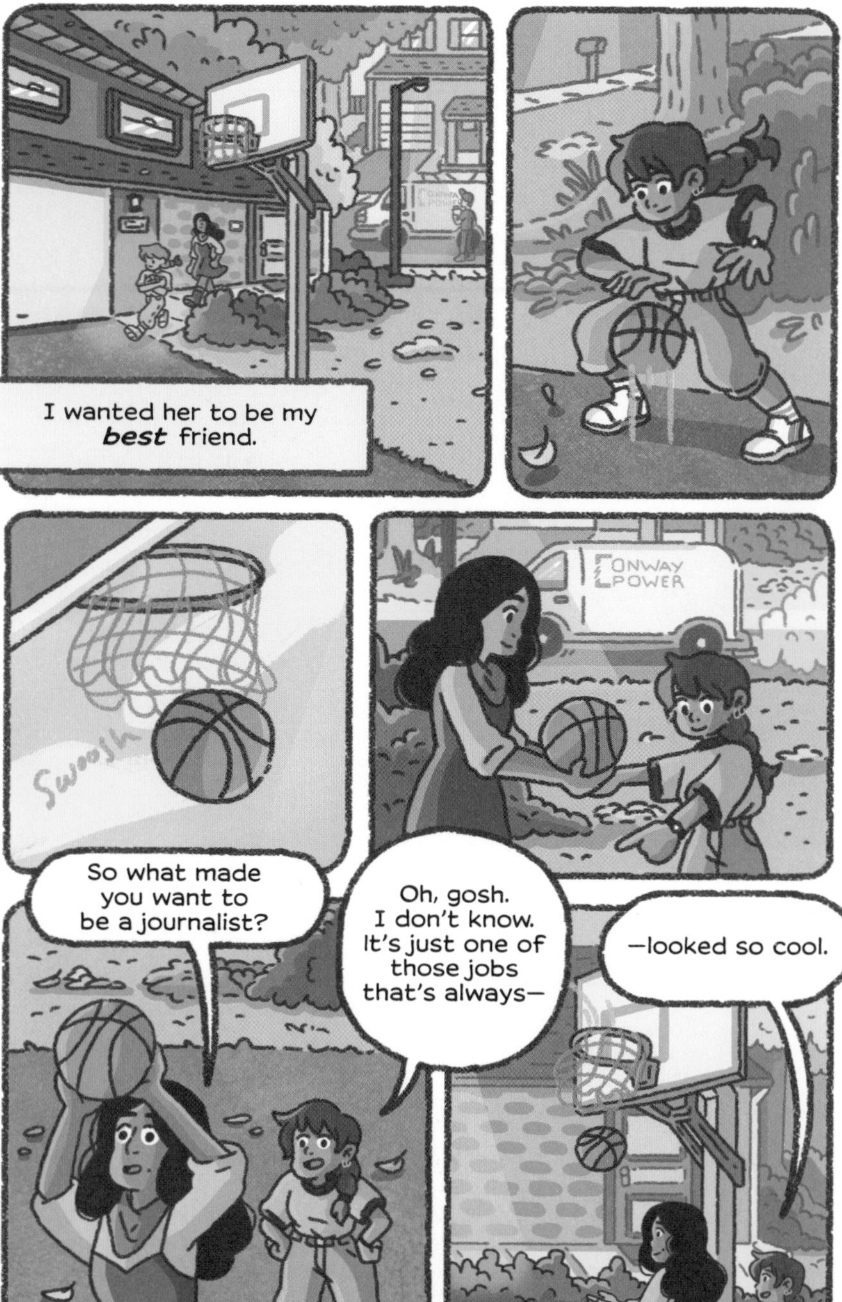
I wanted her to be my ***best*** friend.
CONWAY POWER
Swoosh
CONWAY POWER
So what made you want to be a journalist?
Oh, gosh. I don't know. It's just one of those jobs that's always—
—looked so cool.

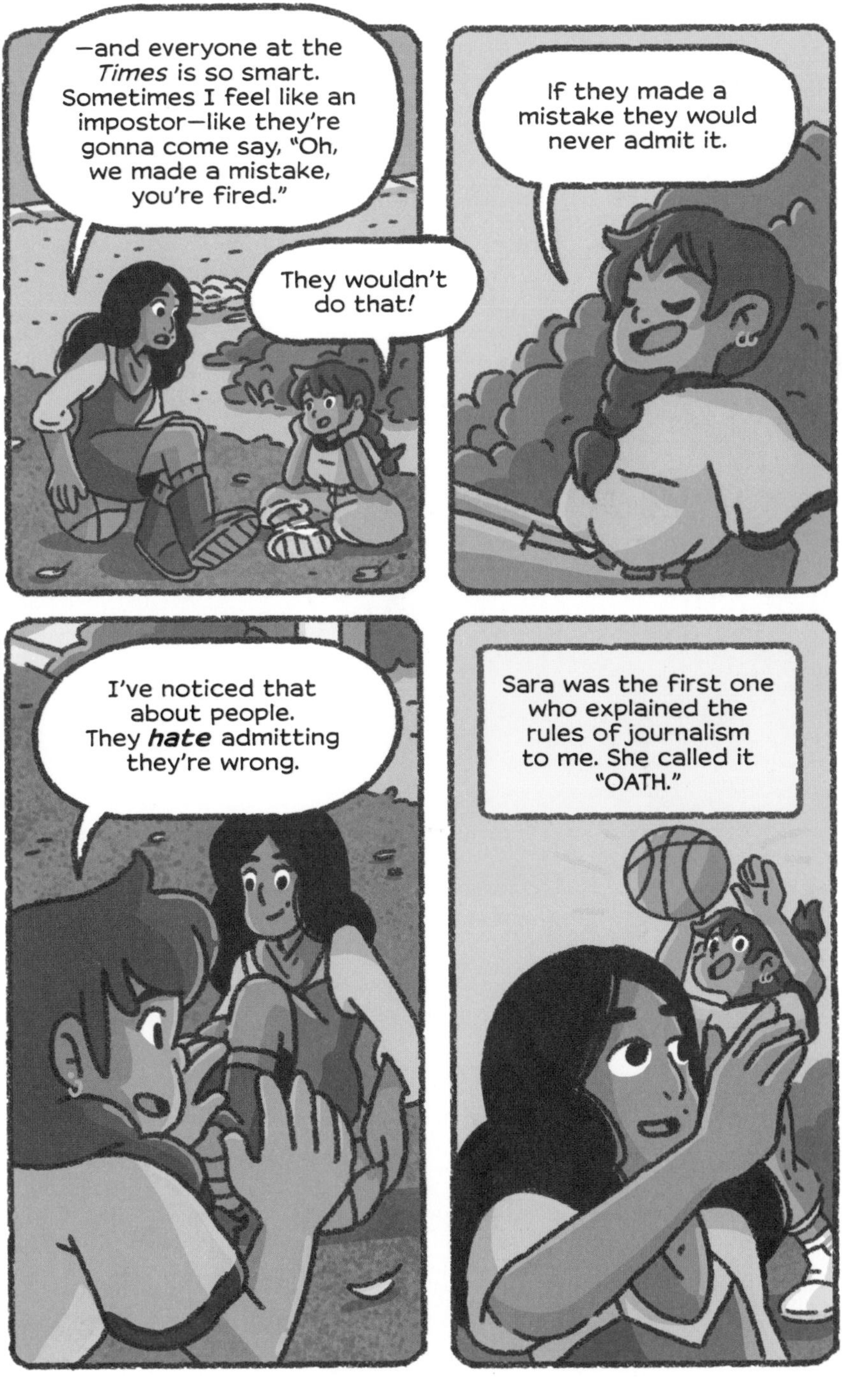
—and everyone at the *Times* is so smart. Sometimes I feel like an impostor—like they're gonna come say, "Oh, we made a mistake, you're fired."
They wouldn't do that!
If they made a mistake they would never admit it.
I've noticed that about people. They ***hate*** admitting they're wrong.
Sara was the first one who explained the rules of journalism to me. She called it "OATH."

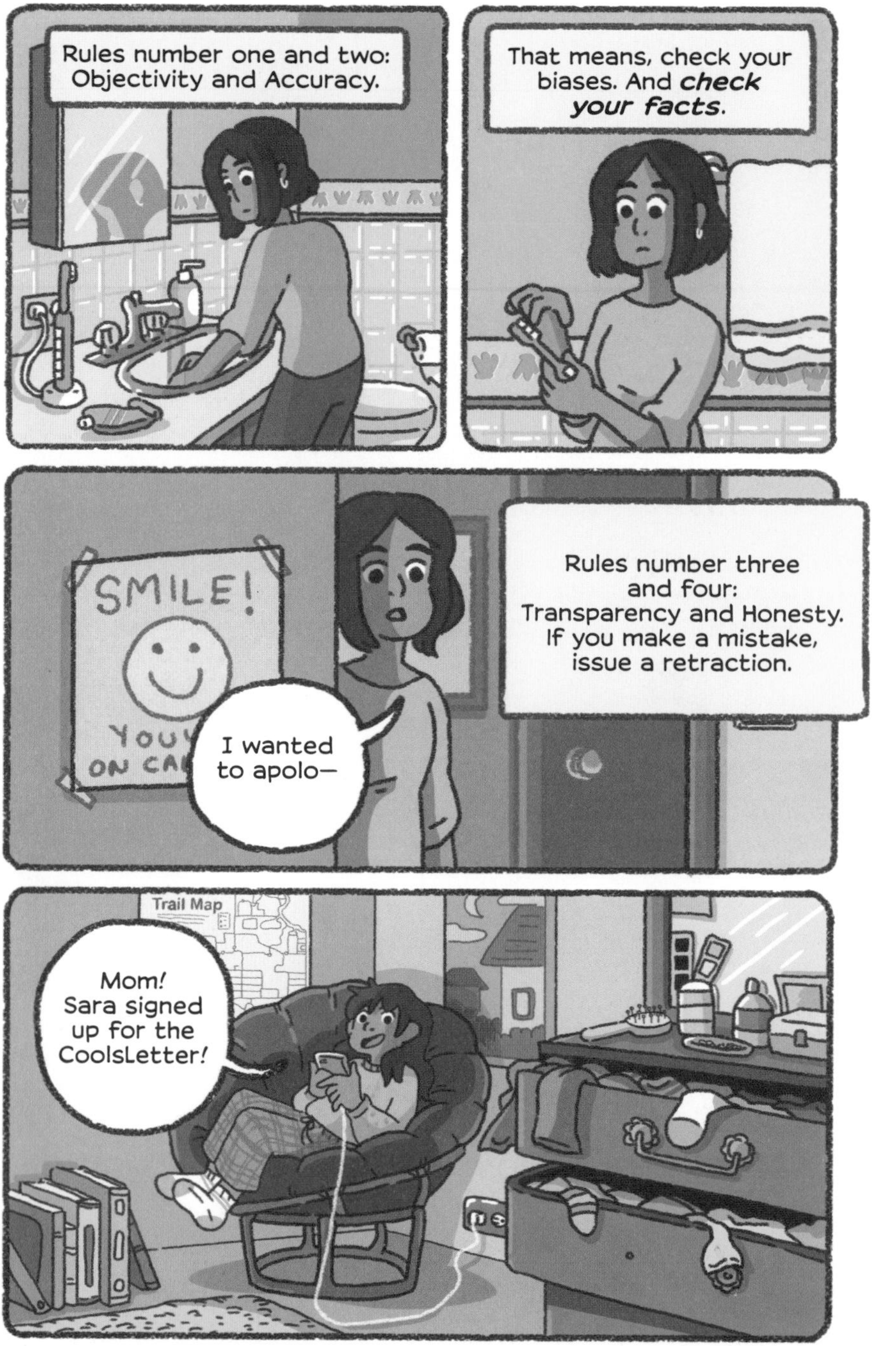
Rules number one and two: Objectivity and Accuracy.
That means, check your biases. And *check your facts*.
SMILE!
Rules number three and four: Transparency and Honesty. If you make a mistake, issue a retraction.
I wanted to apolo—
Trail Map
Mom! Sara signed up for the CoolsLetter!

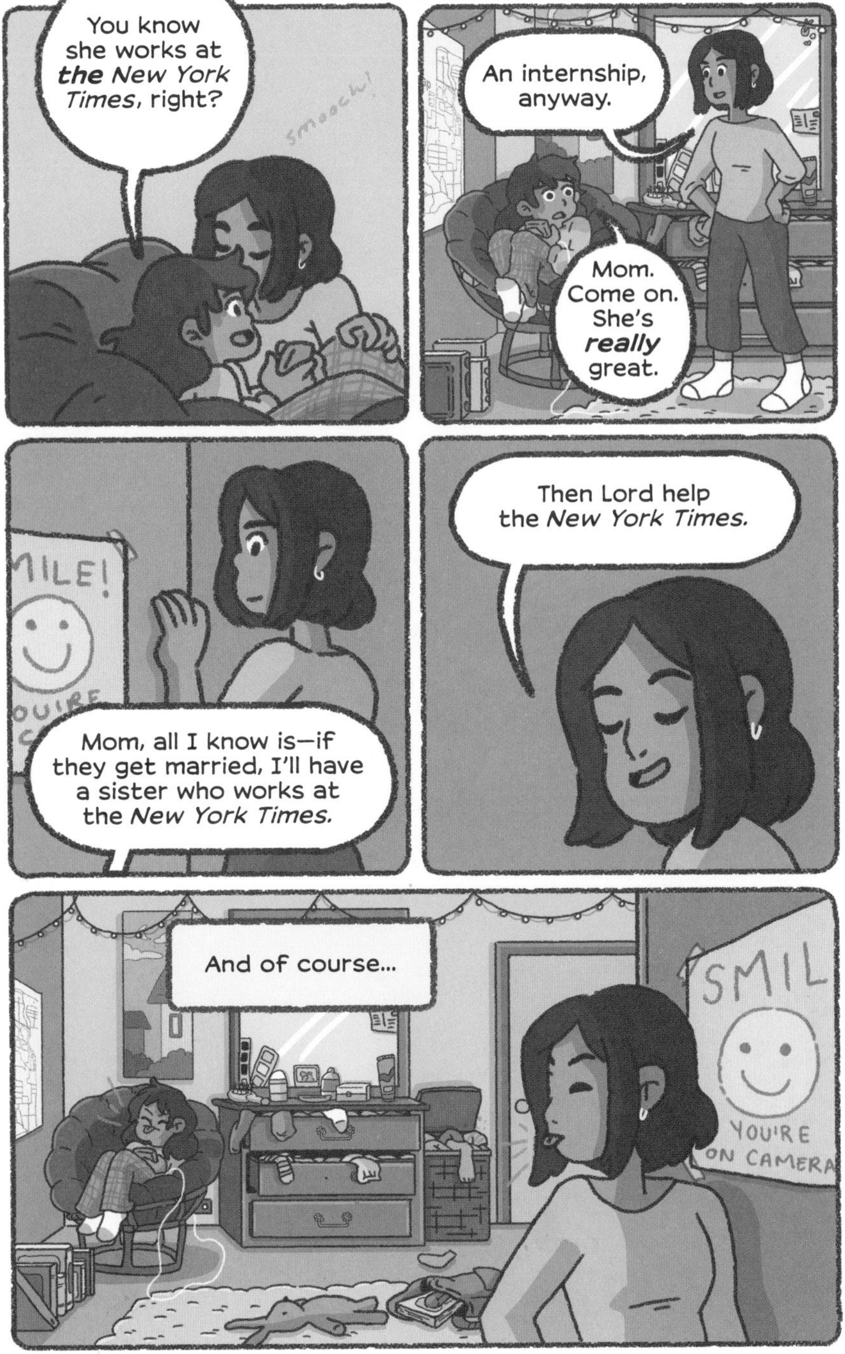
You know she works at ***the*** *New York Times*, right?
smooch!
An internship, anyway.
Mom. Come on. She's ***really*** great.
Mom, all I know is—if they get married, I'll have a sister who works at the *New York Times.*
Then Lord help the *New York Times.*
And of course...
YOU'RE ON CAMERA

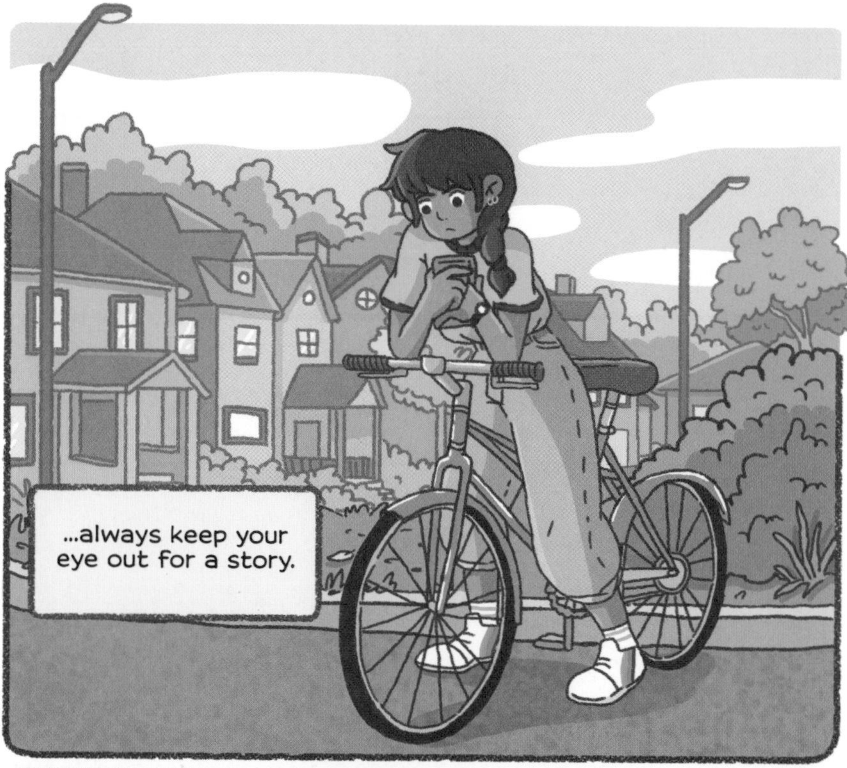
...always keep your eye out for a story.

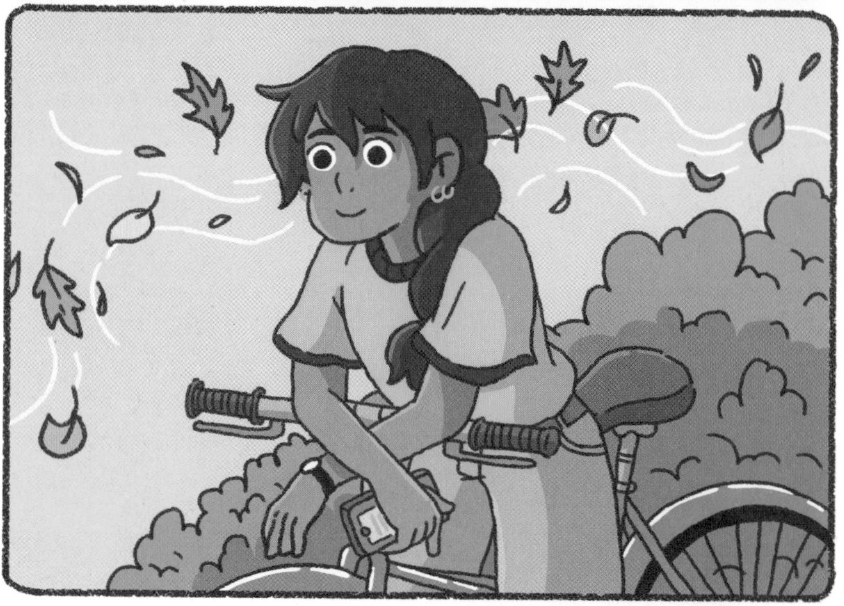

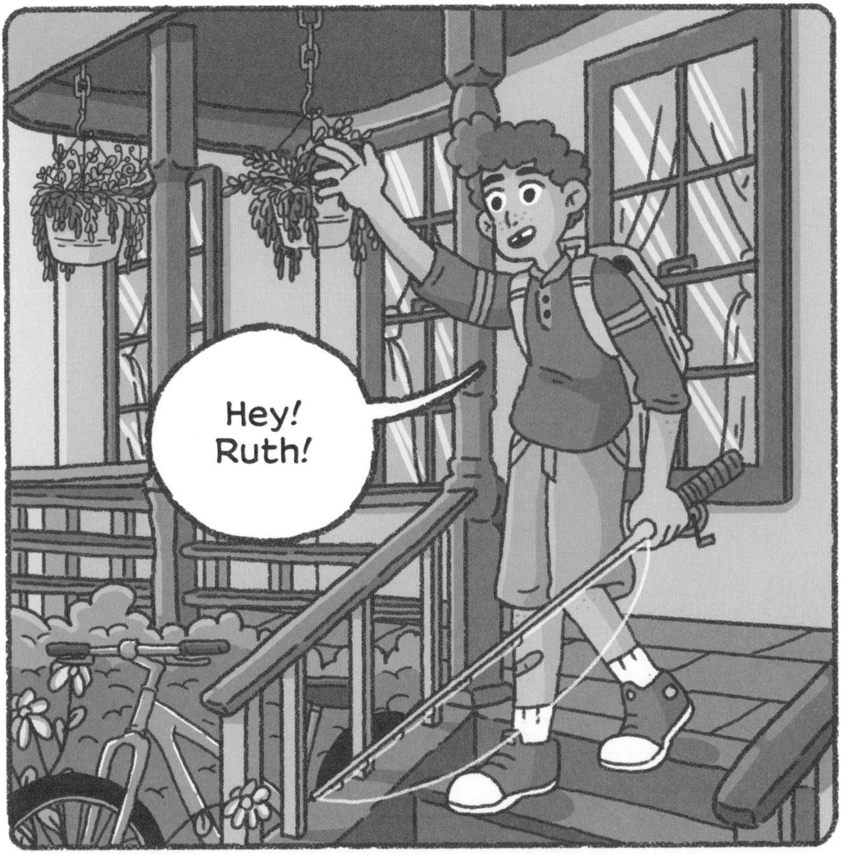
Hey!
Ruth!

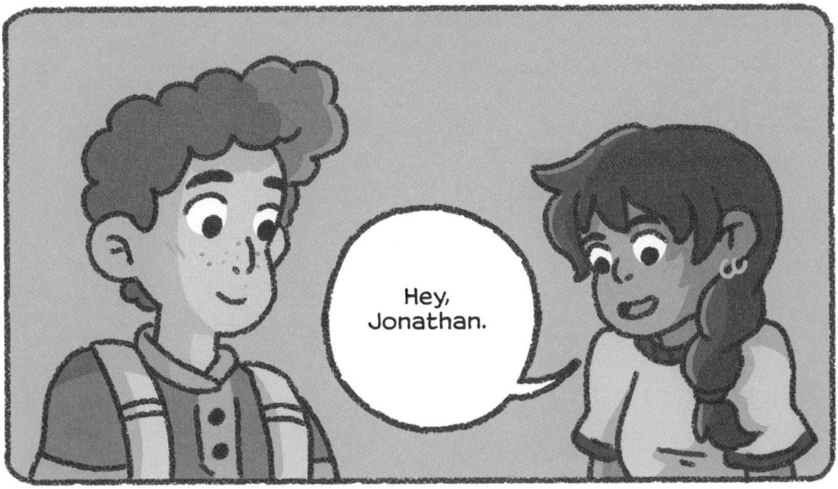
Hey,
Jonathan.

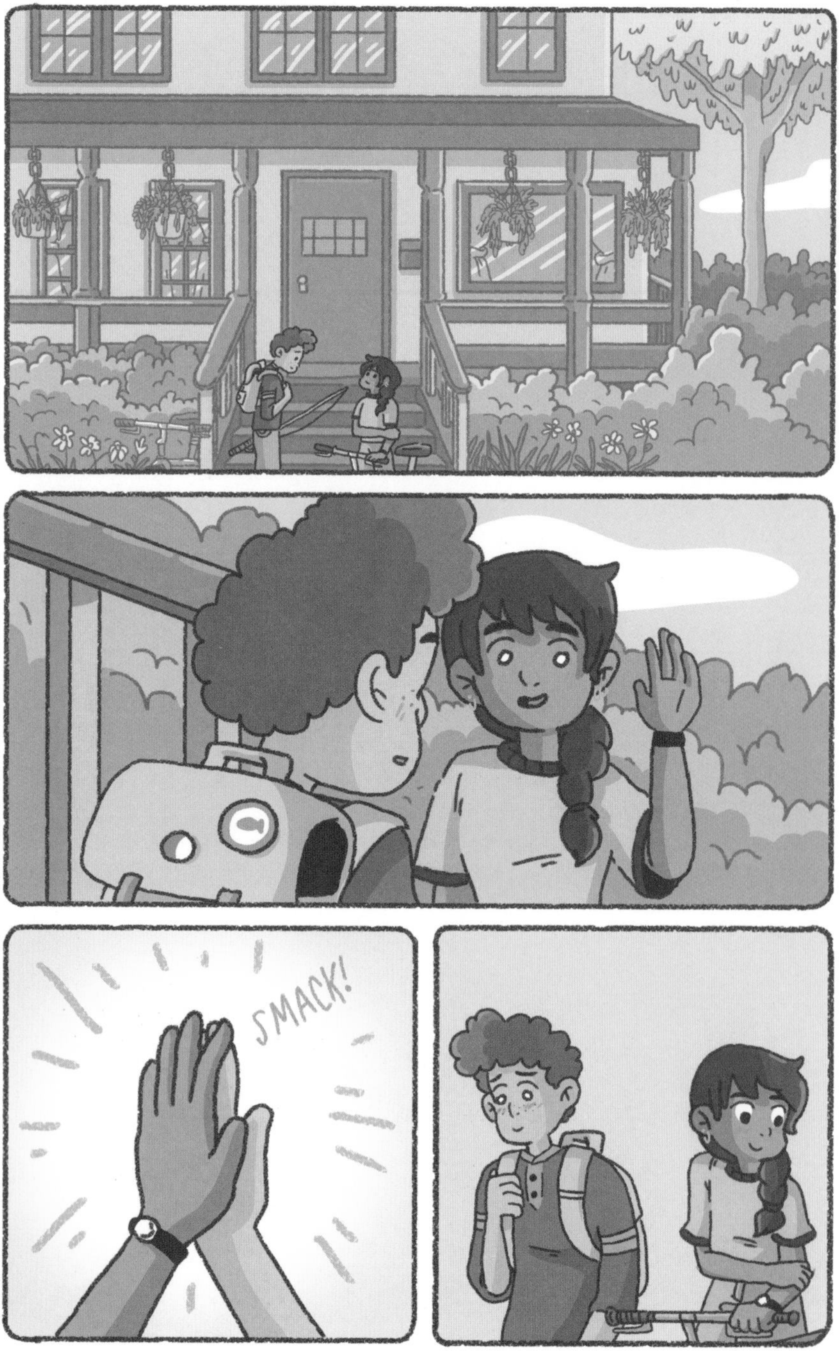
SMACK!

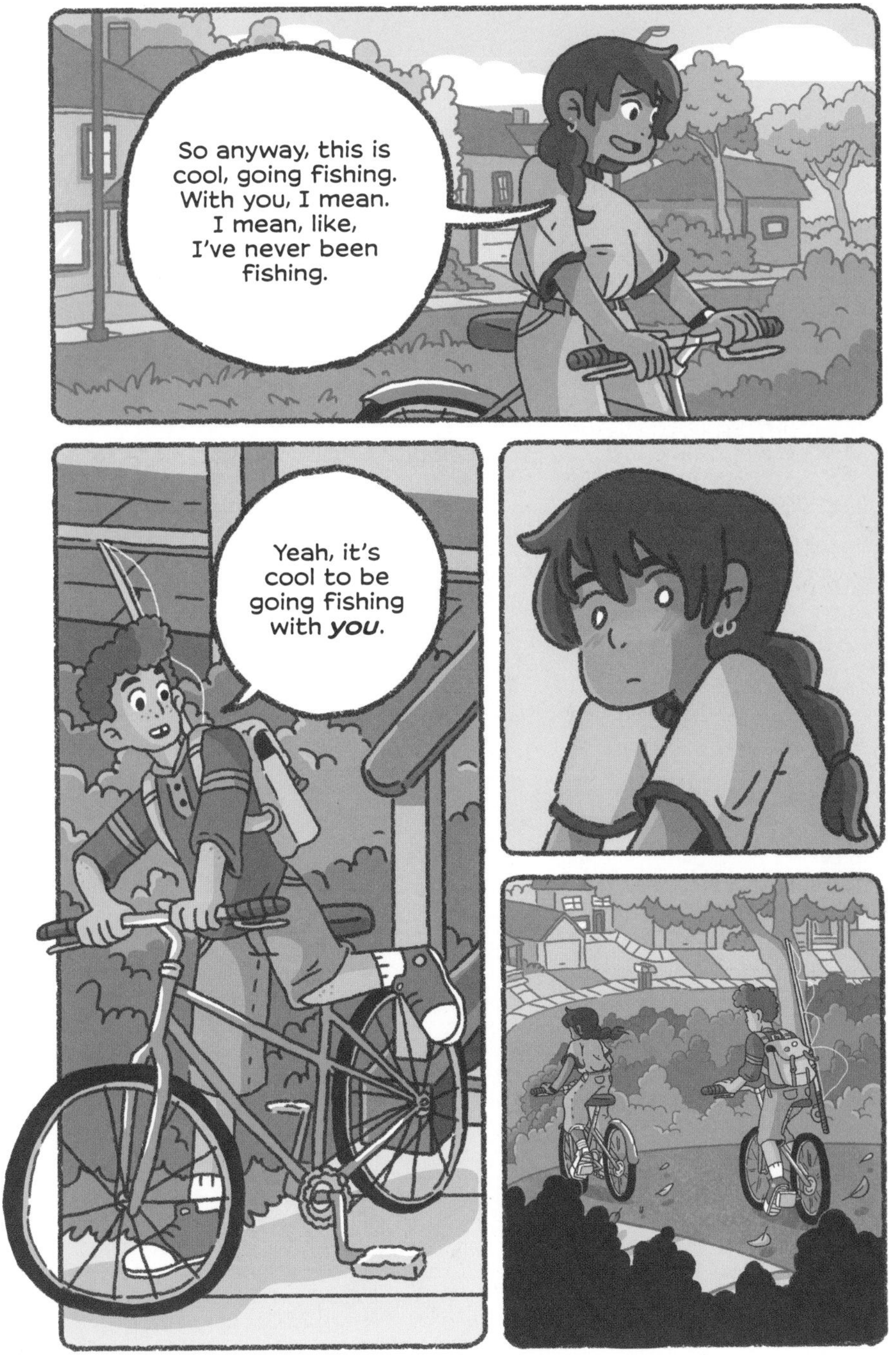
So anyway, this is cool, going fishing. With you, I mean. I mean, like, I've never been fishing.
Yeah, it's cool to be going fishing with *you*.

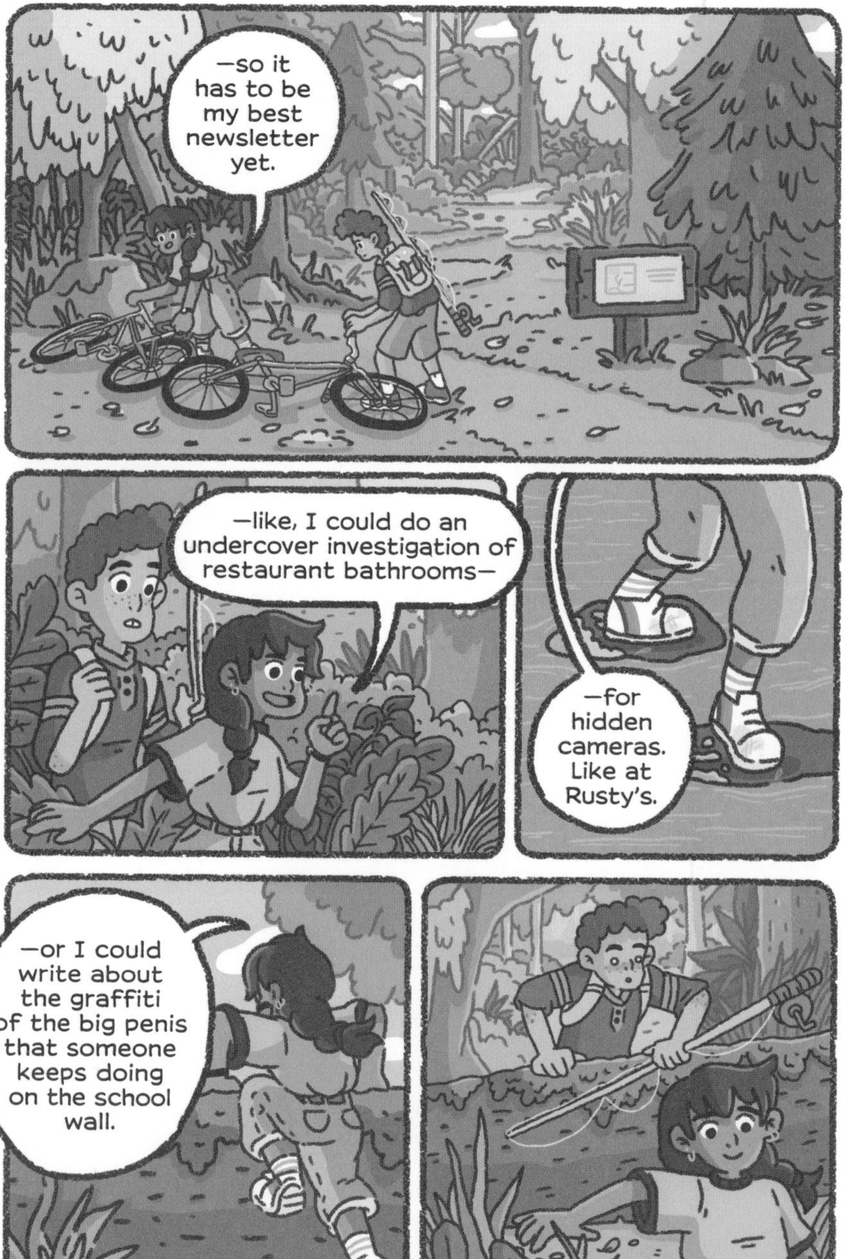
—so it has to be my best newsletter yet.
—like, I could do an undercover investigation of restaurant bathrooms—
—for hidden cameras. Like at Rusty's.
—or I could write about the graffiti of the big penis that someone keeps doing on the school wall.

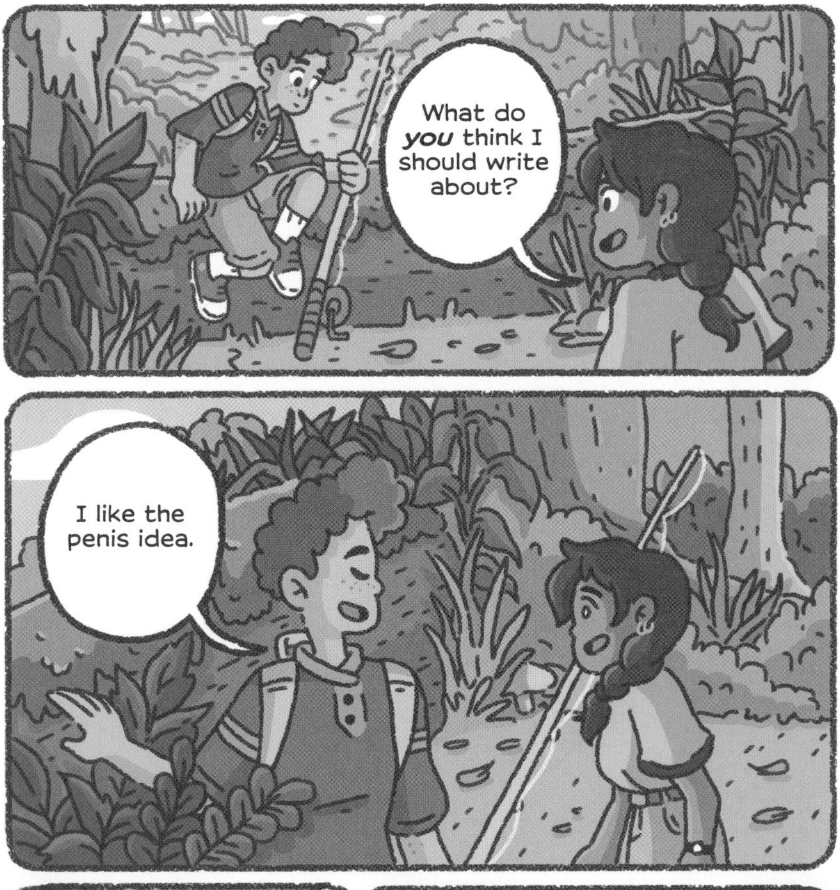
What do *you* think I should write about?
I like the penis idea.
It's a real meaty subject, you know?
You're horrible!
You brought it up!

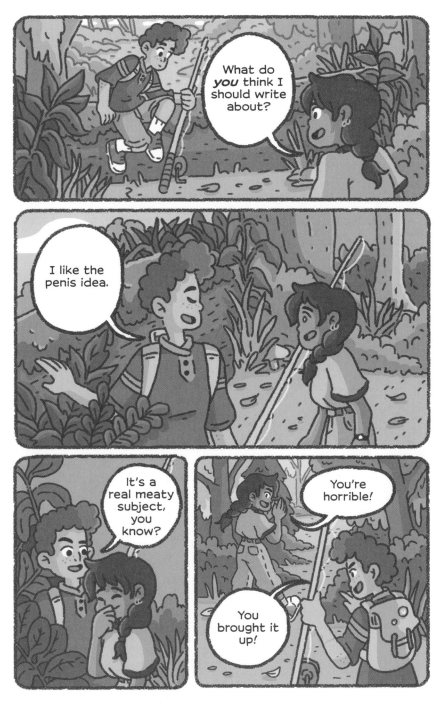

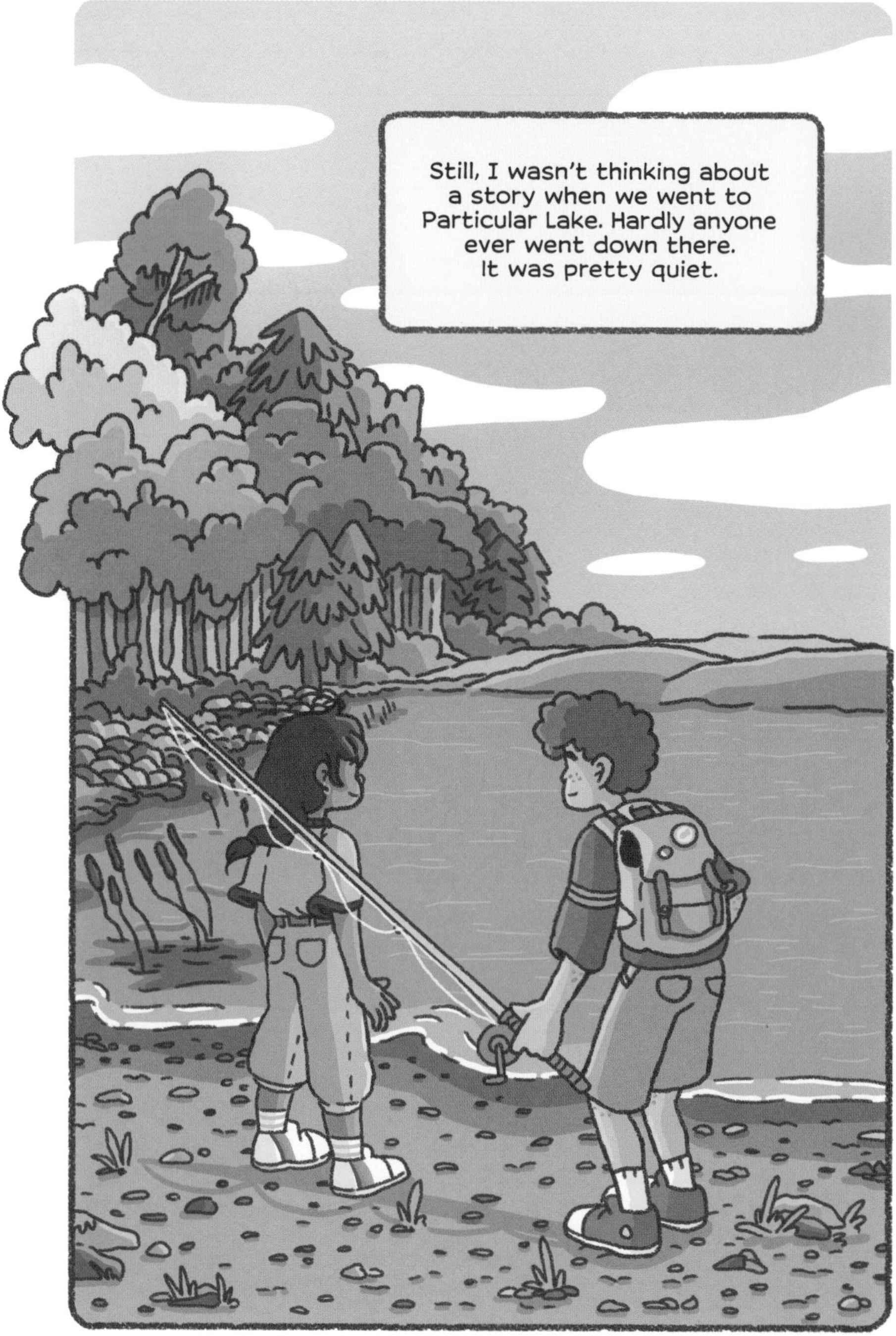
Still, I wasn't thinking about a story when we went to Particular Lake. Hardly anyone ever went down there. It was pretty quiet.

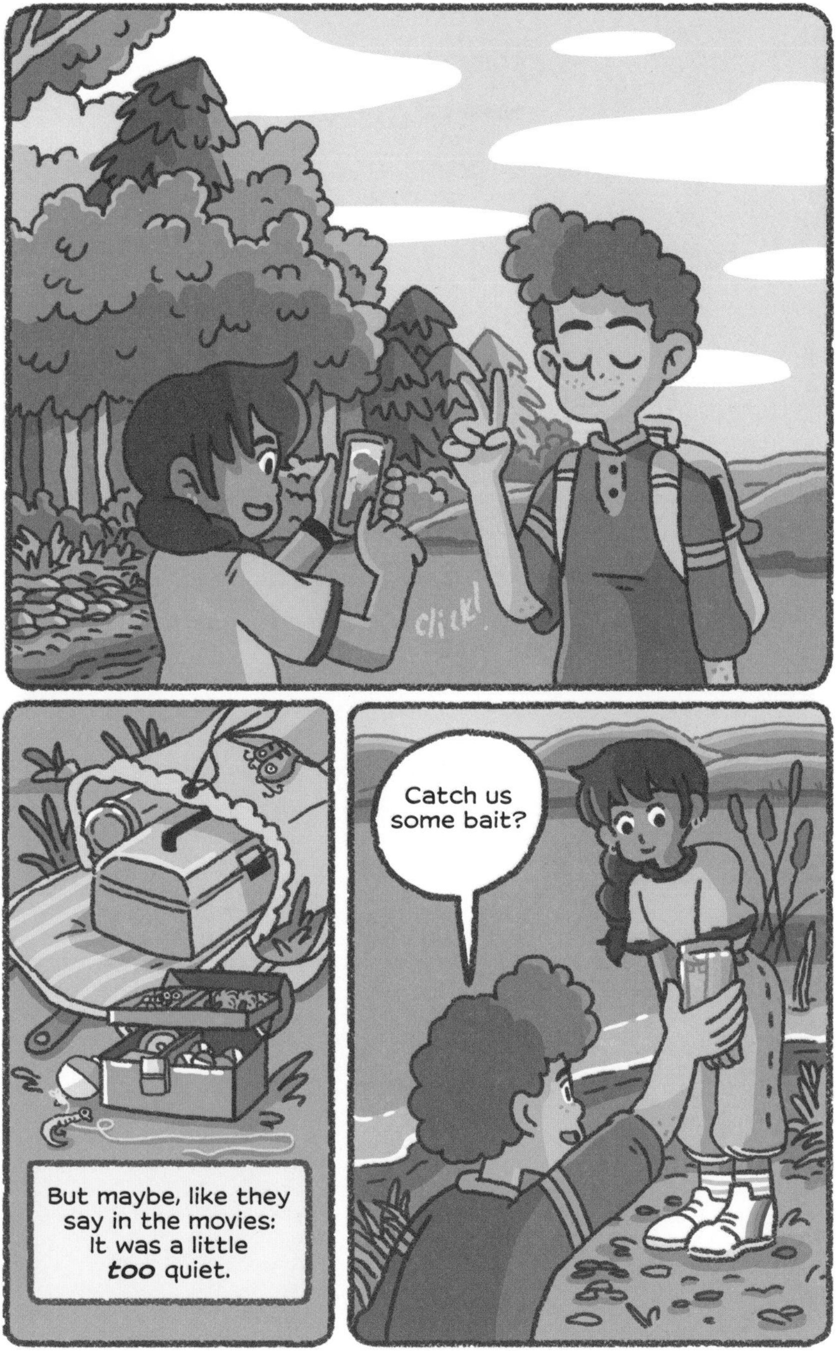
click!
But maybe, like they say in the movies: It was a little ***too*** quiet.
Catch us some bait?

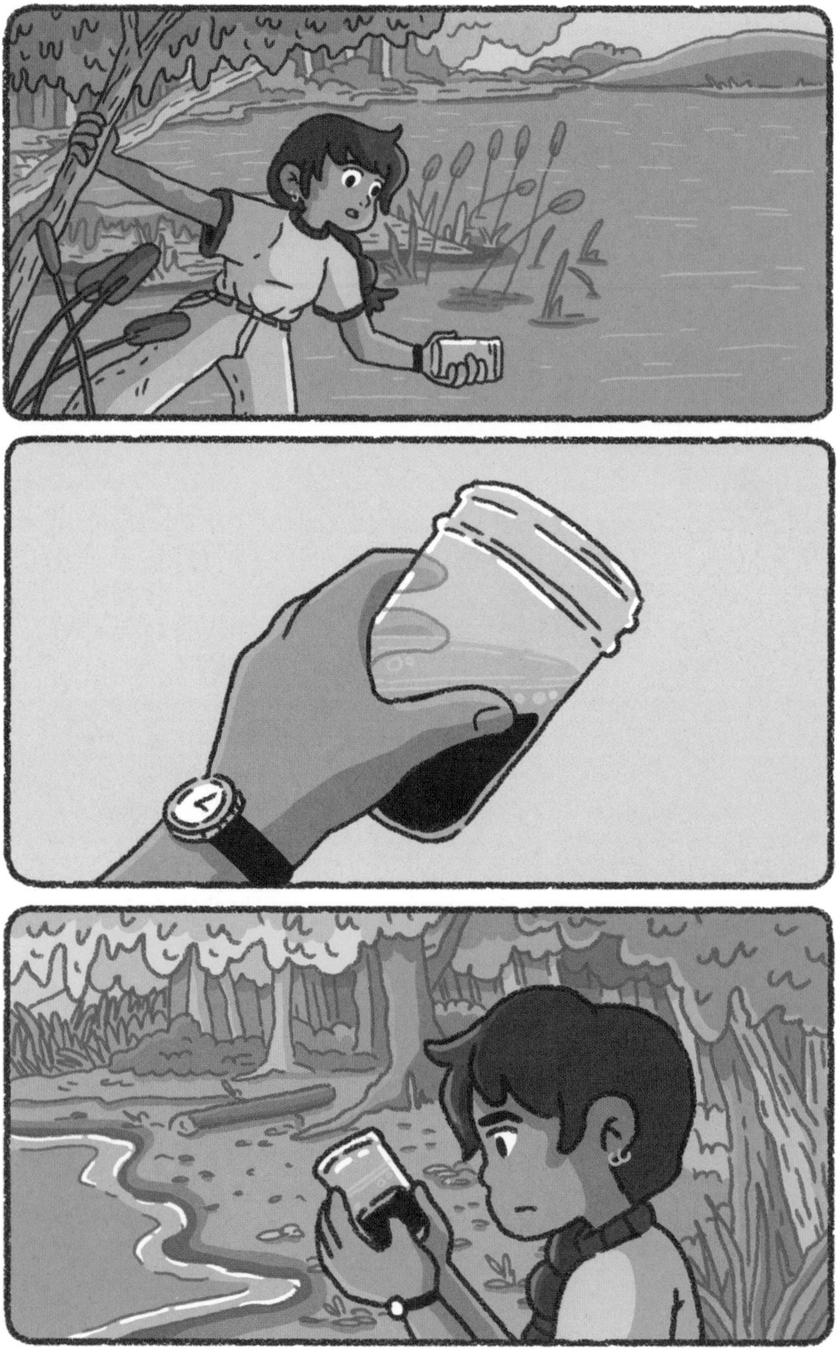

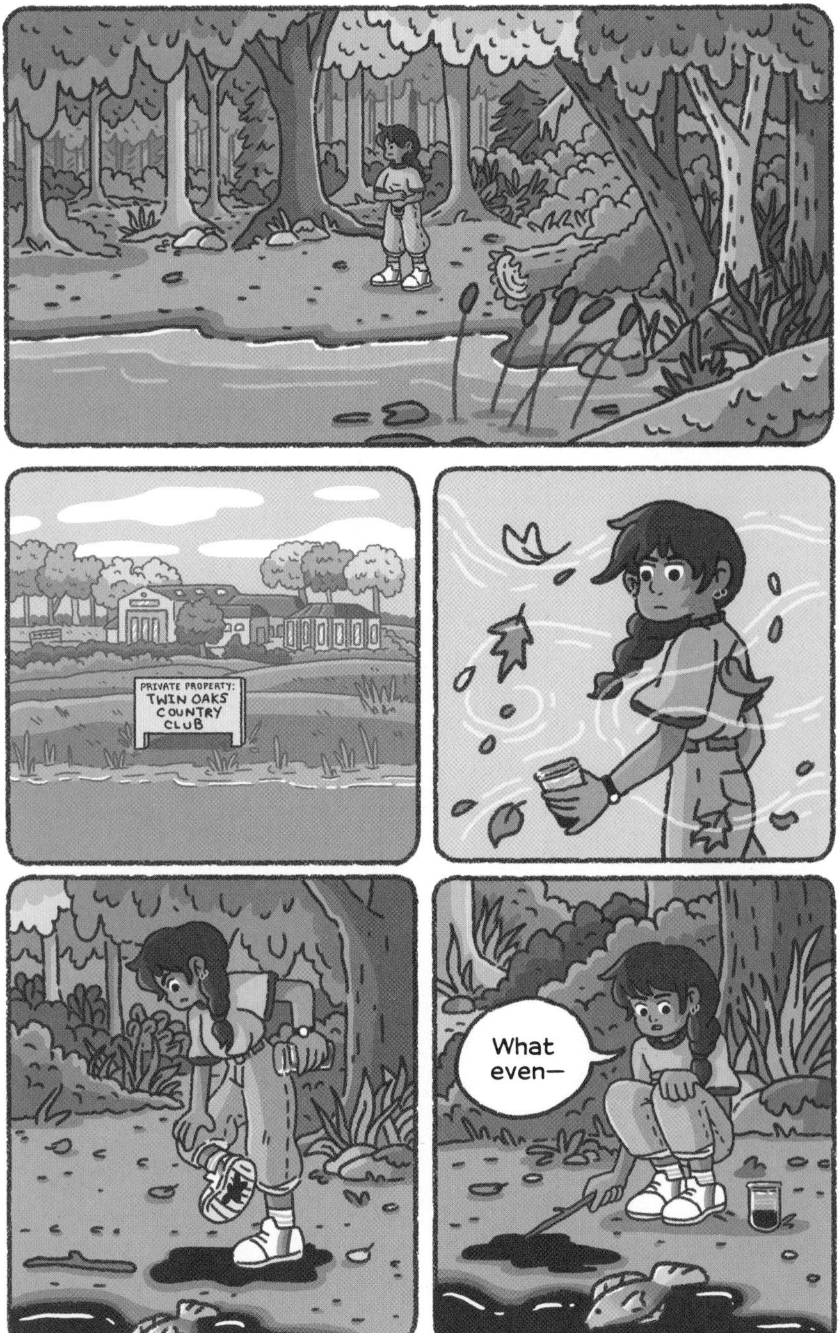
PRIVATE PROPERTY:
TWIN OAKS
COUNTRY
CLUB
What
even—

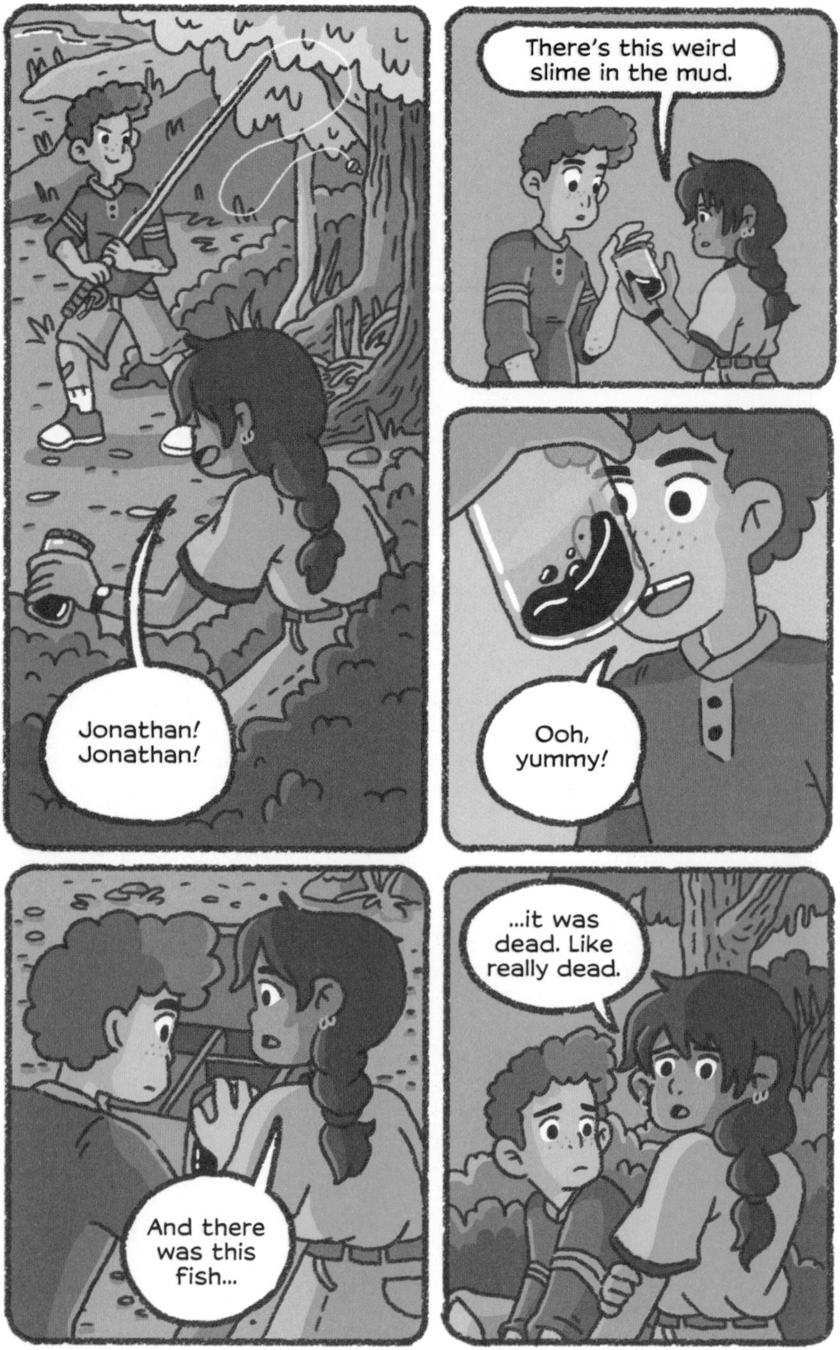
Jonathan!
Jonathan!
There's this weird
slime in the mud.
Ooh,
yummy!
And there
was this
fish...
...it was
dead. Like
really dead.

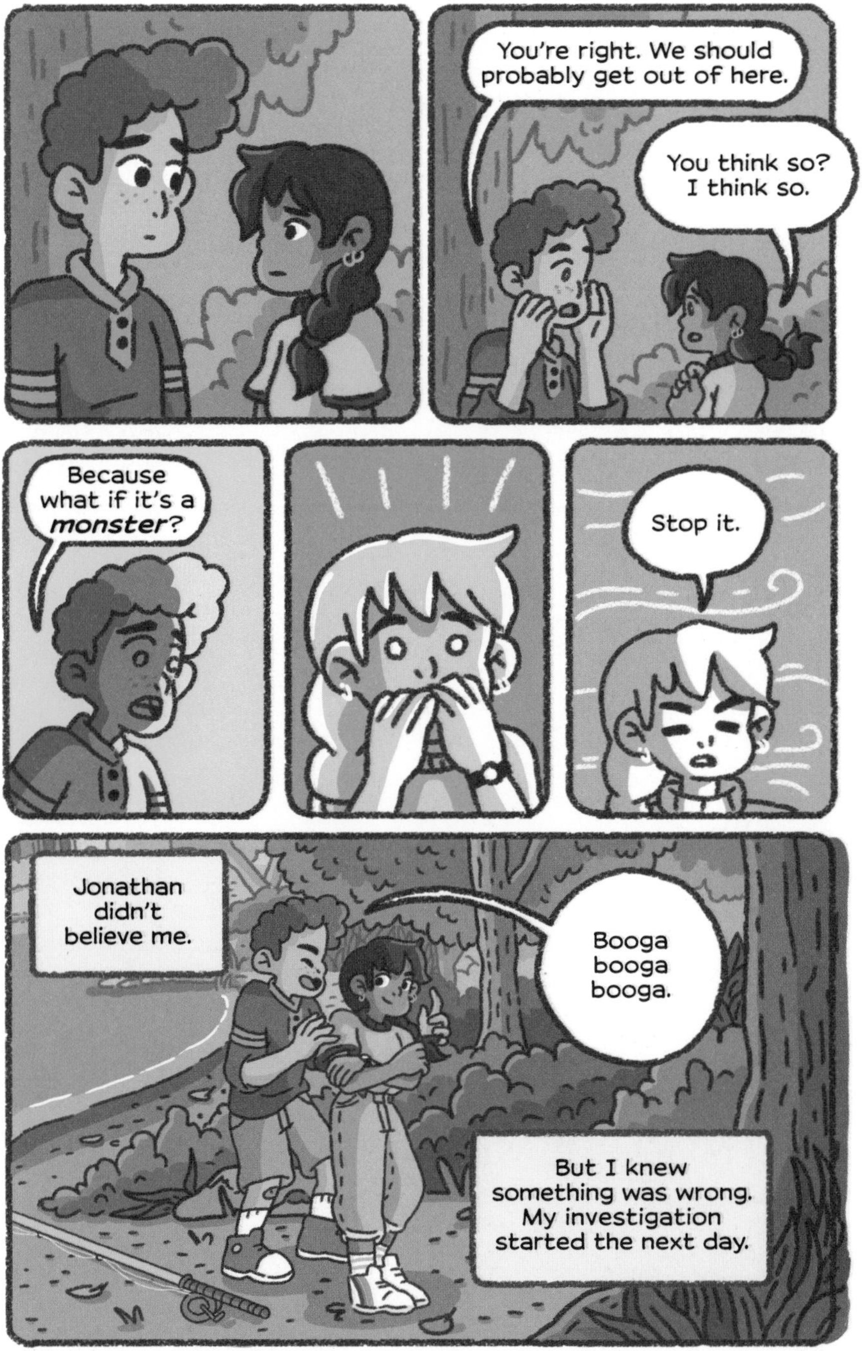
You're right. We should probably get out of here.
You think so? I think so.
Because what if it's a *monster*?
Stop it.
Jonathan didn't believe me.
Booga booga booga.
But I knew something was wrong. My investigation started the next day.

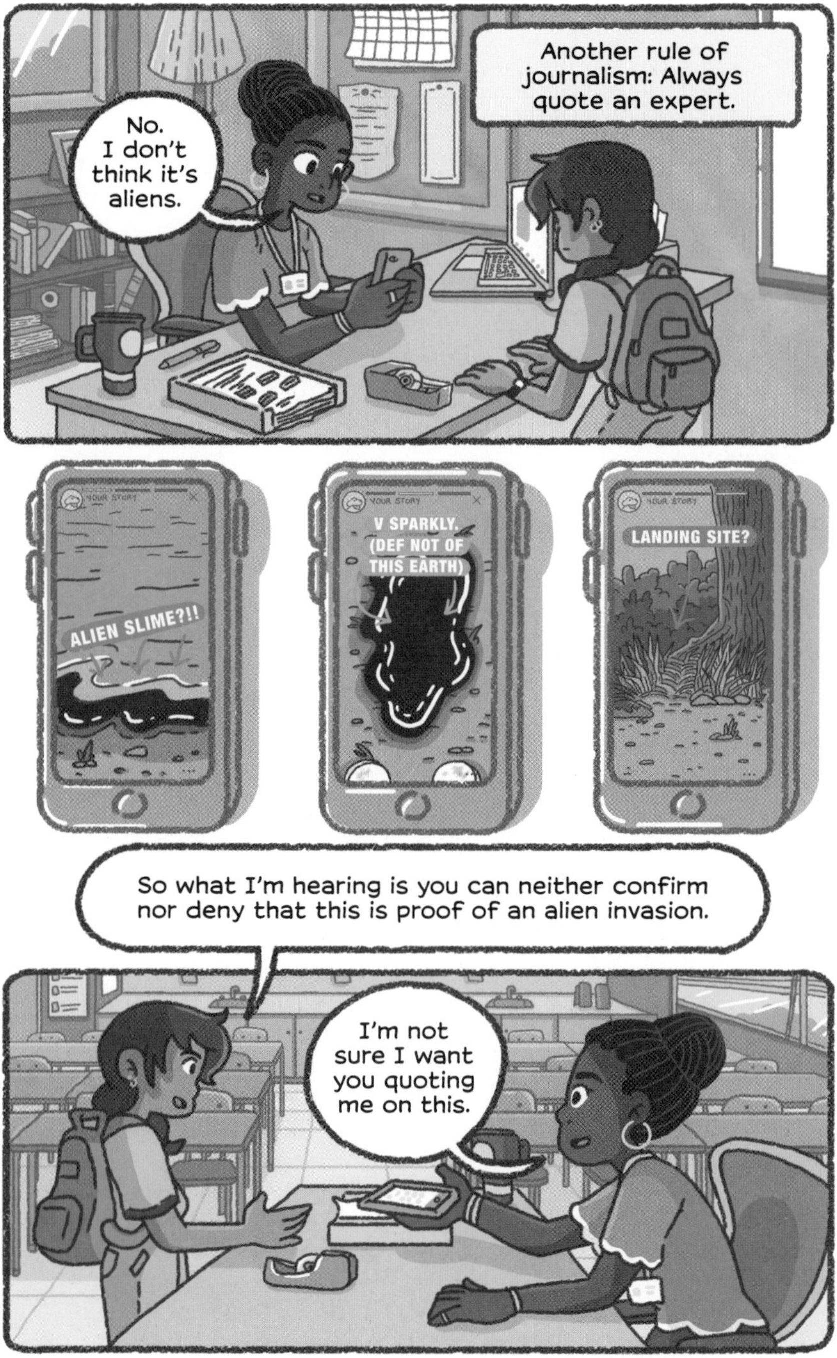
Another rule of journalism: Always quote an expert.
No. I don't think it's aliens.
YOUR STORY
ALIEN SLIME?!!
YOUR STORY
V SPARKLY. (DEF NOT OF THIS EARTH)
YOUR STORY
LANDING SITE?
So what I'm hearing is you can neither confirm nor deny that this is proof of an alien invasion.
I'm not sure I want you quoting me on this.

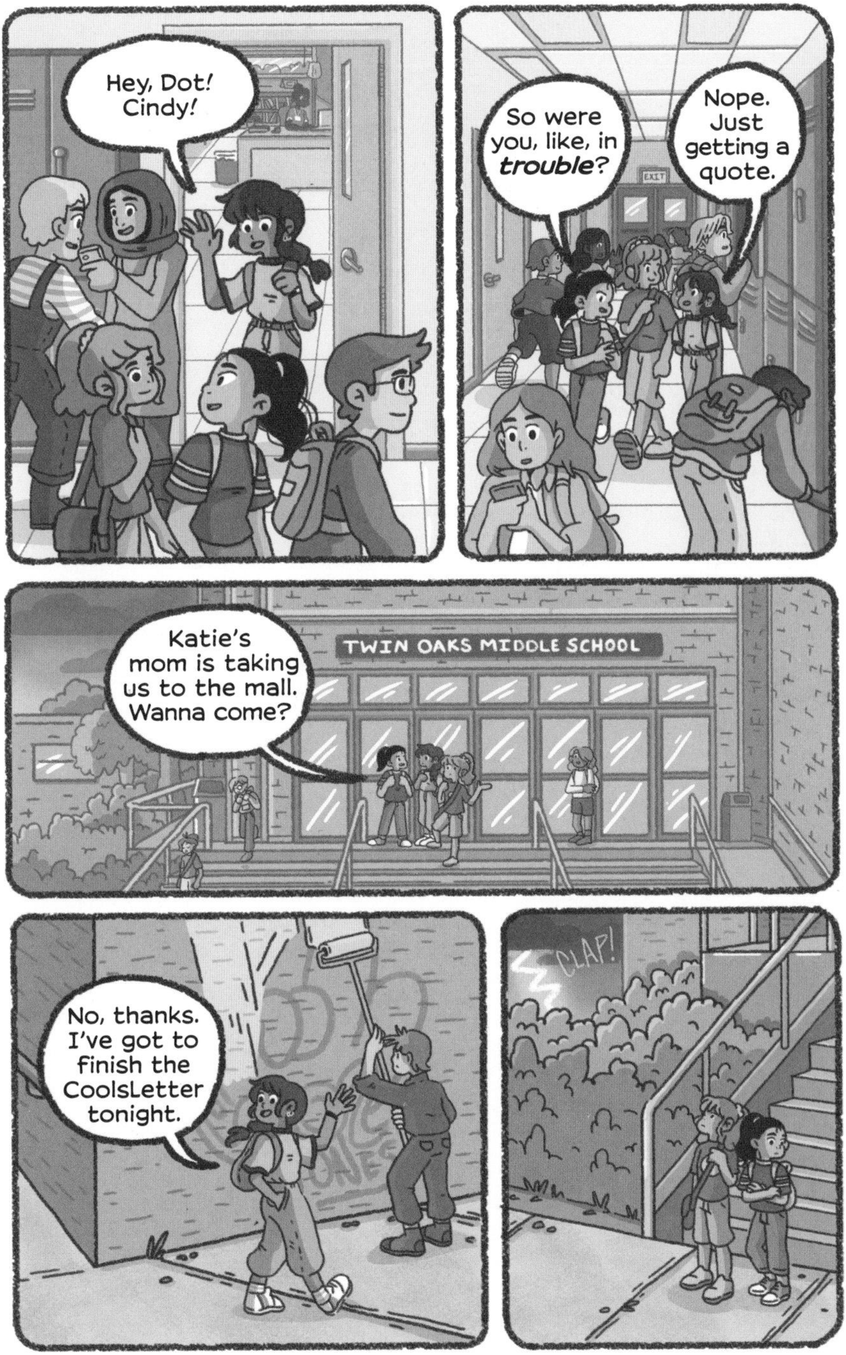
Hey, Dot! Cindy!
So were you, like, in *trouble*?
Nope. Just getting a quote.
TWIN OAKS MIDDLE SCHOOL
Katie's mom is taking us to the mall. Wanna come?
No, thanks. I've got to finish the CoolsLetter tonight.
CLAP!

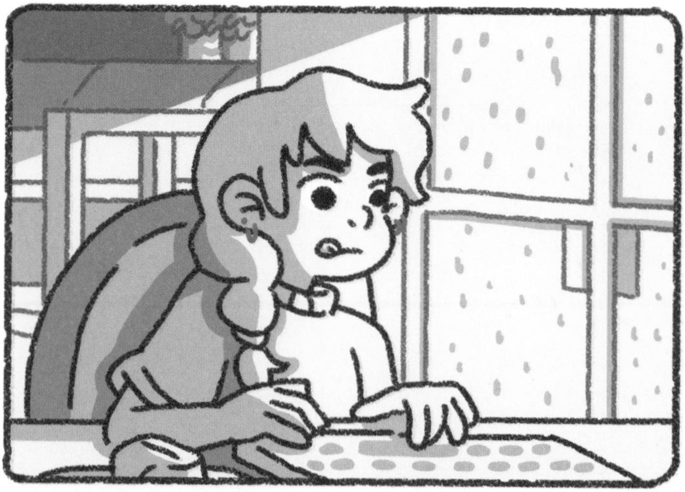

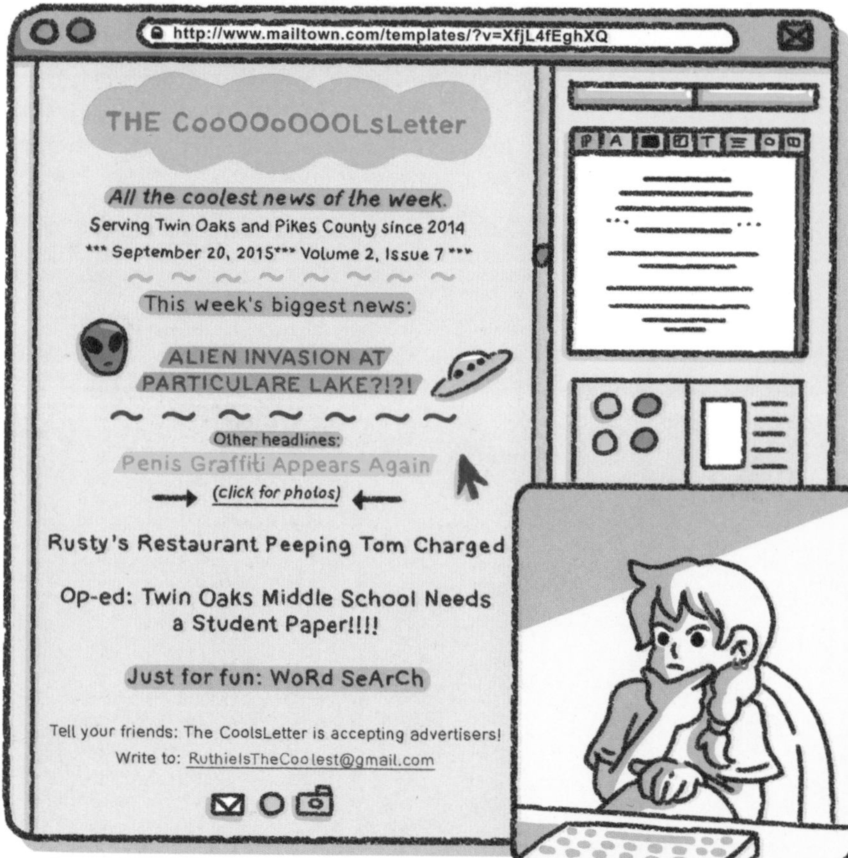
http://www.mailtown.com/templates/?v=XfjL4fEghXQ
THE CooOOoOOOLsLetter
All the coolest news of the week.
Serving Twin Oaks and Pikes County since 2014
*** September 20, 2015*** Volume 2, Issue 7 ***
This week's biggest news:
ALIEN INVASION AT PARTICULARE LAKE?!?!
Other headlines:
Penis Graffiti Appears Again
(click for photos)
Rusty's Restaurant Peeping Tom Charged
Op-ed: Twin Oaks Middle School Needs a Student Paper!!!!
Just for fun: WoRd SeArCh
Tell your friends: The CoolsLetter is accepting advertisers!
Write to: RuthieIsTheCoolest@gmail.com

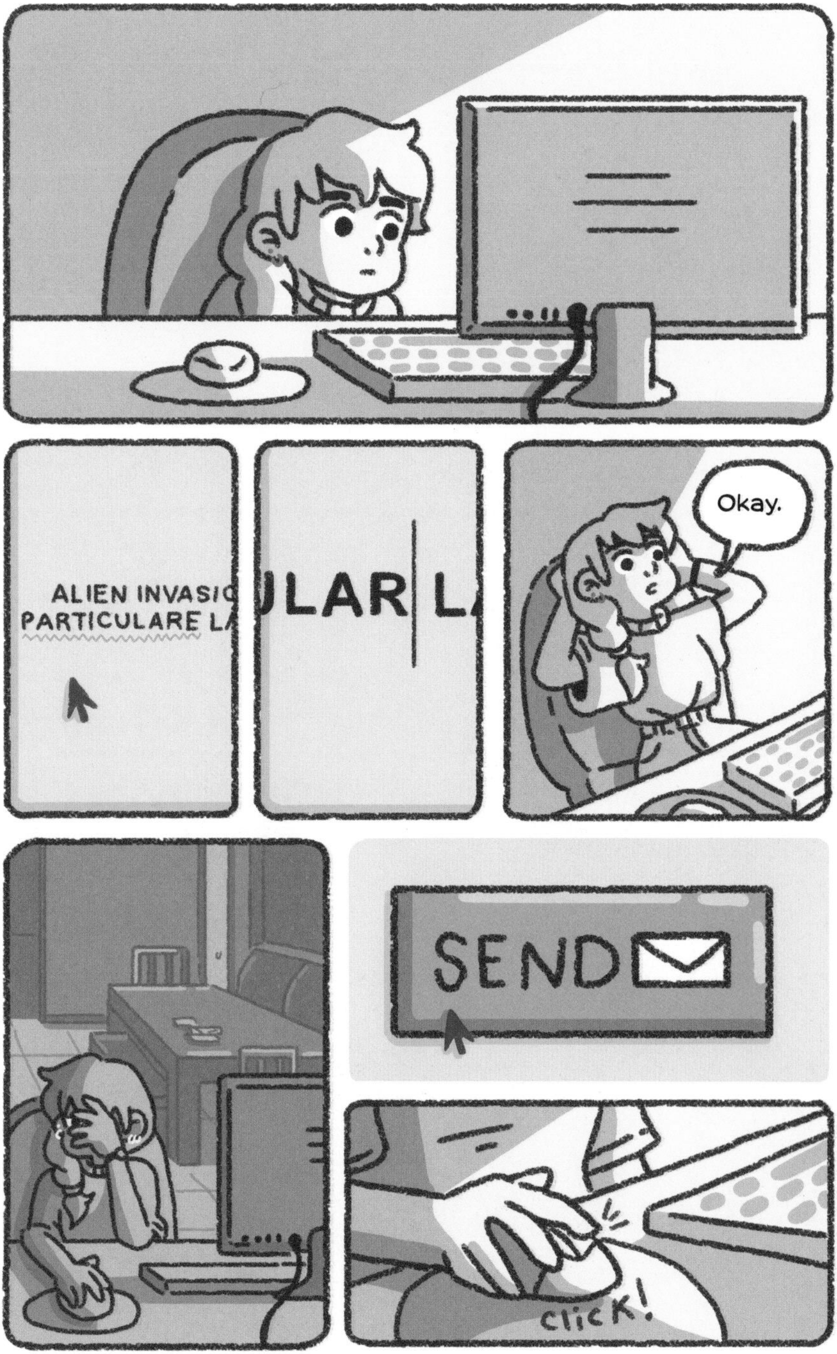
ALIEN INVASIC
PARTICULARE LA
ULAR LA
Okay.
SEND
click!

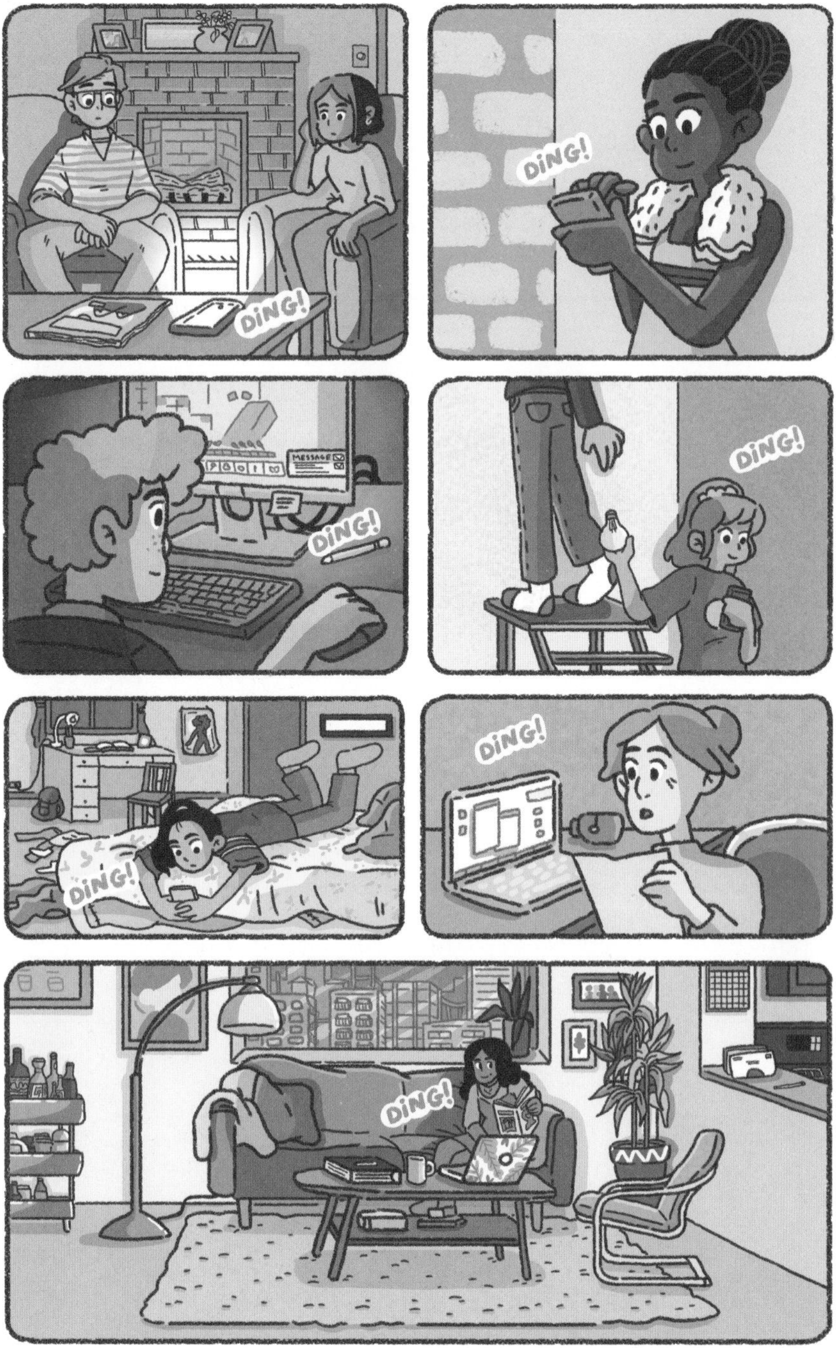
DING!
DING!
MESSAGE
DING!
DING!
DING!
DING!
DING!

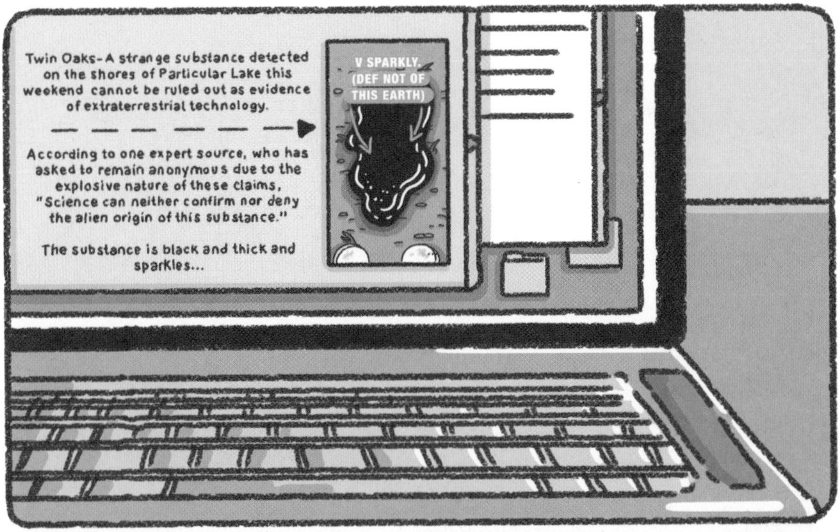
Twin Oaks- A strange substance detected on the shores of Particular Lake this weekend cannot be ruled out as evidence of extraterrestrial technology.
According to one expert source, who has asked to remain anonymous due to the explosive nature of these claims, "Science can neither confirm nor deny the alien origin of this substance."
The substance is black and thick and sparkles...
V SPARKLY. (DEF NOT OF THIS EARTH)

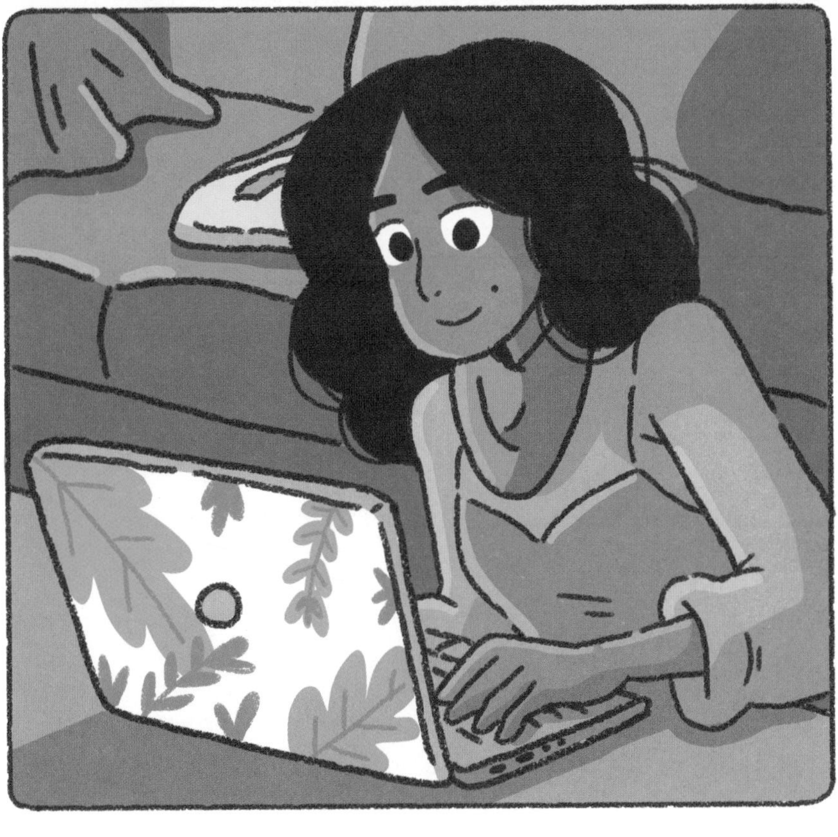

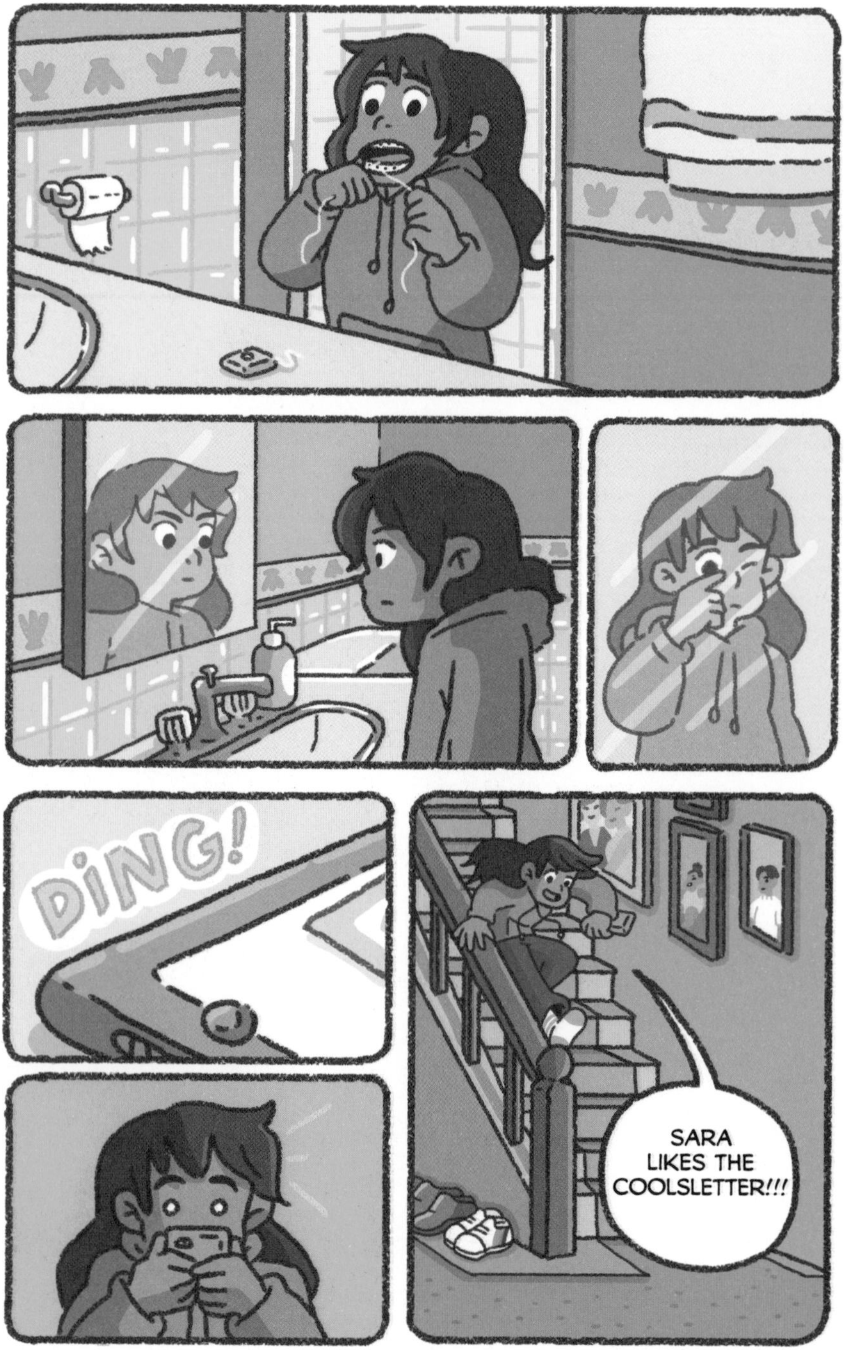
DING!
SARA
LIKES THE
COOLSLETTER!!!

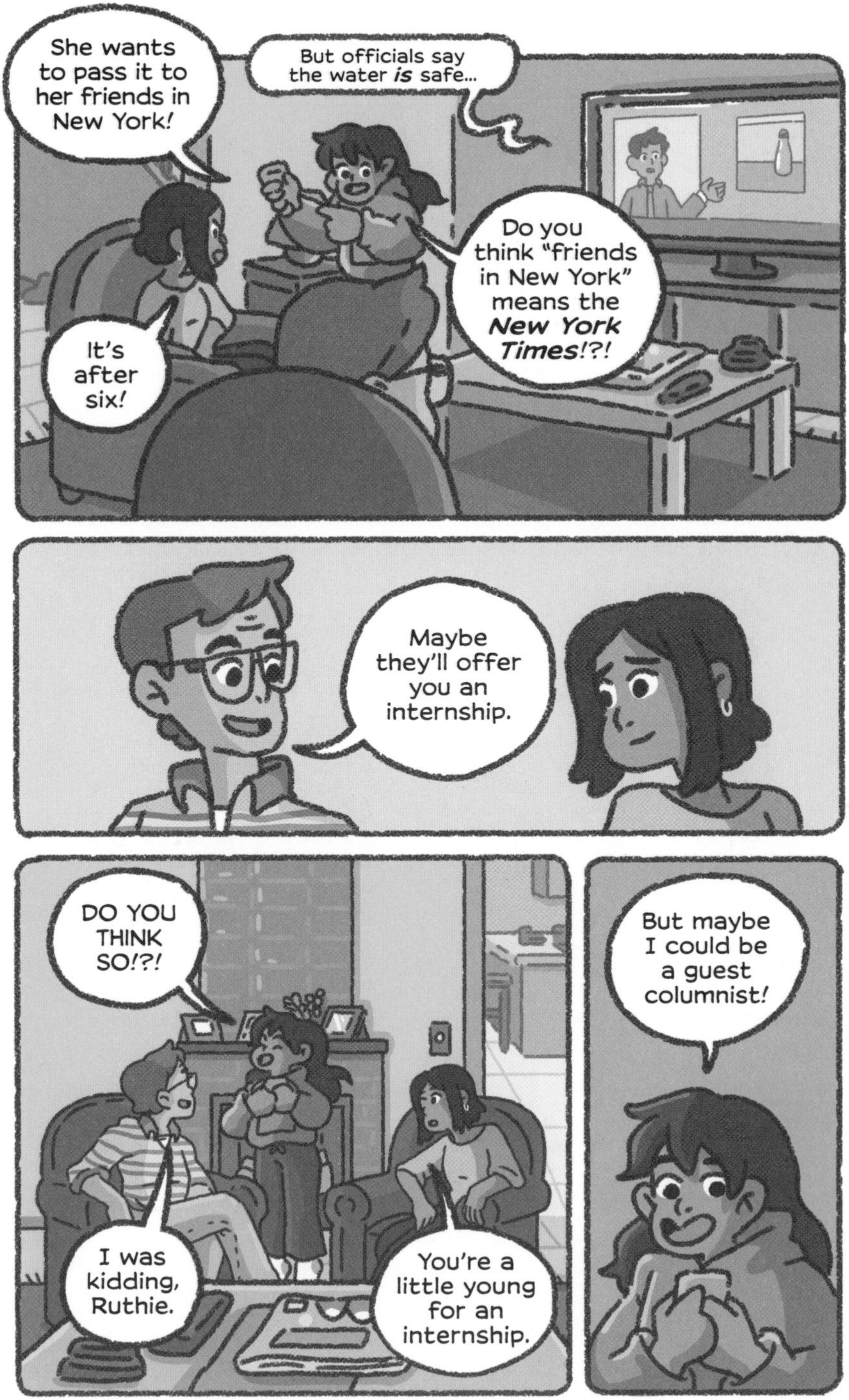

She wants to pass it to her friends in New York!
But officials say the water *is* safe...
It's after six!
Do you think "friends in New York" means the ***New York Times***!?!
Maybe they'll offer you an internship.
DO YOU THINK SO!?!
I was kidding, Ruthie.
You're a little young for an internship.
But maybe I could be a guest columnist!

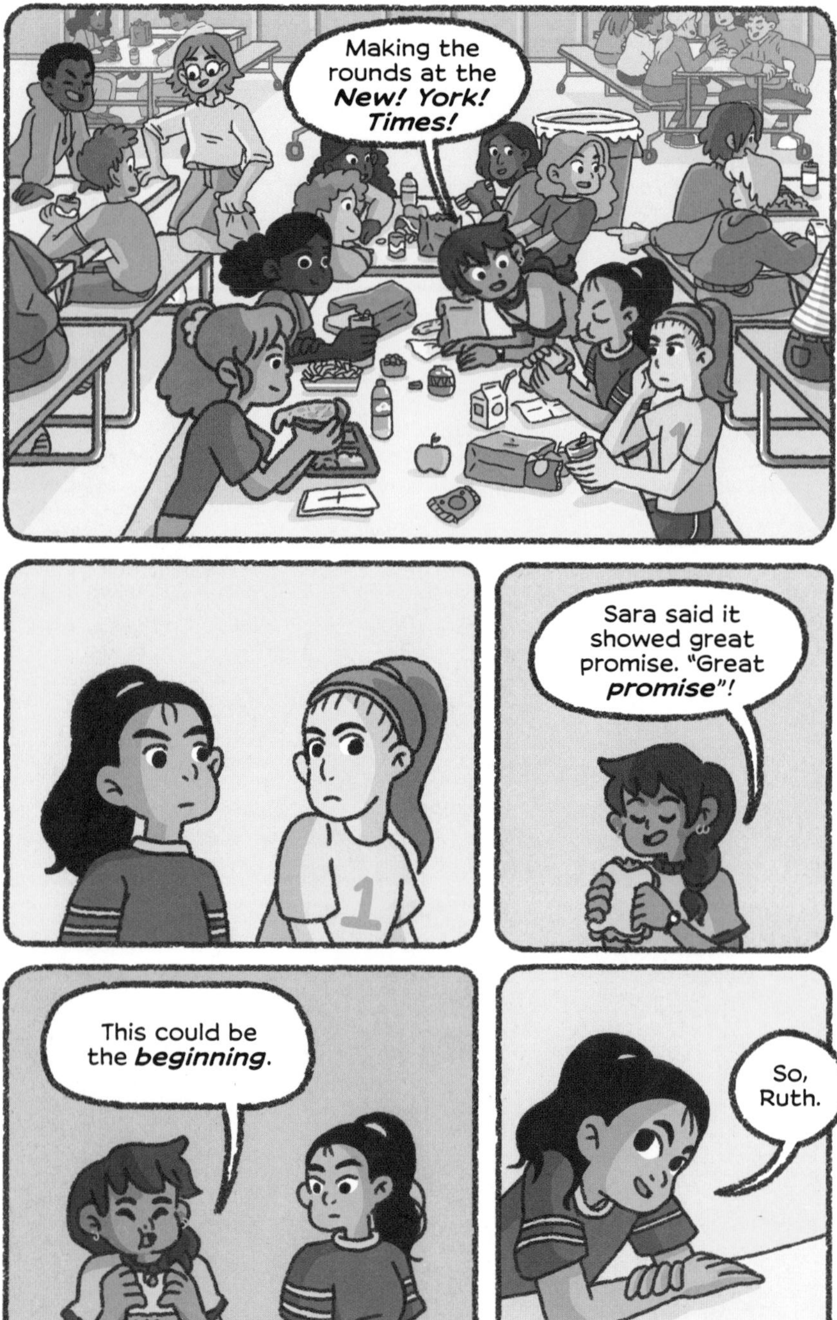
Making the rounds at the *New! York! Times!*
Sara said it showed great promise. "Great *promise*"!
This could be the *beginning*.
So, Ruth.

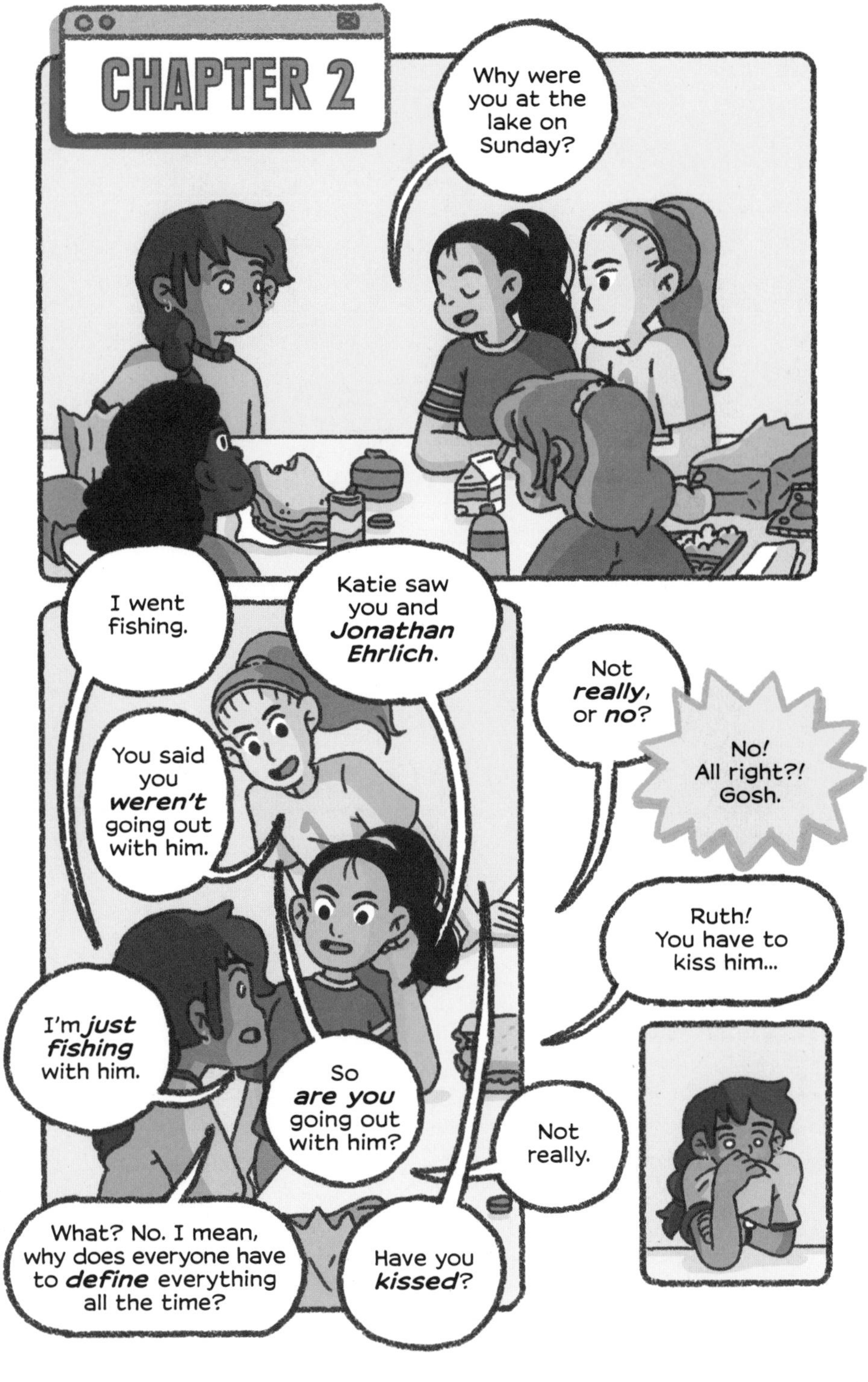
CHAPTER 2
Why were you at the lake on Sunday?
I went fishing.
Katie saw you and *Jonathan Ehrlich*.
You said you ***weren't*** going out with him.
I'm ***just fishing*** with him.
So ***are you*** going out with him?
What? No. I mean, why does everyone have to ***define*** everything all the time?
Have you ***kissed***?
Not really.
Not ***really***, or ***no***?
No! All right?! Gosh.
Ruth! You have to kiss him...

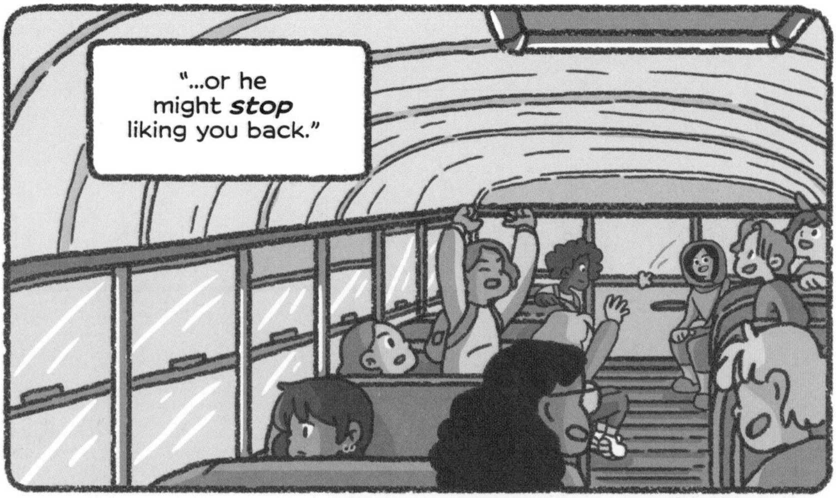
"...or he might *stop* liking you back."

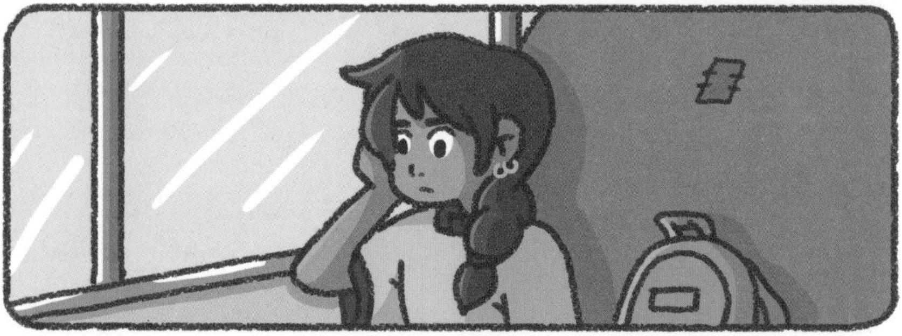

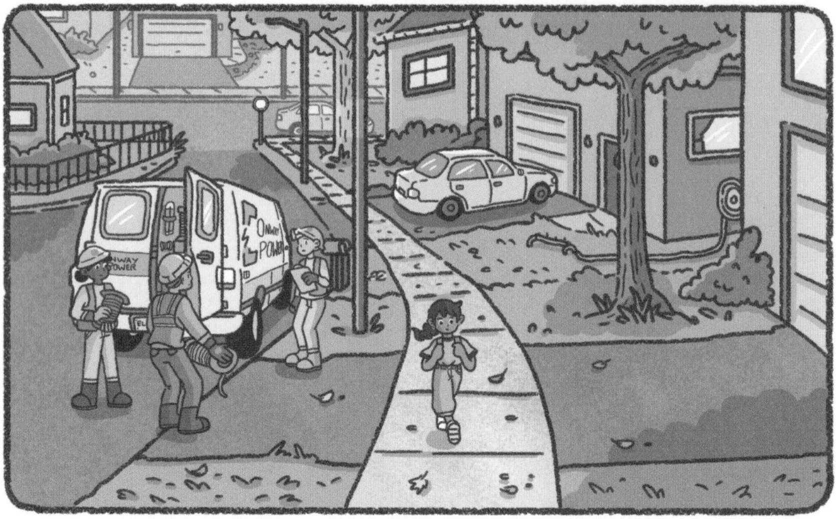

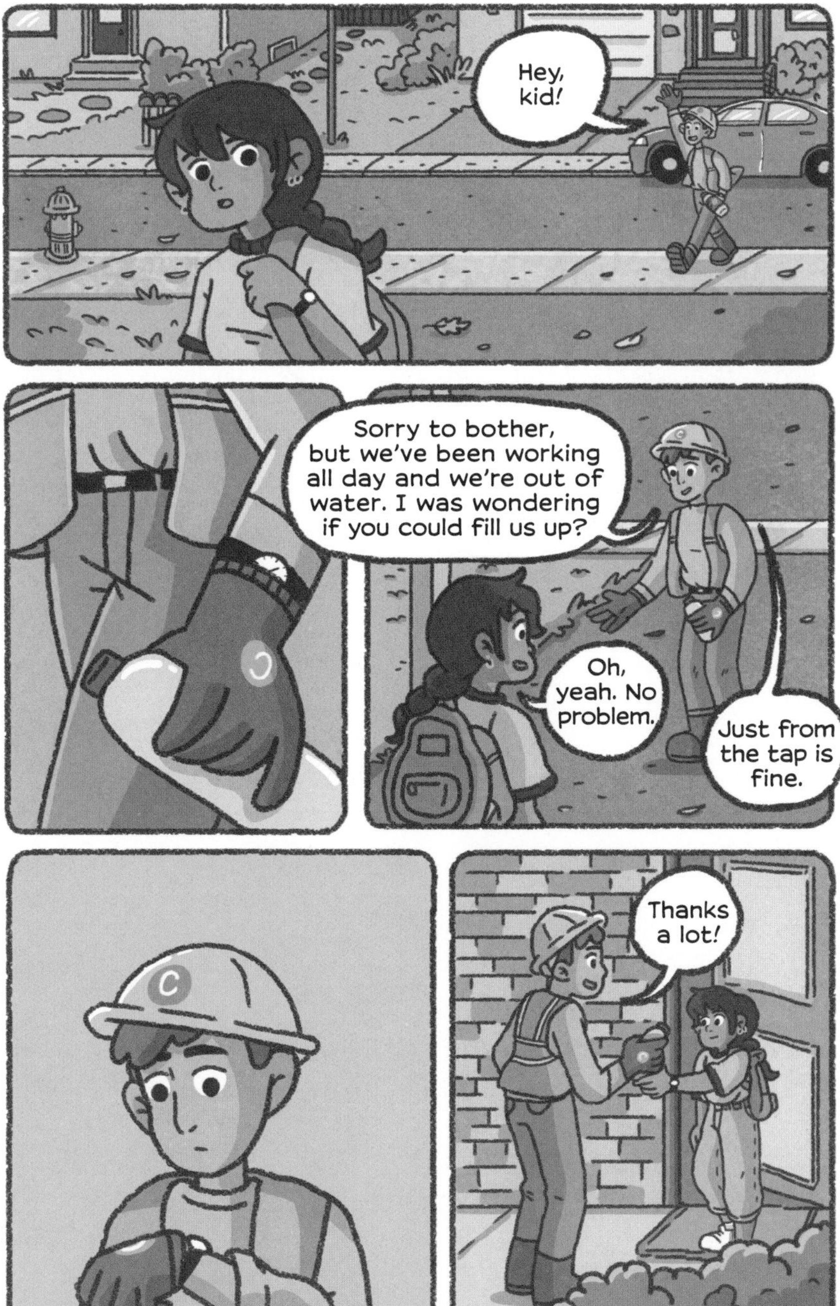
Hey, kid!
Sorry to bother, but we've been working all day and we're out of water. I was wondering if you could fill us up?
Oh, yeah. No problem.
Just from the tap is fine.
Thanks a lot!

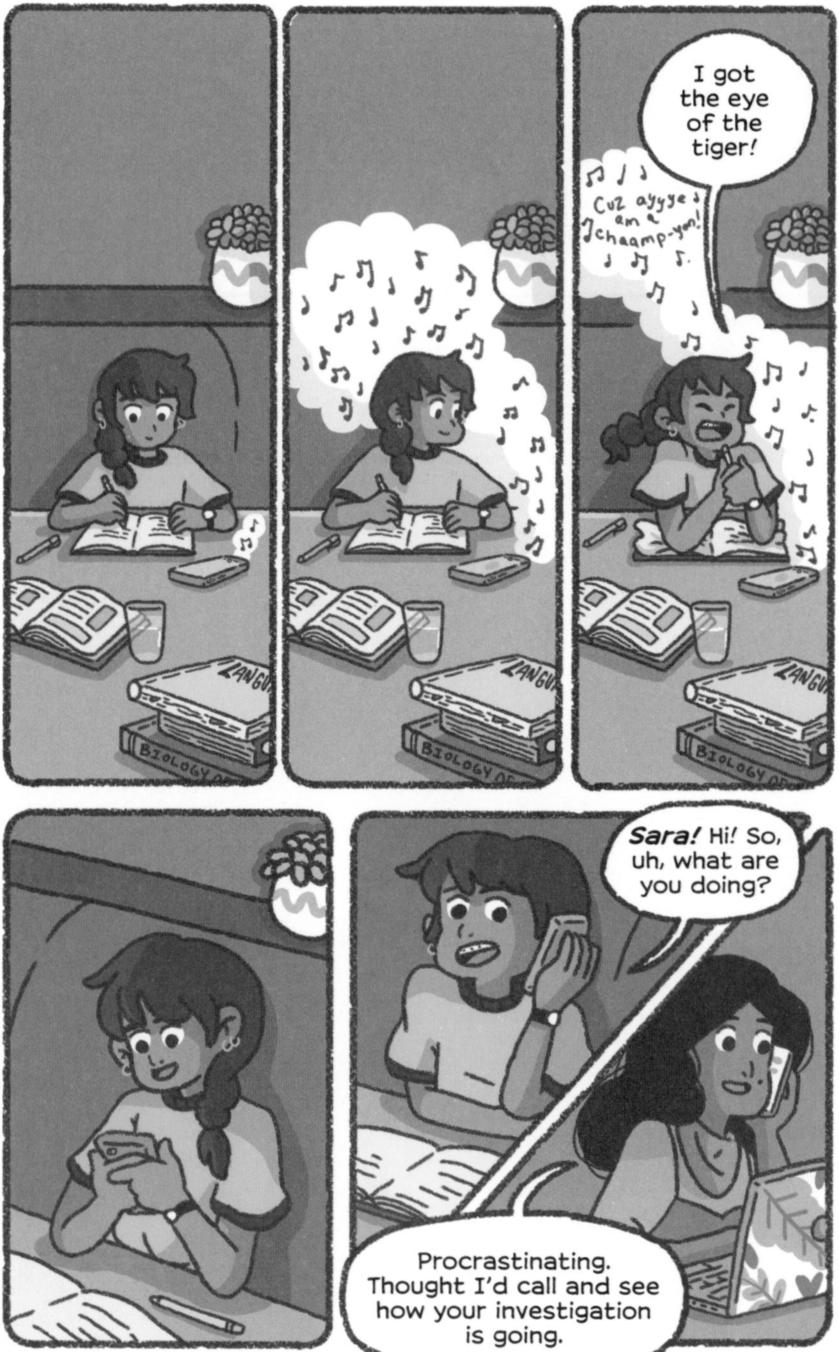
Cuz ayyye am a chaamp-yon!
I got the eye of the tiger!
Sara! Hi! So, uh, what are you doing?
Procrastinating. Thought I'd call and see how your investigation is going.

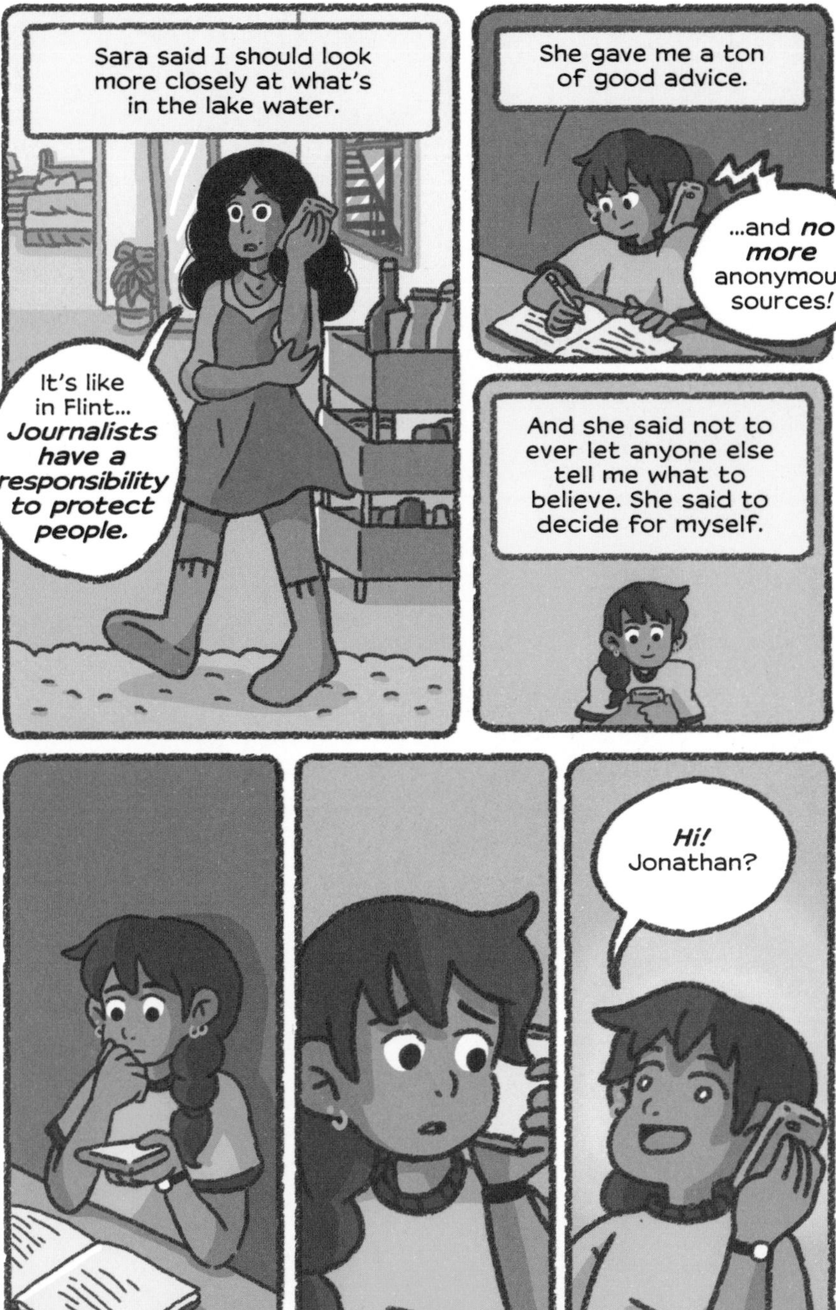
Sara said I should look more closely at what's in the lake water.
It's like in Flint... *Journalists have a responsibility to protect people.*
She gave me a ton of good advice.
...and *no more* anonymous sources!
And she said not to ever let anyone else tell me what to believe. She said to decide for myself.
Hi! Jonathan?

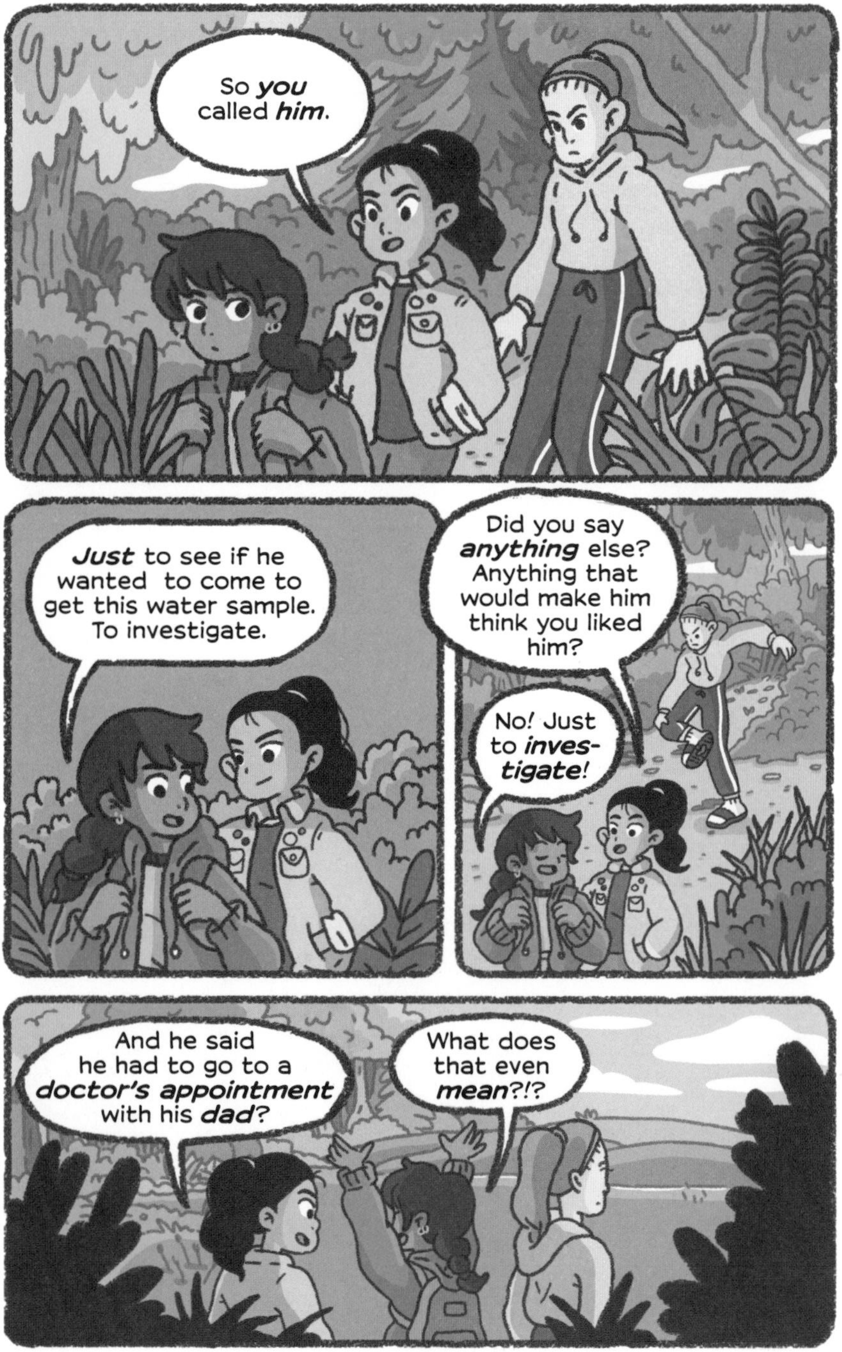

So *you* called *him*.
Just to see if he wanted to come to get this water sample. To investigate.
Did you say *anything* else? Anything that would make him think you liked him?
No! Just to *inves-tigate*!
And he said he had to go to a *doctor's appointment* with his *dad*?
What does that even *mean*?!?

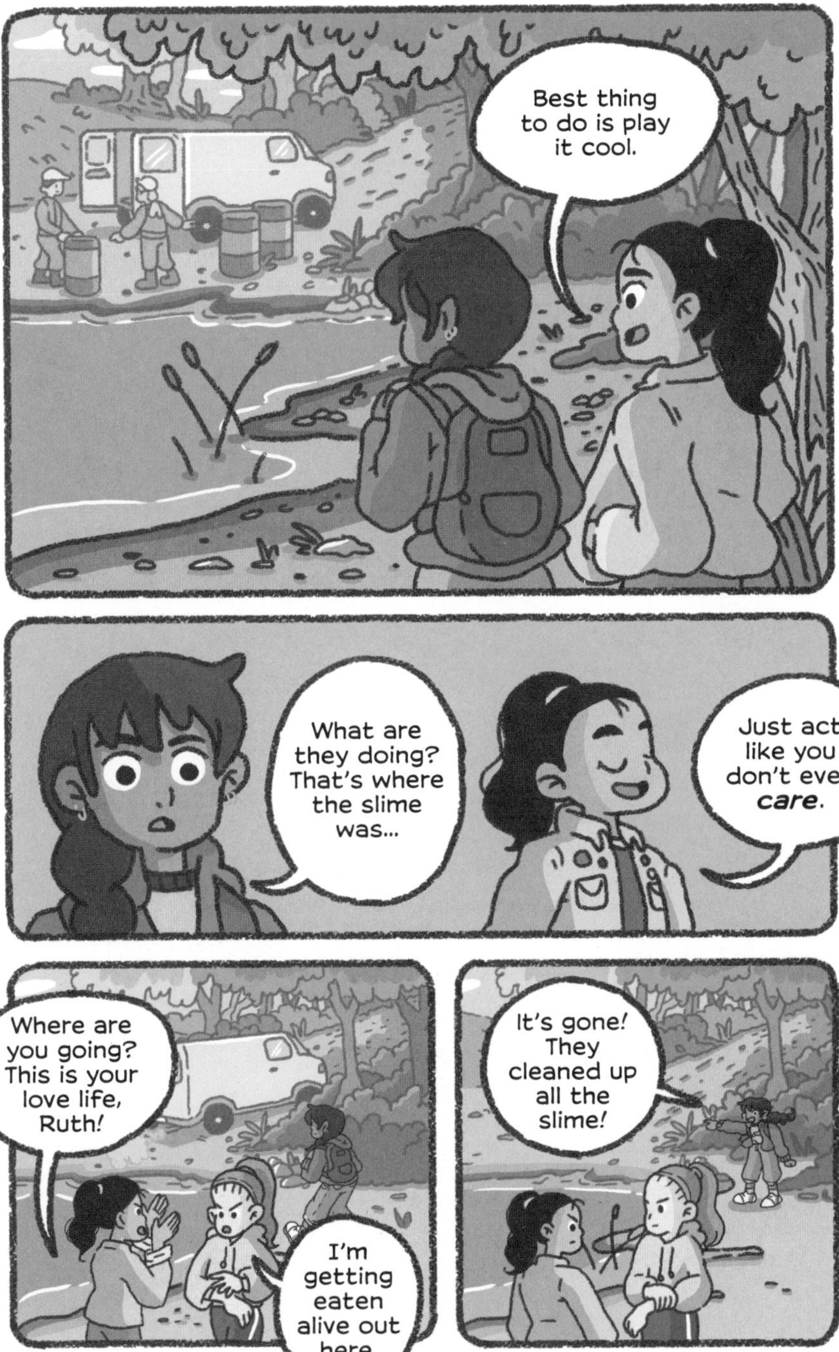
Best thing to do is play it cool.
What are they doing? That's where the slime was...
Just act like you don't even *care*.
Where are you going? This is your love life, Ruth!
I'm getting eaten alive out here.
It's gone! They cleaned up all the slime!

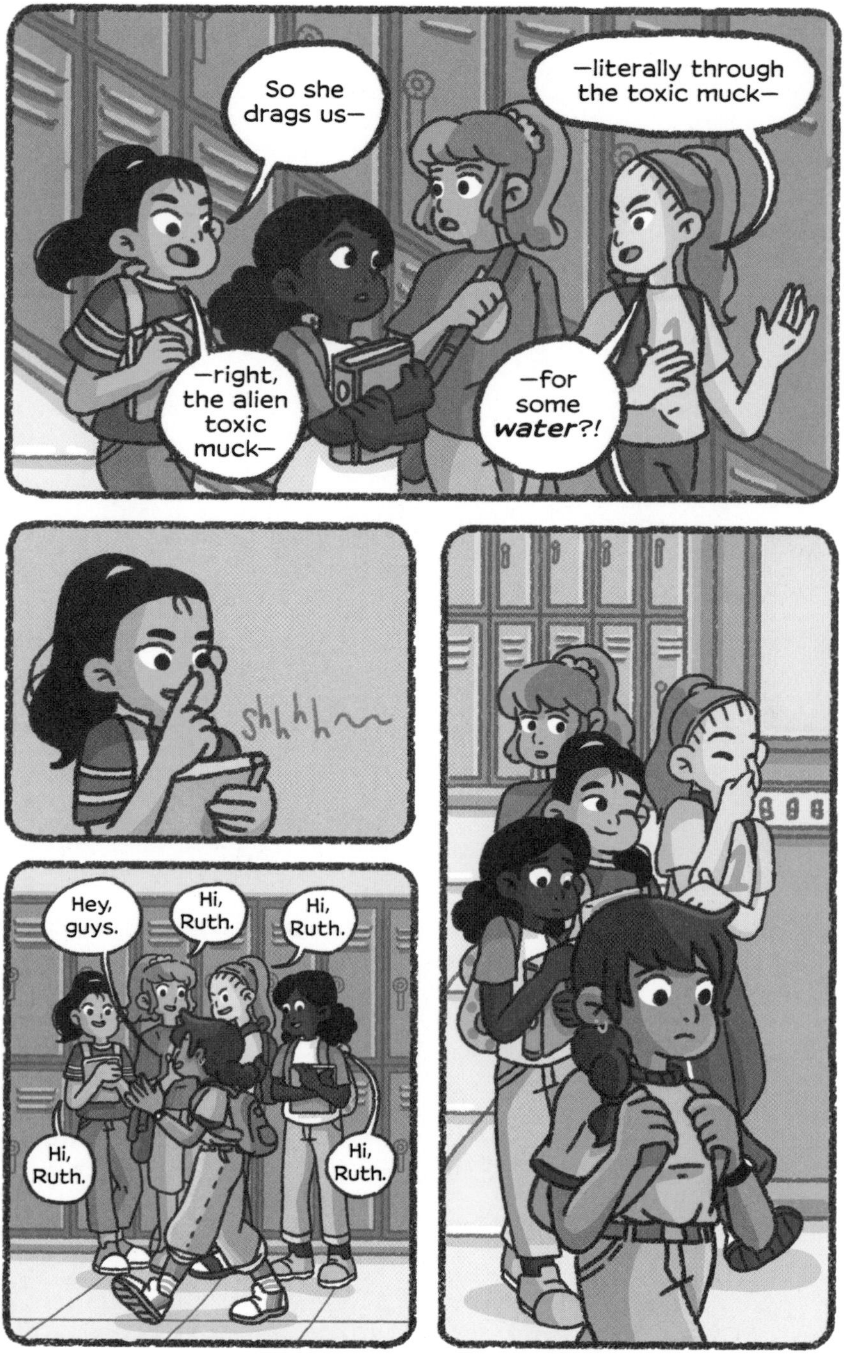
So she drags us—
—literally through the toxic muck—
—right, the alien toxic muck—
—for some *water*?!
shhhh~~
Hey, guys.
Hi, Ruth.
Hi, Ruth.
Hi, Ruth.
Hi, Ruth.

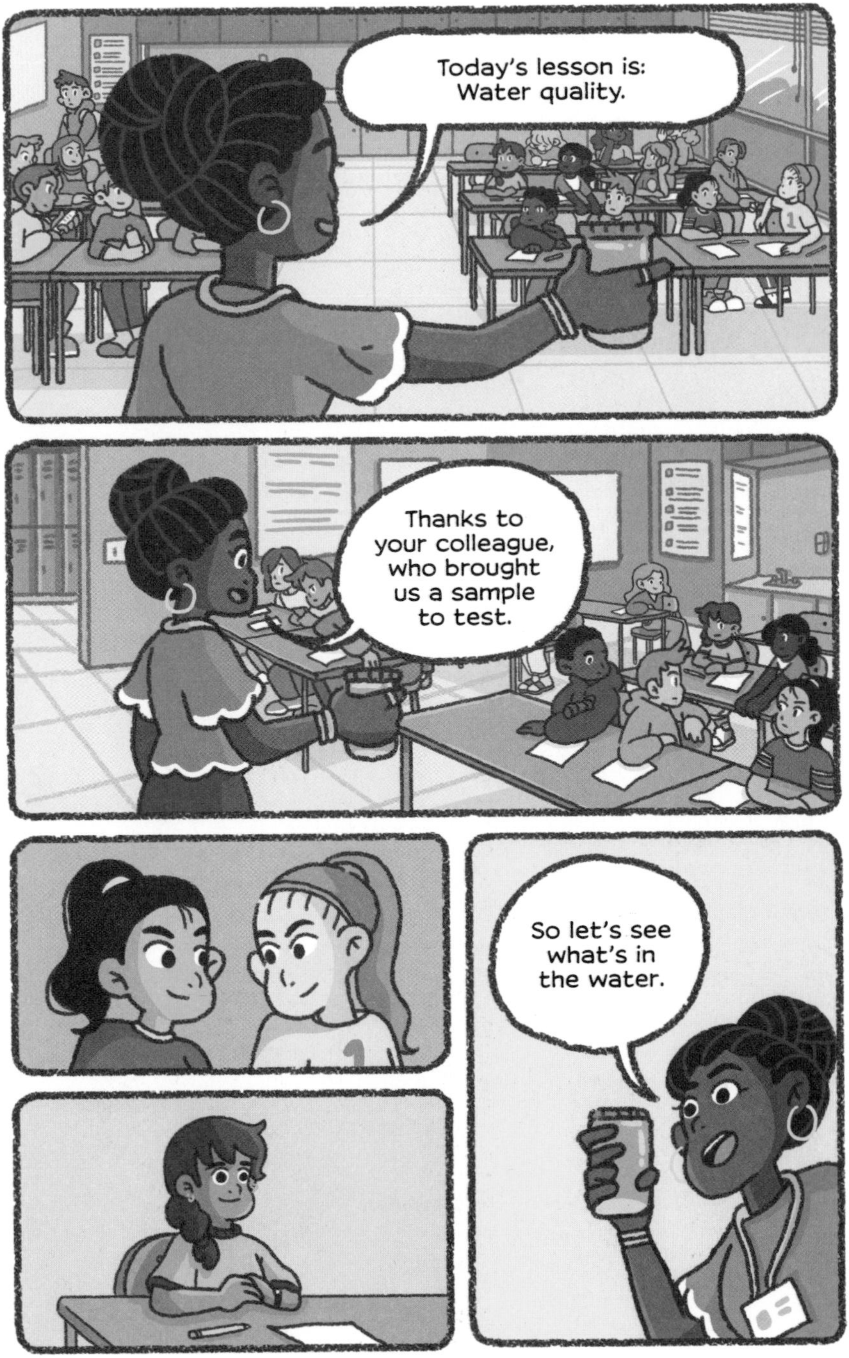
Today's lesson is:
Water quality.
Thanks to
your colleague,
who brought
us a sample
to test.
So let's see
what's in
the water.

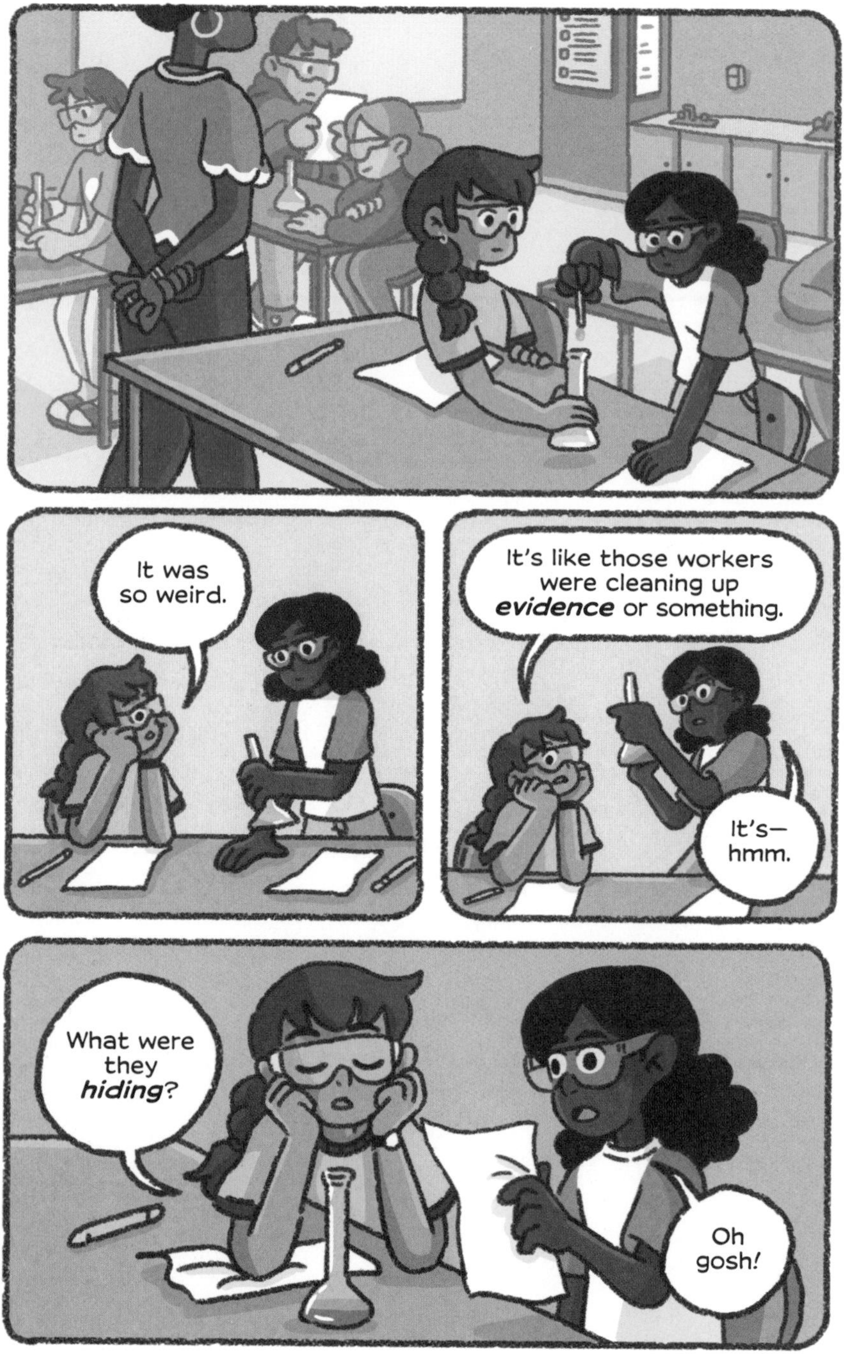
It was so weird.
It's like those workers were cleaning up *evidence* or something.
It's—hmm.
What were they *hiding*?
Oh gosh!

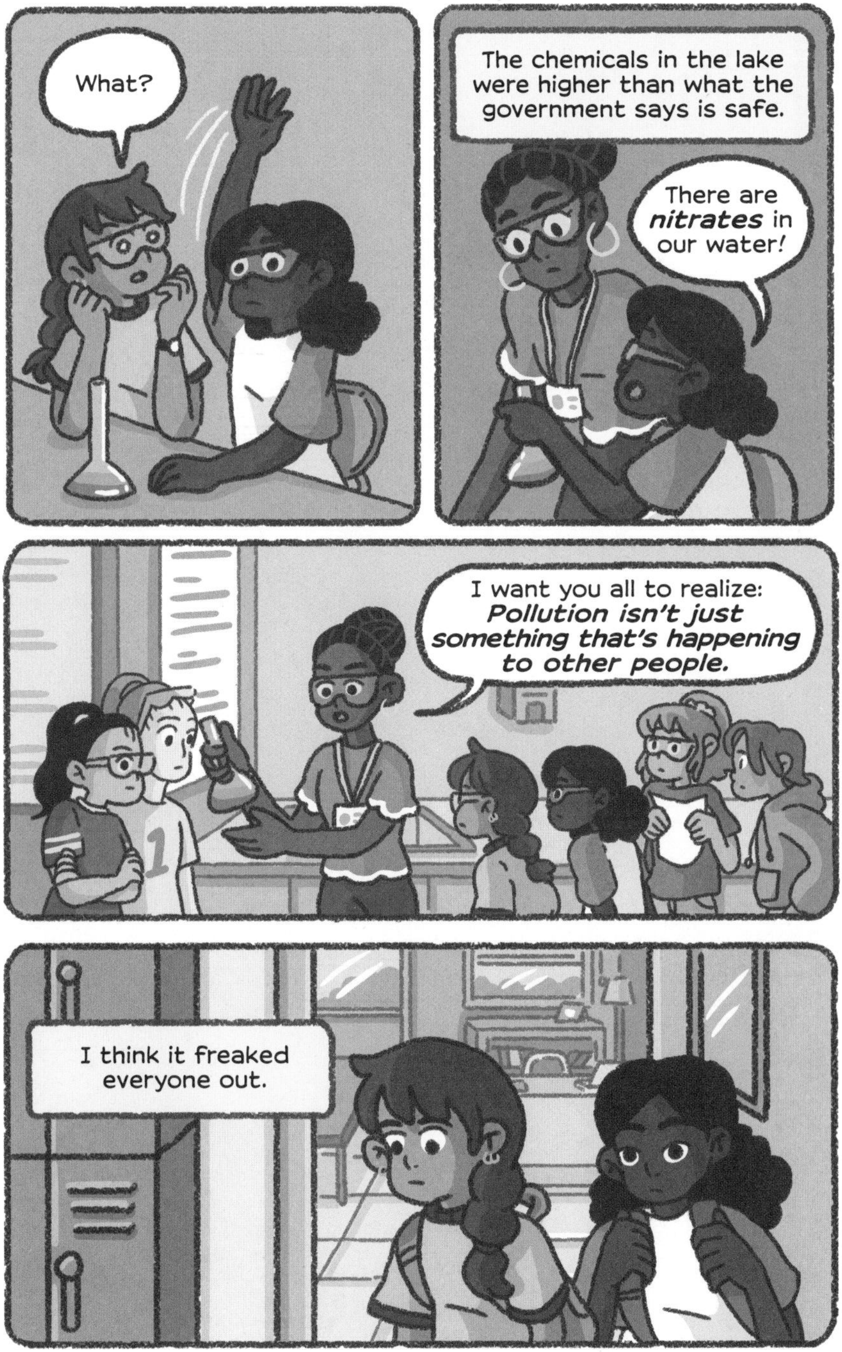
What?
The chemicals in the lake were higher than what the government says is safe.
There are *nitrates* in our water!
I want you all to realize: ***Pollution isn't just something that's happening to other people.***
I think it freaked everyone out.

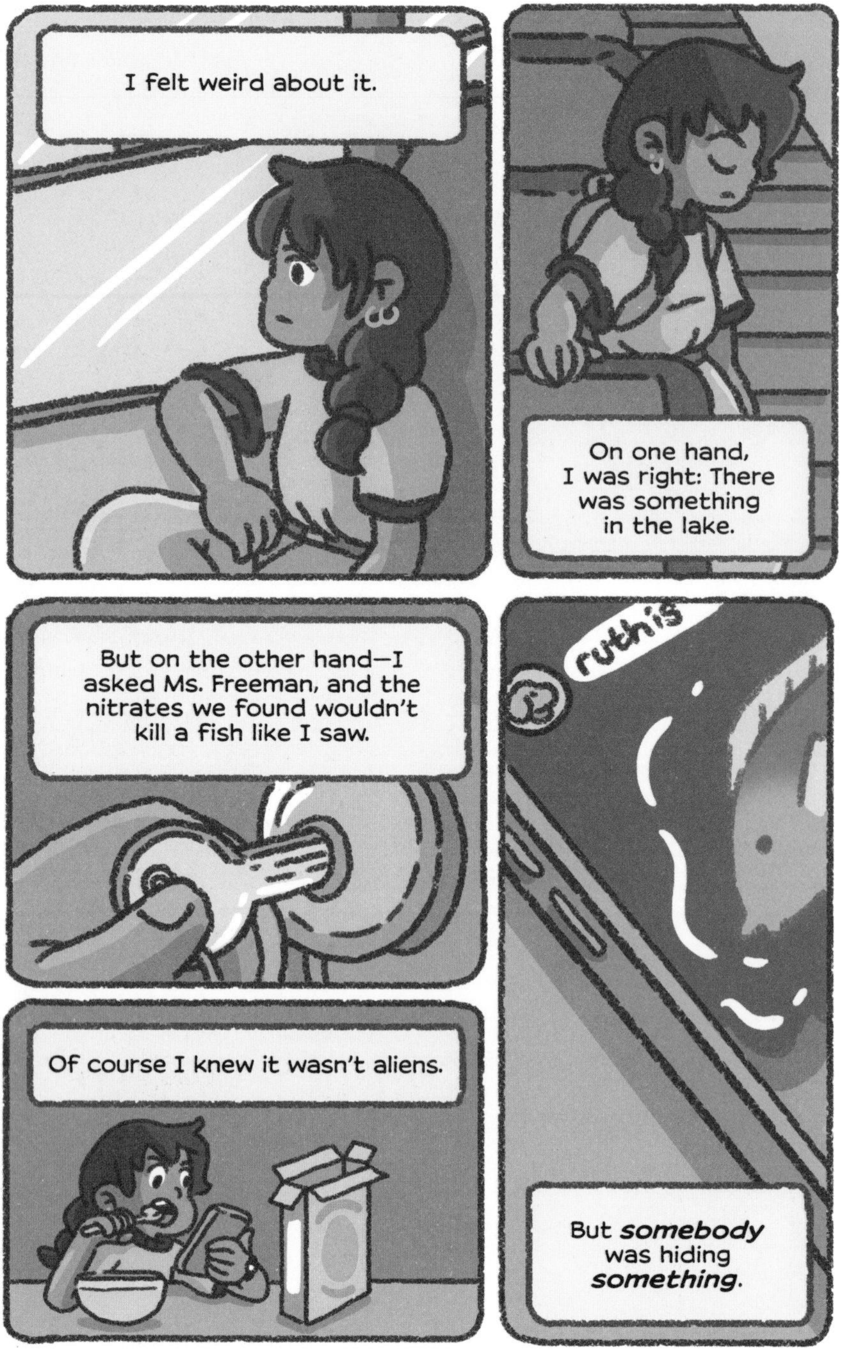
I felt weird about it.
On one hand, I was right: There was something in the lake.
But on the other hand—I asked Ms. Freeman, and the nitrates we found wouldn't kill a fish like I saw.
ruthis
Of course I knew it wasn't aliens.
But *somebody* was hiding ***something***.

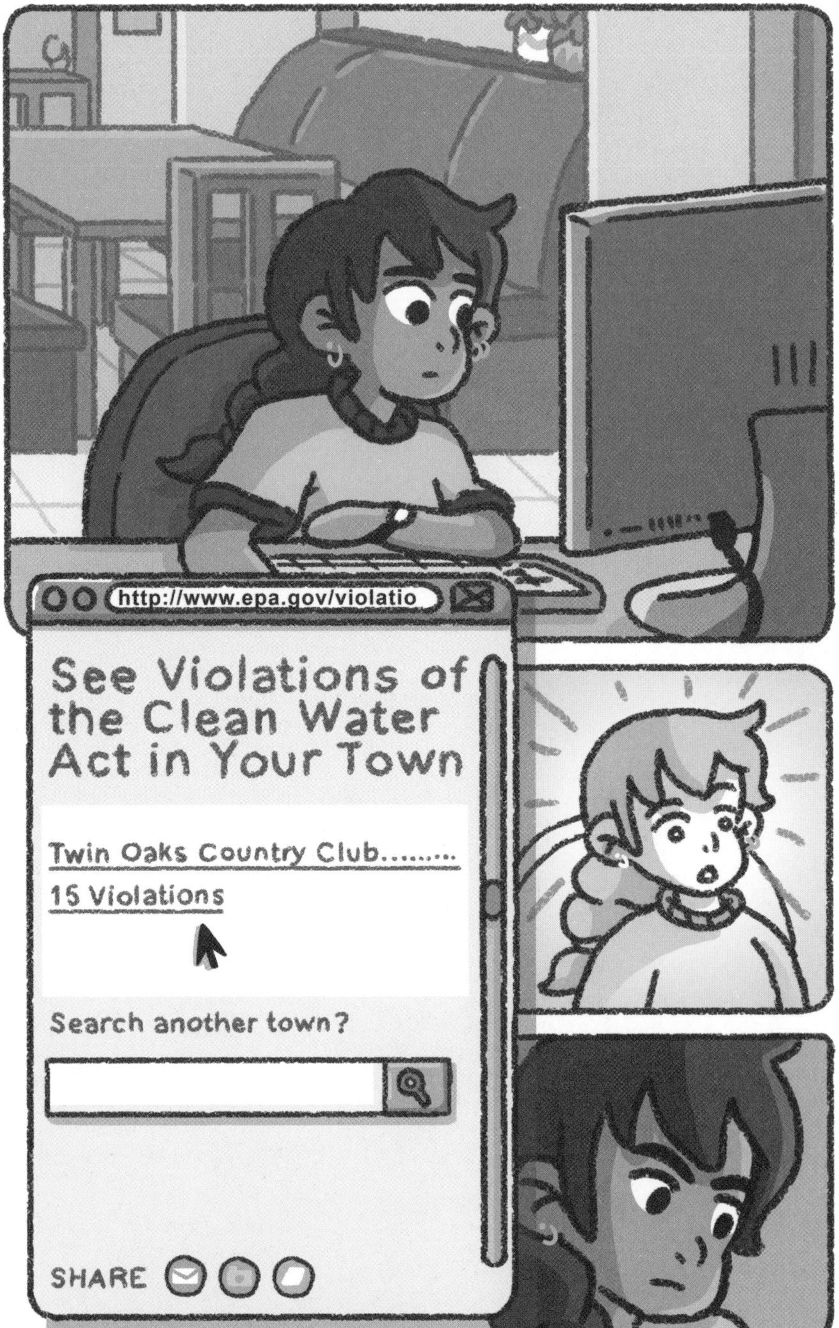
http://www.epa.gov/violatio
See Violations of the Clean Water Act in Your Town
Twin Oaks Country Club.........
15 Violations
Search another town?
SHARE

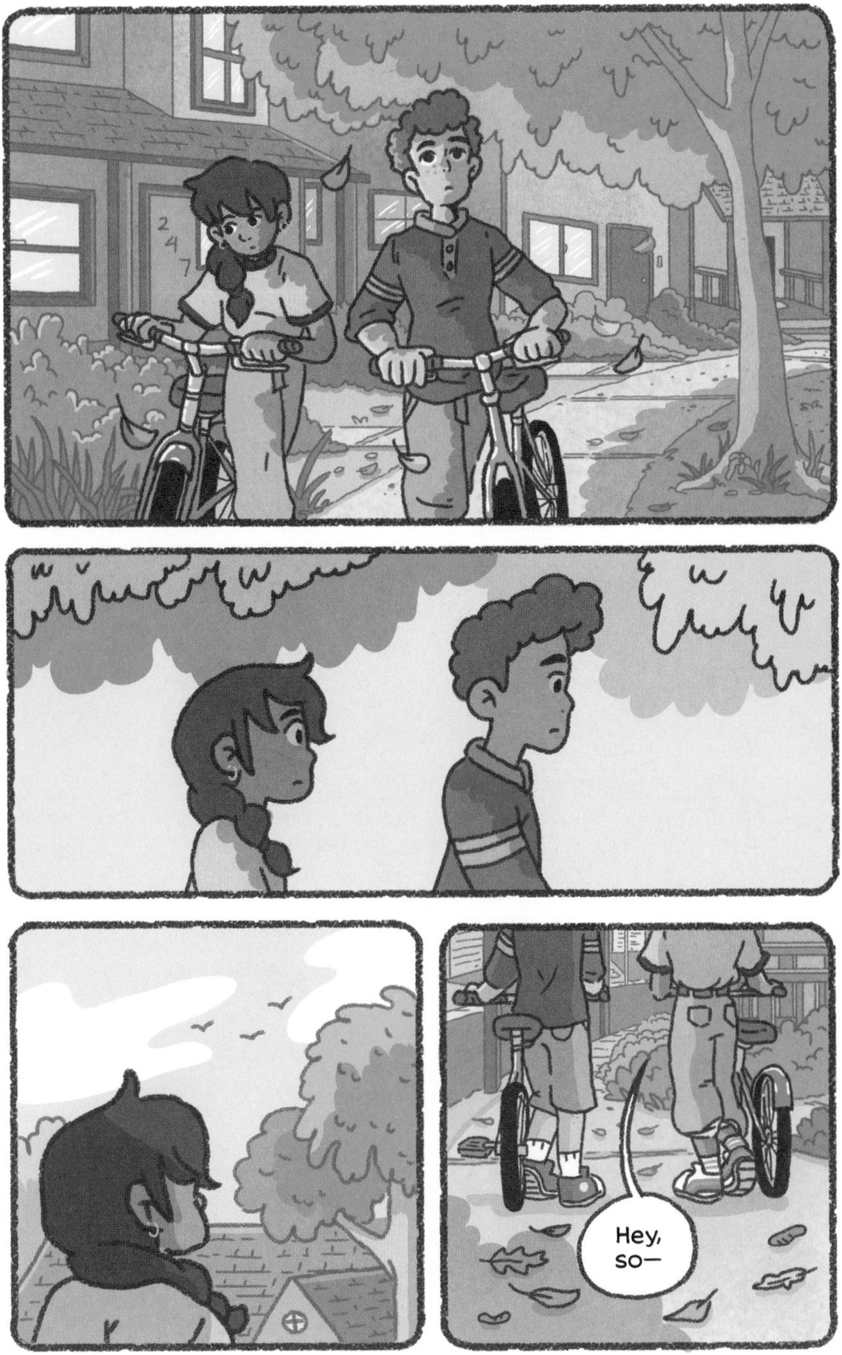
Hey,
so—

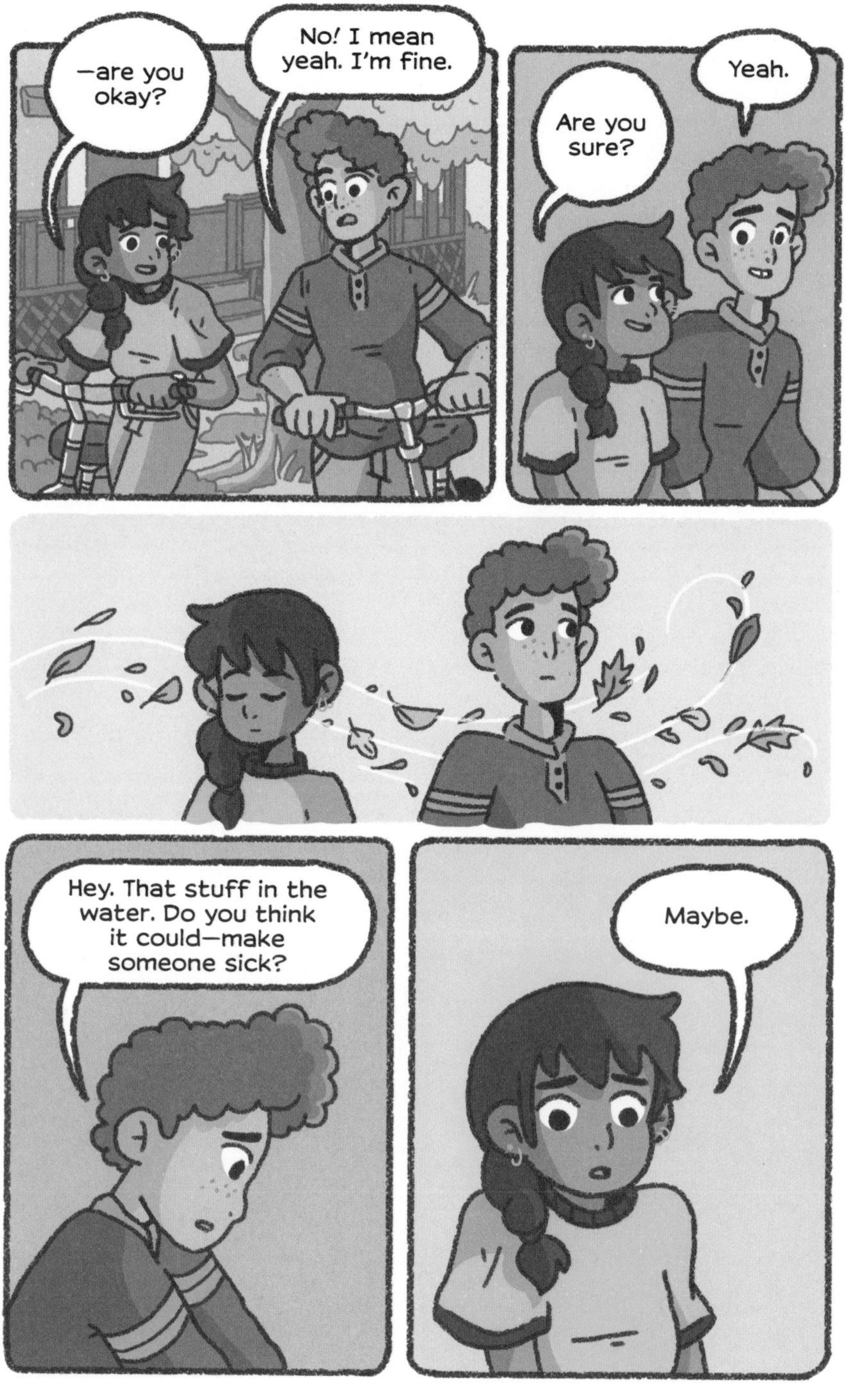
—are you okay?
No! I mean yeah. I'm fine.
Are you sure?
Yeah.
Hey. That stuff in the water. Do you think it could—make someone sick?
Maybe.

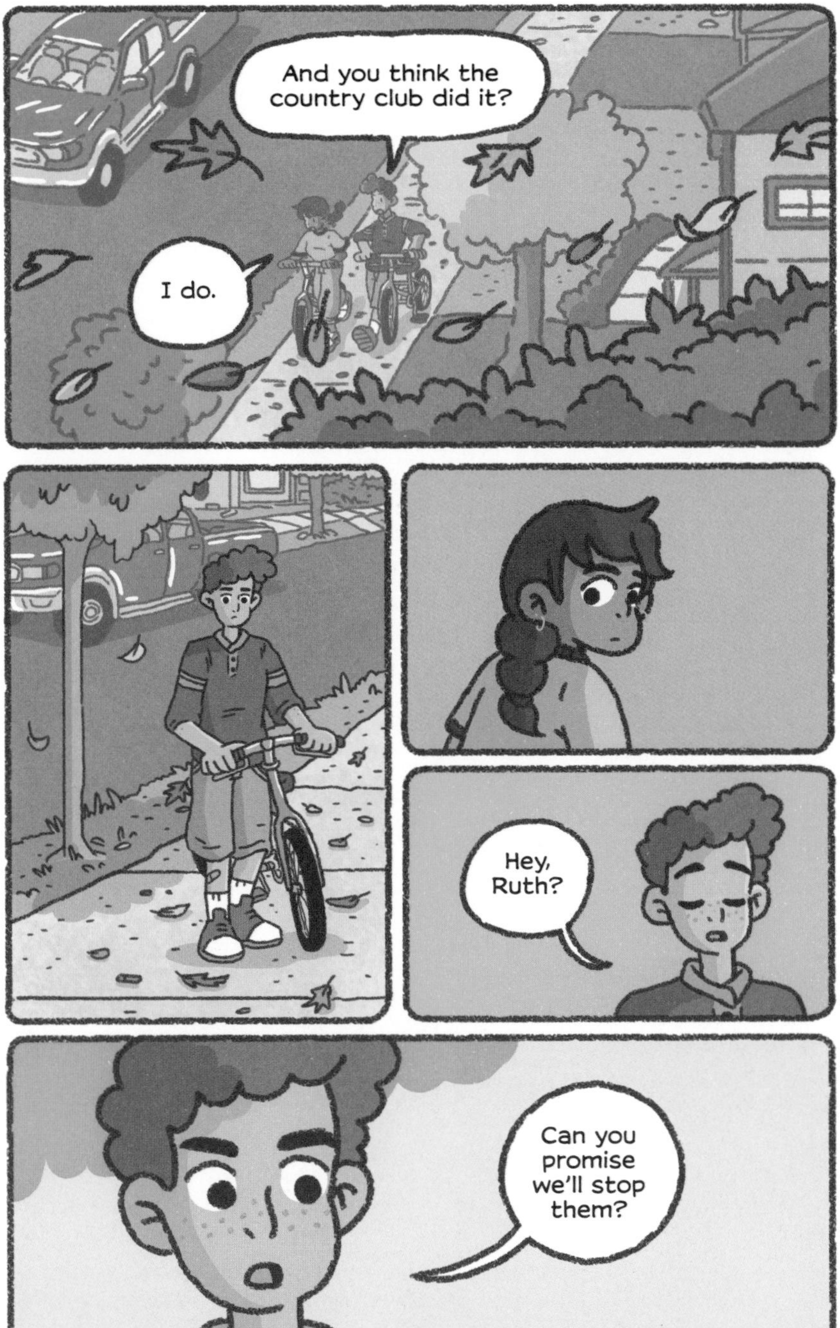
And you think the country club did it?
I do.
Hey, Ruth?
Can you promise we'll stop them?

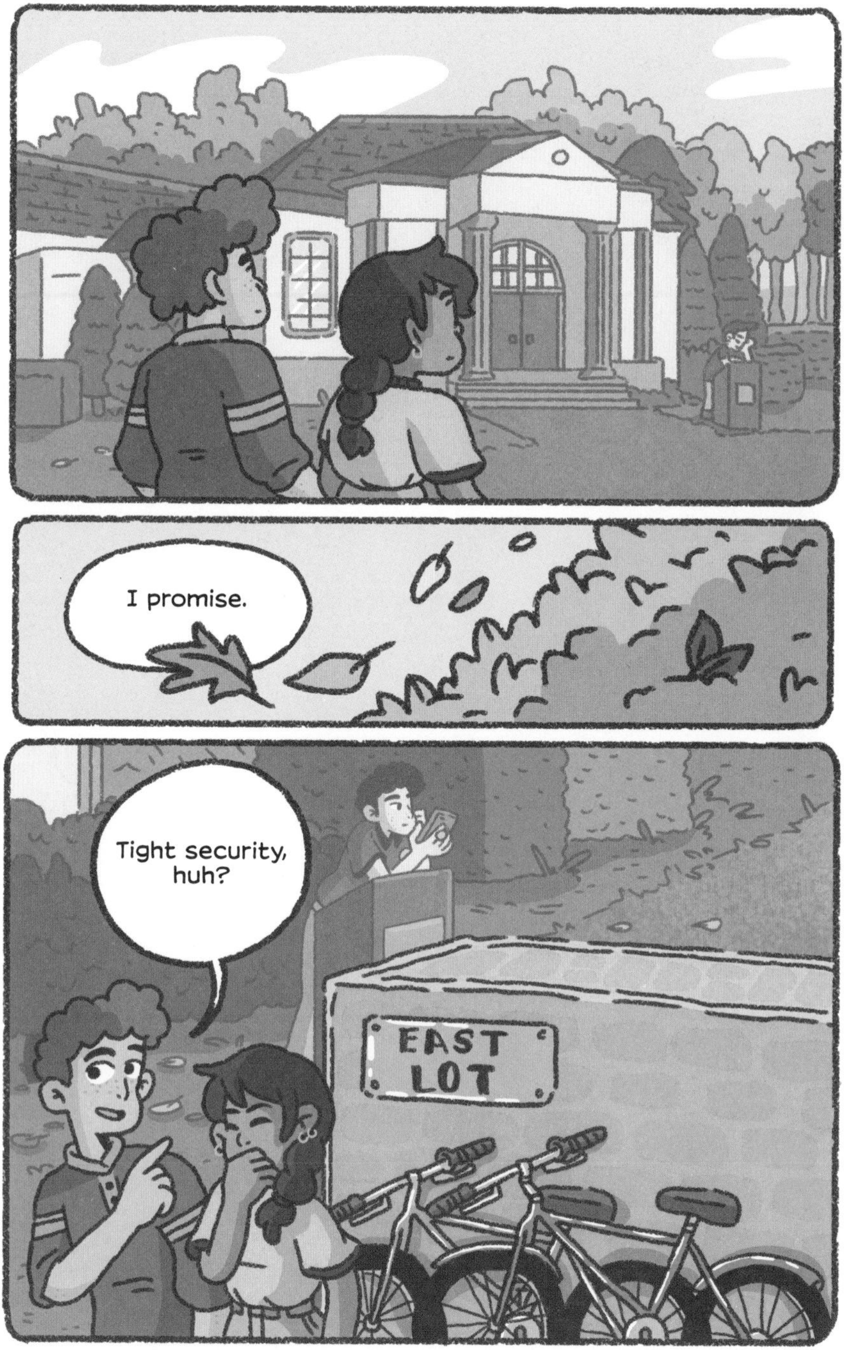
I promise.
Tight security, huh?
EAST LOT

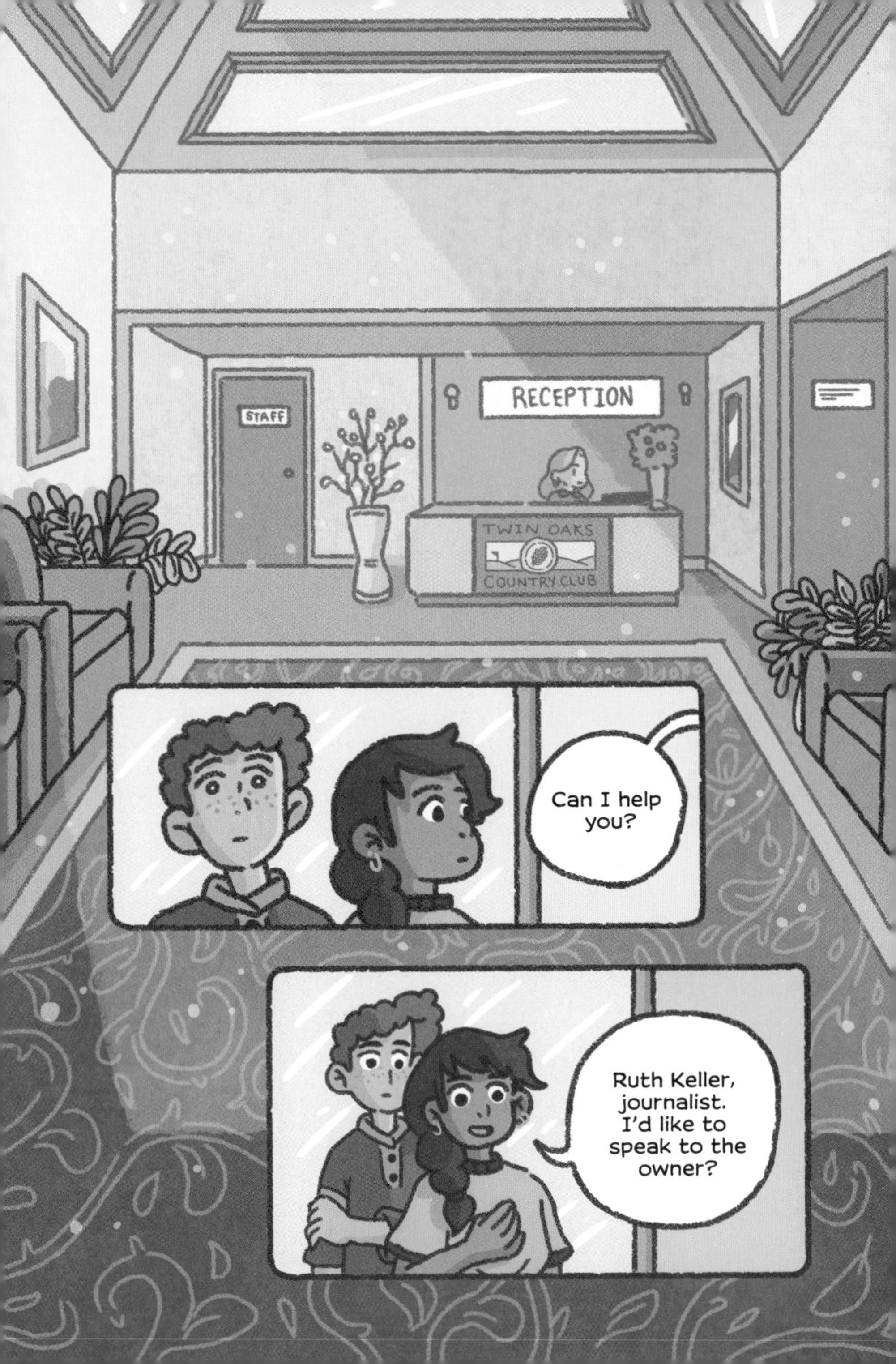
RECEPTION
STAFF
TWIN OAKS
COUNTRY CLUB
Can I help you?
Ruth Keller, journalist. I'd like to speak to the owner?

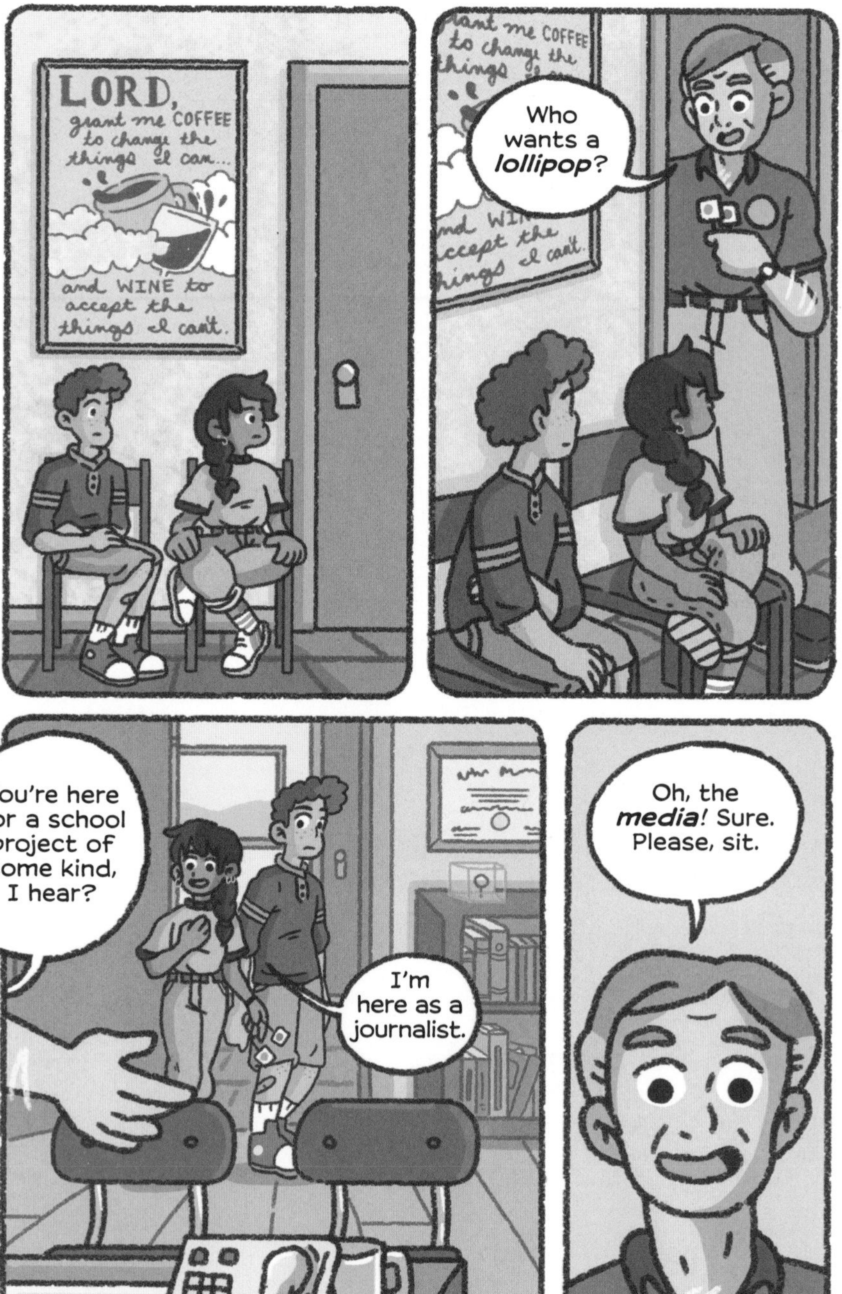
LORD,
grant me COFFEE
to change the
things I can...
and WINE to
accept the
things I can't.
Who wants a *lollipop*?
You're here for a school project of some kind, I hear?
I'm here as a journalist.
Oh, the *media*! Sure. Please, sit.

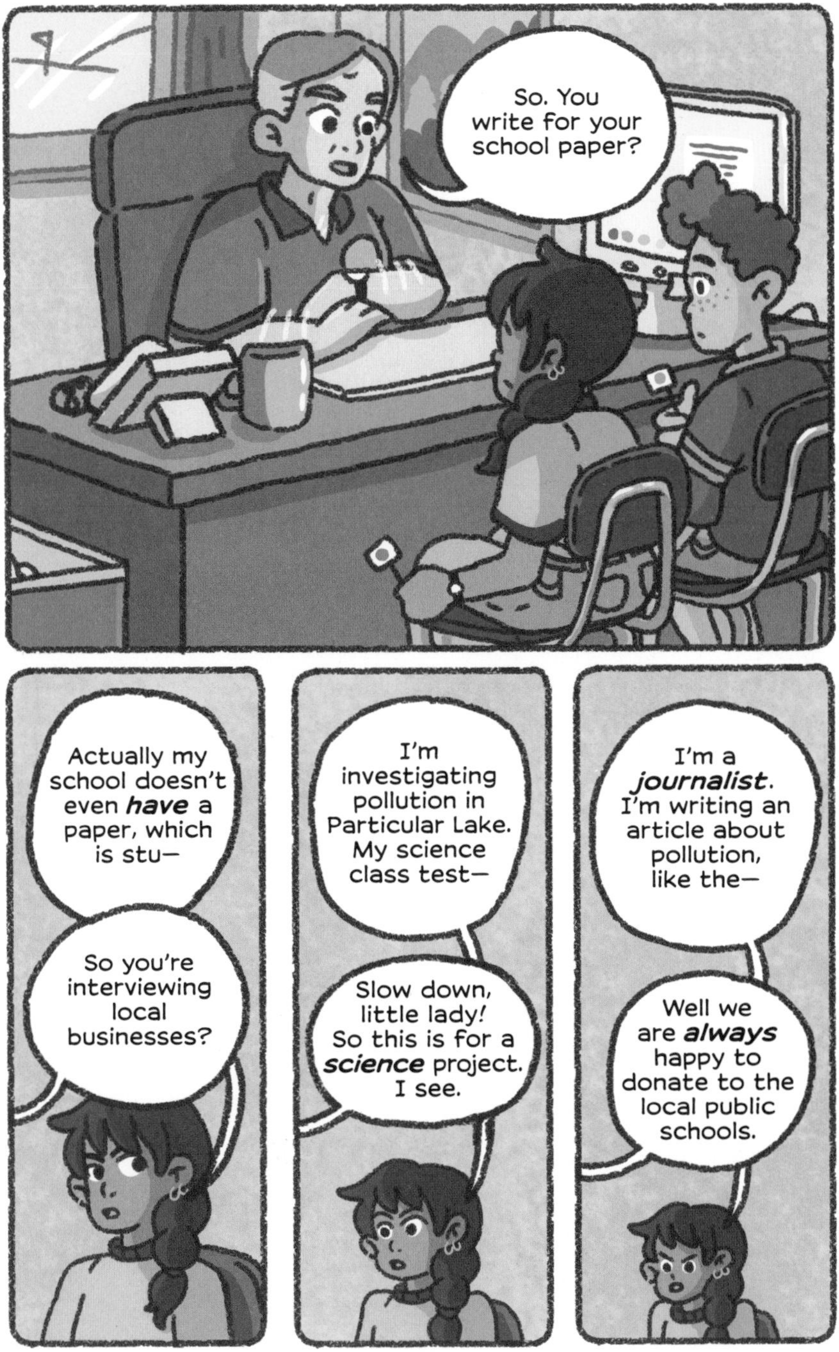
So. You write for your school paper?
Actually my school doesn't even *have* a paper, which is stu—
So you're interviewing local businesses?
I'm investigating pollution in Particular Lake. My science class test—
Slow down, little lady! So this is for a *science* project. I see.
I'm a *journalist*. I'm writing an article about pollution, like the—
Well we are *always* happy to donate to the local public schools.

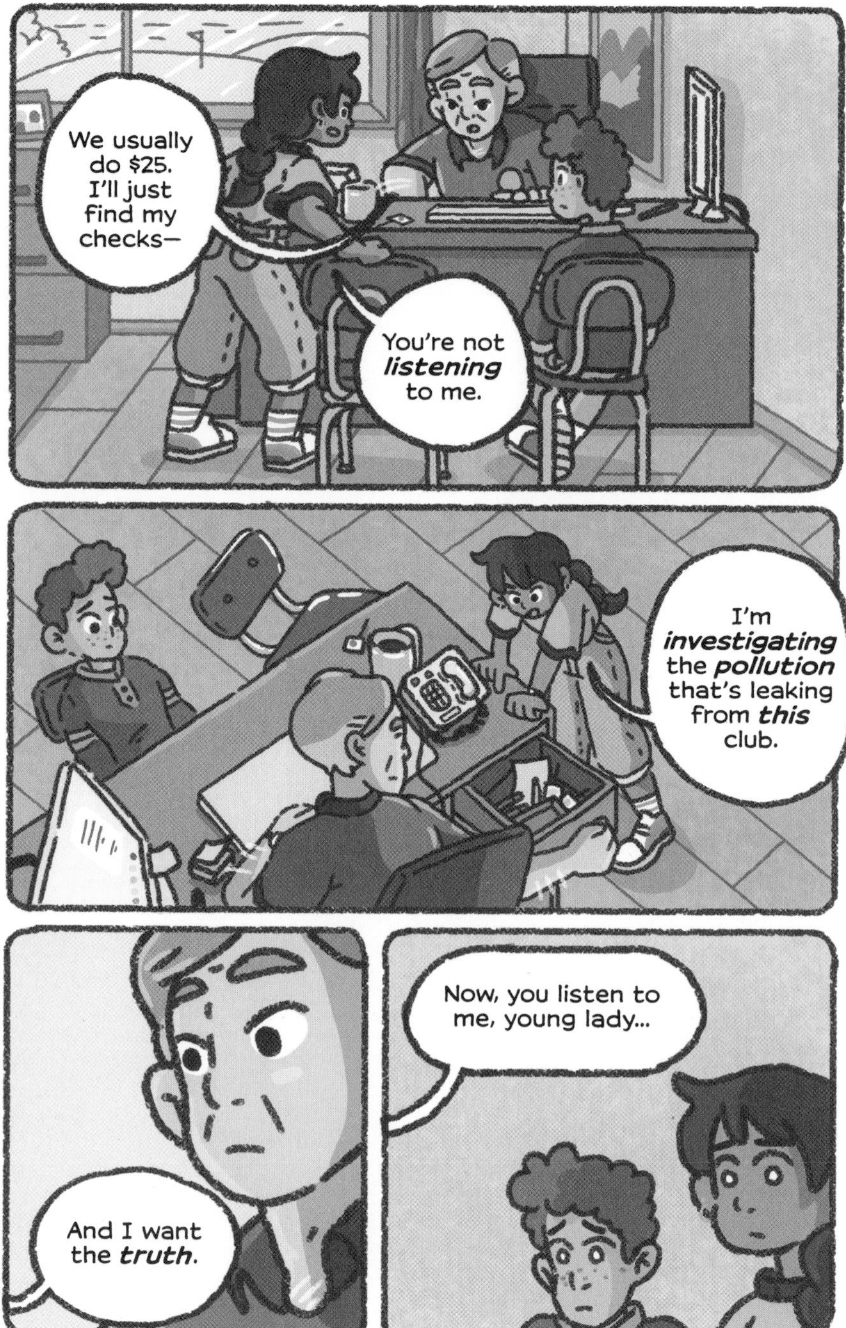
We usually do $25. I'll just find my checks—
You're not *listening* to me.
I'm *investigating* the *pollution* that's leaking from *this* club.
And I want the *truth*.
Now, you listen to me, young lady...

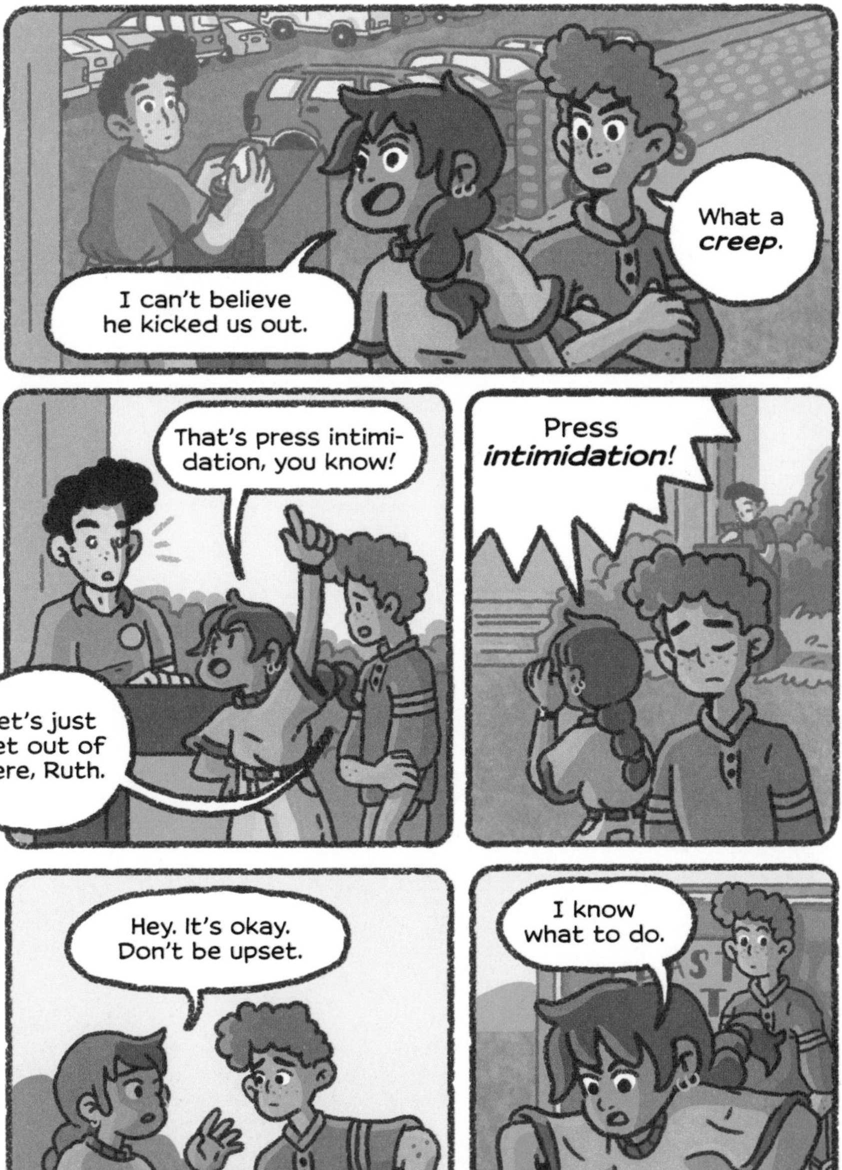
I can't believe
he kicked us out.
What a *creep*.
That's press intimi-
dation, you know!
Let's just
get out of
here, Ruth.
Press
intimidation!
Hey. It's okay.
Don't be upset.
I know
what to do.

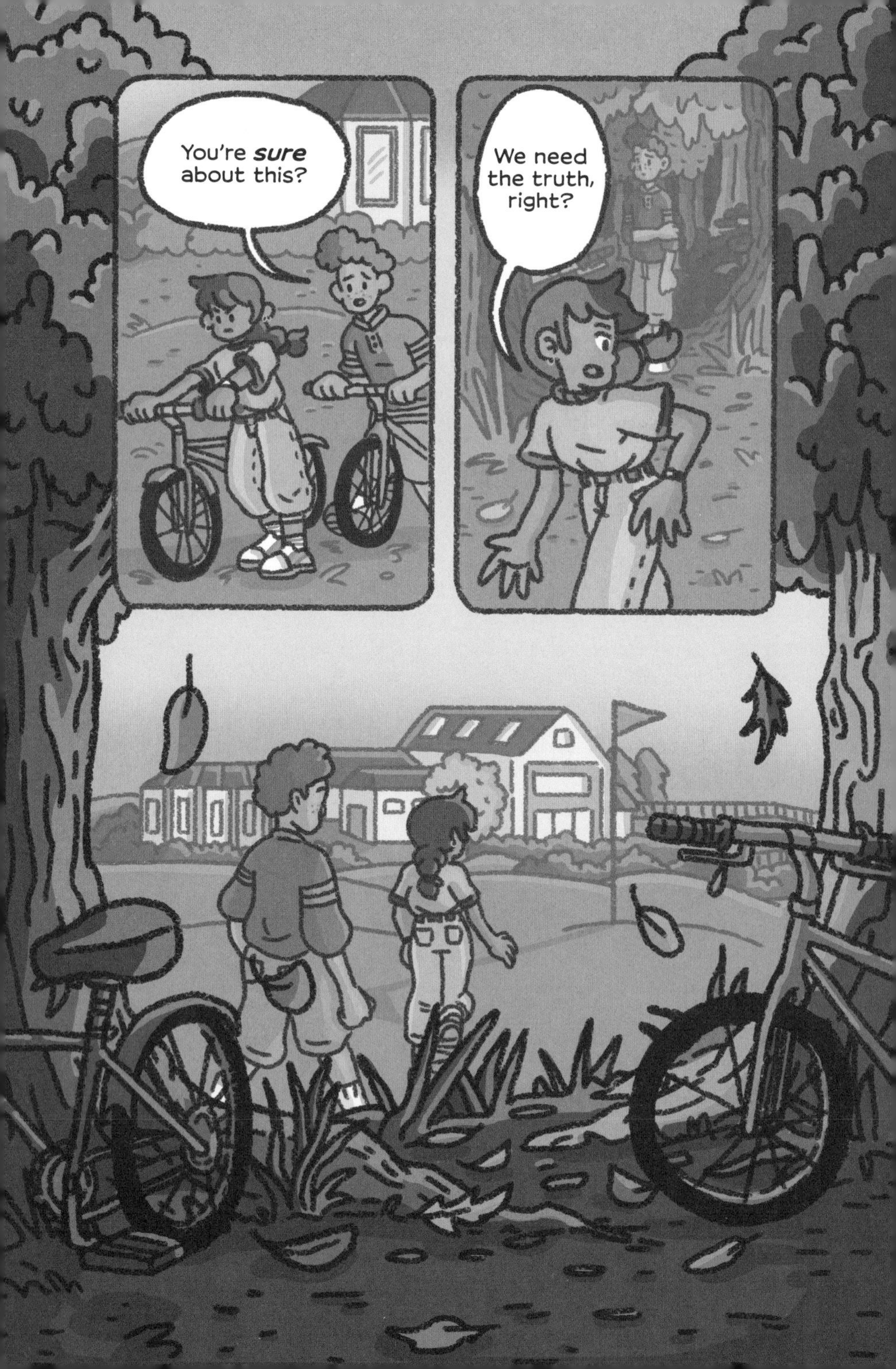
You're ***sure*** about this?
We need the truth, right?

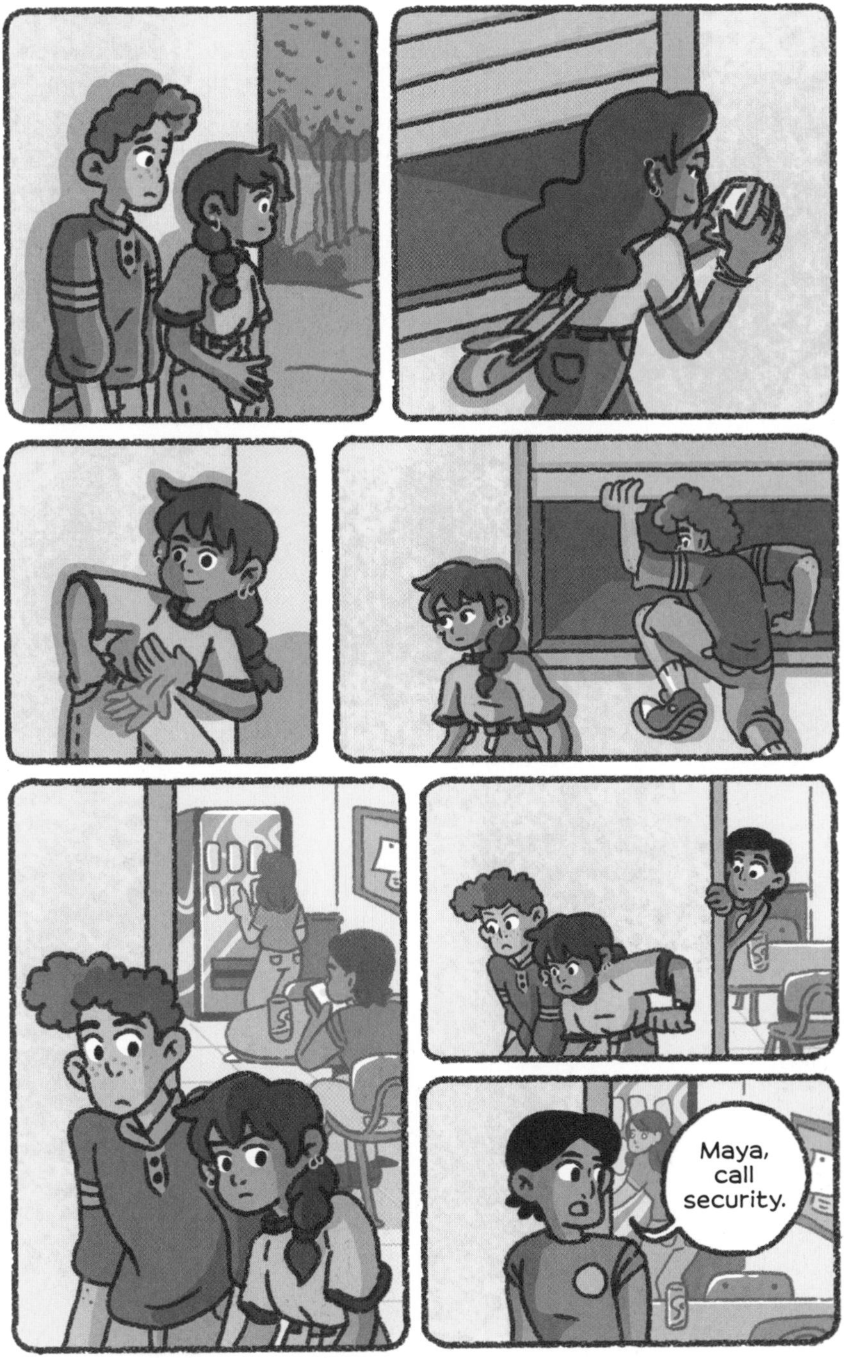
Maya,
call
security.

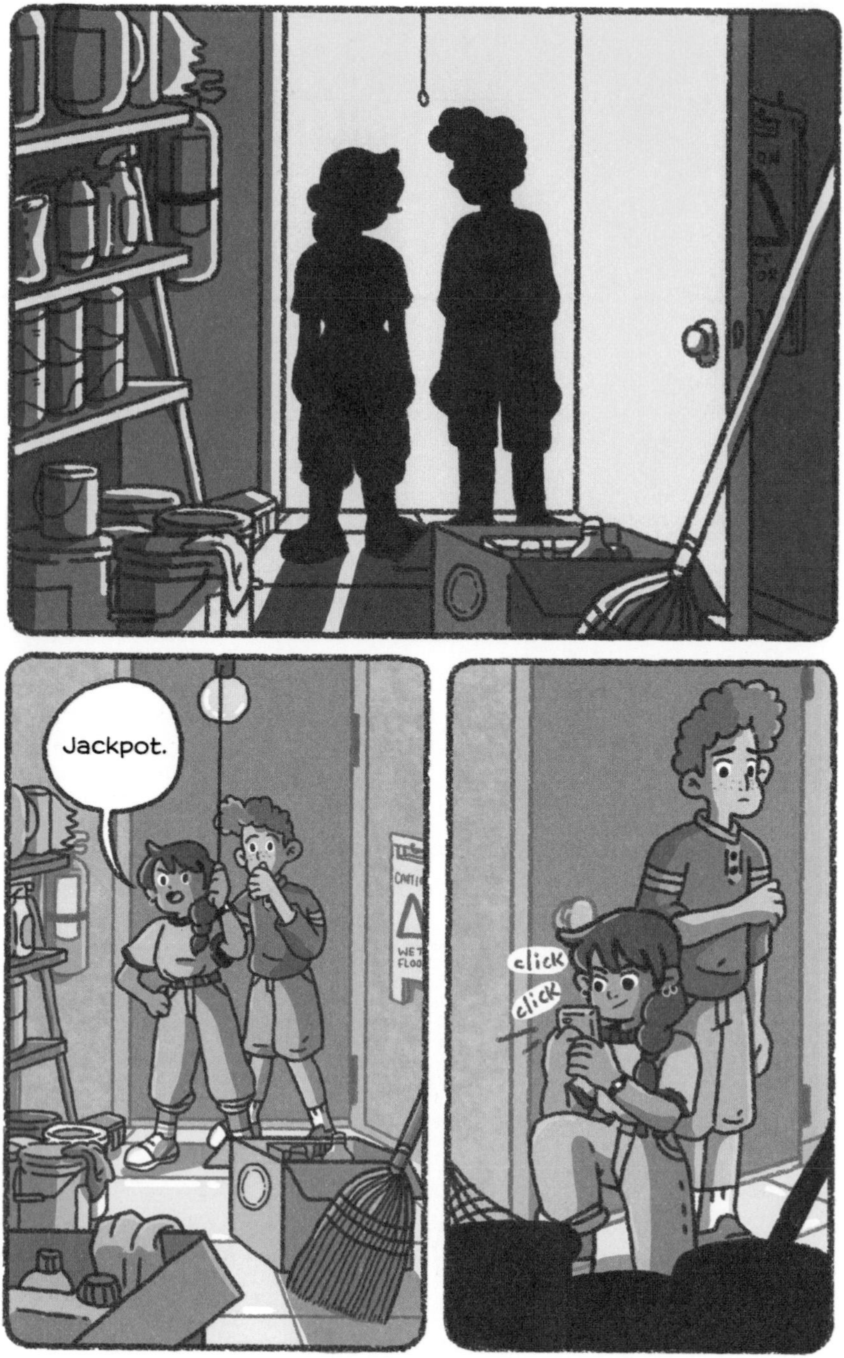
Jackpot.
click
click

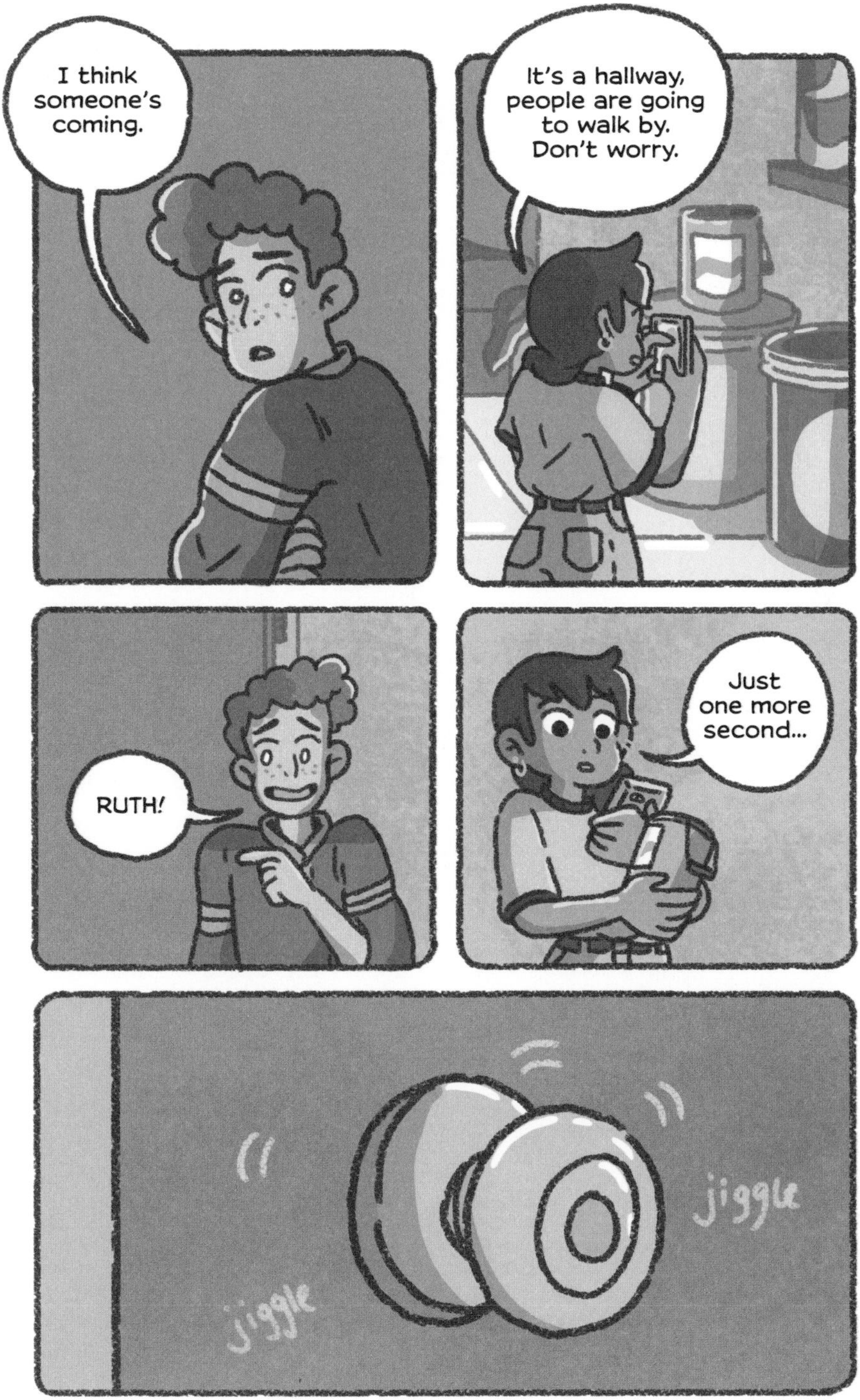
I think someone's coming.
It's a hallway, people are going to walk by. Don't worry.
RUTH!
Just one more second...
jiggle
jiggle

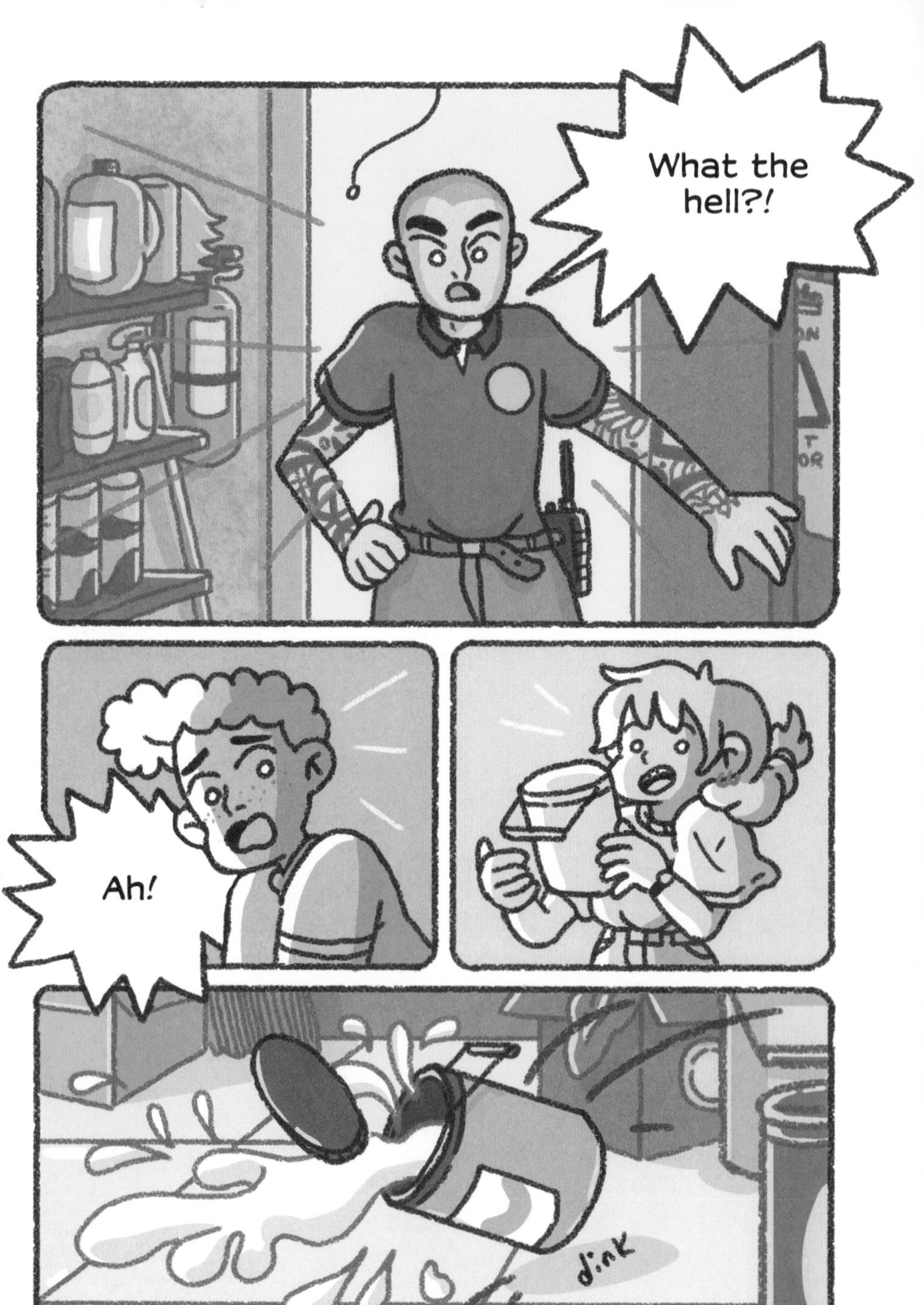
What the hell?!
Ah!
dink

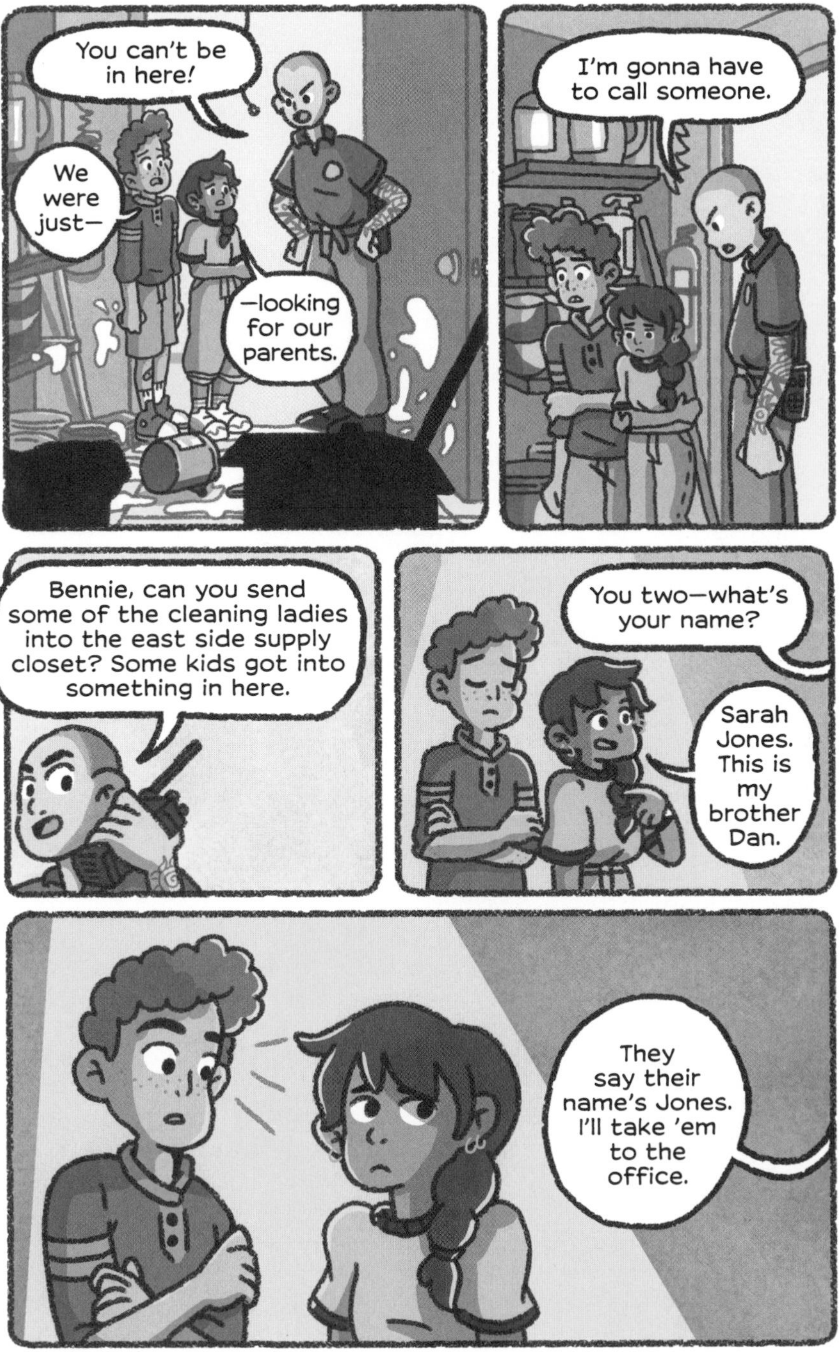
You can't be in here!
We were just—
—looking for our parents.
I'm gonna have to call someone.
Bennie, can you send some of the cleaning ladies into the east side supply closet? Some kids got into something in here.
You two—what's your name?
Sarah Jones. This is my brother Dan.
They say their name's Jones. I'll take 'em to the office.

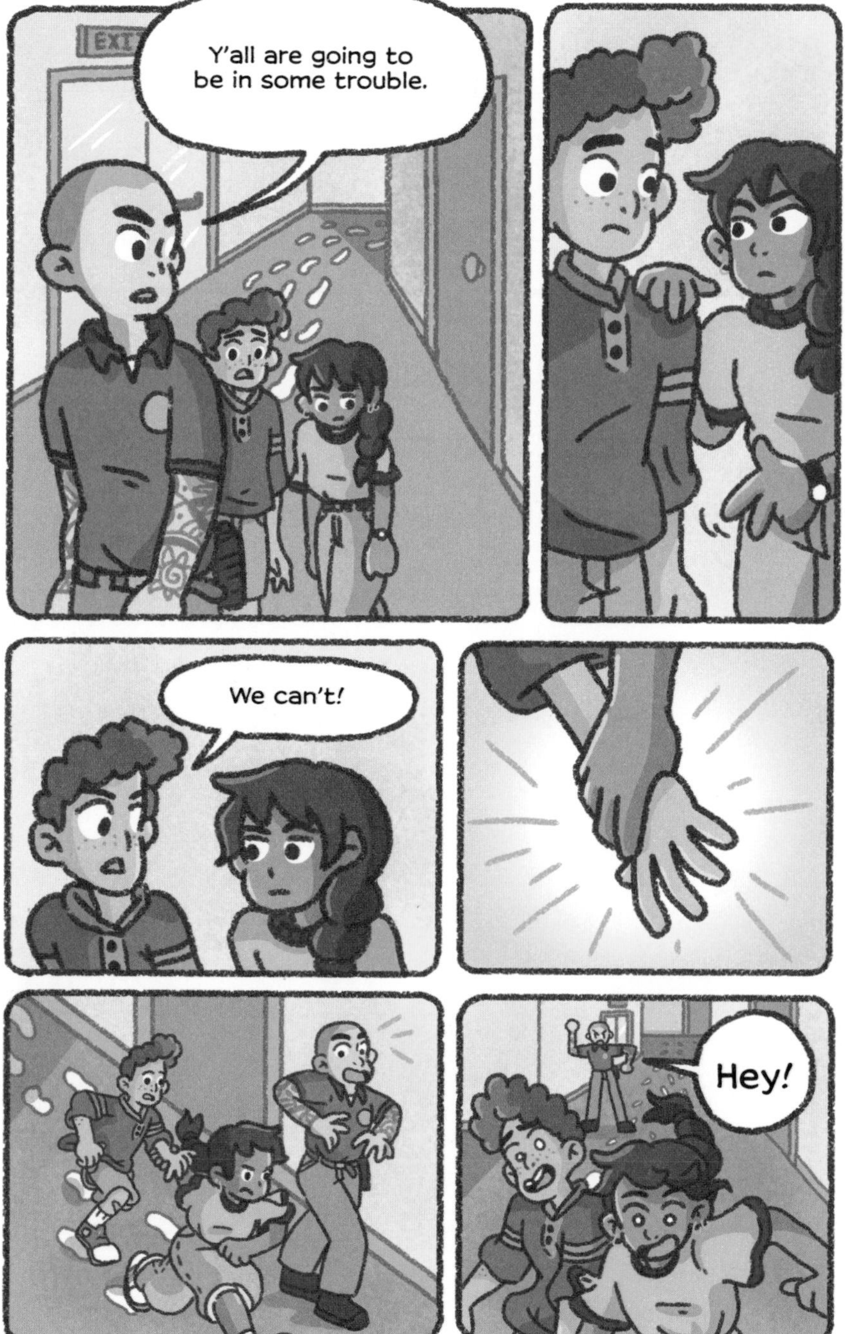
EXIT
Y'all are going to be in some trouble.
We can't!
Hey!

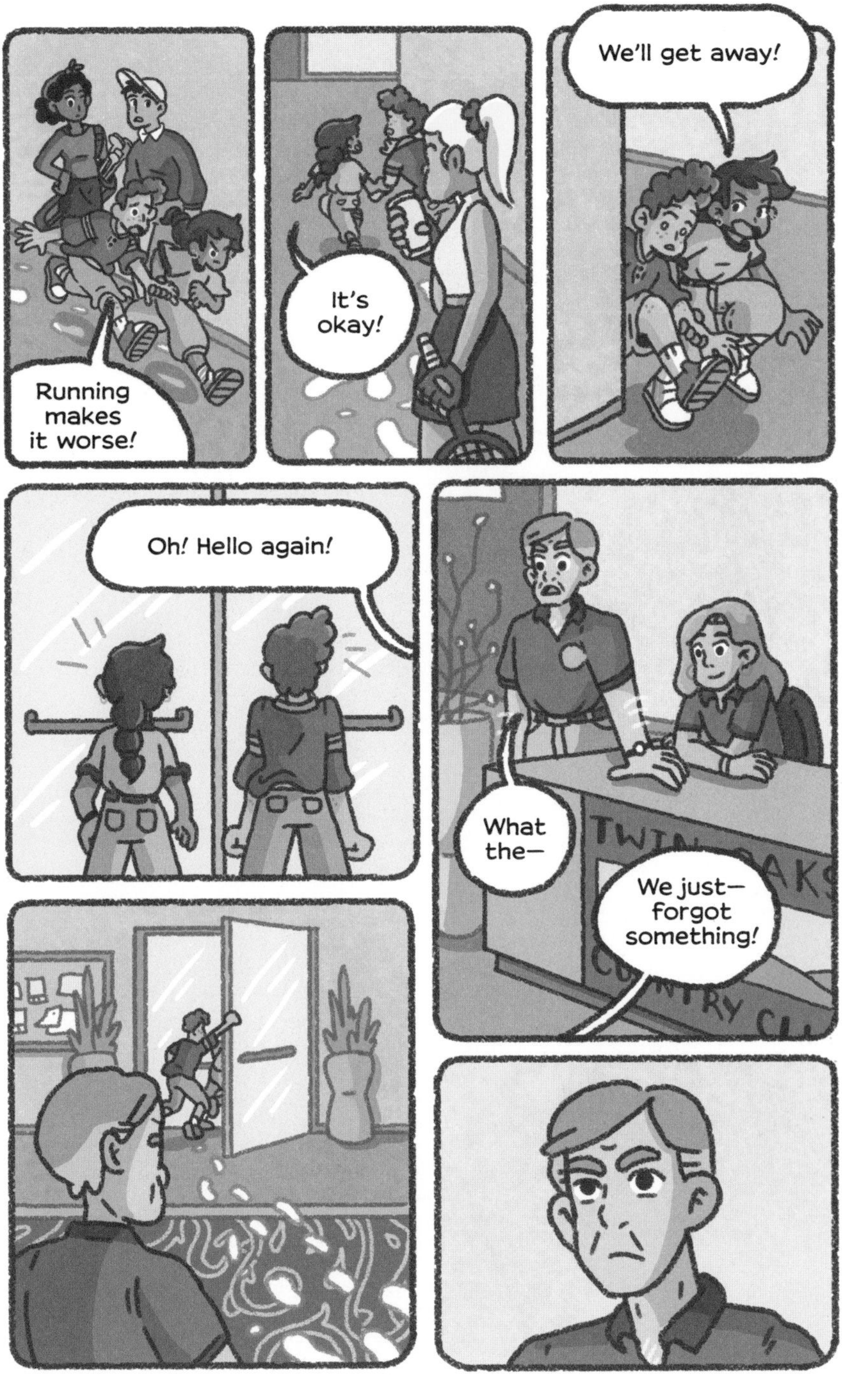
Running makes it worse!
It's okay!
We'll get away!
Oh! Hello again!
What the—
We just—forgot something!

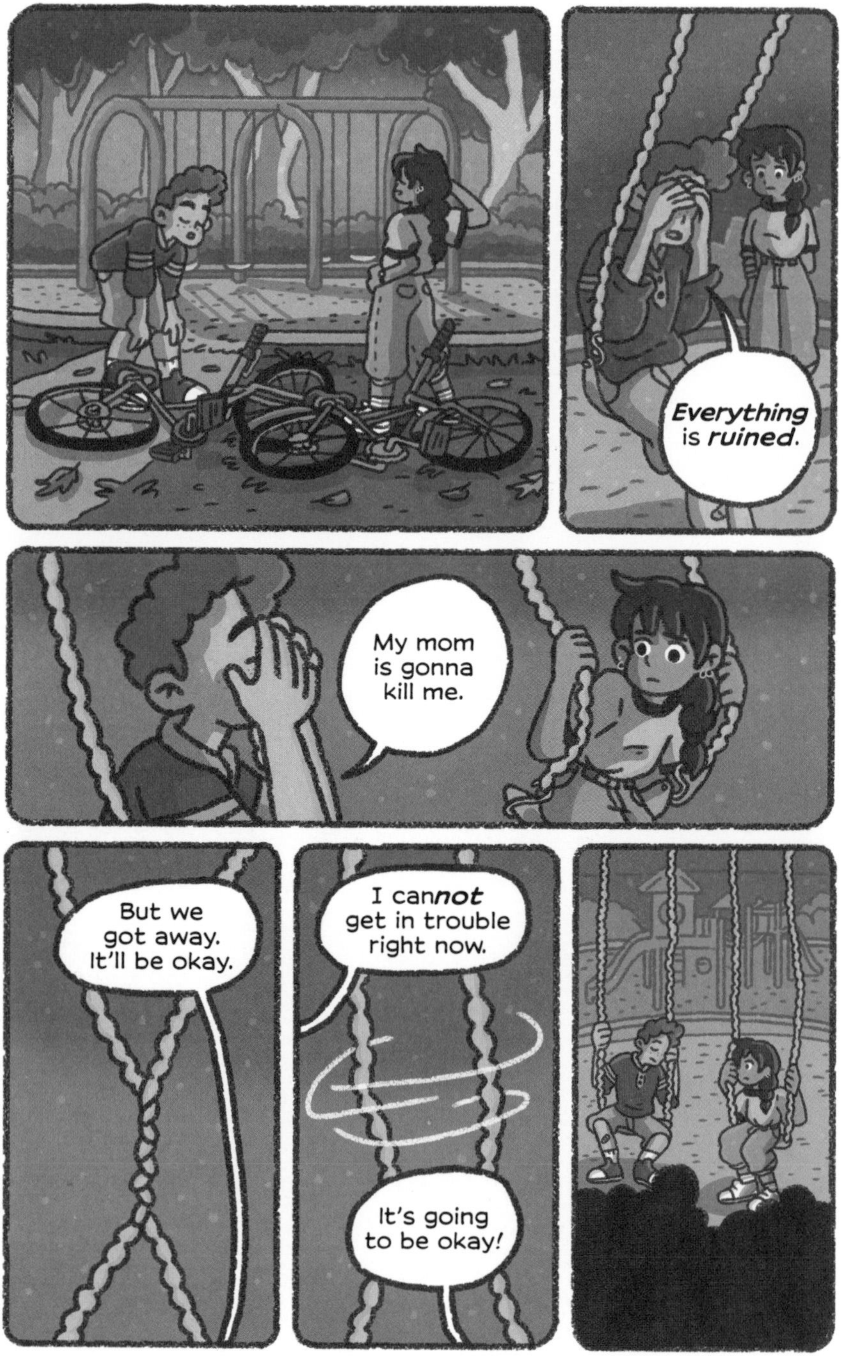
Everything is ruined.
My mom is gonna kill me.
But we got away. It'll be okay.
I cannot get in trouble right now.
It's going to be okay!

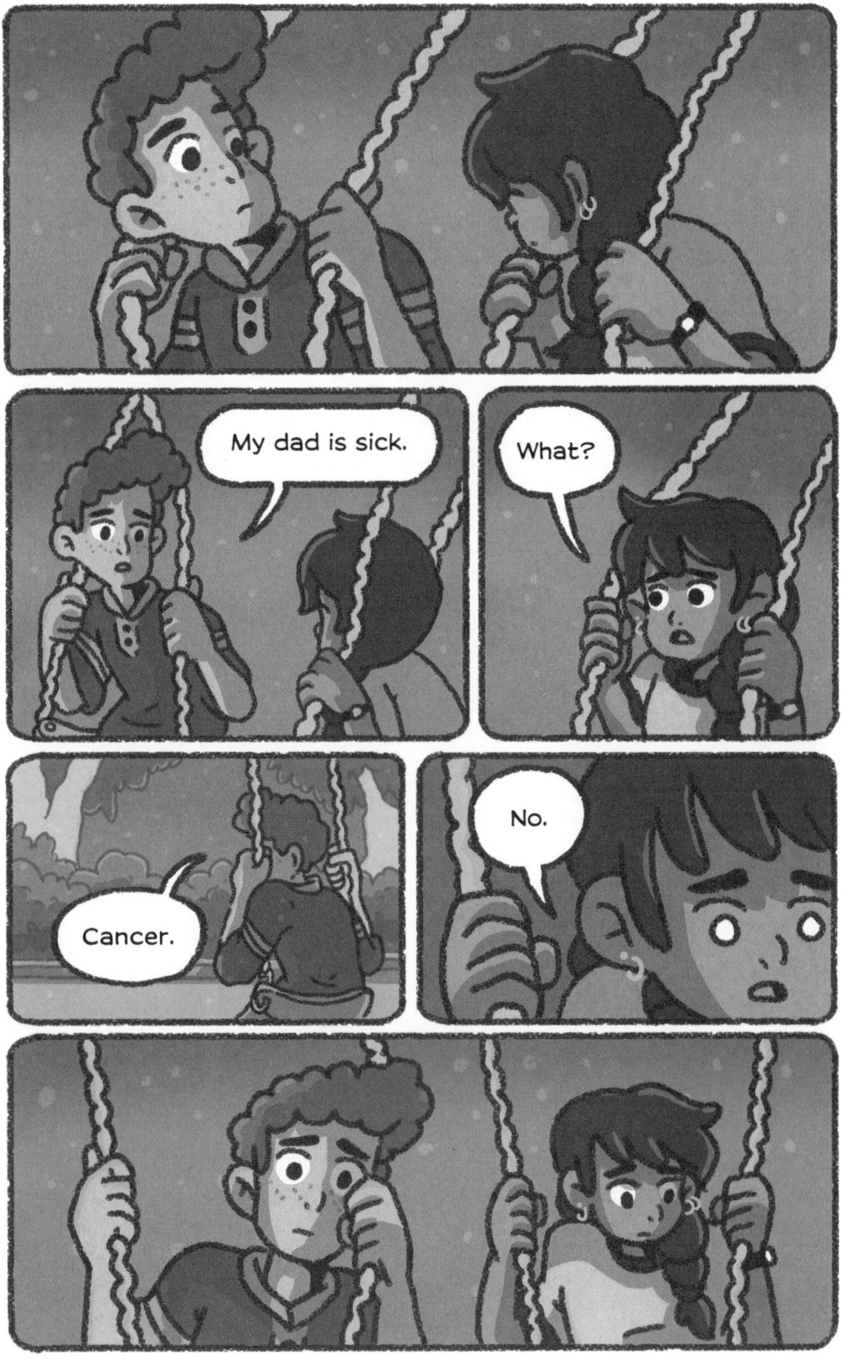
My dad is sick.
What?
Cancer.
No.

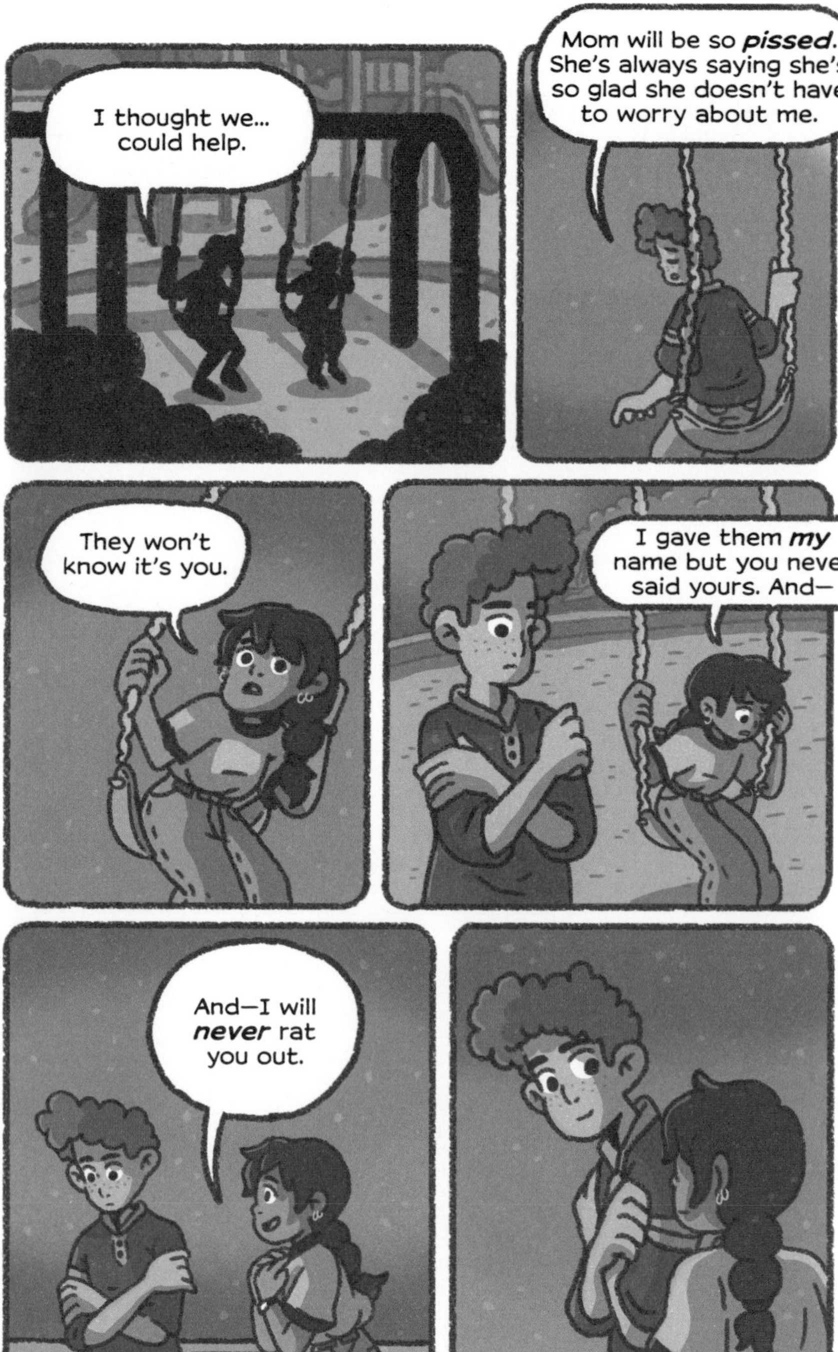
I thought we... could help.
Mom will be so ***pissed***. She's always saying she's so glad she doesn't have to worry about me.
They won't know it's you.
I gave them ***my*** name but you never said yours. And—
And—I will ***never*** rat you out.

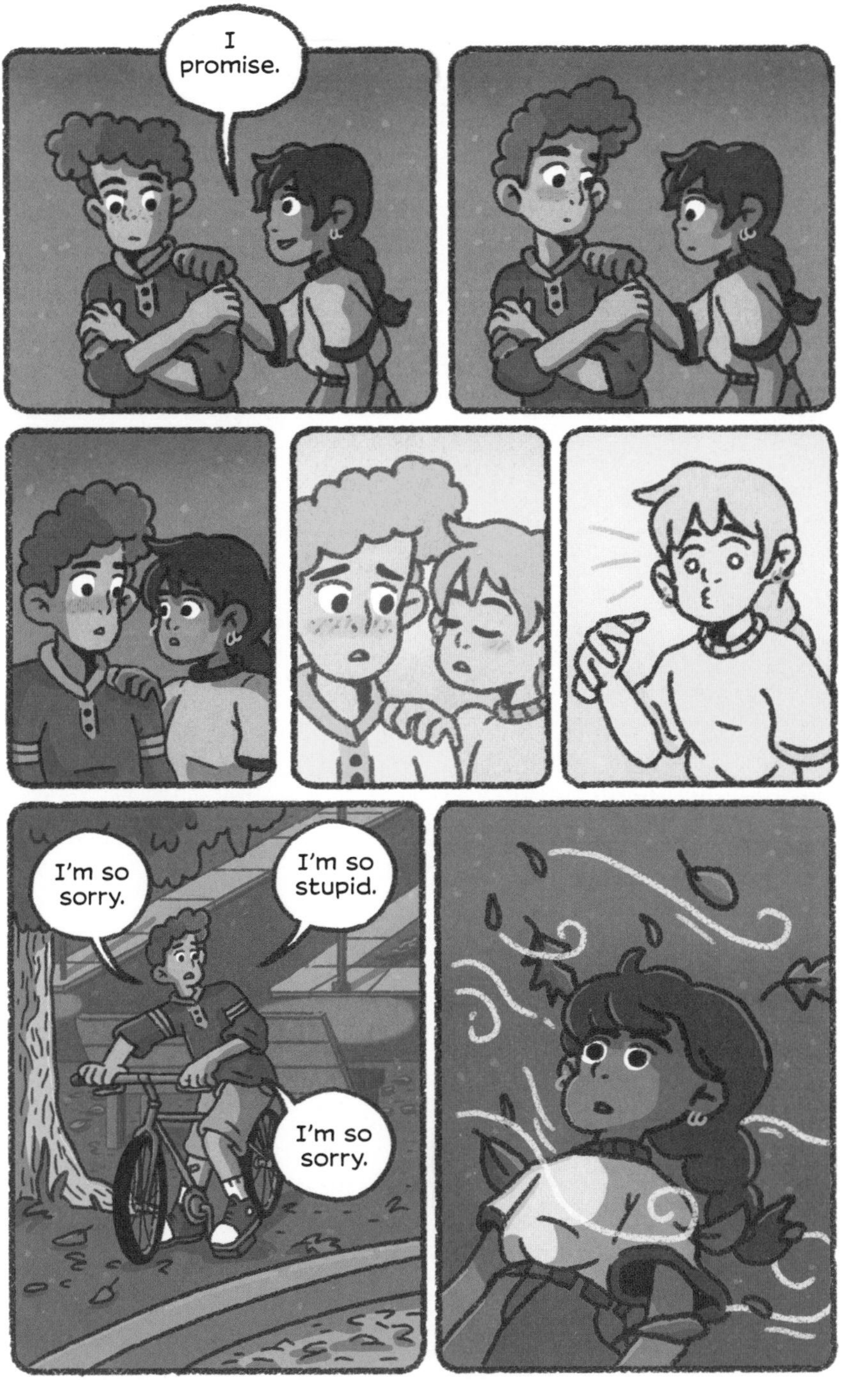
I promise.
I'm so sorry.
I'm so stupid.
I'm so sorry.

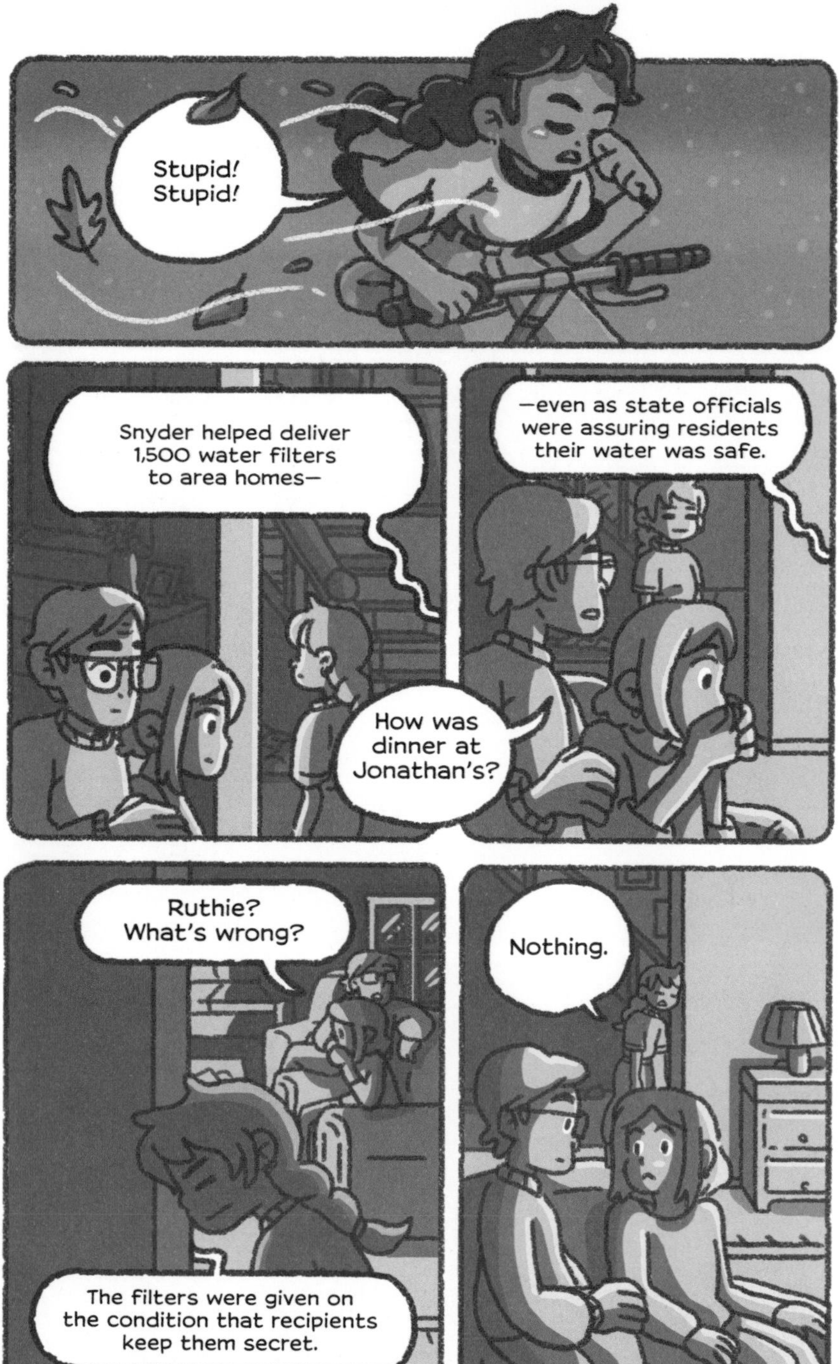
Stupid! Stupid!
Snyder helped deliver 1,500 water filters to area homes—
—even as state officials were assuring residents their water was safe.
How was dinner at Jonathan's?
Ruthie? What's wrong?
The filters were given on the condition that recipients keep them secret.
Nothing.

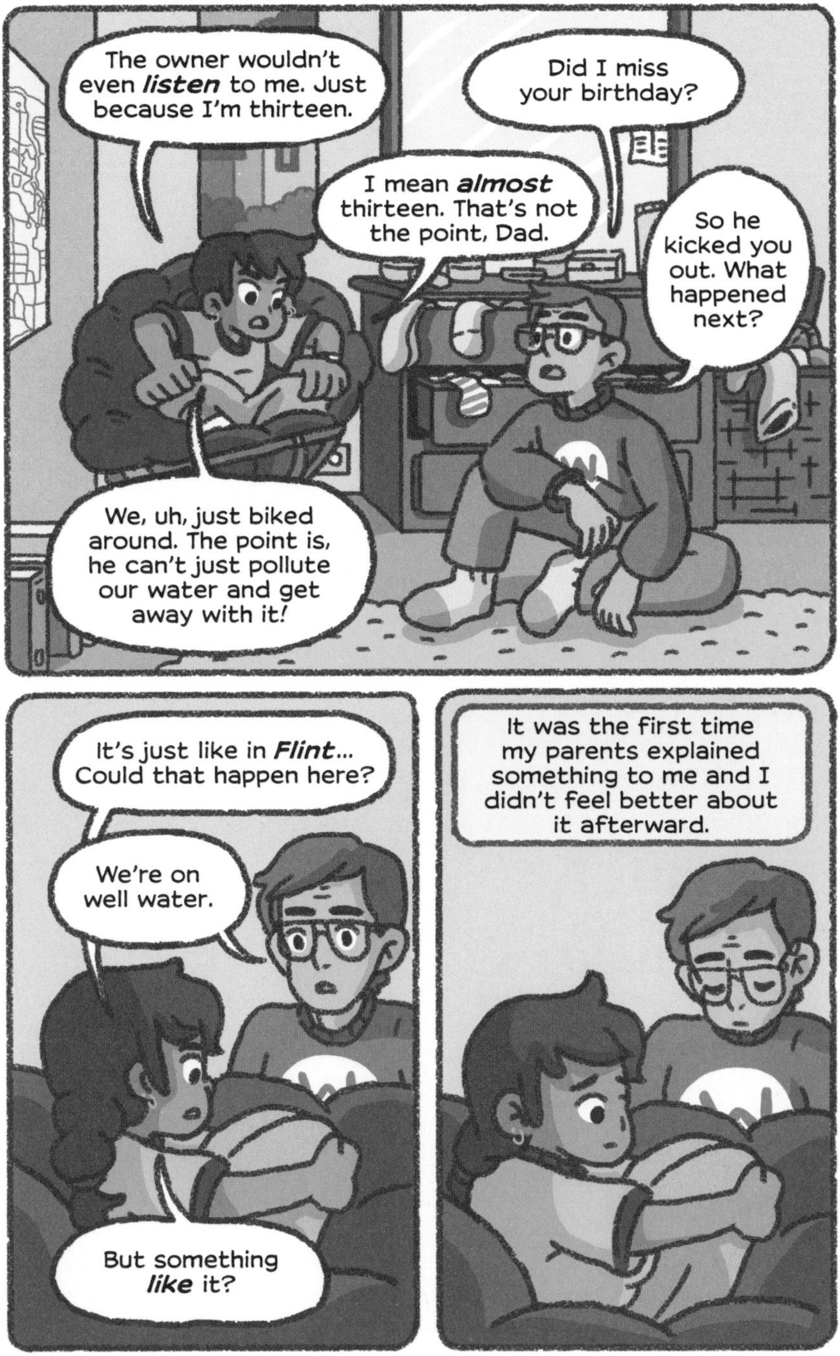
The owner wouldn't even *listen* to me. Just because I'm thirteen.
Did I miss your birthday?
I mean *almost* thirteen. That's not the point, Dad.
So he kicked you out. What happened next?
We, uh, just biked around. The point is, he can't just pollute our water and get away with it!
It's just like in *Flint*... Could that happen here?
We're on well water.
But something *like* it?
It was the first time my parents explained something to me and I didn't feel better about it afterward.

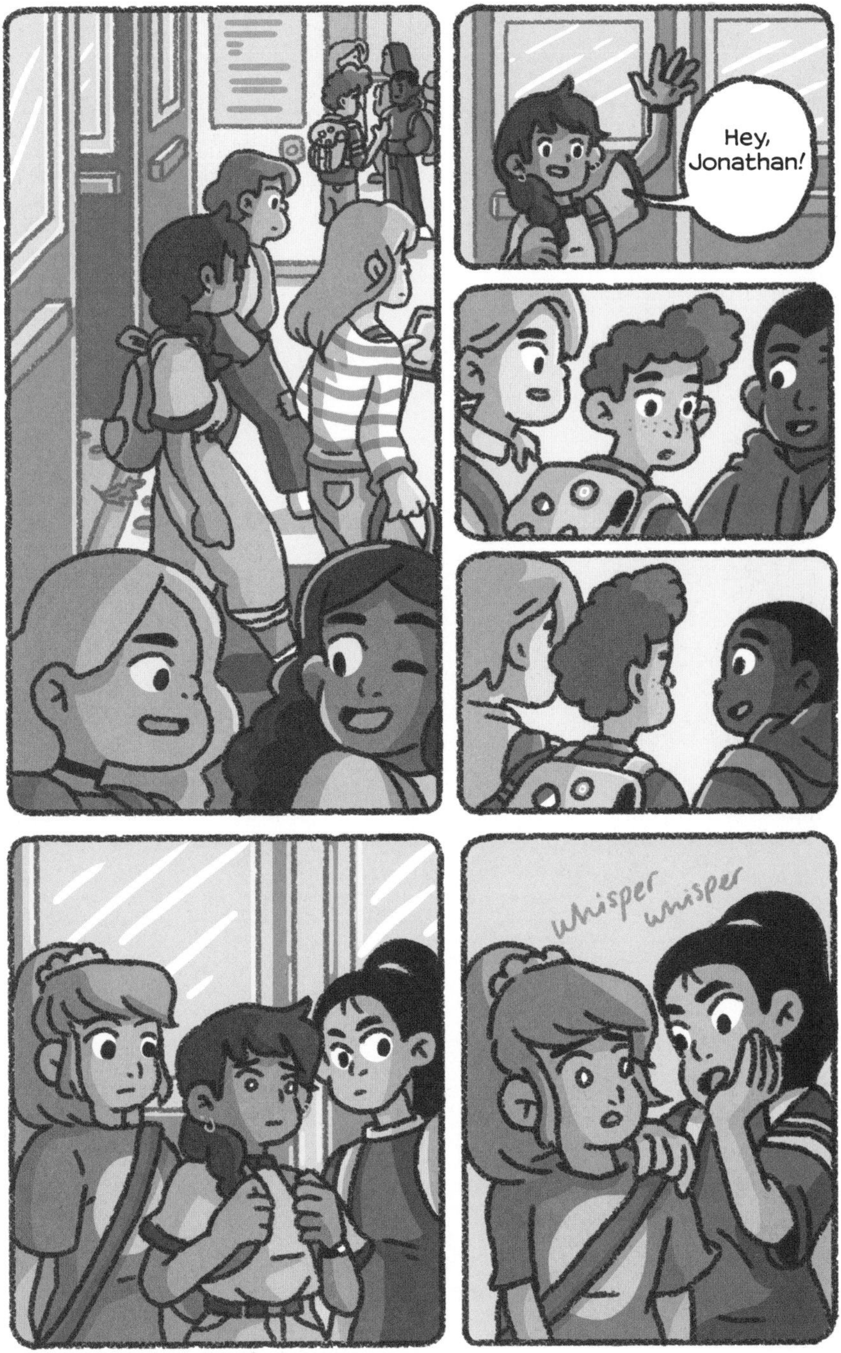
Hey, Jonathan!
whisper whisper

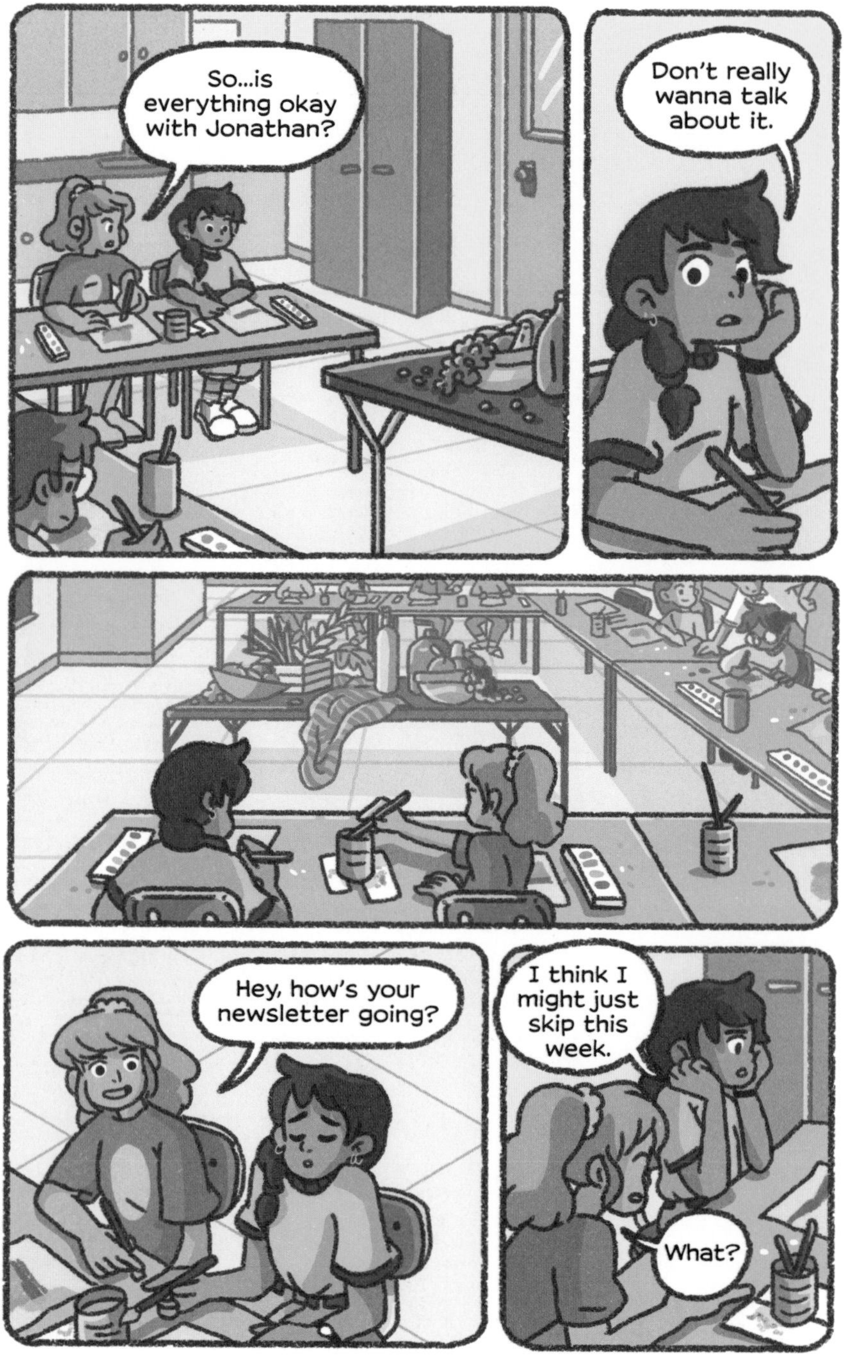
So...is everything okay with Jonathan?
Don't really wanna talk about it.
Hey, how's your newsletter going?
I think I might just skip this week.
What?

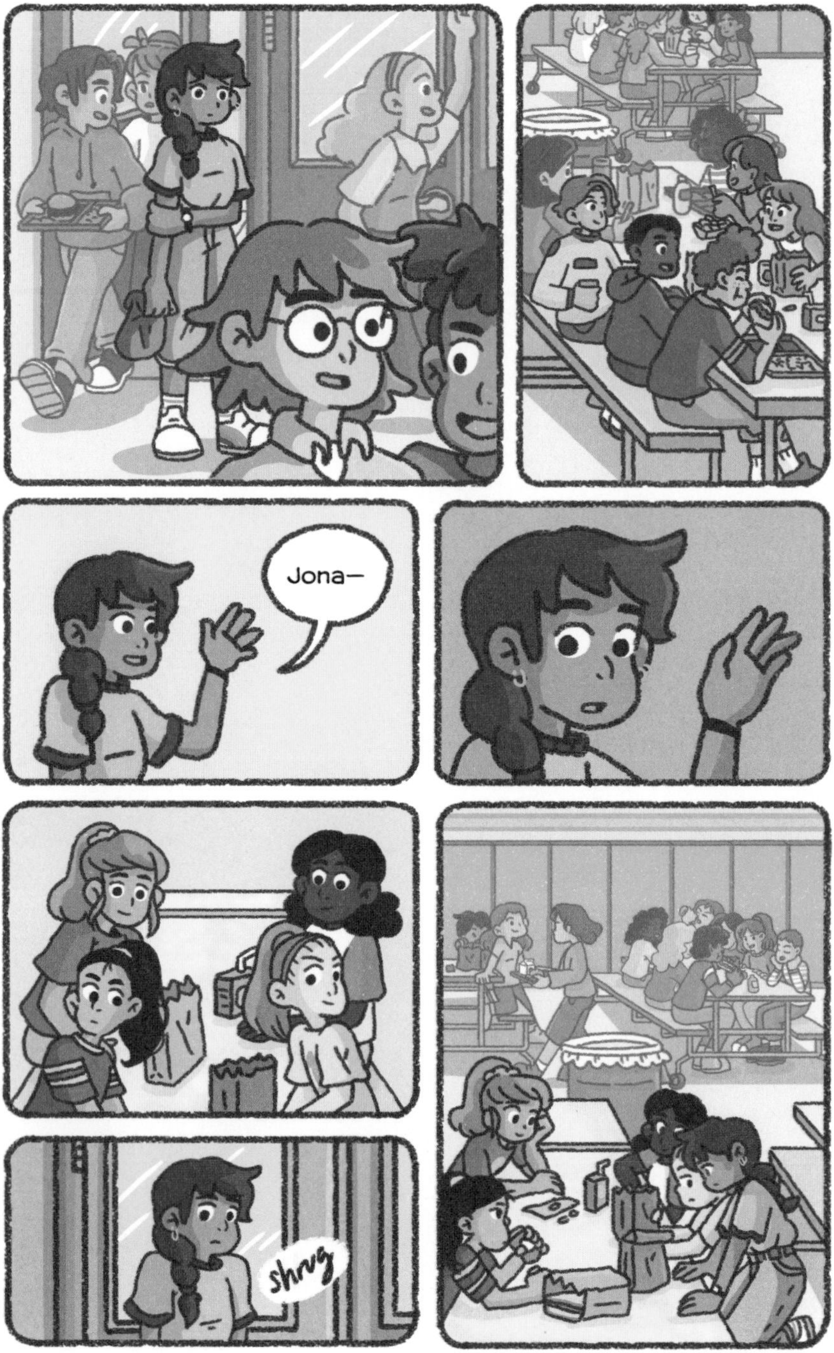
Jona—
shrug

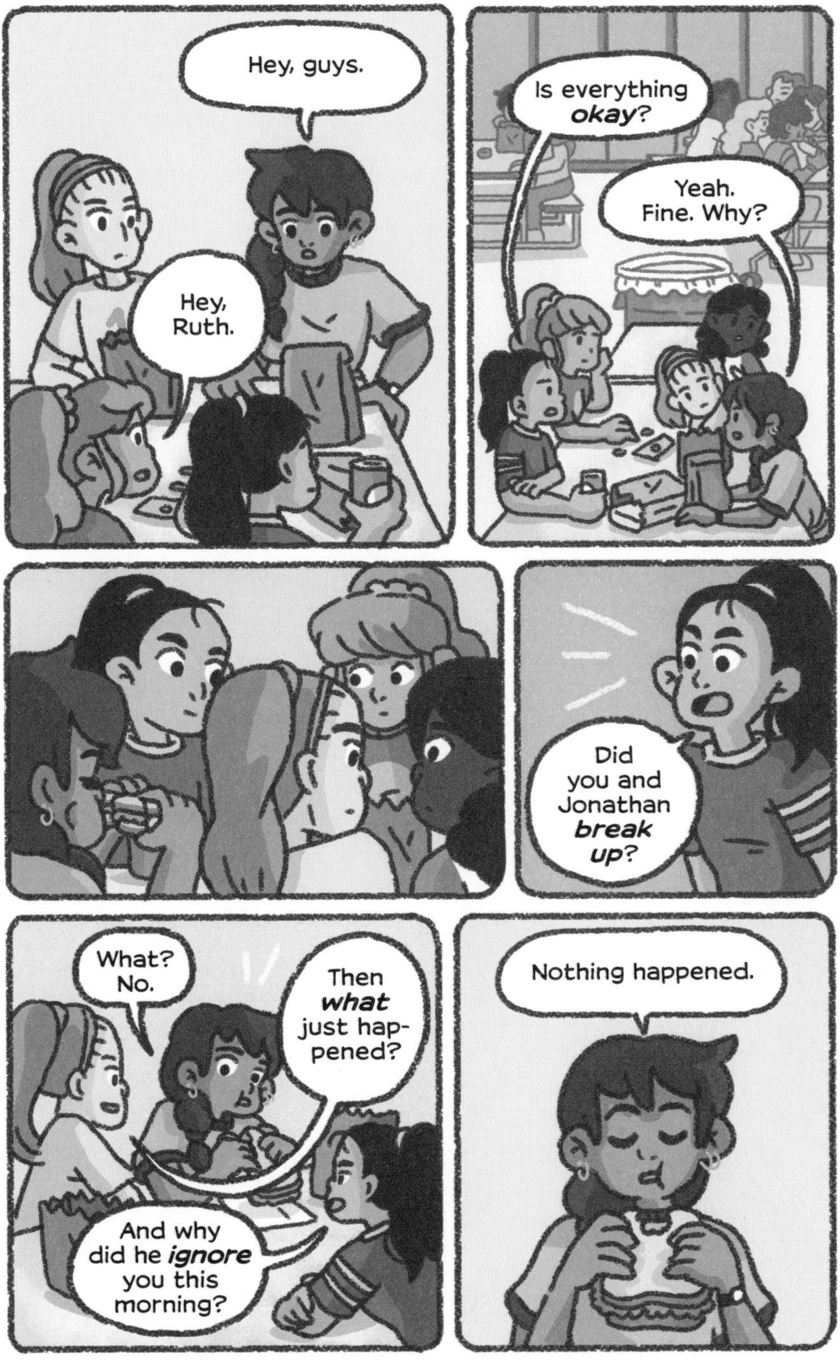
Hey, guys.
Hey, Ruth.
Is everything *okay*?
Yeah. Fine. Why?
Did you and Jonathan *break up*?
What? No.
Then *what* just happened?
And why did he *ignore* you this morning?
Nothing happened.

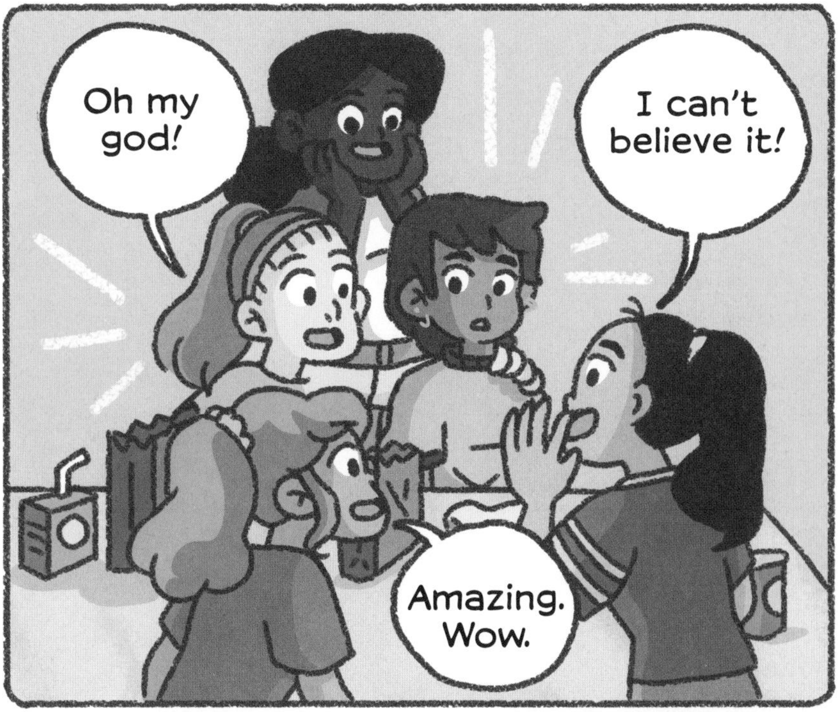
Oh my god!
I can't believe it!
Amazing. Wow.

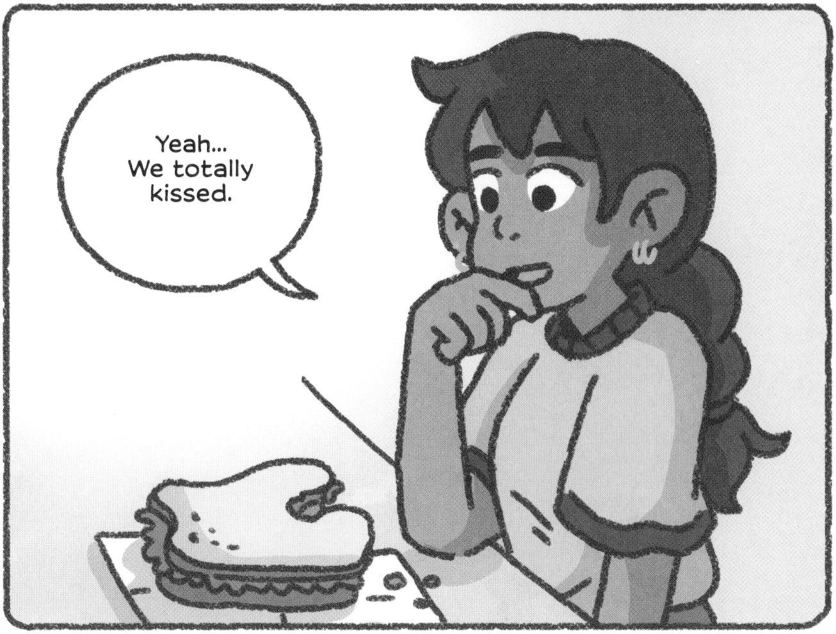
Yeah... We totally kissed.

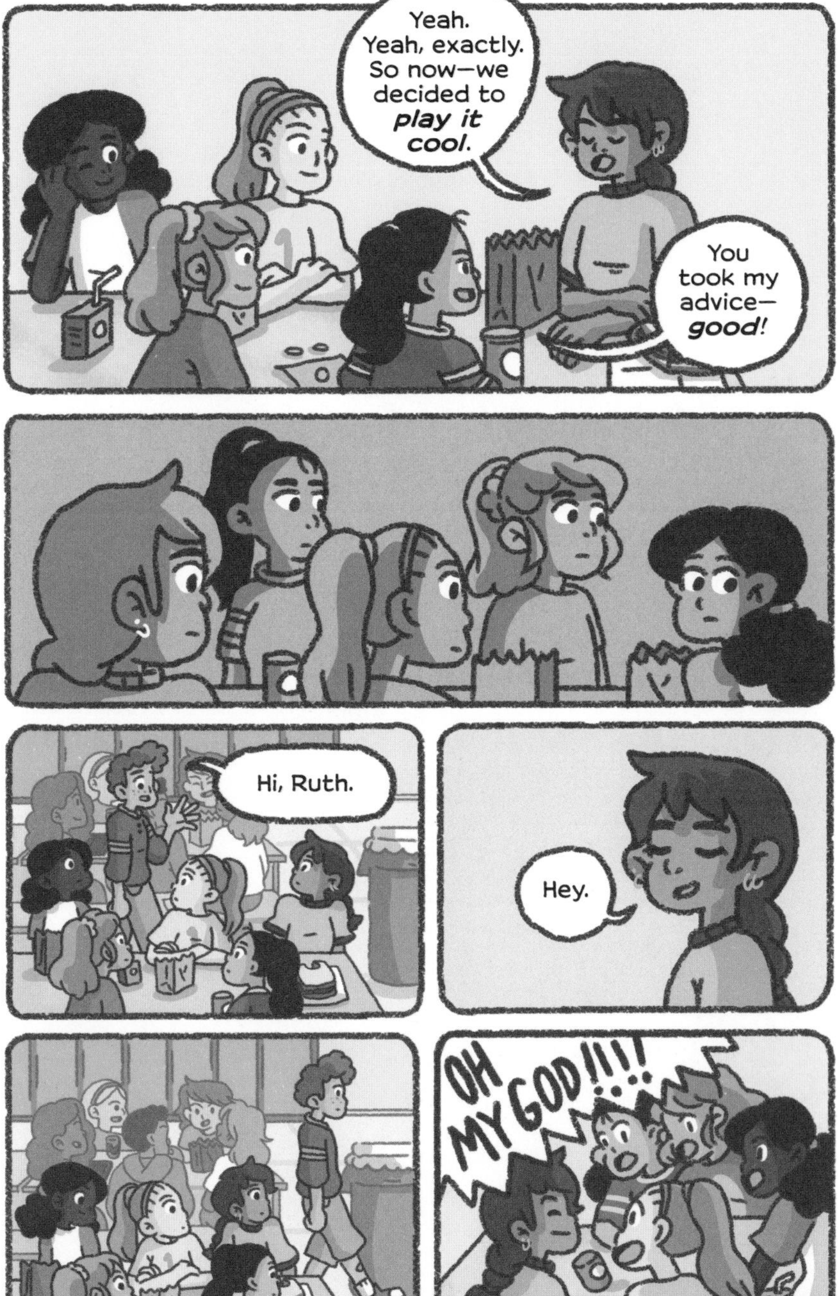
Yeah. Yeah, exactly. So now—we decided to ***play it cool***.
You took my advice—***good!***
Hi, Ruth.
Hey.
OH MY GOD!!!!

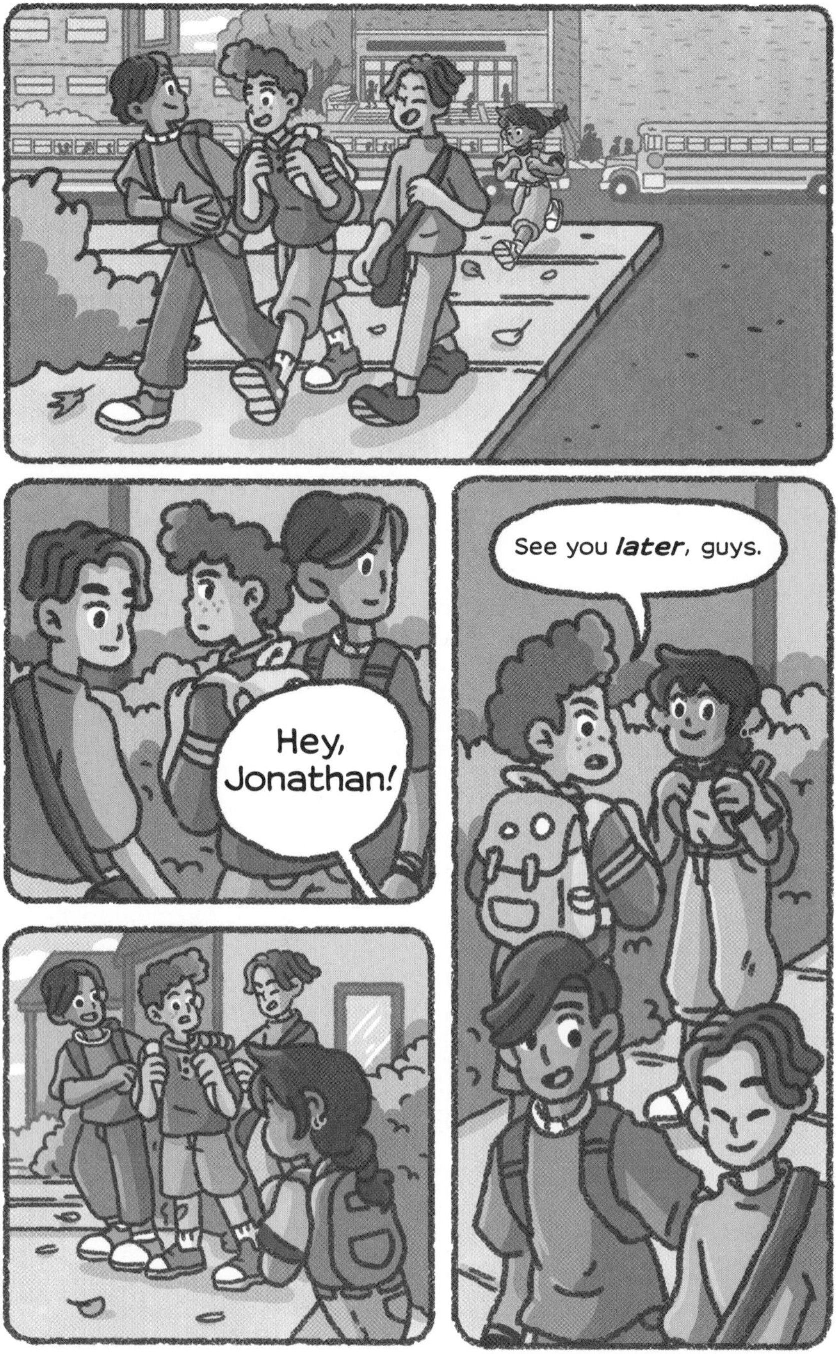
Hey, Jonathan!
See you *later*, guys.

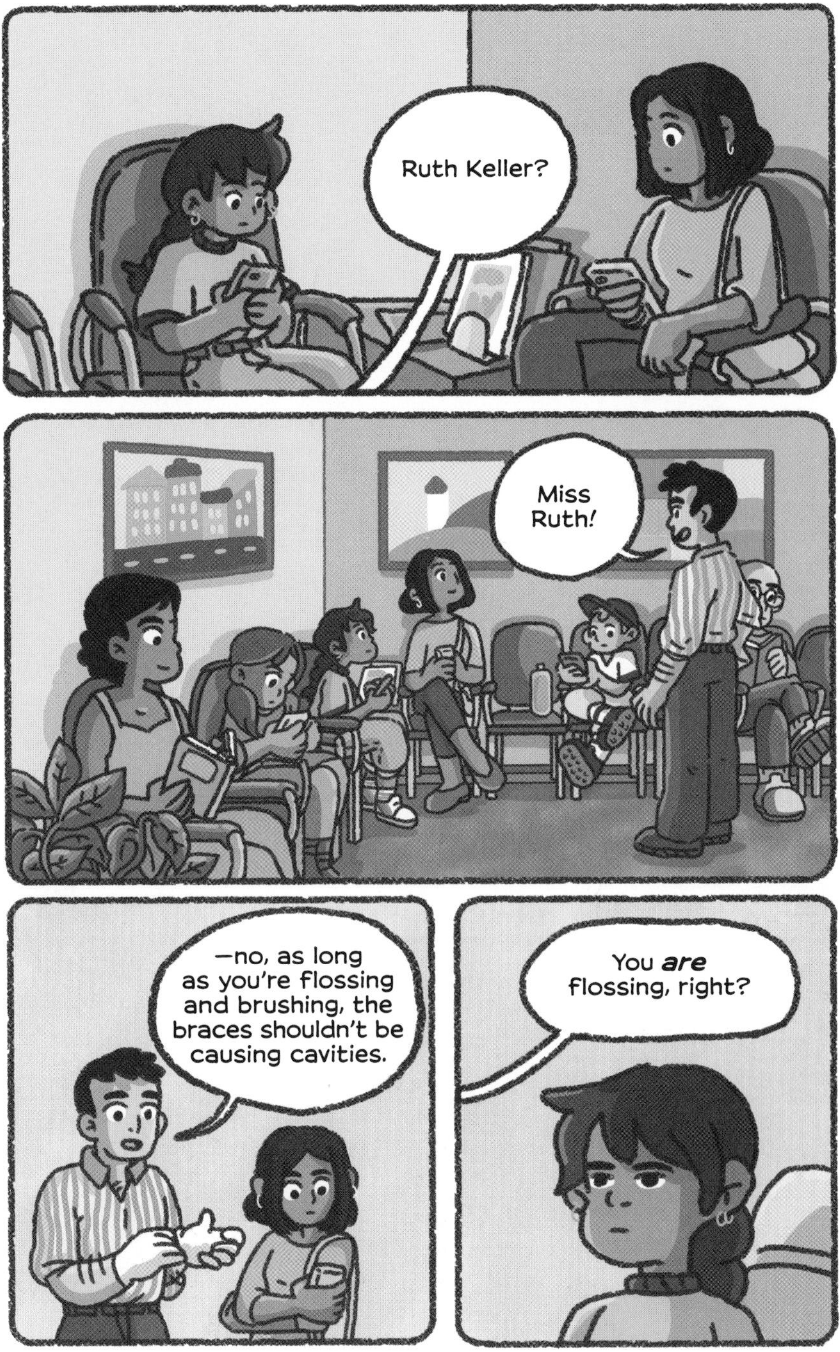
Ruth Keller?
Miss Ruth!
—no, as long as you're flossing and brushing, the braces shouldn't be causing cavities.
You *are* flossing, right?

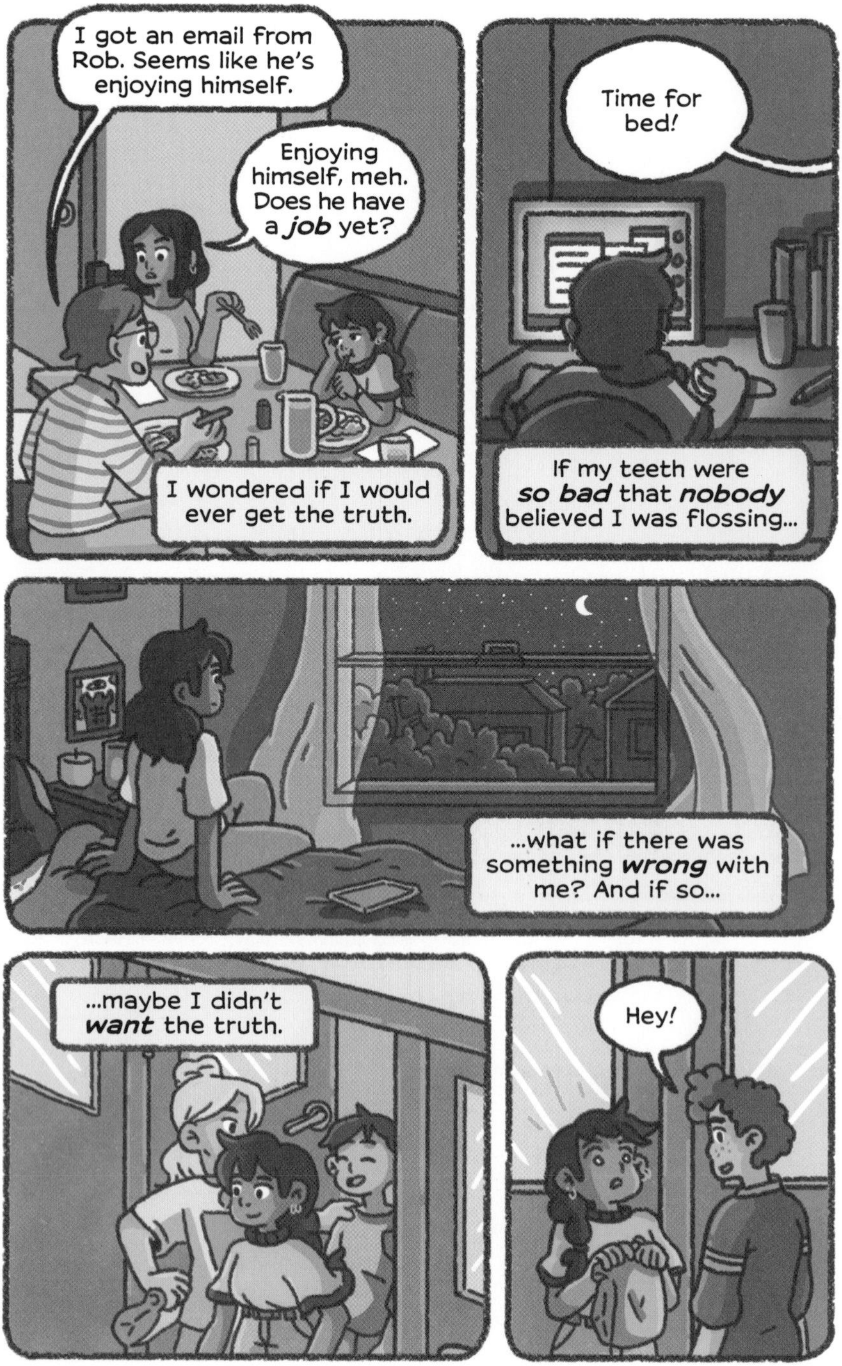
I got an email from Rob. Seems like he's enjoying himself.
Enjoying himself, meh. Does he have a *job* yet?
I wondered if I would ever get the truth.
Time for bed!
If my teeth were *so bad* that *nobody* believed I was flossing...
...what if there was something *wrong* with me? And if so...
...maybe I didn't *want* the truth.
Hey!

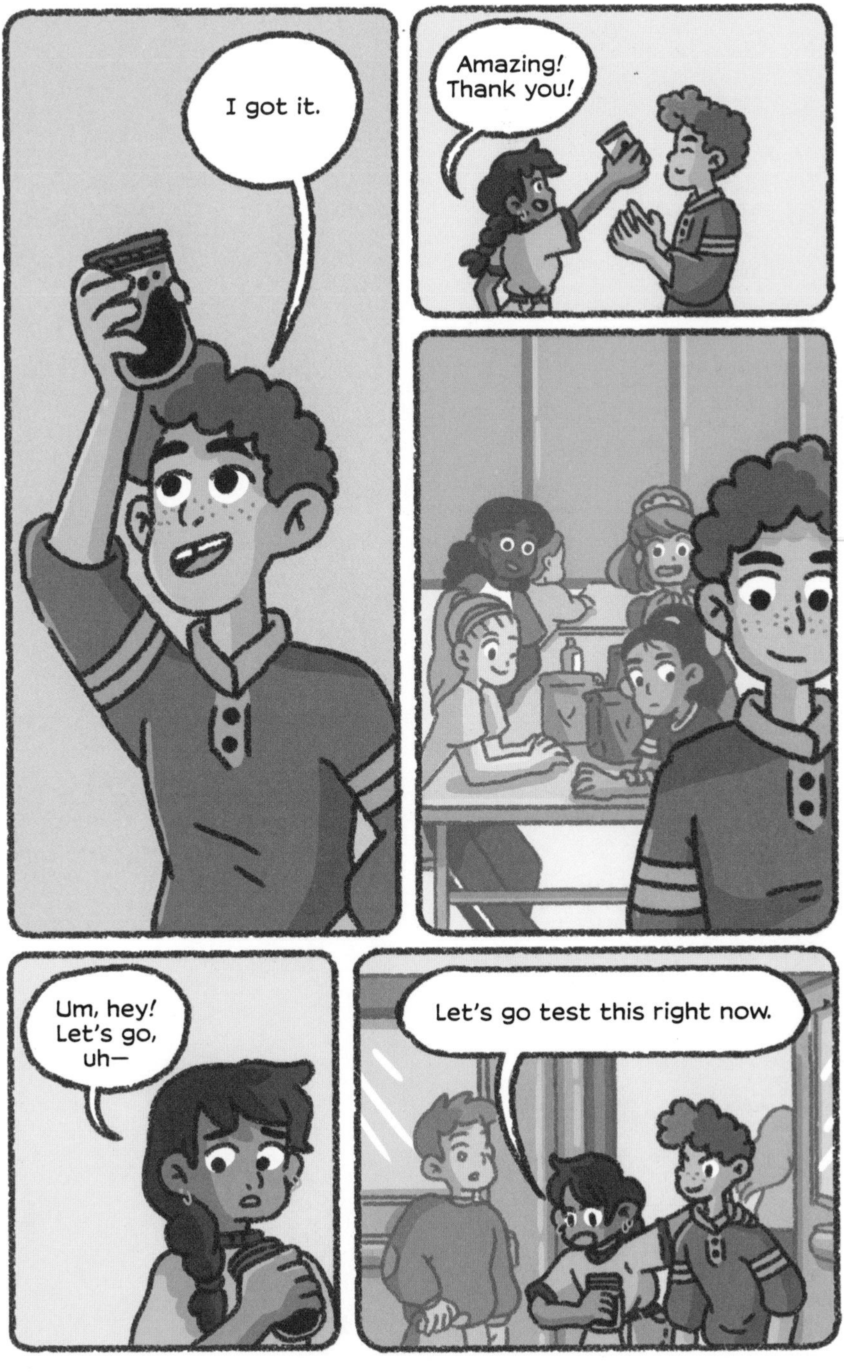
I got it.
Amazing! Thank you!
Um, hey! Let's go, uh—
Let's go test this right now.

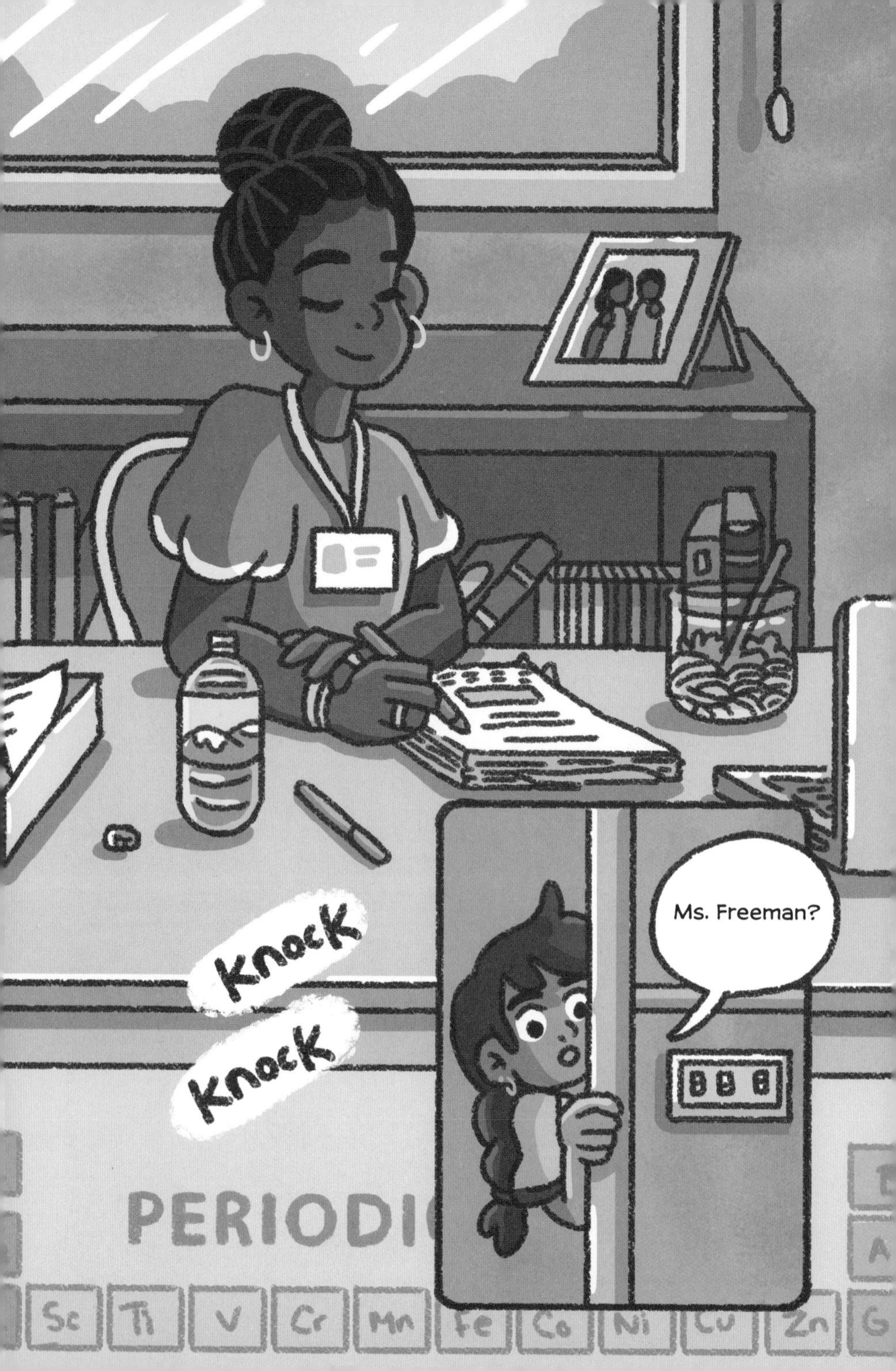
Knock
Knock
Ms. Freeman?
PERIODIC
Sc
Ti
V
Cr
Mn
Fe
Co
Ni
Cu
Zn

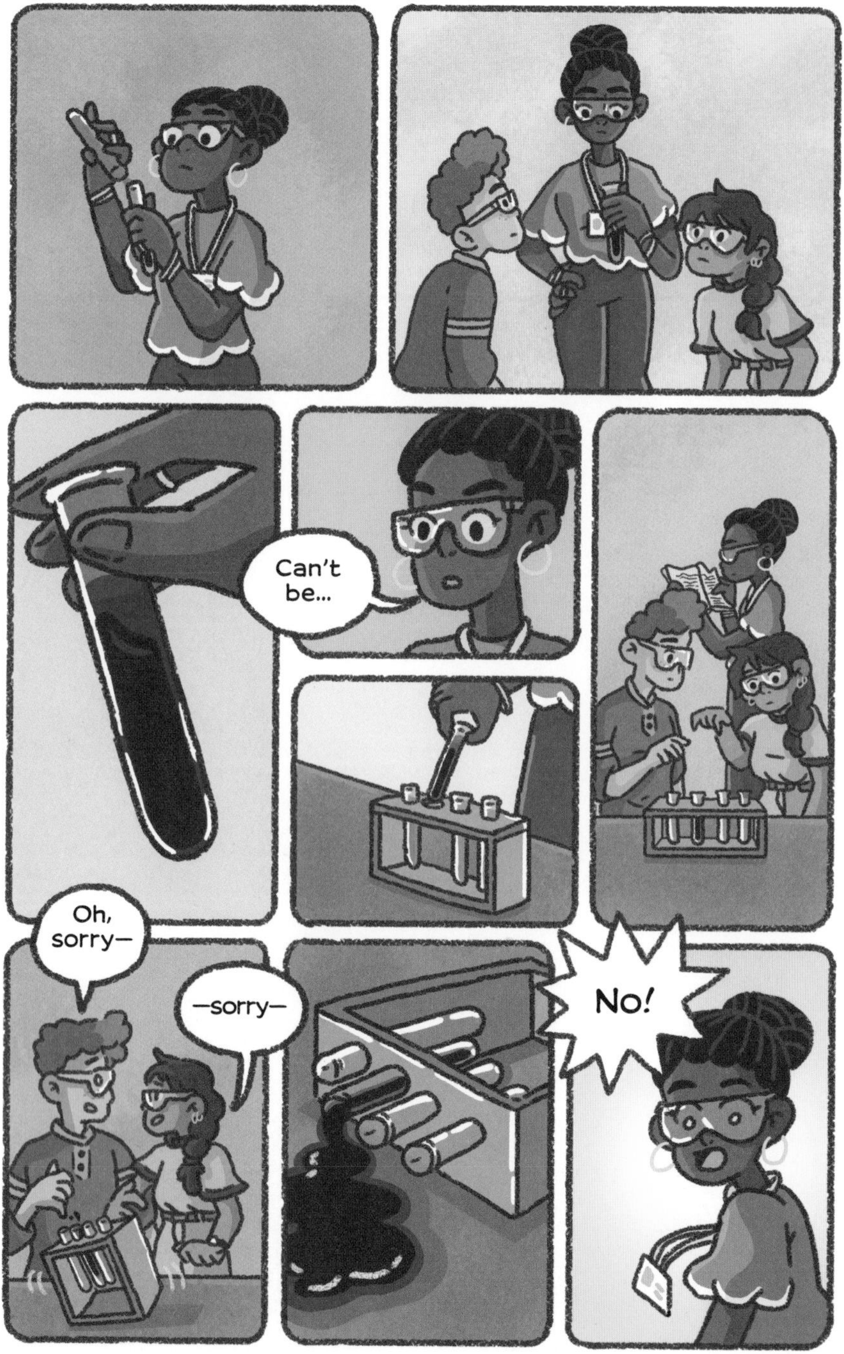
Can't be...
Oh, sorry—
—sorry—
No!

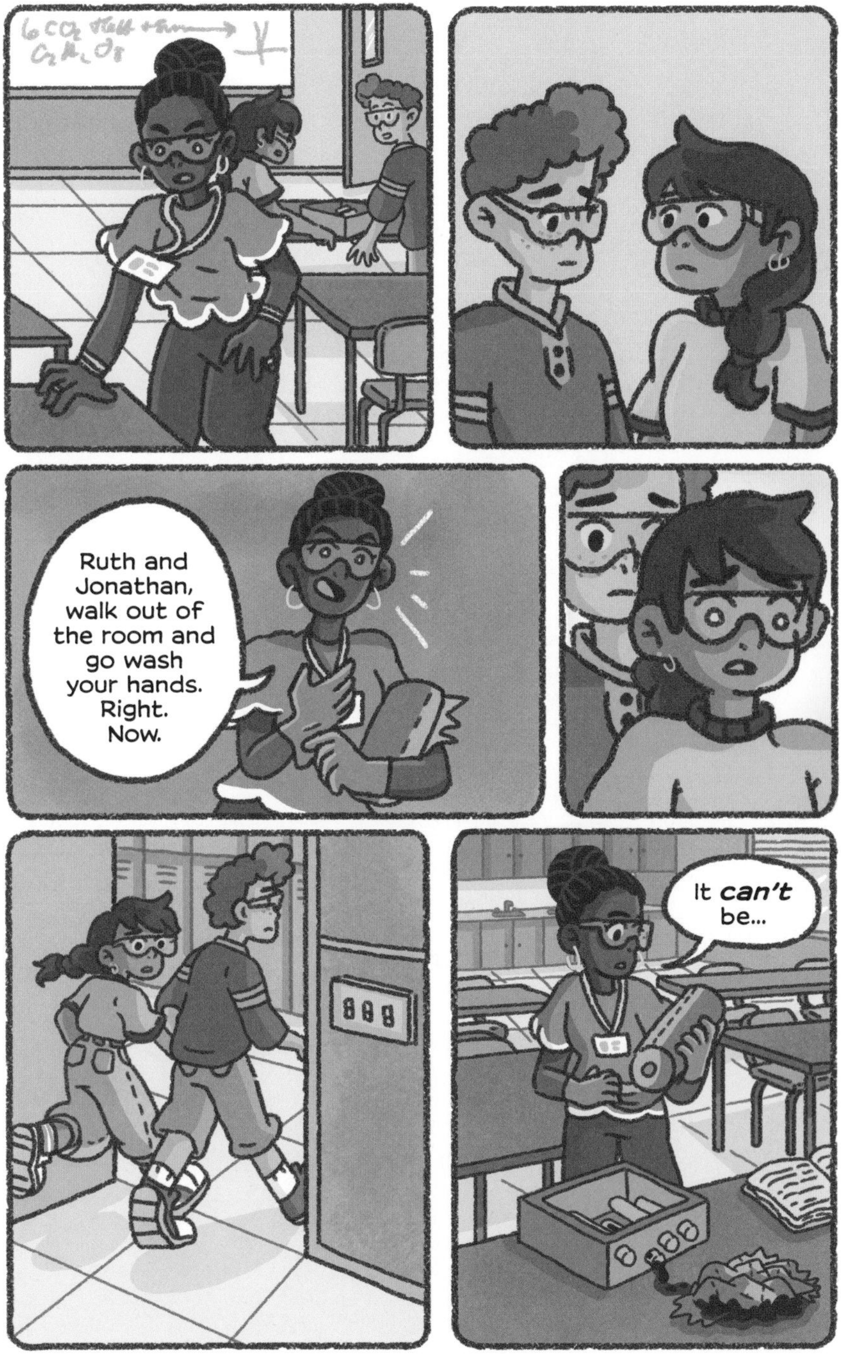
Ruth and Jonathan, walk out of the room and go wash your hands. Right. Now.
It *can't* be...

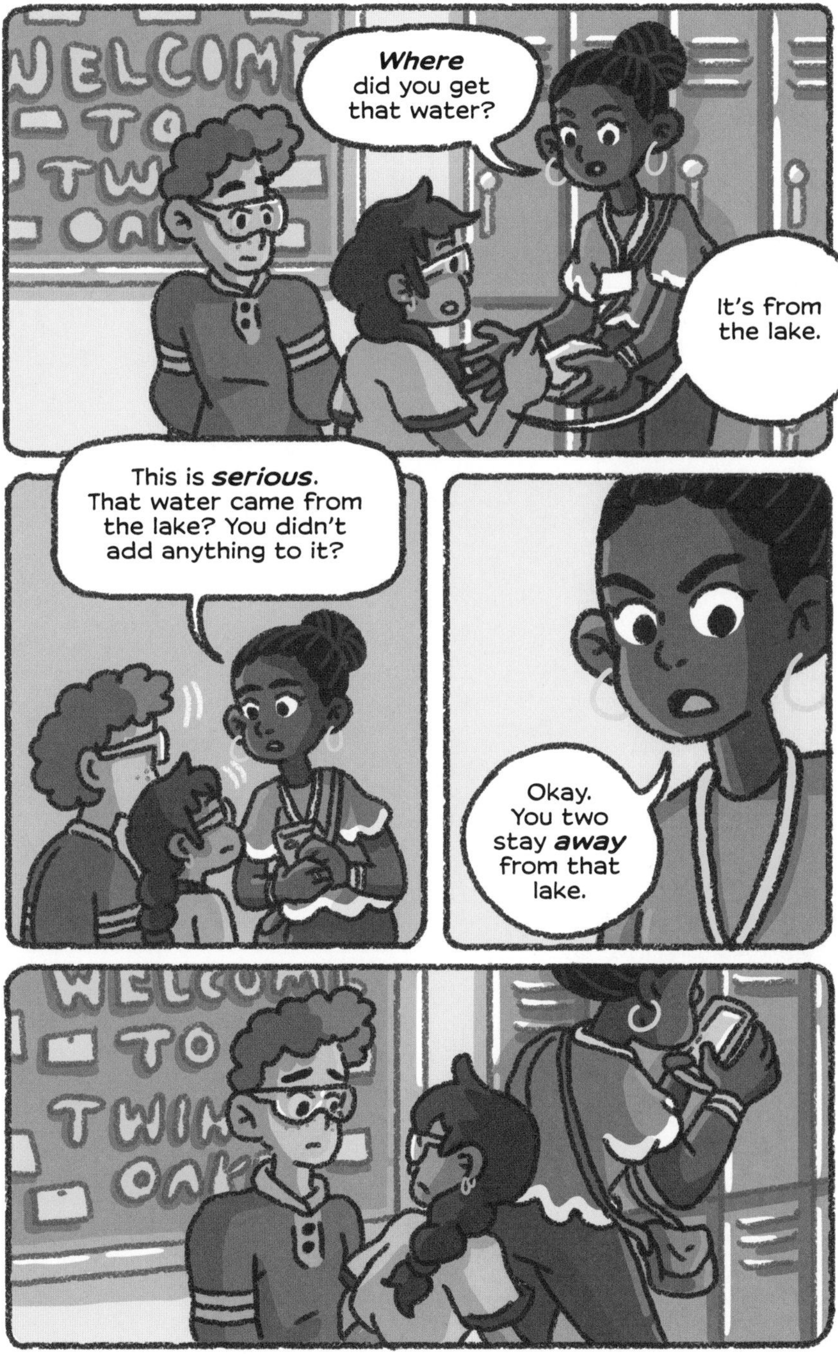
WELCOME TO TWIN ON
Where did you get that water?
It's from the lake.
This is ***serious***. That water came from the lake? You didn't add anything to it?
Okay. You two stay ***away*** from that lake.
WELCOME TO TWIN ON

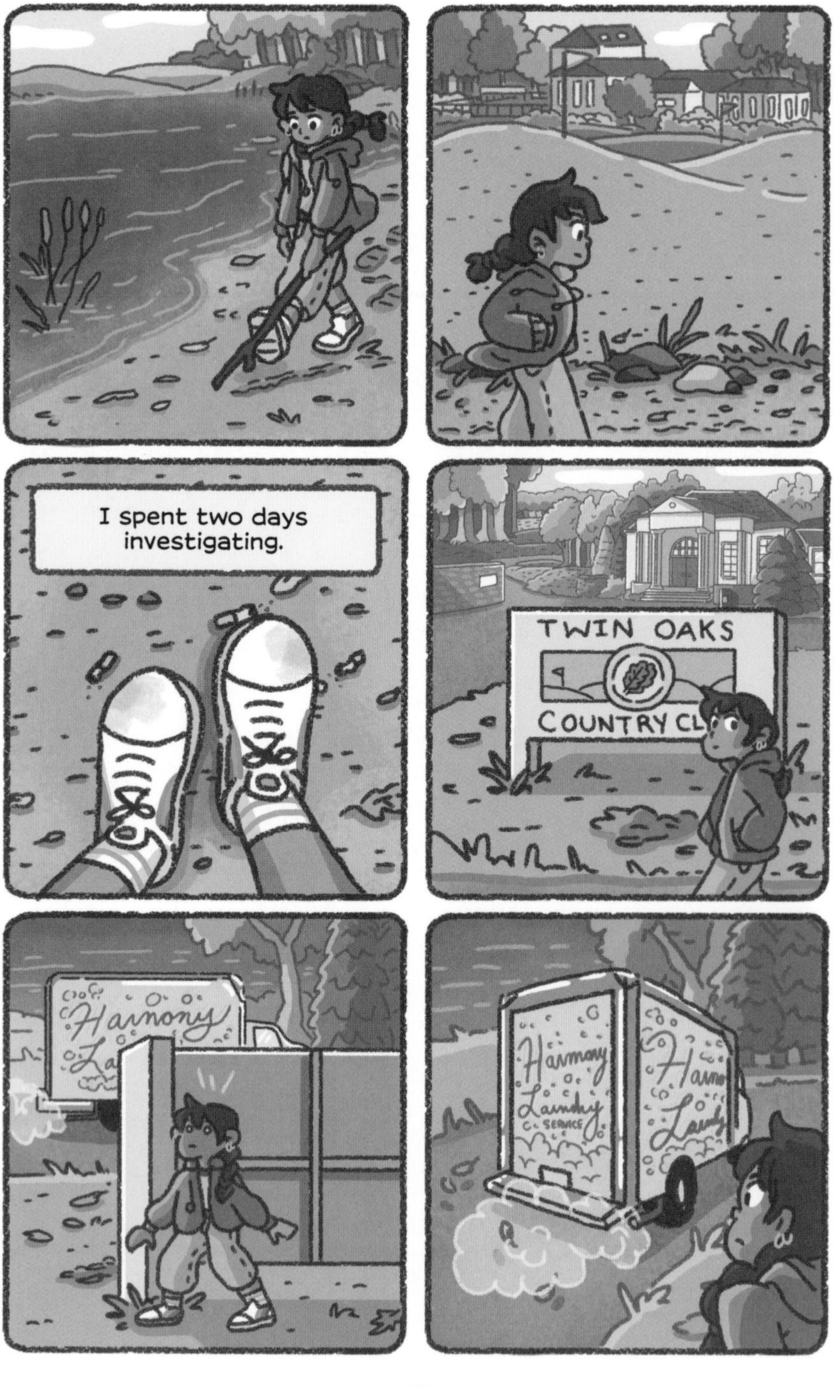
I spent two days investigating.
TWIN OAKS
COUNTRY CL
Harmony
Harmony
Laundry
SERVICE
Harmo
Laundy

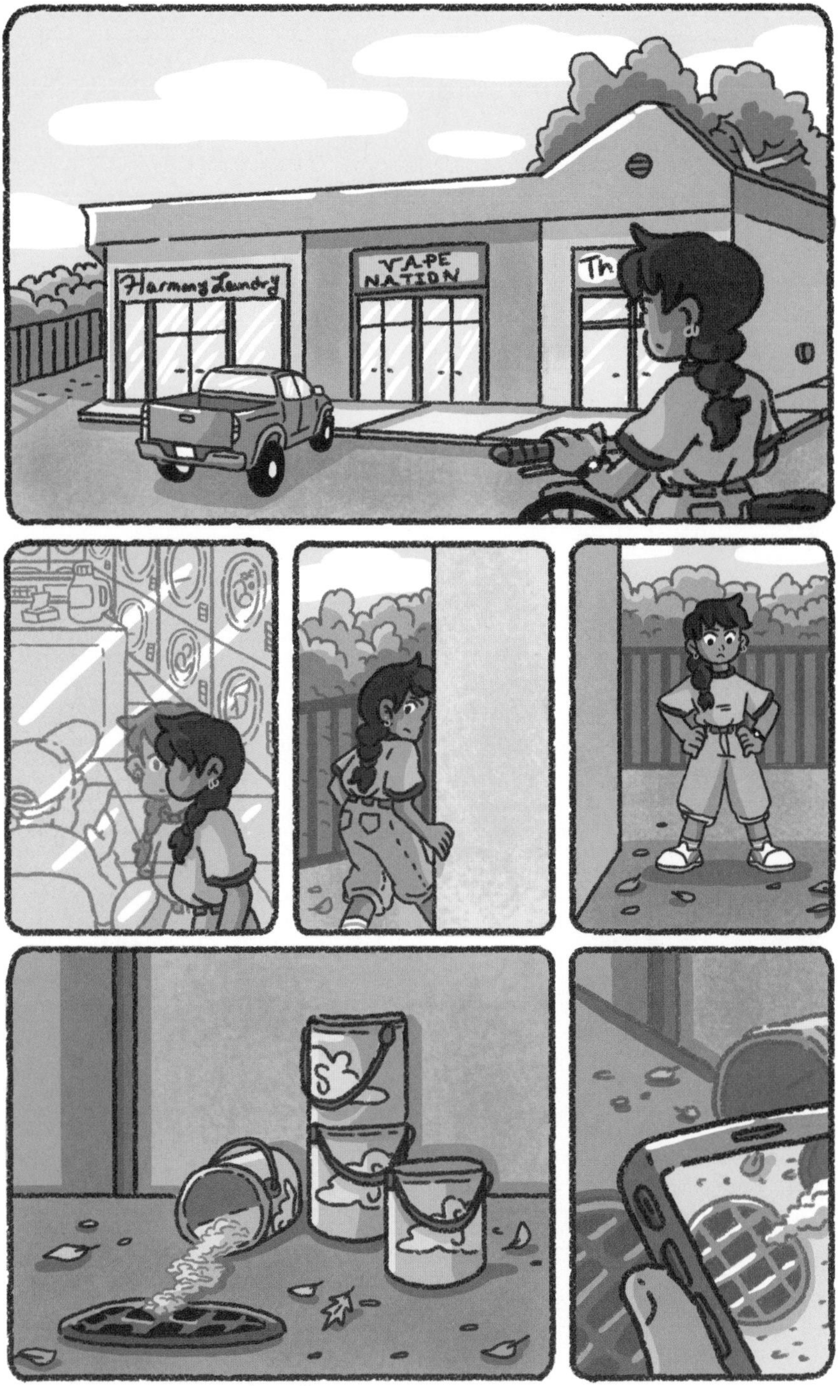
Harmony Laundry
VAPE NATION
Th

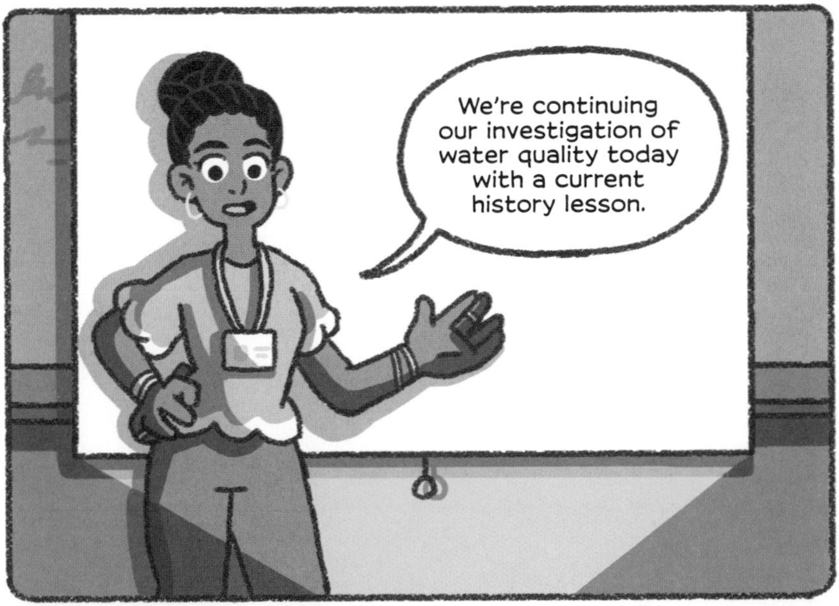
We're continuing our investigation of water quality today with a current history lesson.

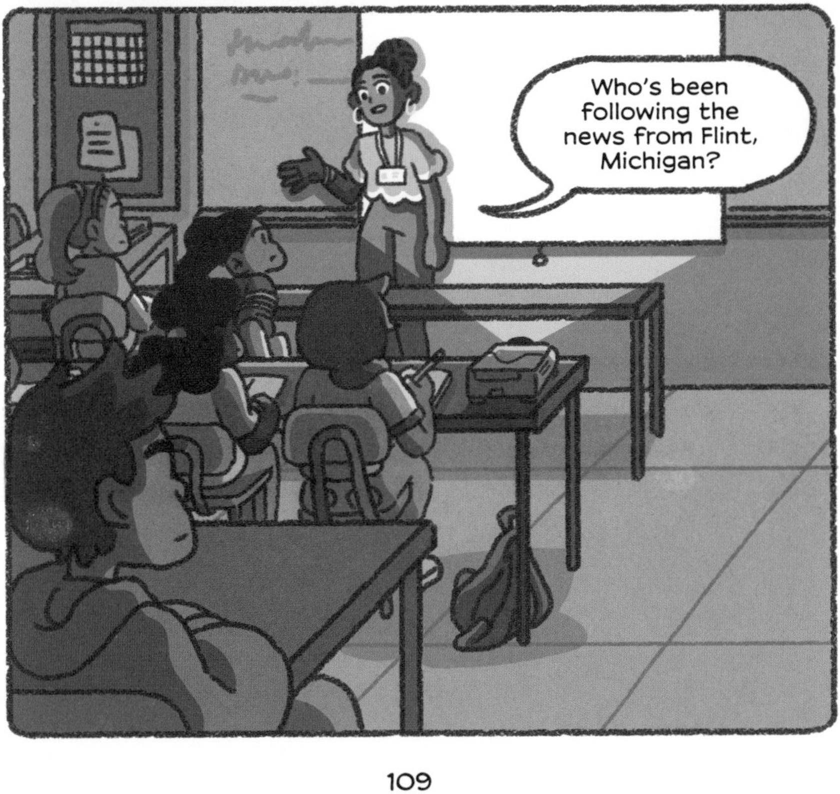
Who's been following the news from Flint, Michigan?

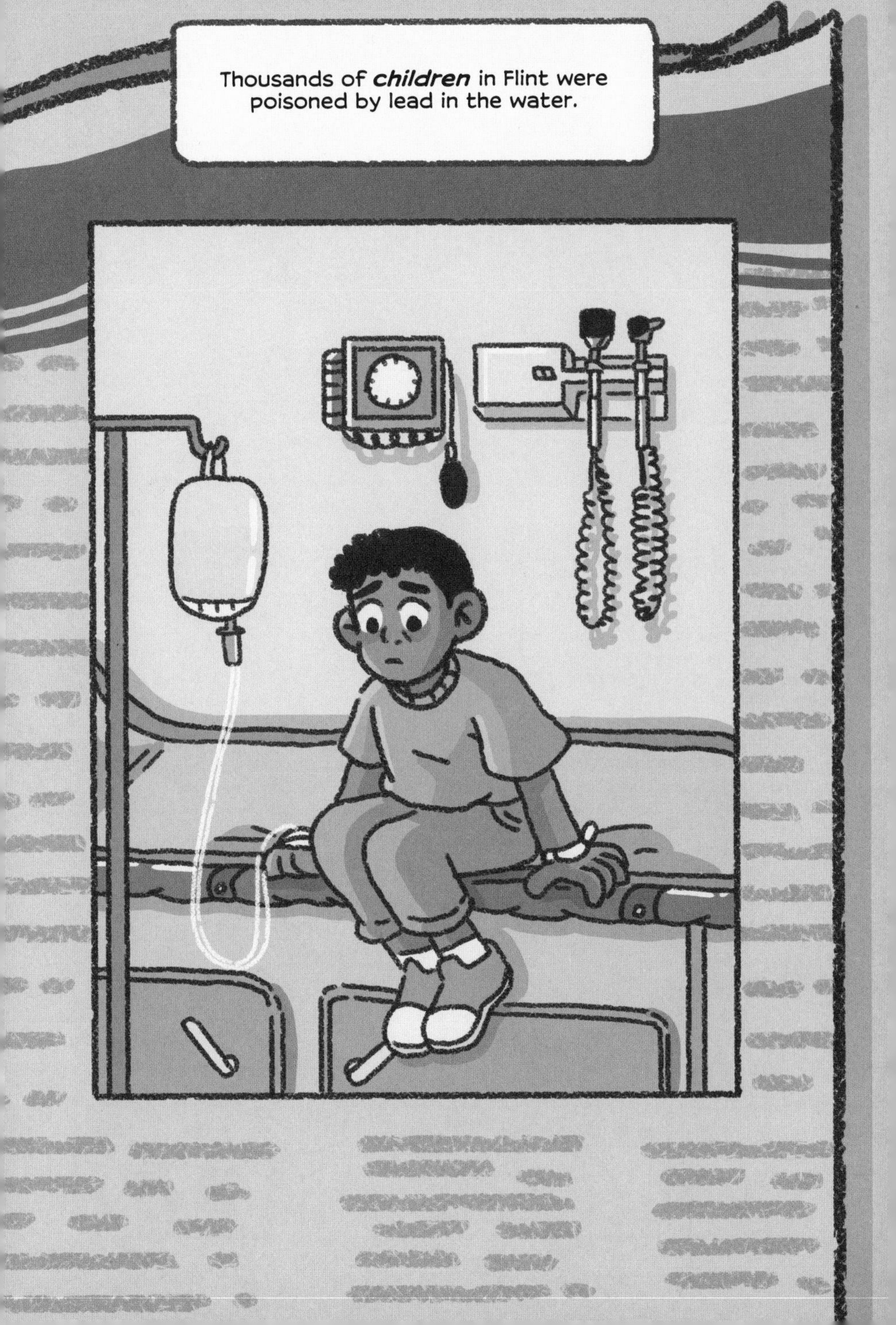
Thousands of ***children*** in Flint were poisoned by lead in the water.

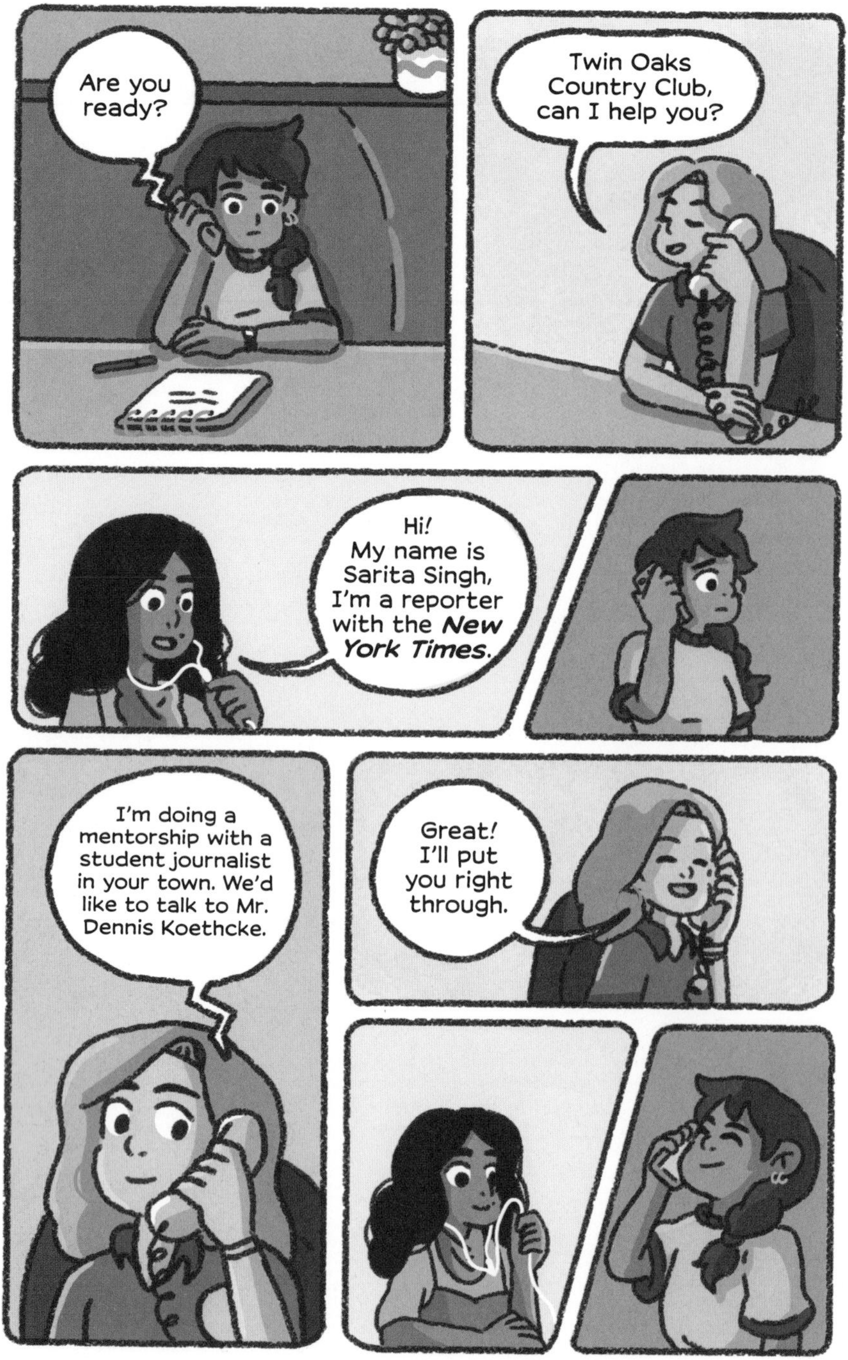
Are you ready?
Twin Oaks Country Club, can I help you?
Hi! My name is Sarita Singh, I'm a reporter with the *New York Times*.
I'm doing a mentorship with a student journalist in your town. We'd like to talk to Mr. Dennis Koethcke.
Great! I'll put you right through.

117

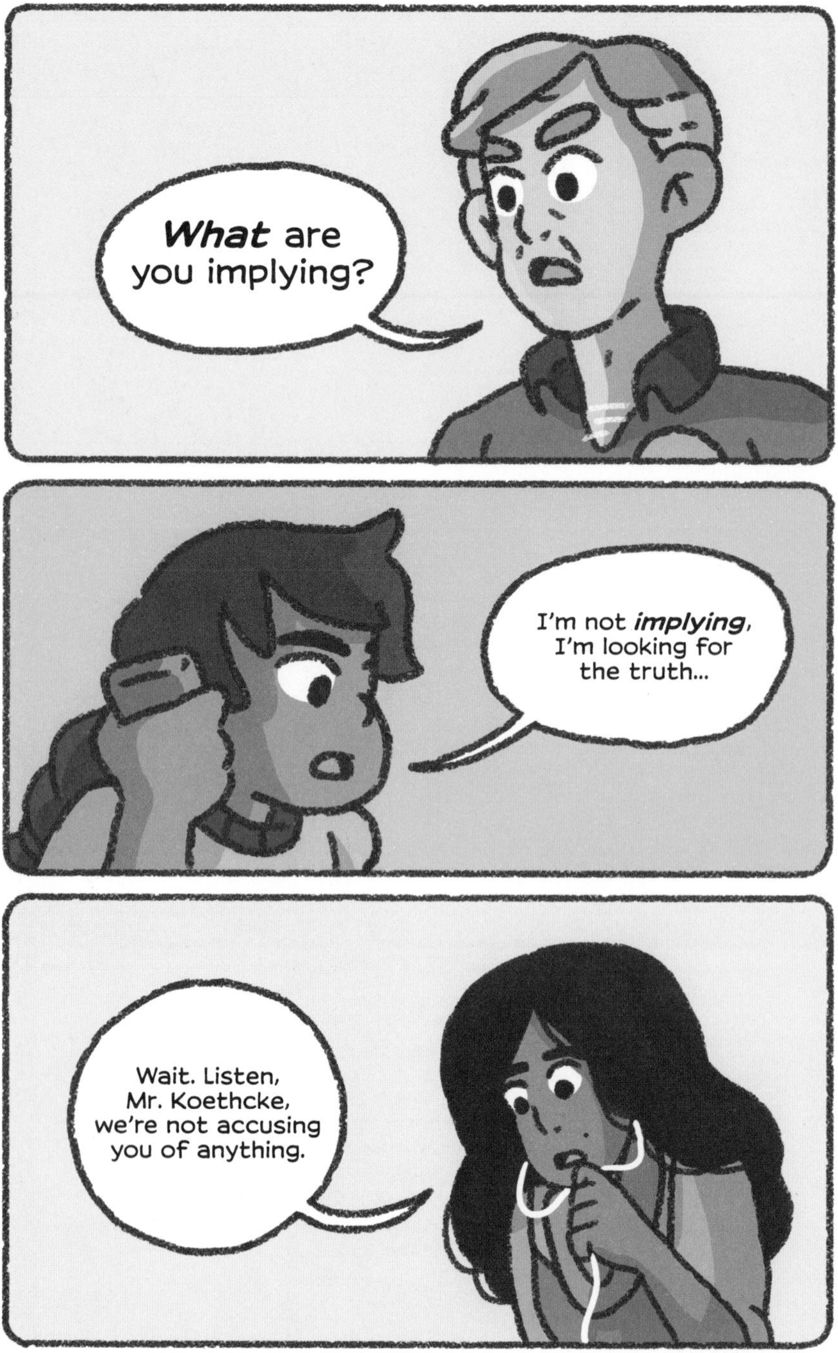
What are you implying?
I'm not *implying*, I'm looking for the truth...
Wait. Listen, Mr. Koethcke, we're not accusing you of anything.

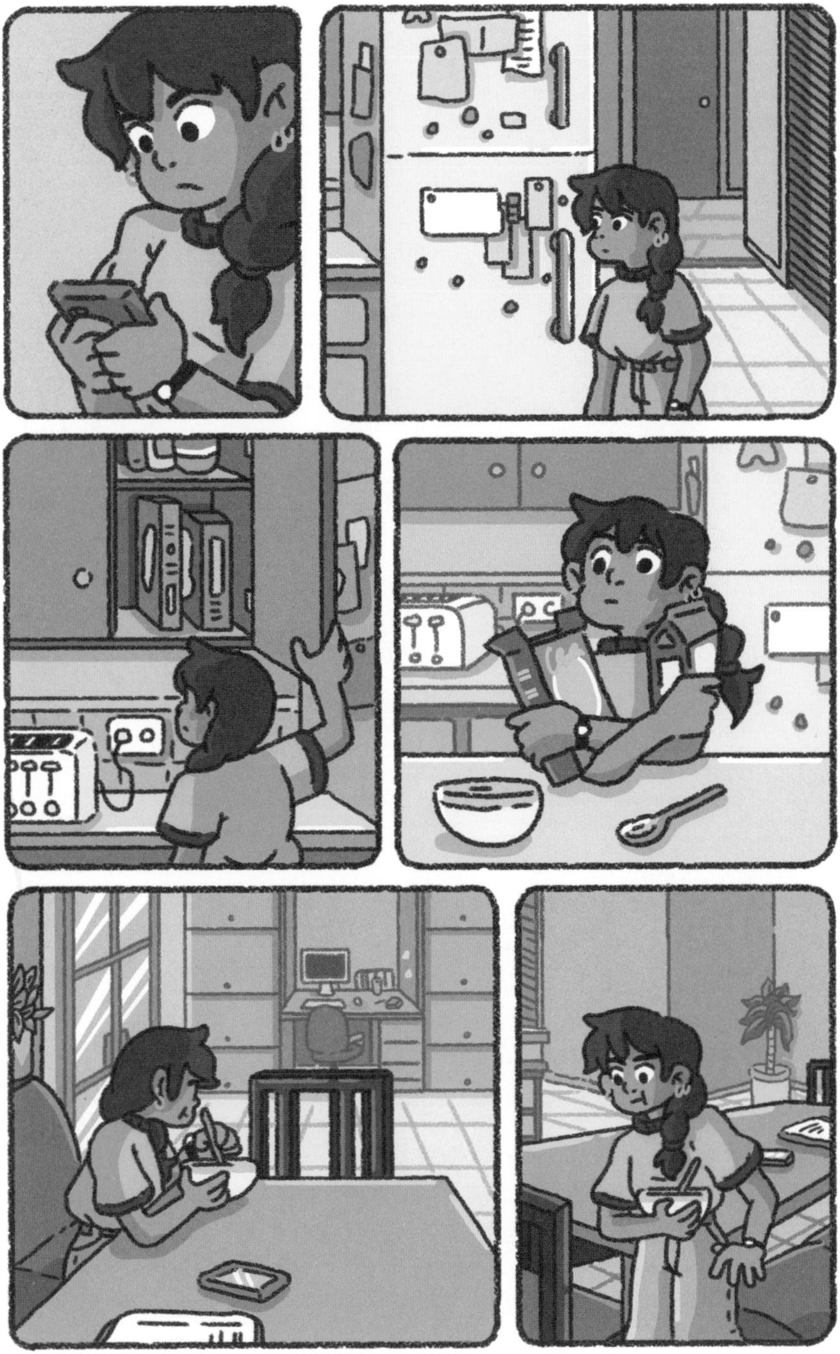

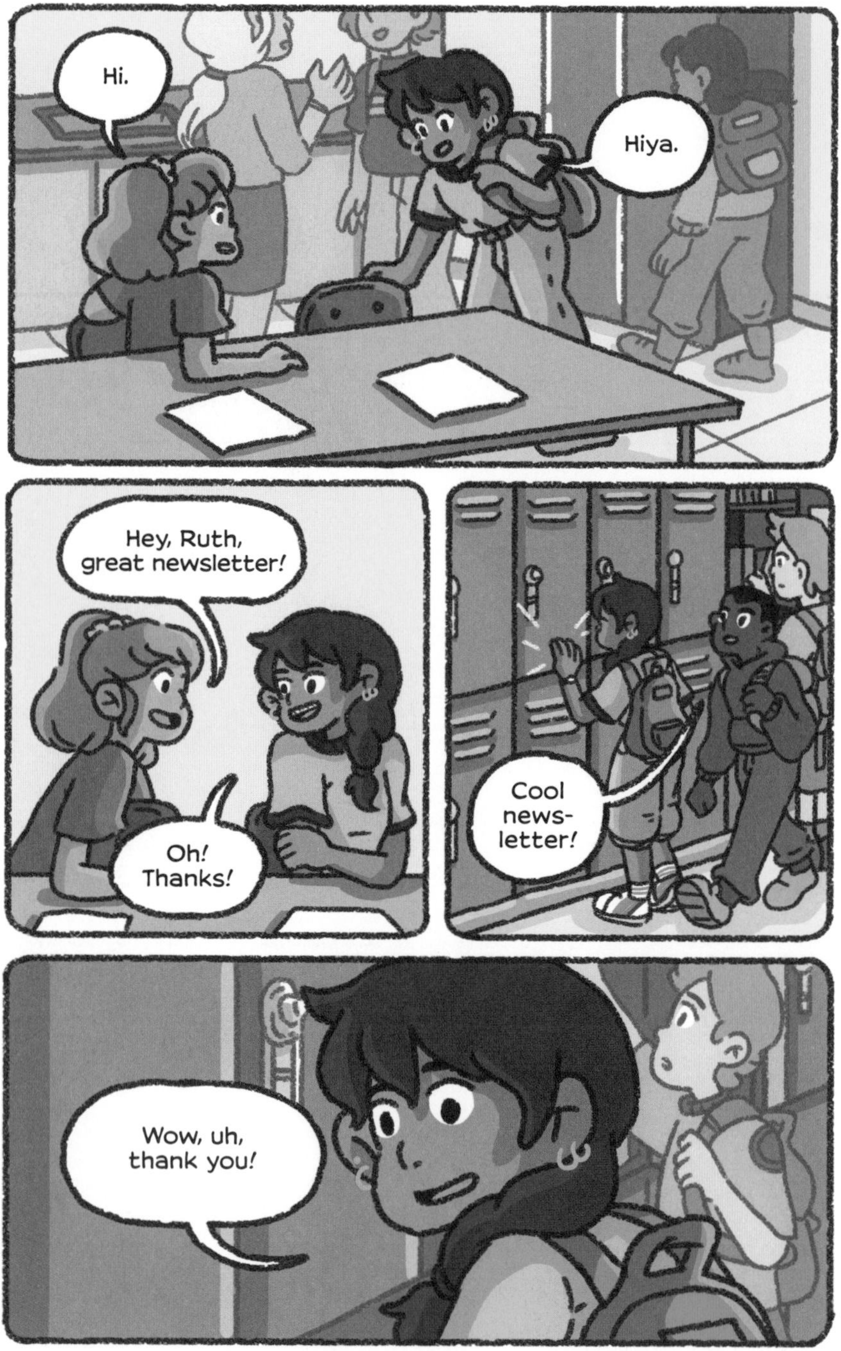
Hi.
Hiya.
Hey, Ruth, great newsletter!
Oh! Thanks!
Cool news-letter!
Wow, uh, thank you!

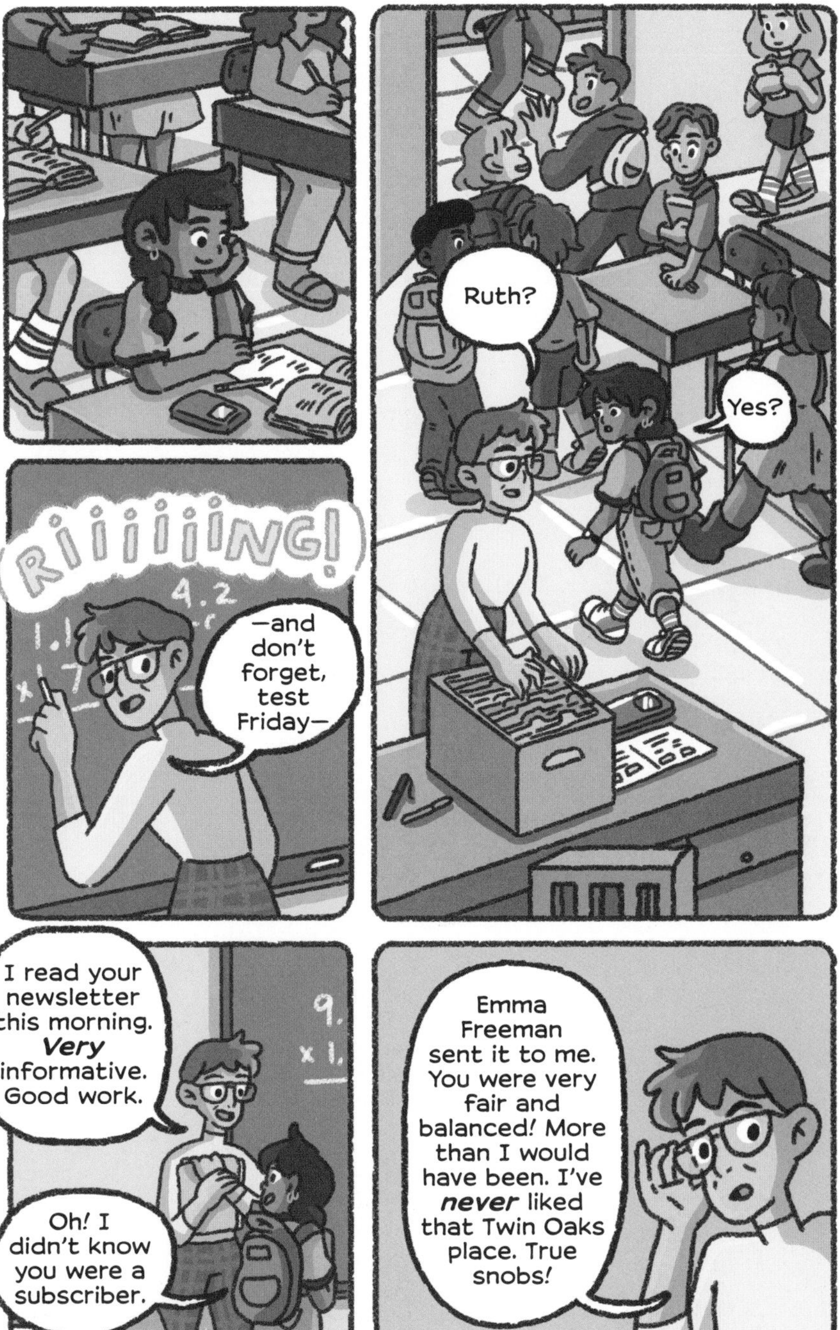
RIIIIING!
4.2
—and don't forget, test Friday—
Ruth?
Yes?
I read your newsletter this morning. *Very* informative. Good work.
Oh! I didn't know you were a subscriber.
Emma Freeman sent it to me. You were very fair and balanced! More than I would have been. I've *never* liked that Twin Oaks place. True snobs!

128

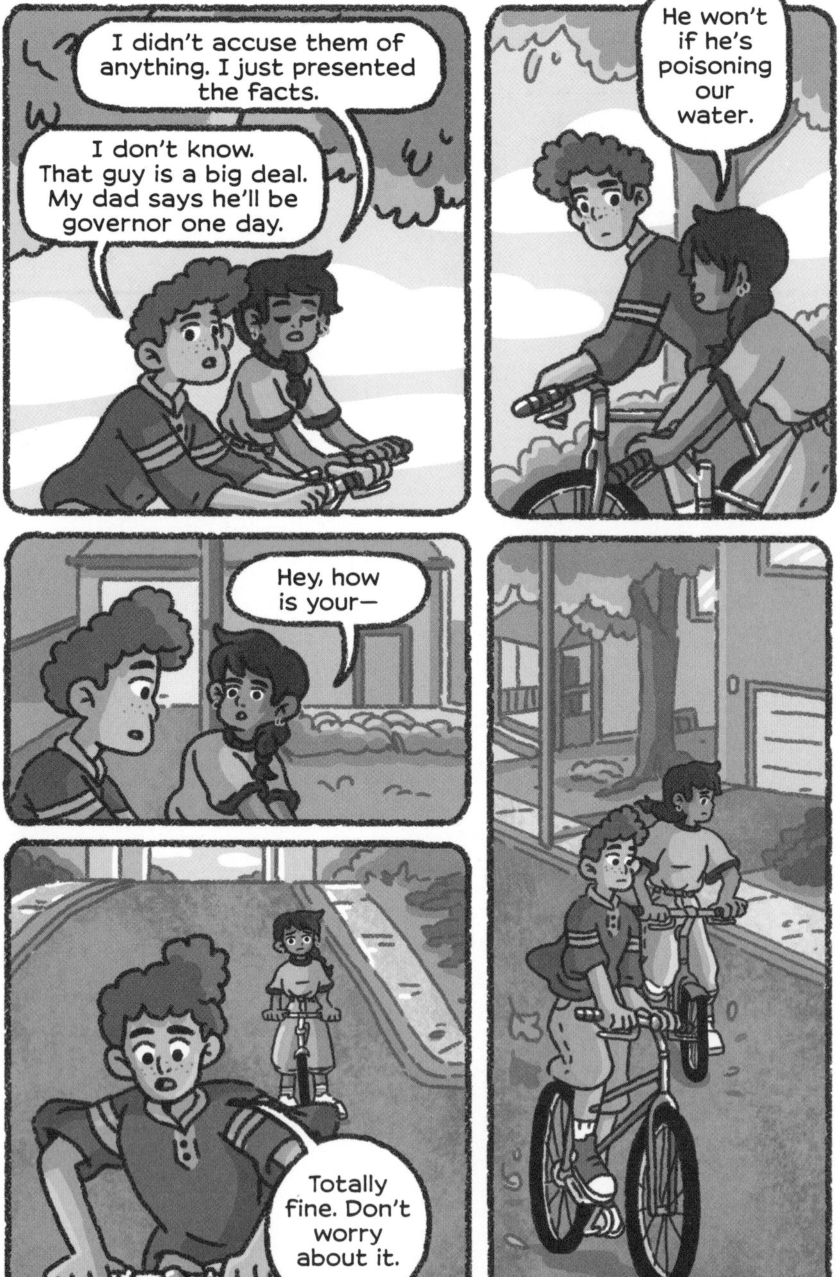
I didn't accuse them of anything. I just presented the facts.
I don't know. That guy is a big deal. My dad says he'll be governor one day.
He won't if he's poisoning our water.
Hey, how is your—
Totally fine. Don't worry about it.

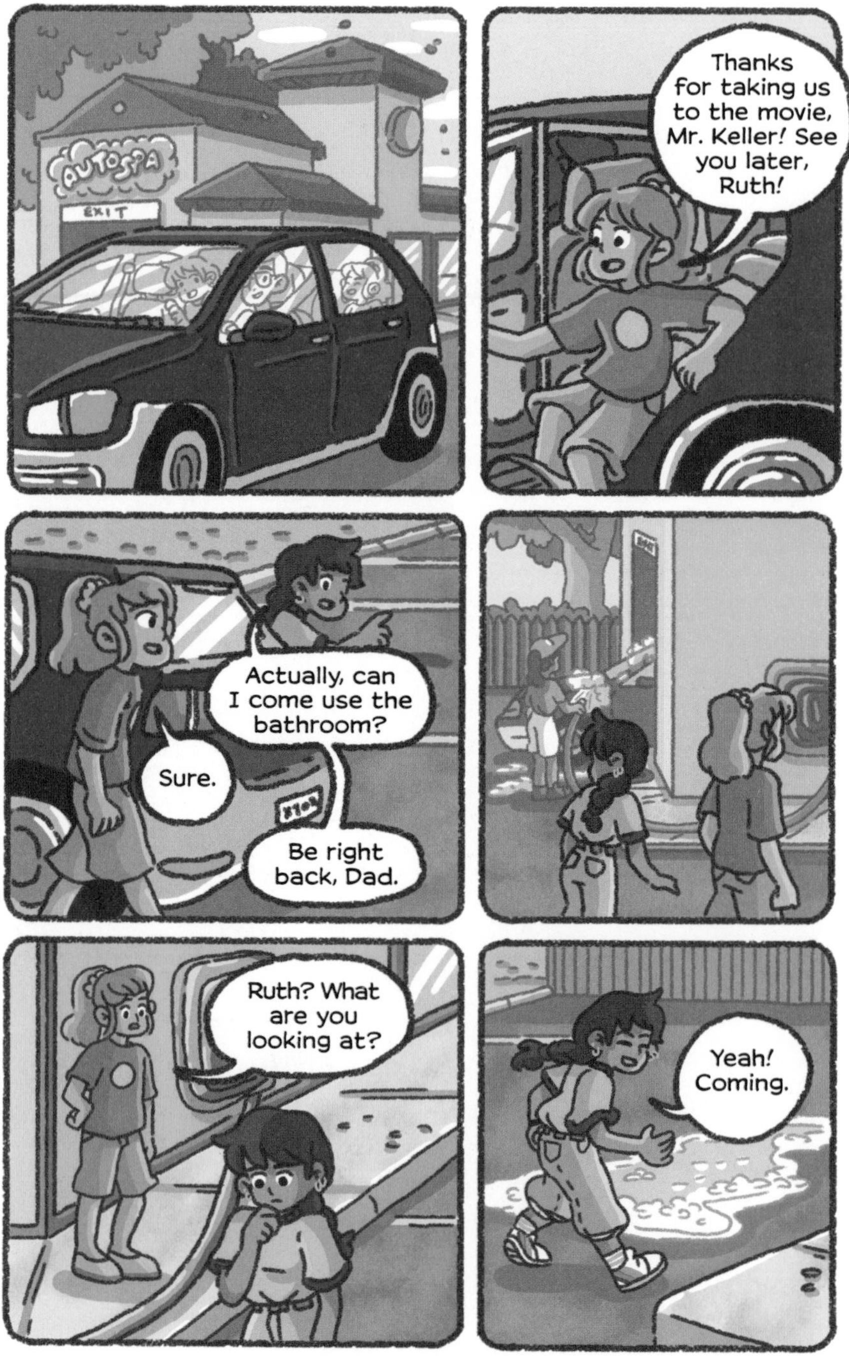
AUTOSPA
EXIT
Thanks for taking us to the movie, Mr. Keller! See you later, Ruth!
Actually, can I come use the bathroom?
Sure.
Be right back, Dad.
Ruth? What are you looking at?
Yeah! Coming.

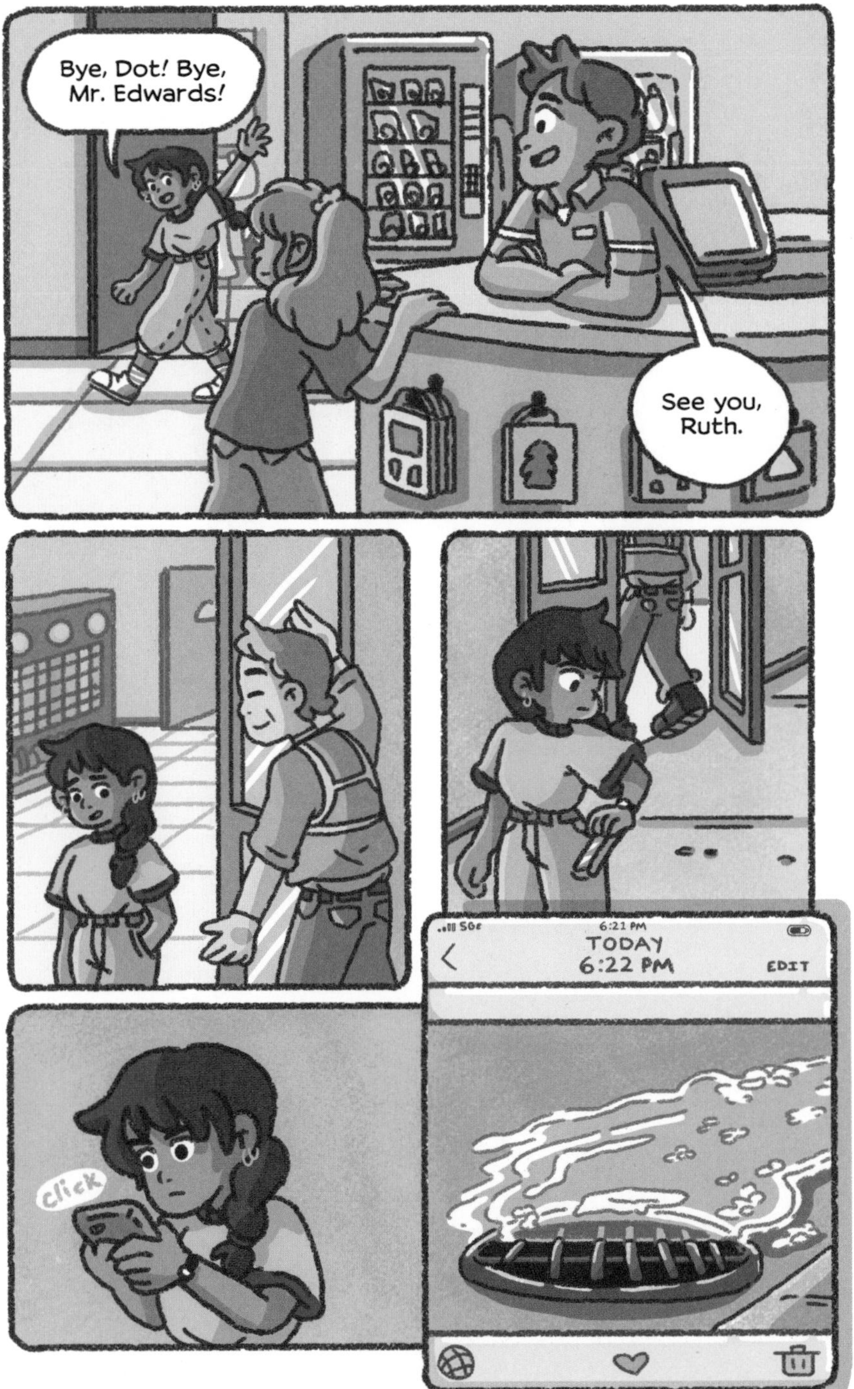
Bye, Dot! Bye, Mr. Edwards!
See you, Ruth.
6:21 PM
TODAY
6:22 PM
EDIT
click

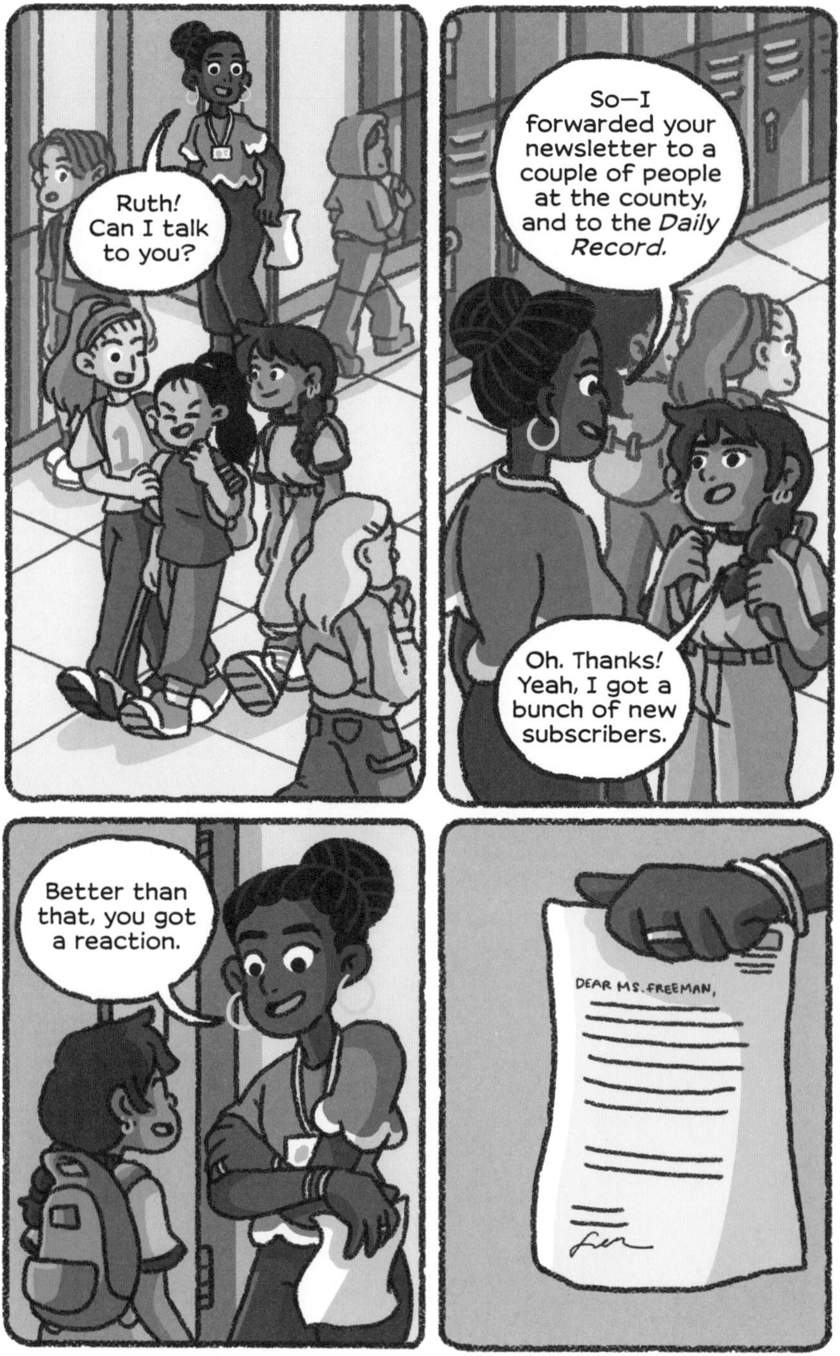
Ruth! Can I talk to you?
So—I forwarded your newsletter to a couple of people at the county, and to the *Daily Record.*
Oh. Thanks! Yeah, I got a bunch of new subscribers.
Better than that, you got a reaction.
DEAR MS. FREEMAN,

135

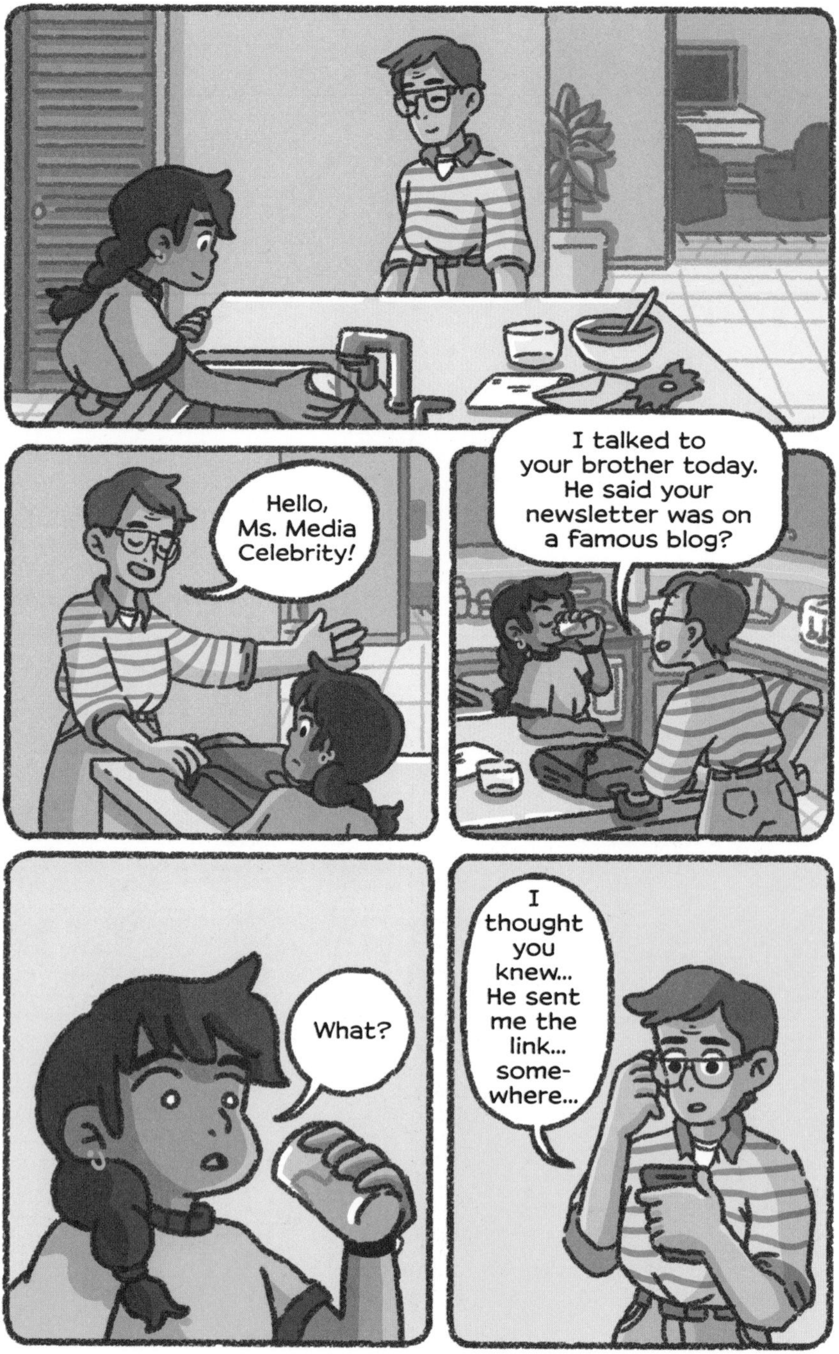
Hello, Ms. Media Celebrity!
I talked to your brother today. He said your newsletter was on a famous blog?
What?
I thought you knew... He sent me the link... some-where...

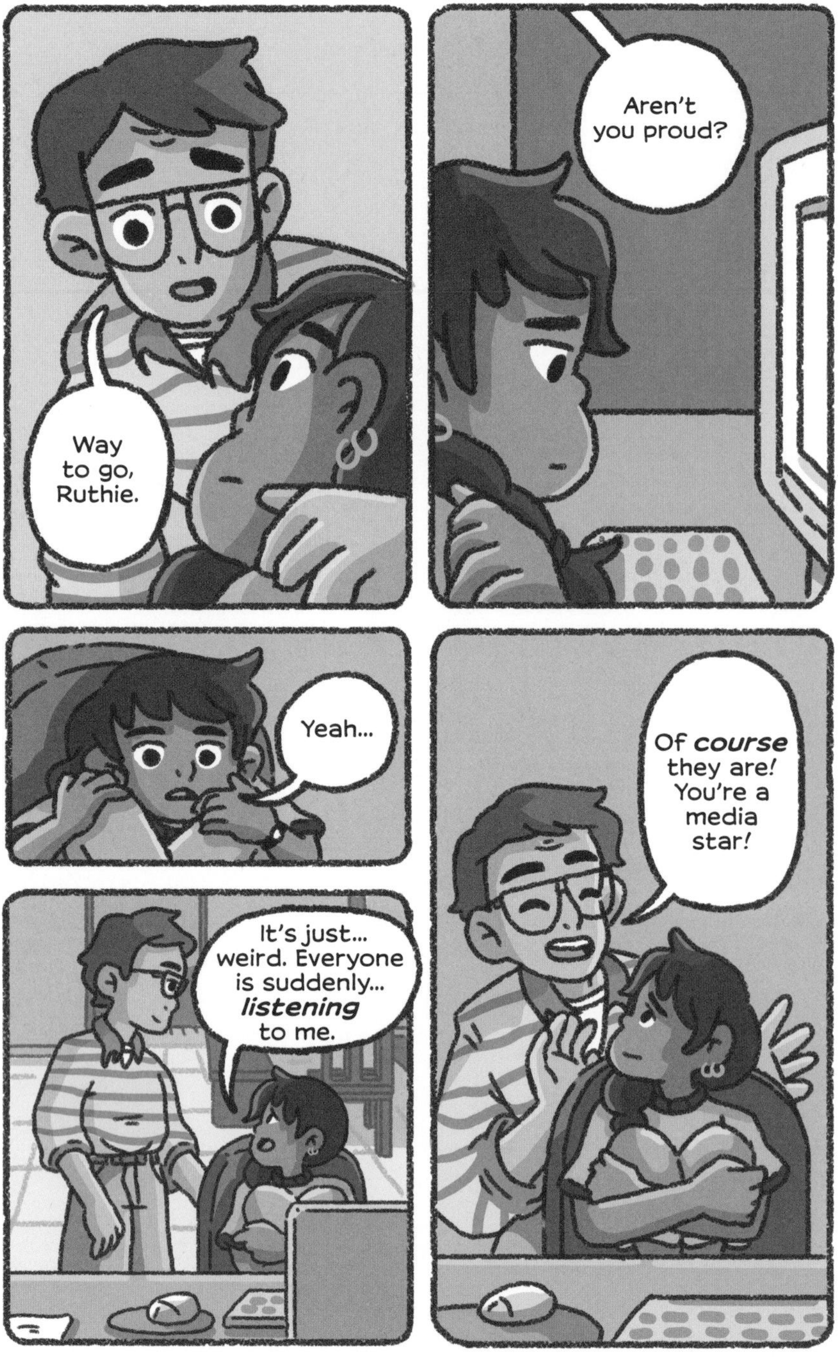
Way to go, Ruthie.
Aren't you proud?
Yeah...
It's just... weird. Everyone is suddenly... *listening* to me.
Of *course* they are! You're a media star!

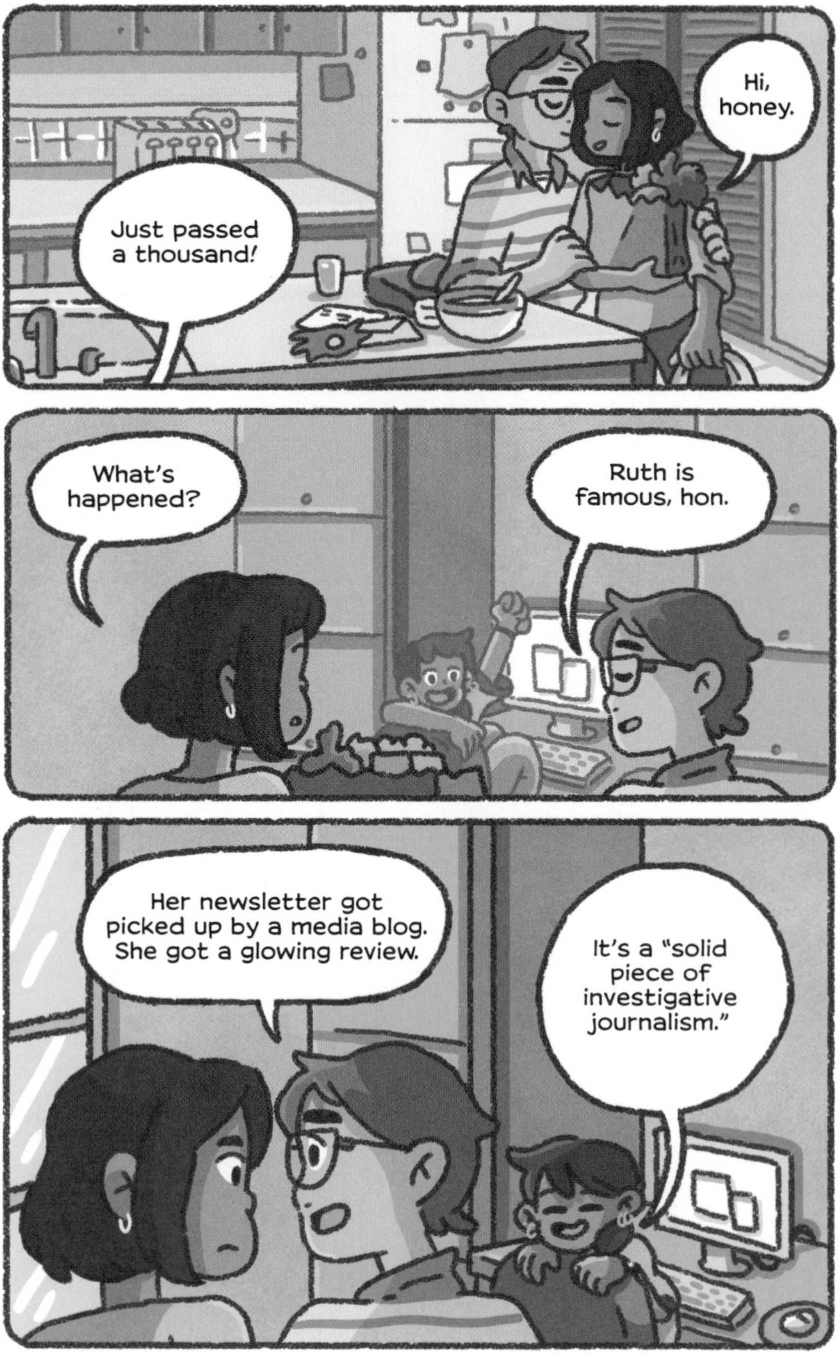

Hi, honey.
Just passed a thousand!
What's happened?
Ruth is famous, hon.
Her newsletter got picked up by a media blog. She got a glowing review.
It's a "solid piece of investigative journalism."

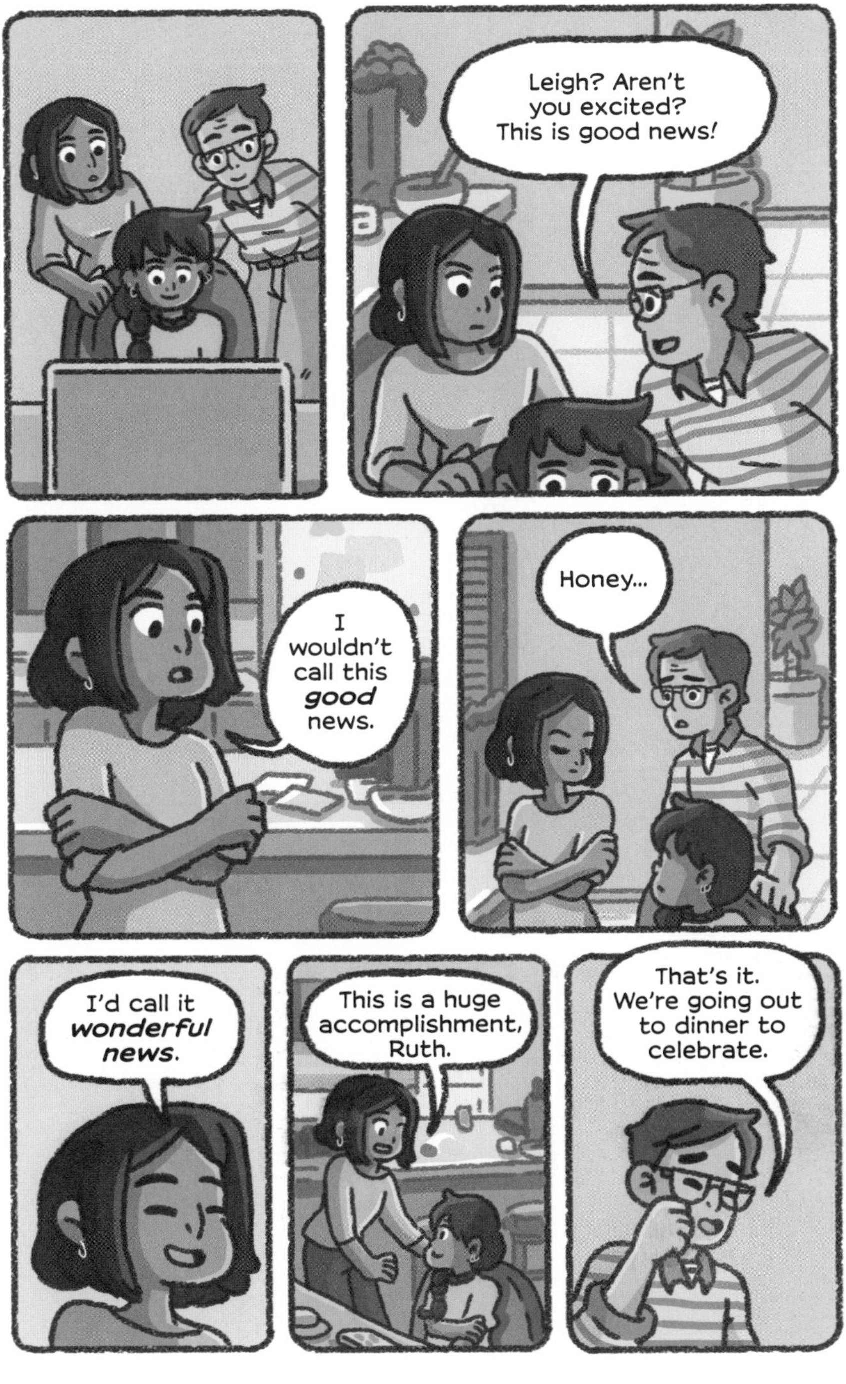
Leigh? Aren't you excited? This is good news!
I wouldn't call this *good* news.
Honey...
I'd call it ***wonderful news***.
This is a huge accomplishment, Ruth.
That's it. We're going out to dinner to celebrate.

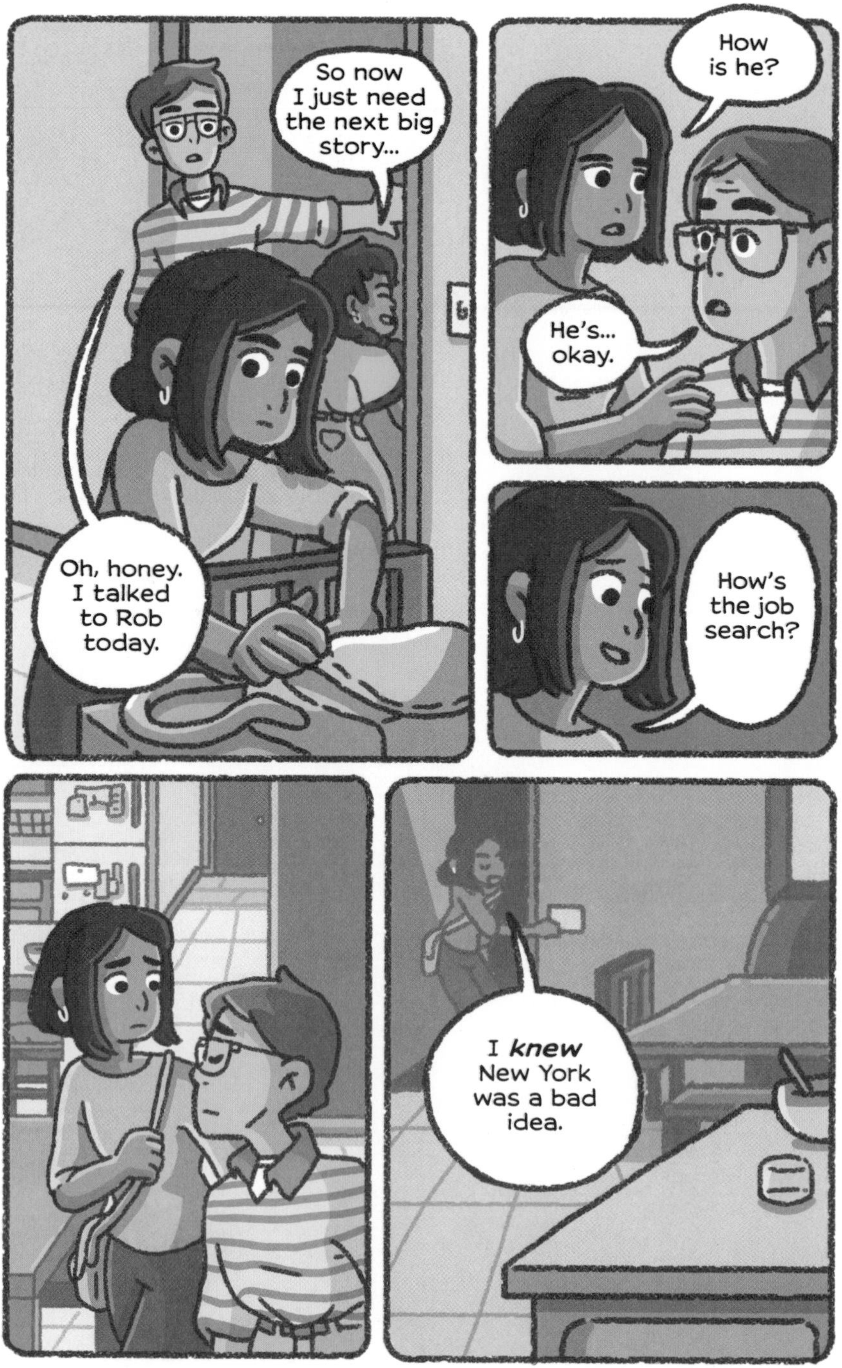
So now I just need the next big story...
Oh, honey. I talked to Rob today.
How is he?
He's... okay.
How's the job search?
I *knew* New York was a bad idea.

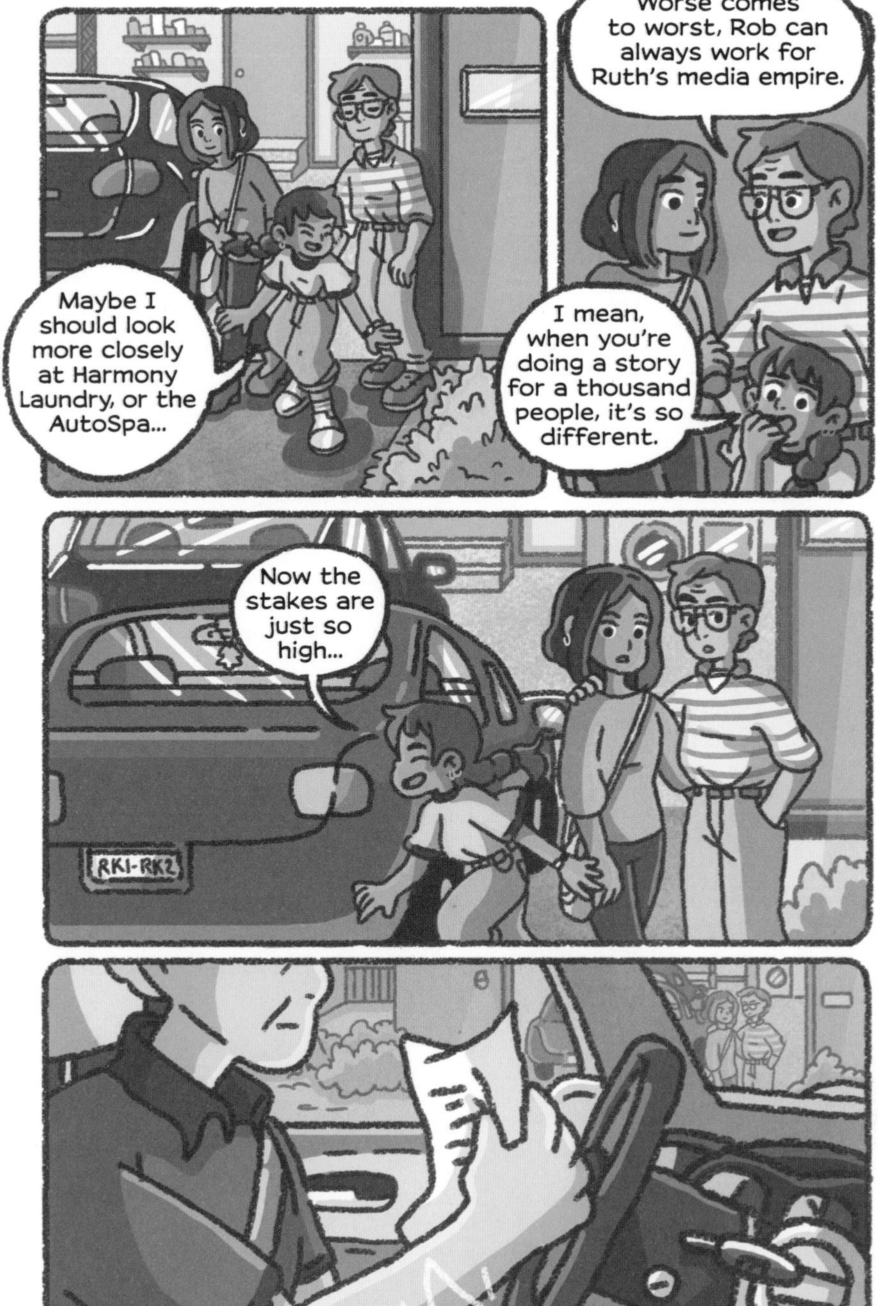
Maybe I should look more closely at Harmony Laundry, or the AutoSpa...
Worse comes to worst, Rob can always work for Ruth's media empire.
I mean, when you're doing a story for a thousand people, it's so different.
Now the stakes are just so high...
RK1-RK2

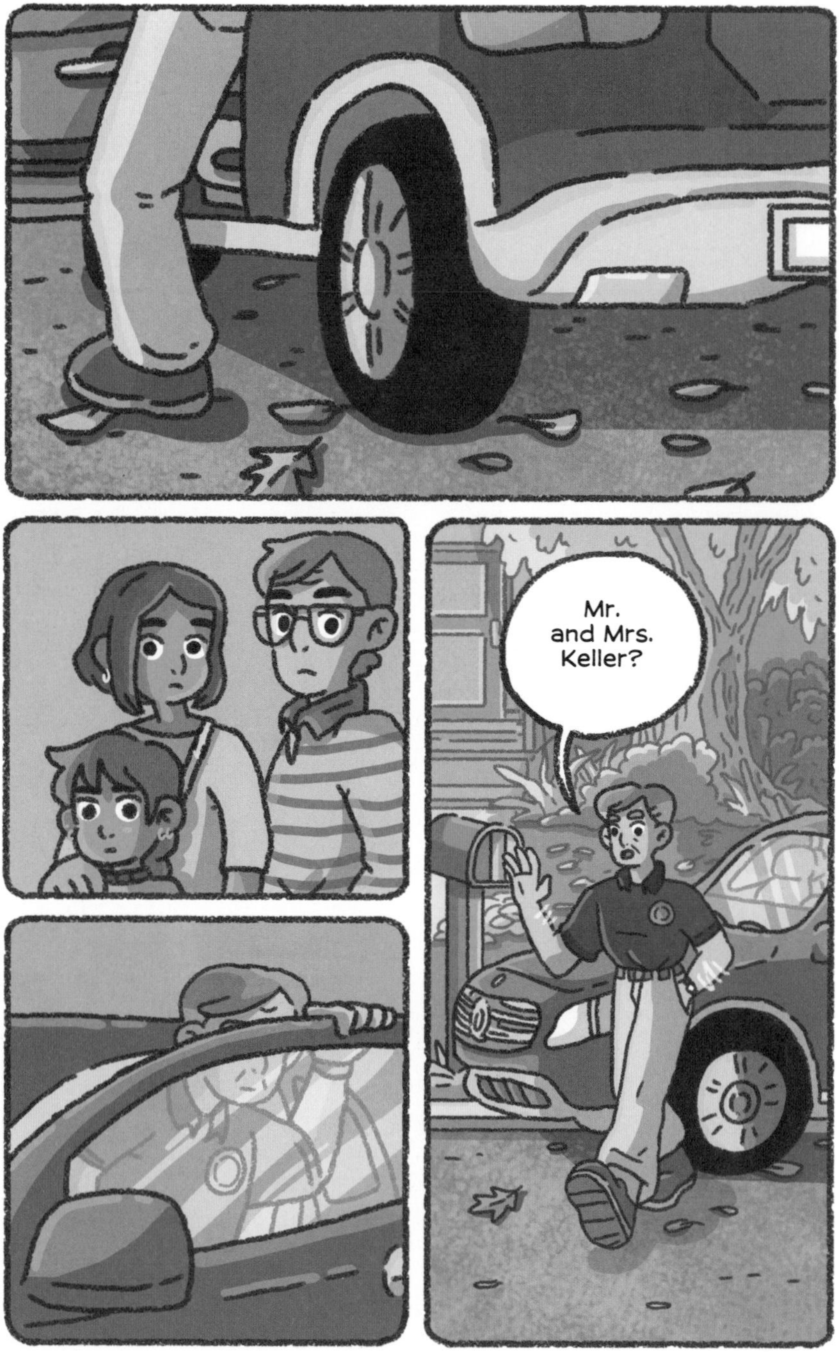
Mr.
and Mrs.
Keller?

145

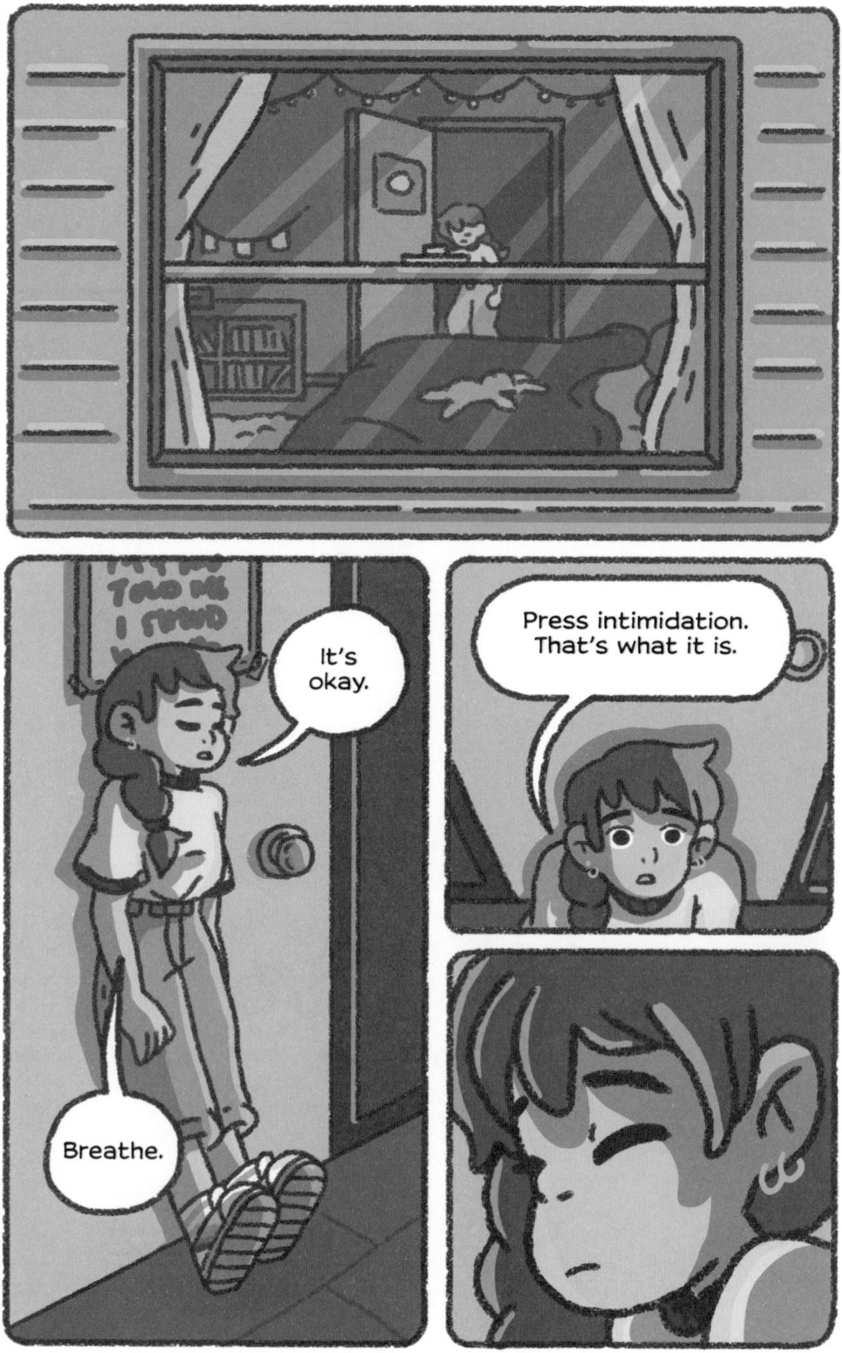
It's okay.
Breathe.
Press intimidation. That's what it is.

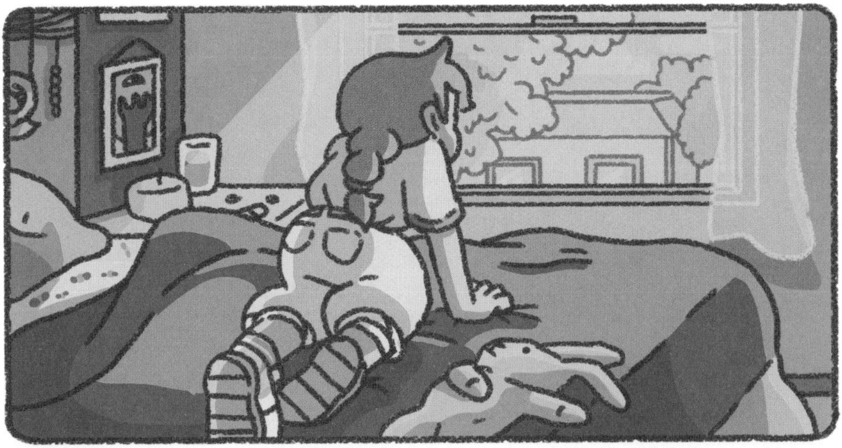

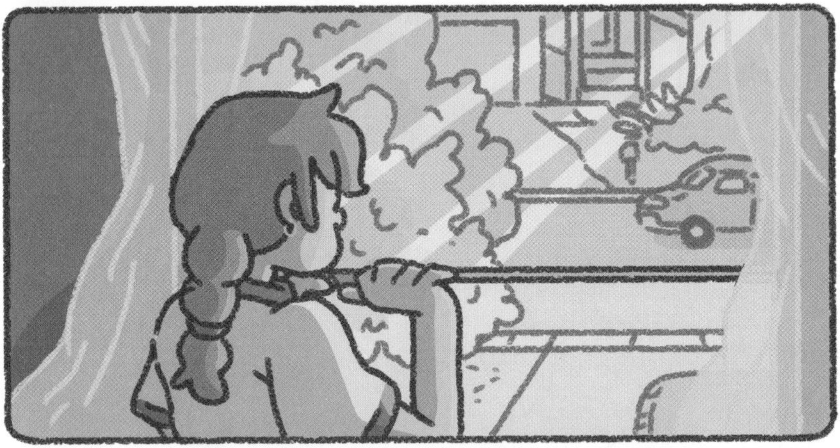

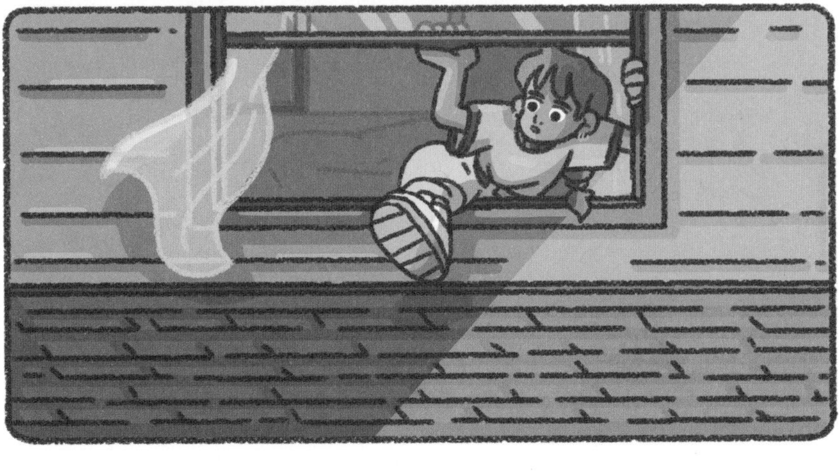

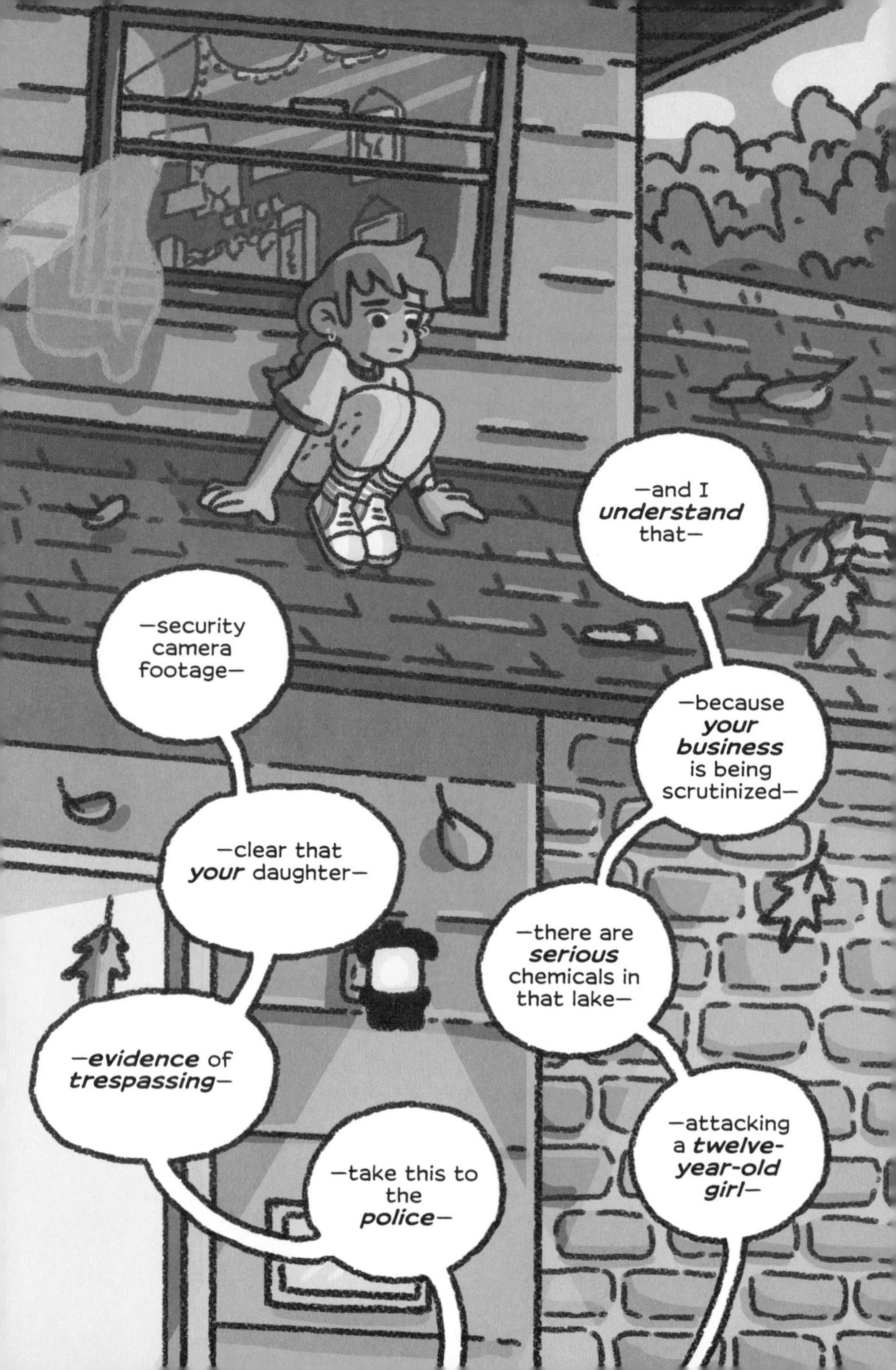
—and I understand that—
—security camera footage—
—because your business is being scrutinized—
—clear that your daughter—
—there are serious chemicals in that lake—
—evidence of trespassing—
—attacking a twelve-year-old girl—
—take this to the police—

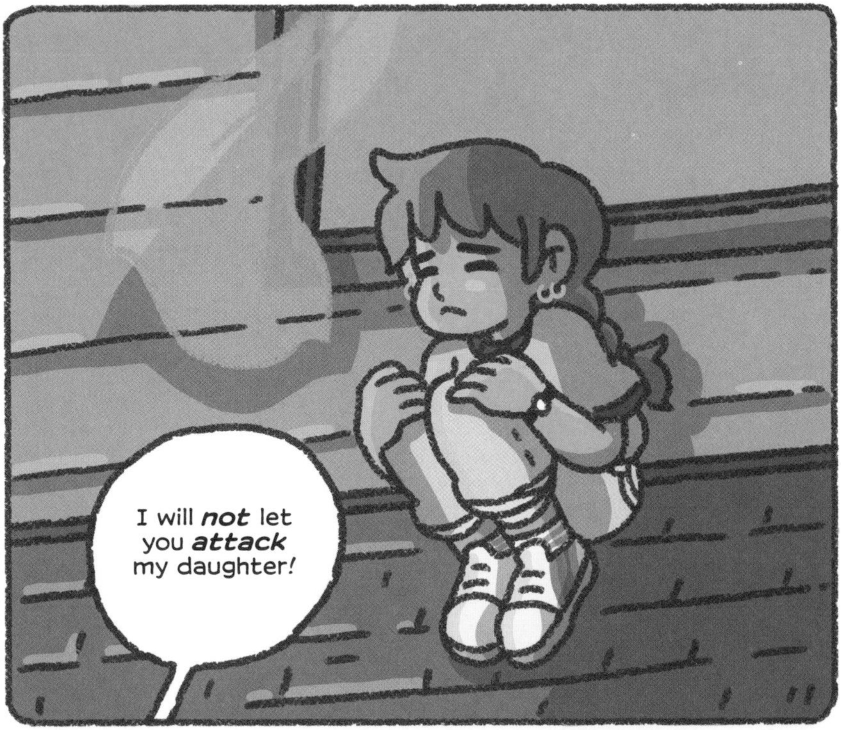
I will ***not*** let you ***attack*** my daughter!

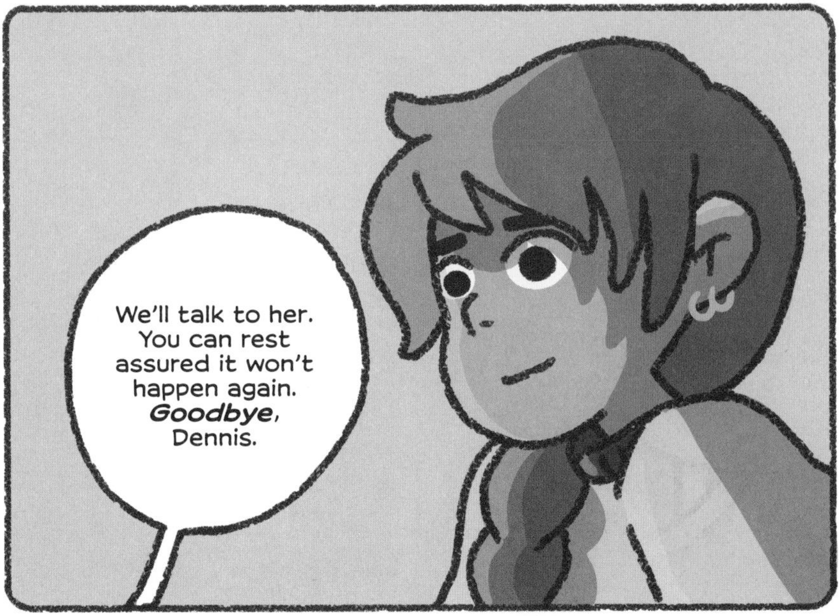
We'll talk to her. You can rest assured it won't happen again. ***Goodbye***, Dennis.

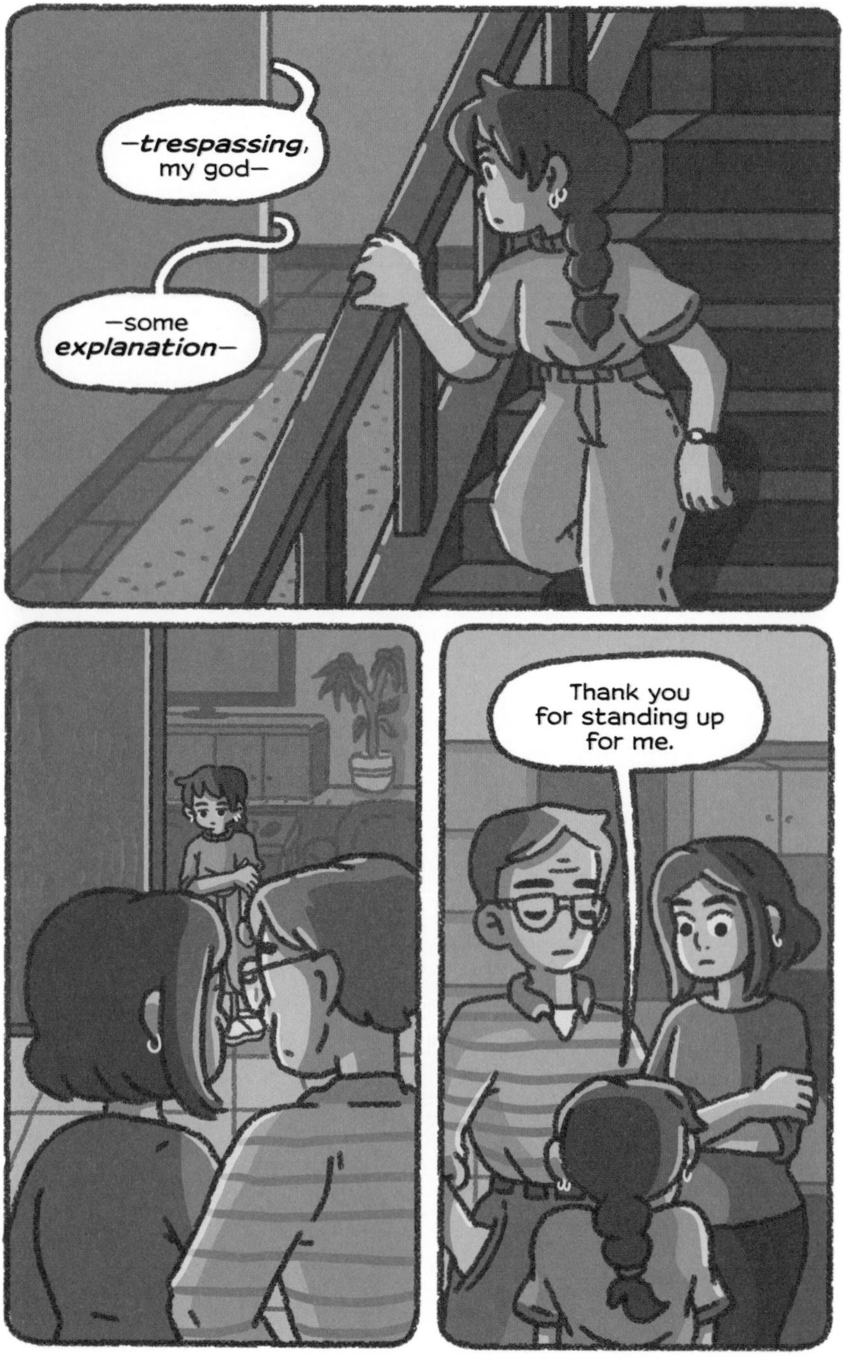

—*trespassing*, my god—
—some *explanation*—
Thank you for standing up for me.

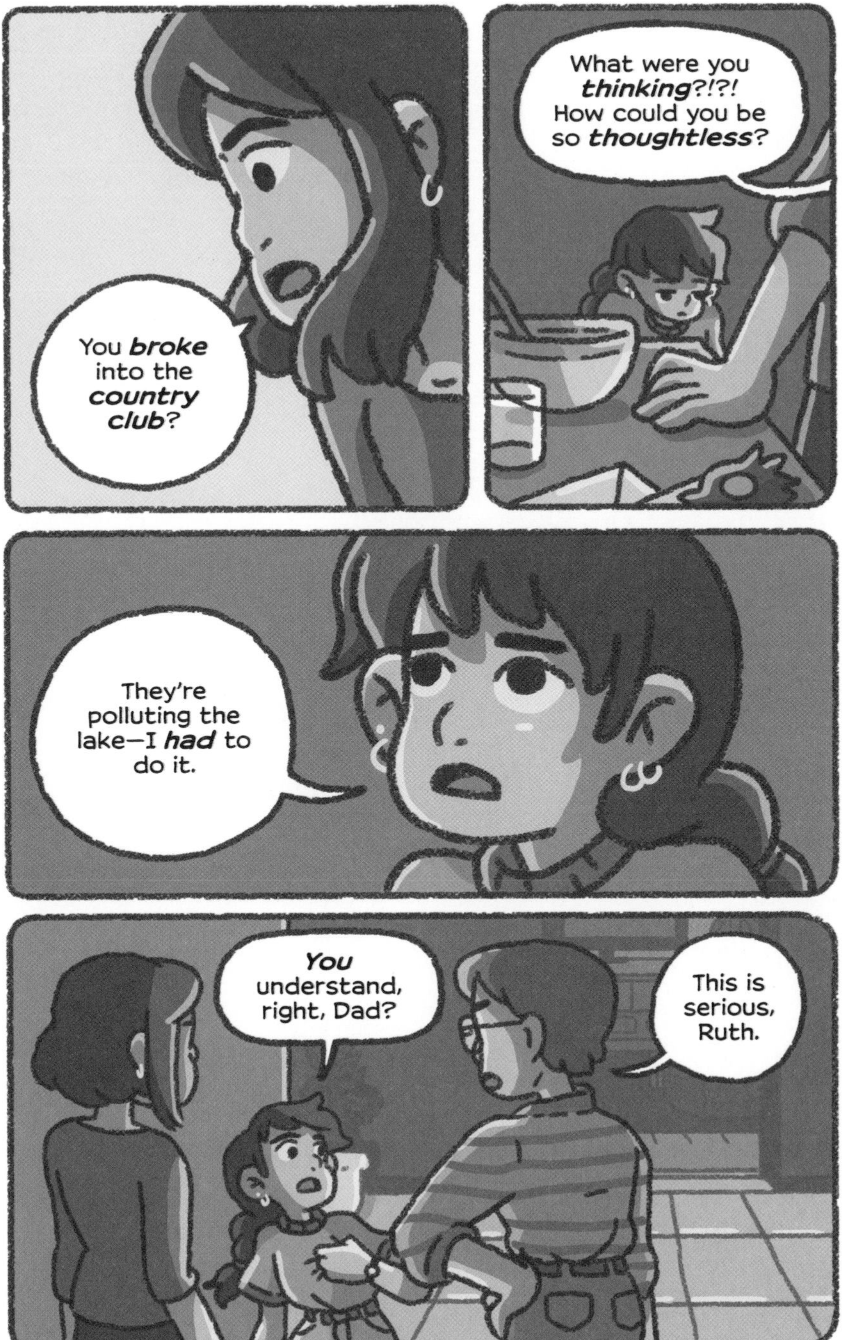
You *broke* into the *country club*?
What were you *thinking*?!?! How could you be so *thoughtless*?
They're polluting the lake—I *had* to do it.
You understand, right, Dad?
This is serious, Ruth.

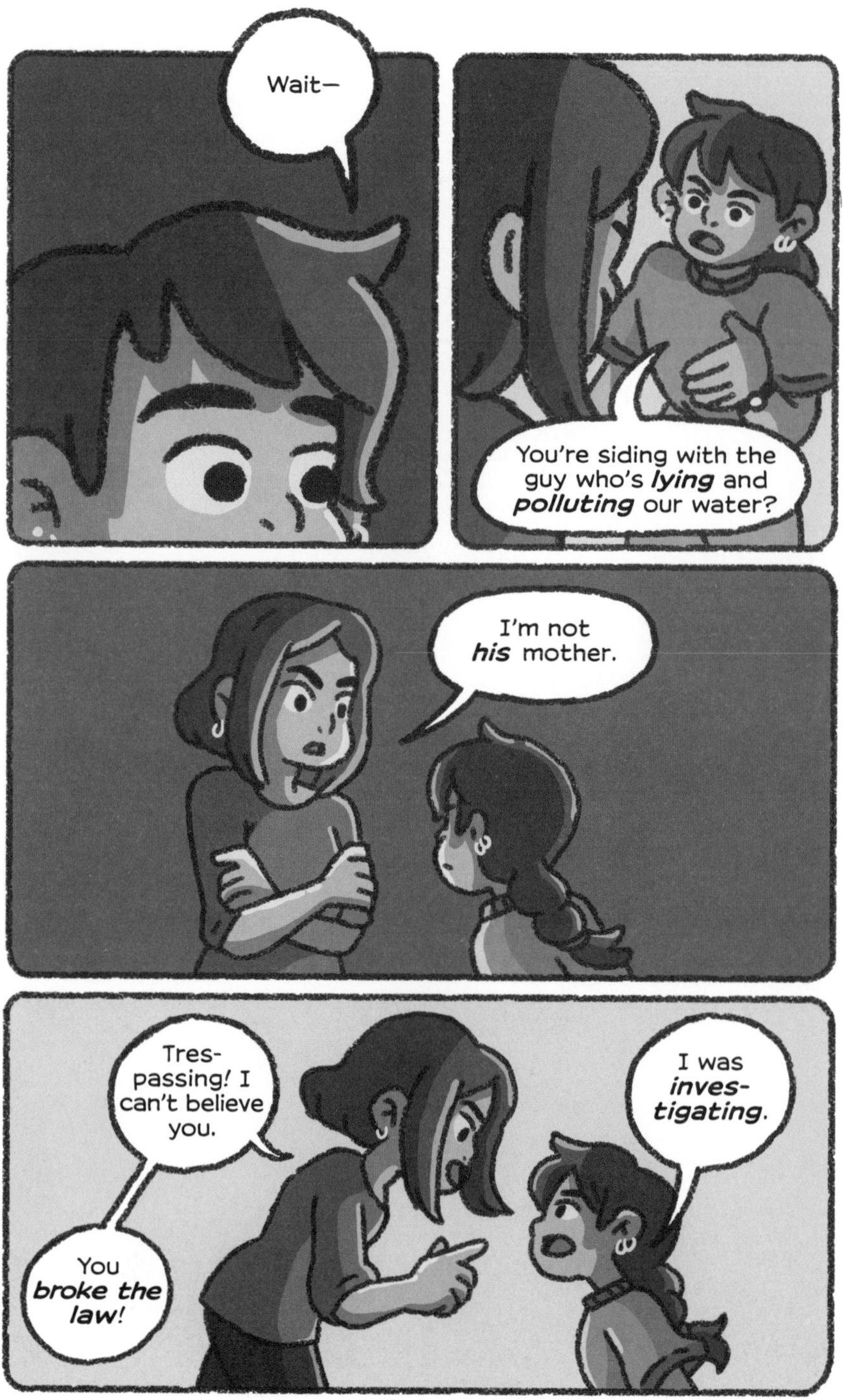
Wait—
You're siding with the guy who's ***lying*** and ***polluting*** our water?
I'm not ***his*** mother.
Tres-passing! I can't believe you.
You ***broke the law***!
I was ***inves-tigating***.

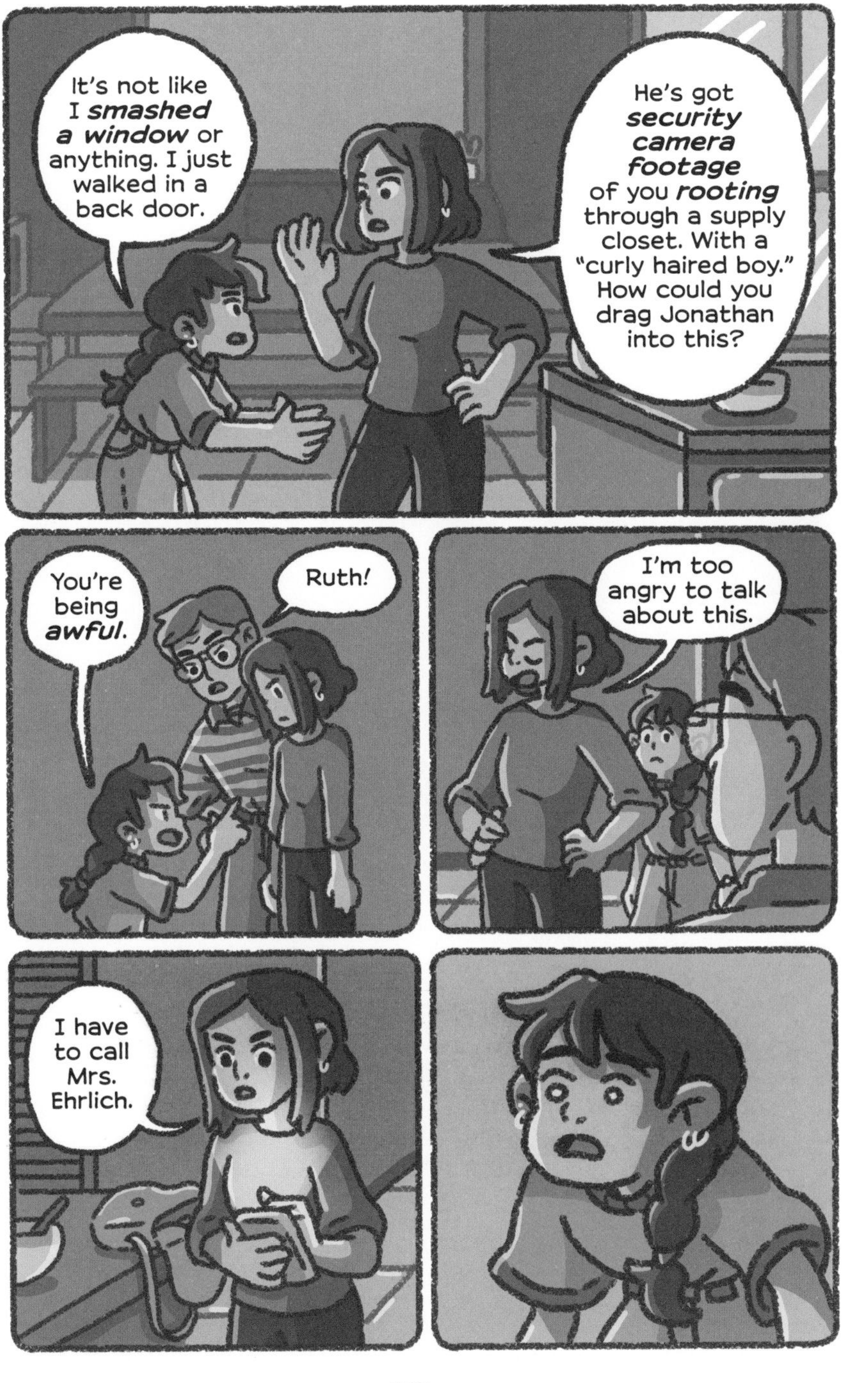
It's not like I ***smashed a window*** or anything. I just walked in a back door.
He's got ***security camera footage*** of you ***rooting*** through a supply closet. With a "curly haired boy." How could you drag Jonathan into this?
You're being ***awful***.
Ruth!
I'm too angry to talk about this.
I have to call Mrs. Ehrlich.

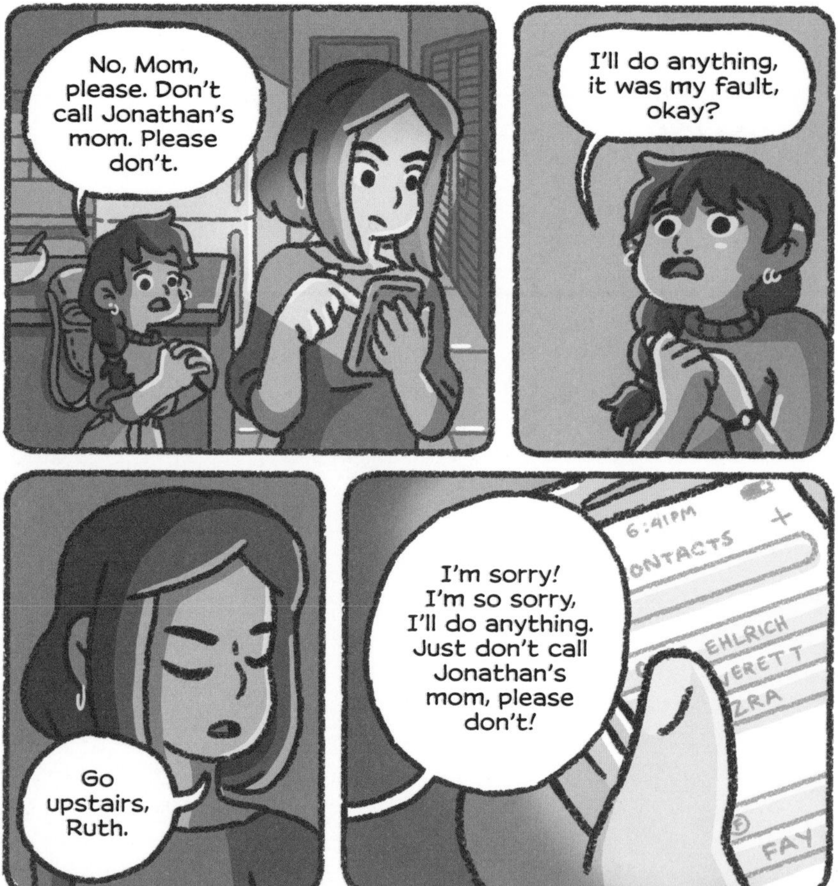
No, Mom, please. Don't call Jonathan's mom. Please don't.
I'll do anything, it was my fault, okay?
Go upstairs, Ruth.
6:41PM
ONTACTS
EHLRICH
VERETT
ZRA
FAY
I'm sorry! I'm so sorry, I'll do anything. Just don't call Jonathan's mom, please don't!
I said go upstairs!!

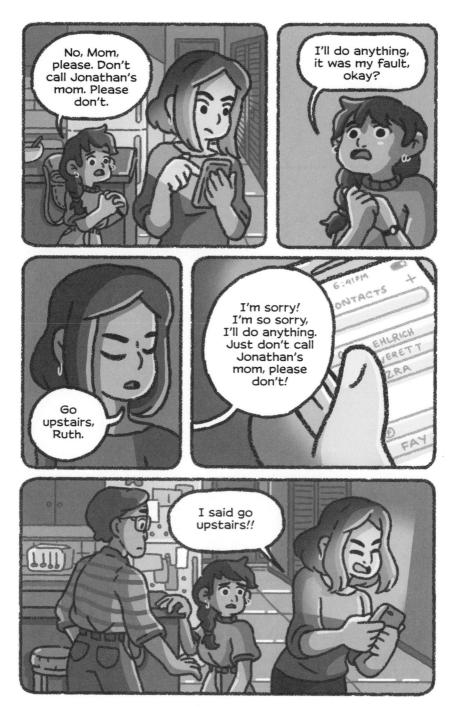

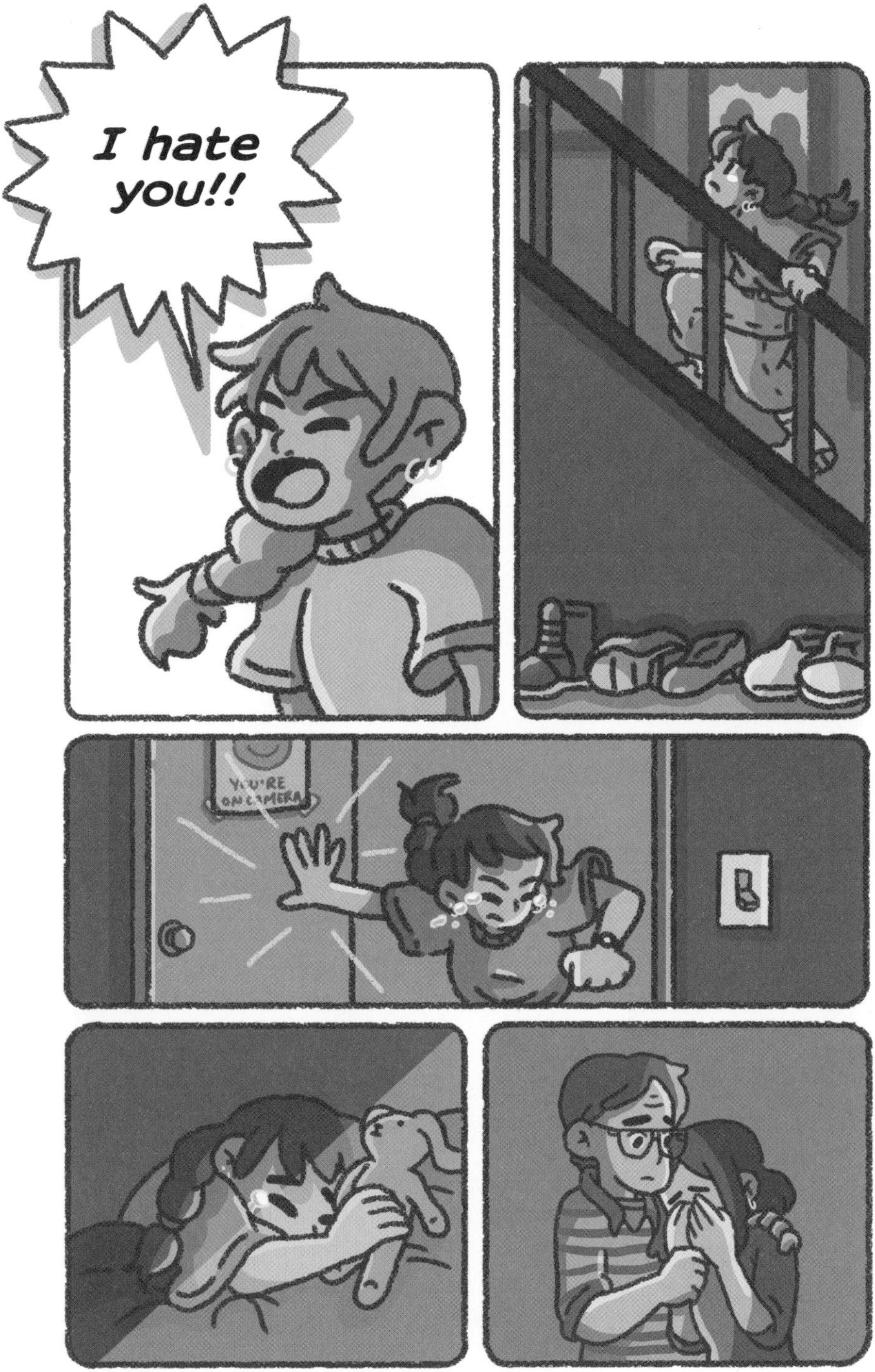
I hate you!!
YOU'RE ON CAMERA

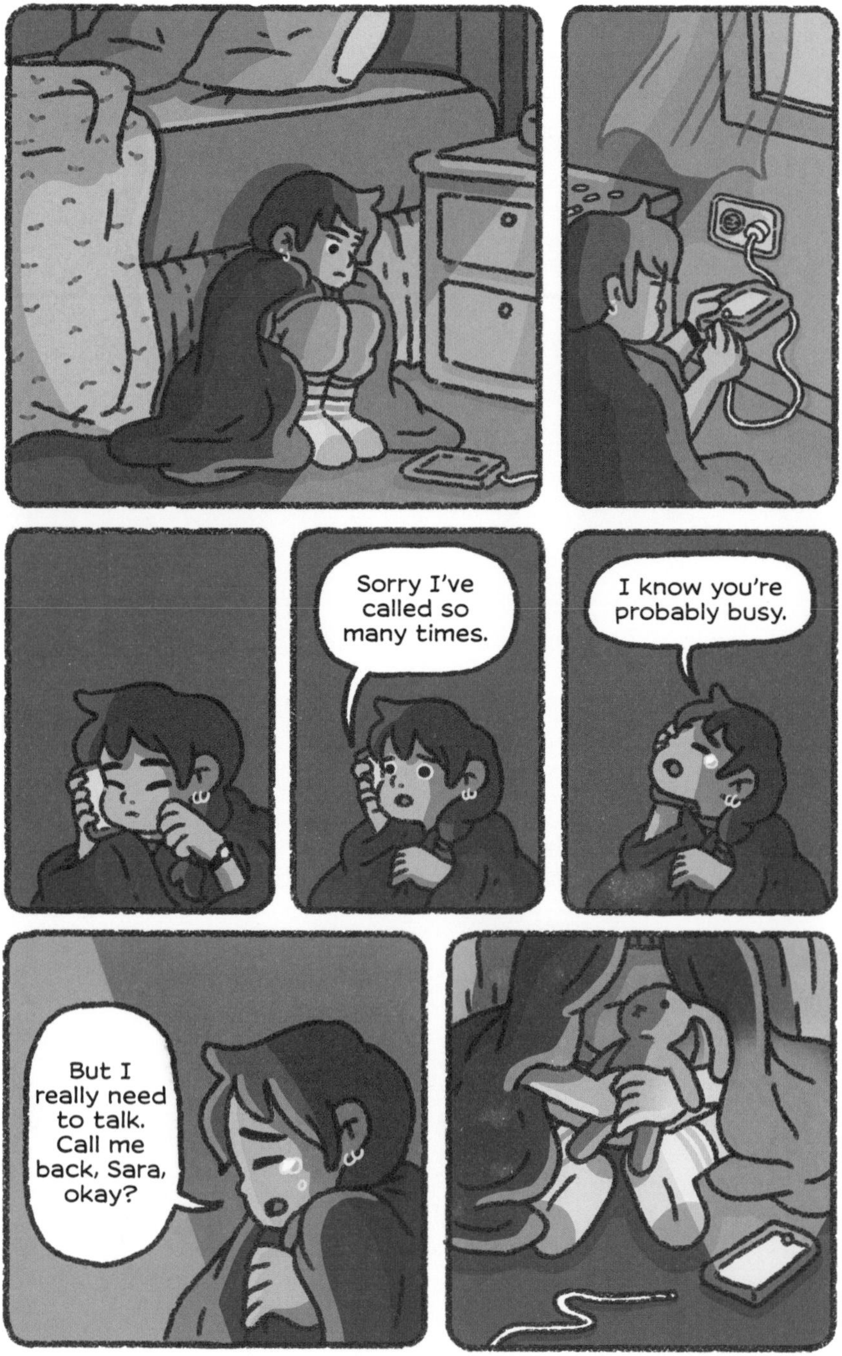
Sorry I've called so many times.
I know you're probably busy.
But I really need to talk. Call me back, Sara, okay?

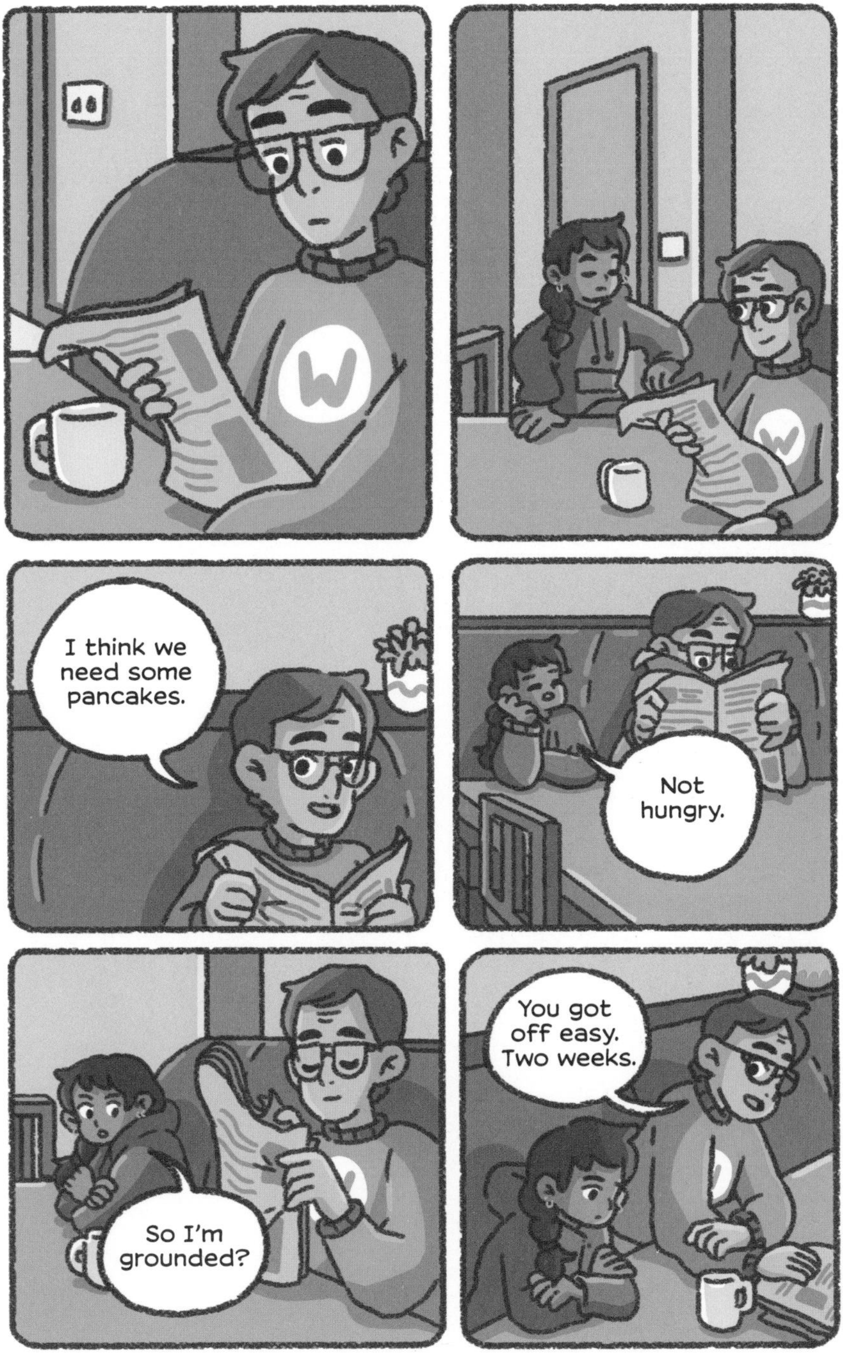
I think we need some pancakes.
Not hungry.
So I'm grounded?
You got off easy. Two weeks.

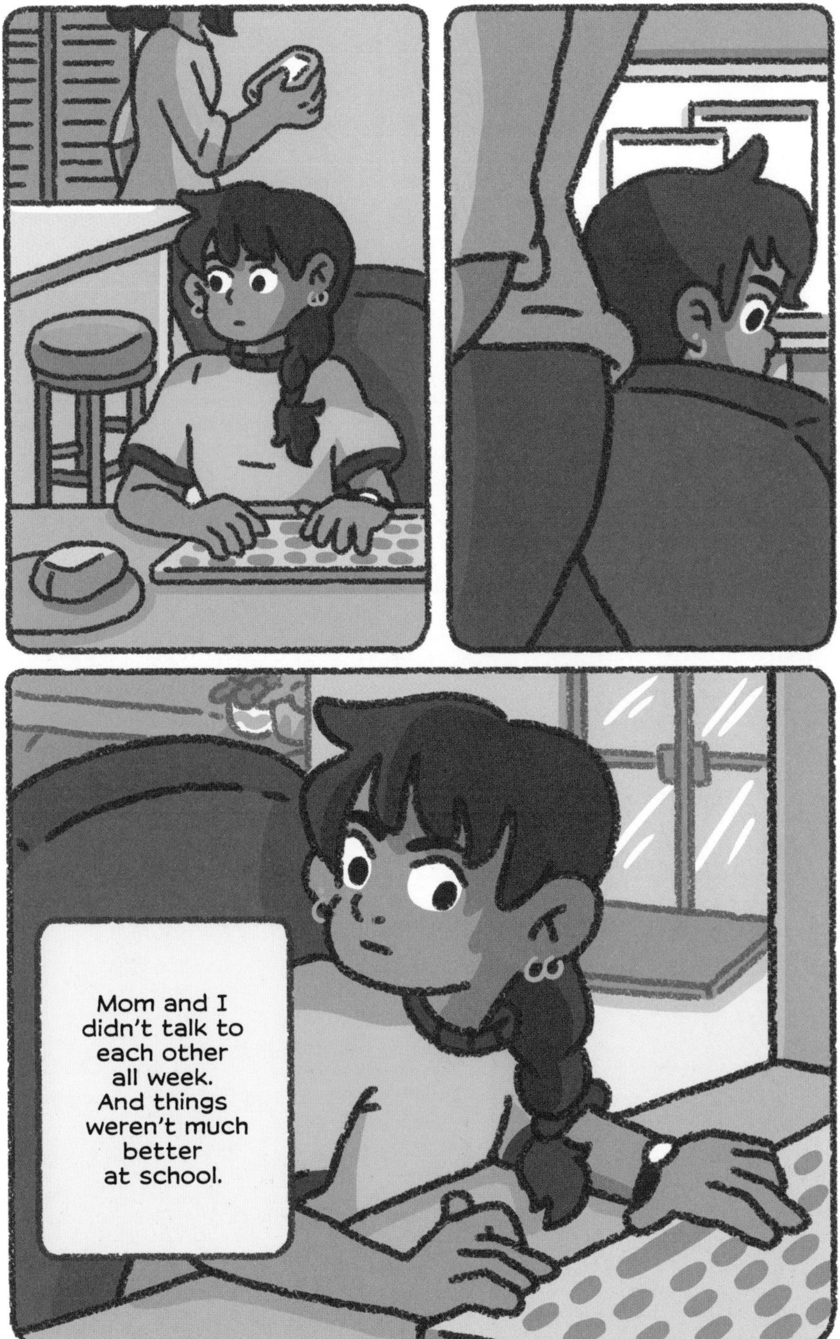
Mom and I didn't talk to each other all week. And things weren't much better at school.

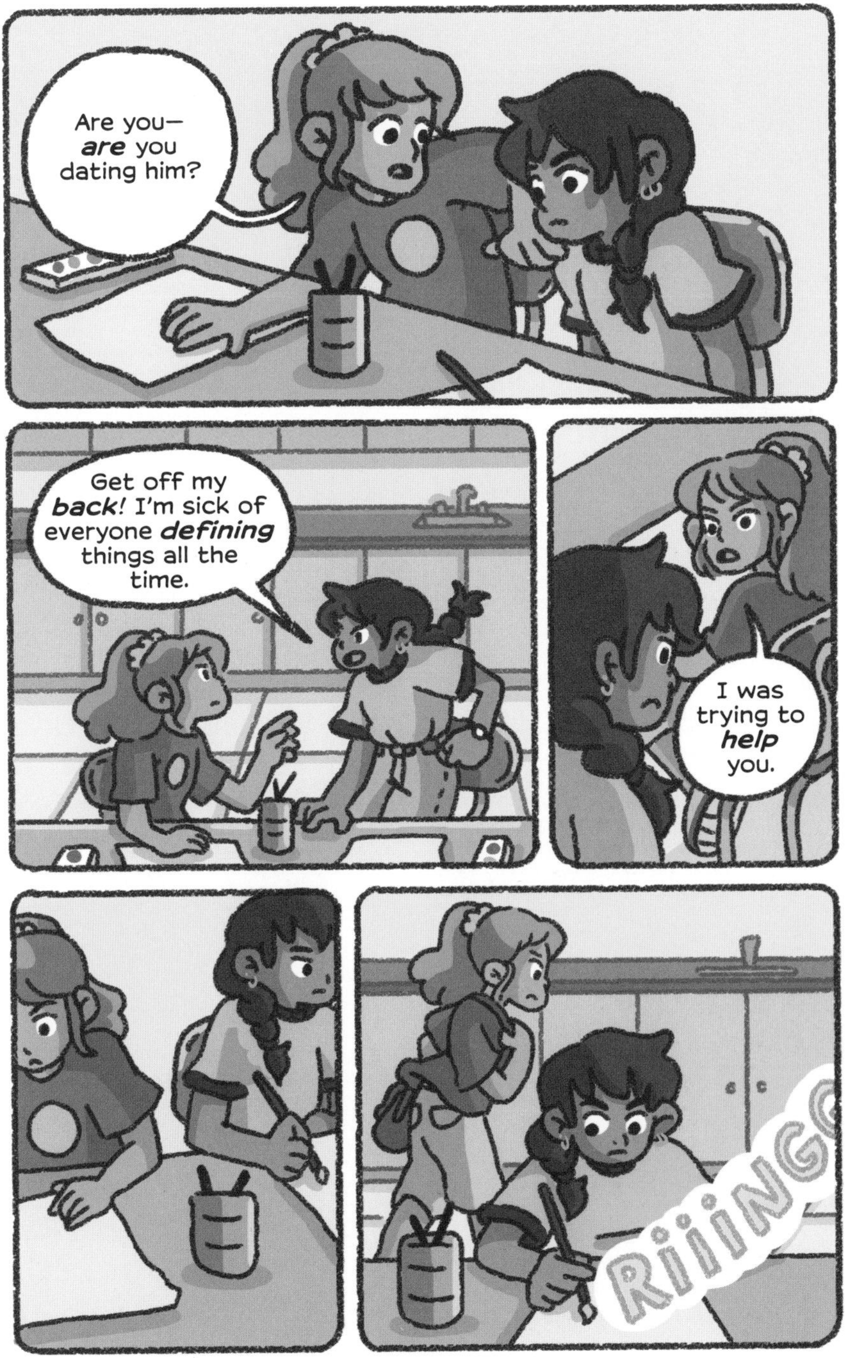
Are you— ***are*** you dating him?
Get off my ***back***! I'm sick of everyone ***defining*** things all the time.
I was trying to ***help*** you.
RiiiNG

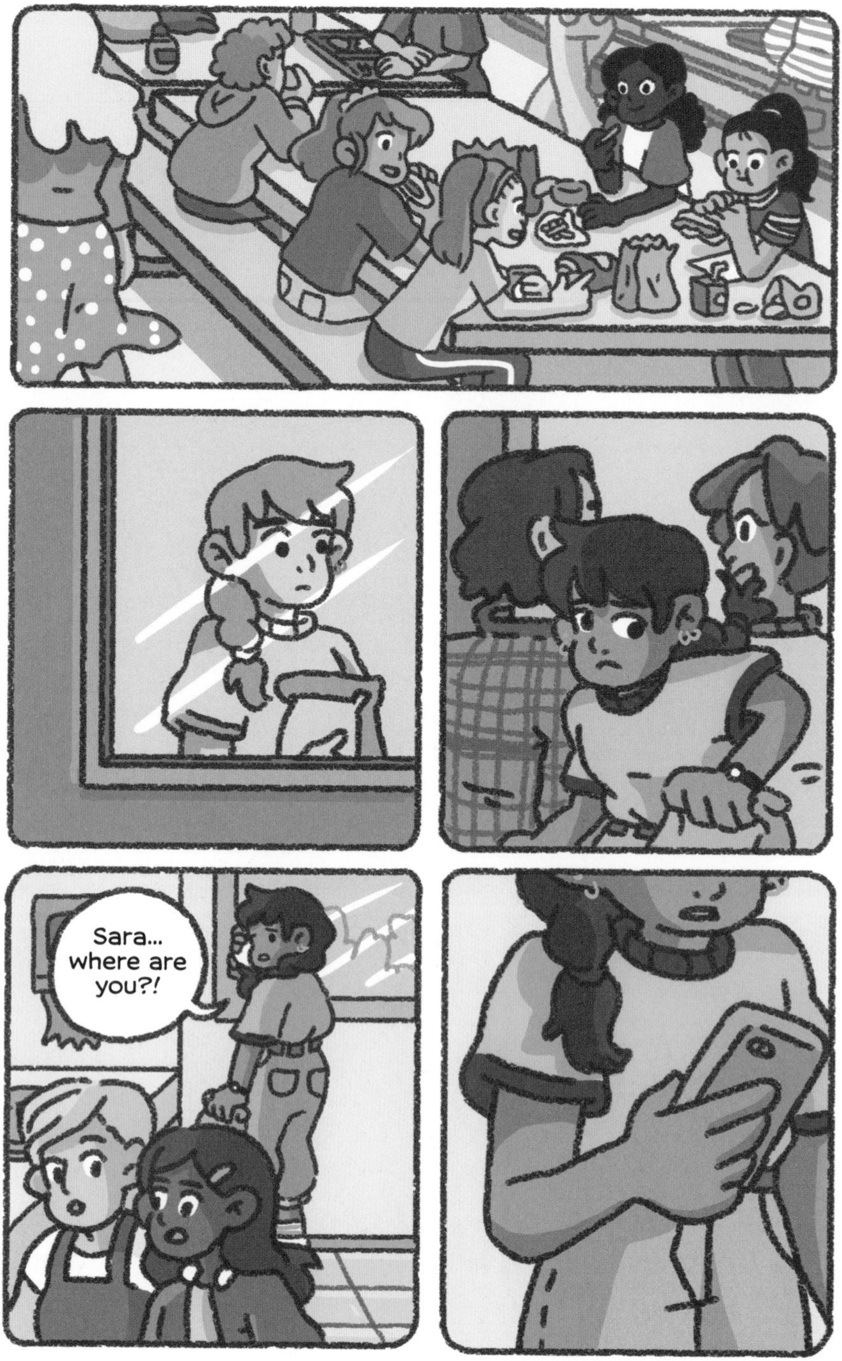
Sara... where are you?!

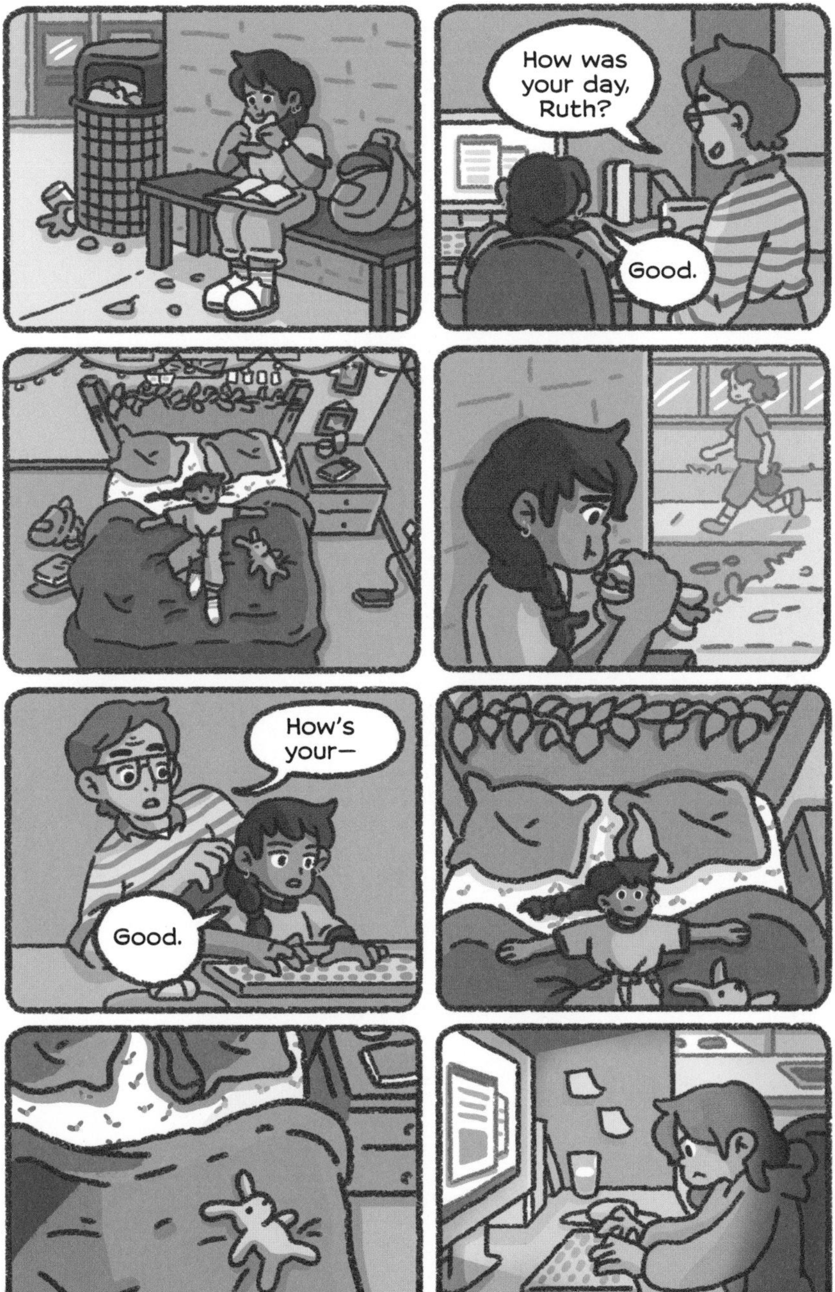
How was your day, Ruth?
Good.
How's your—
Good.

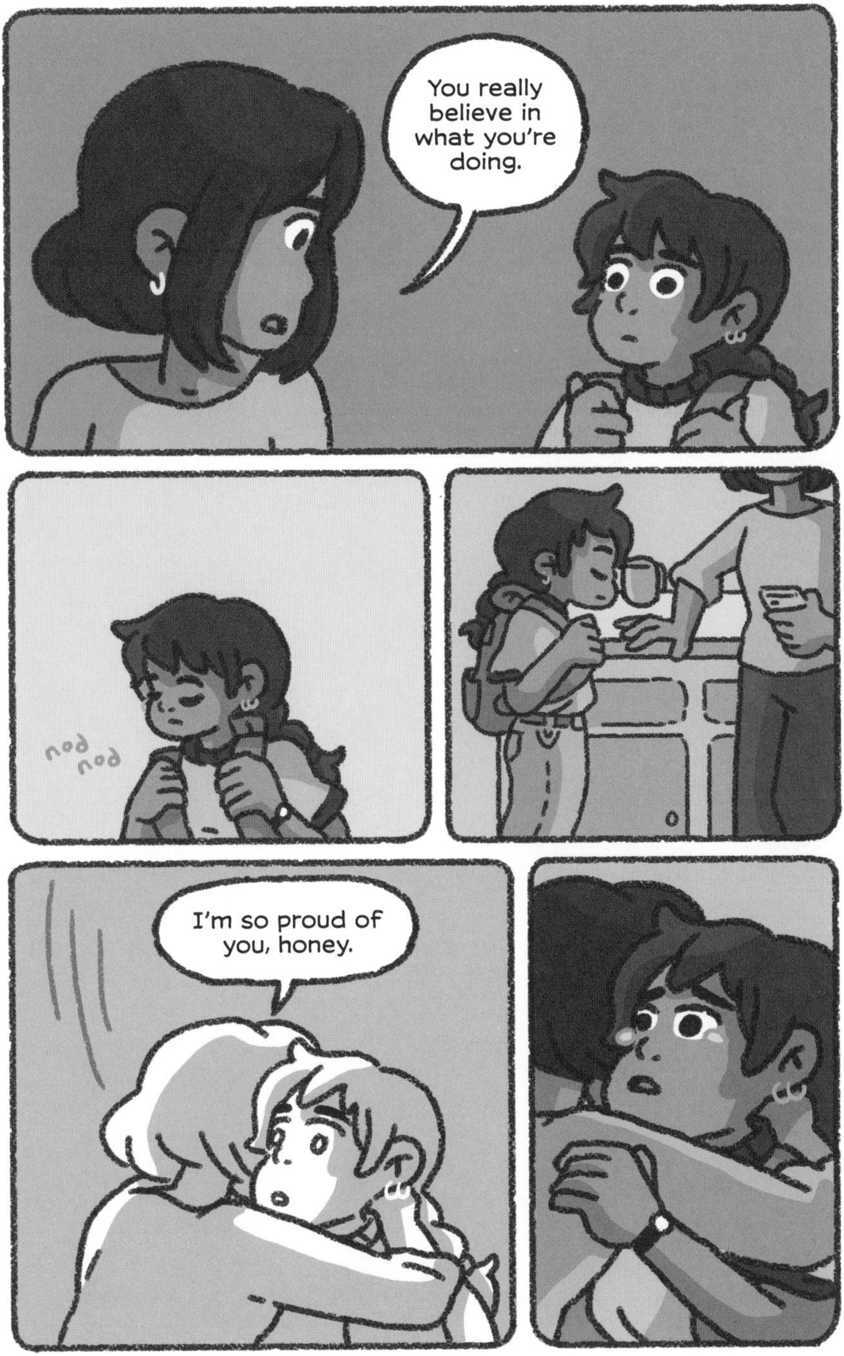
You really believe in what you're doing.
nod nod
I'm so proud of you, honey.

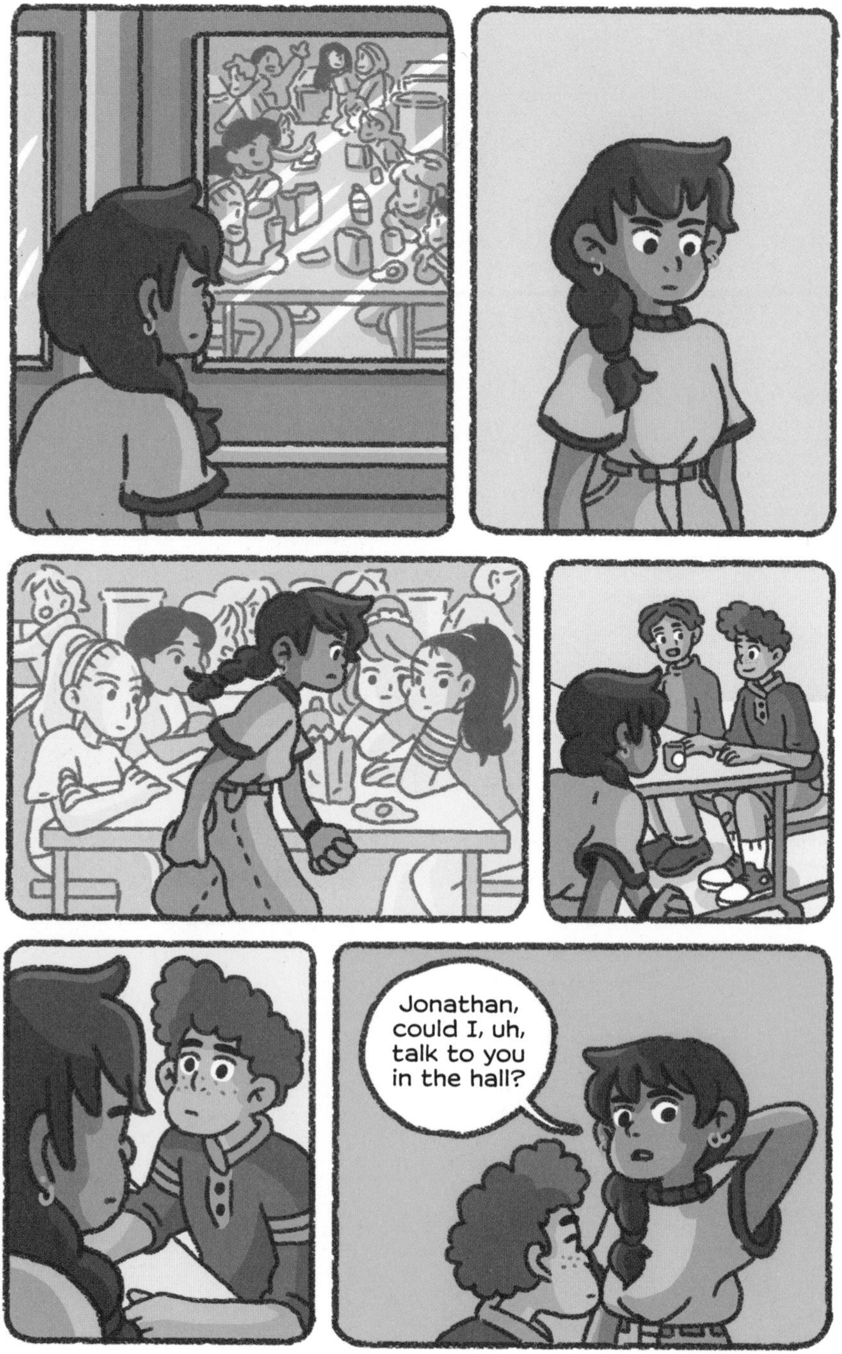
Jonathan, could I, uh, talk to you in the hall?

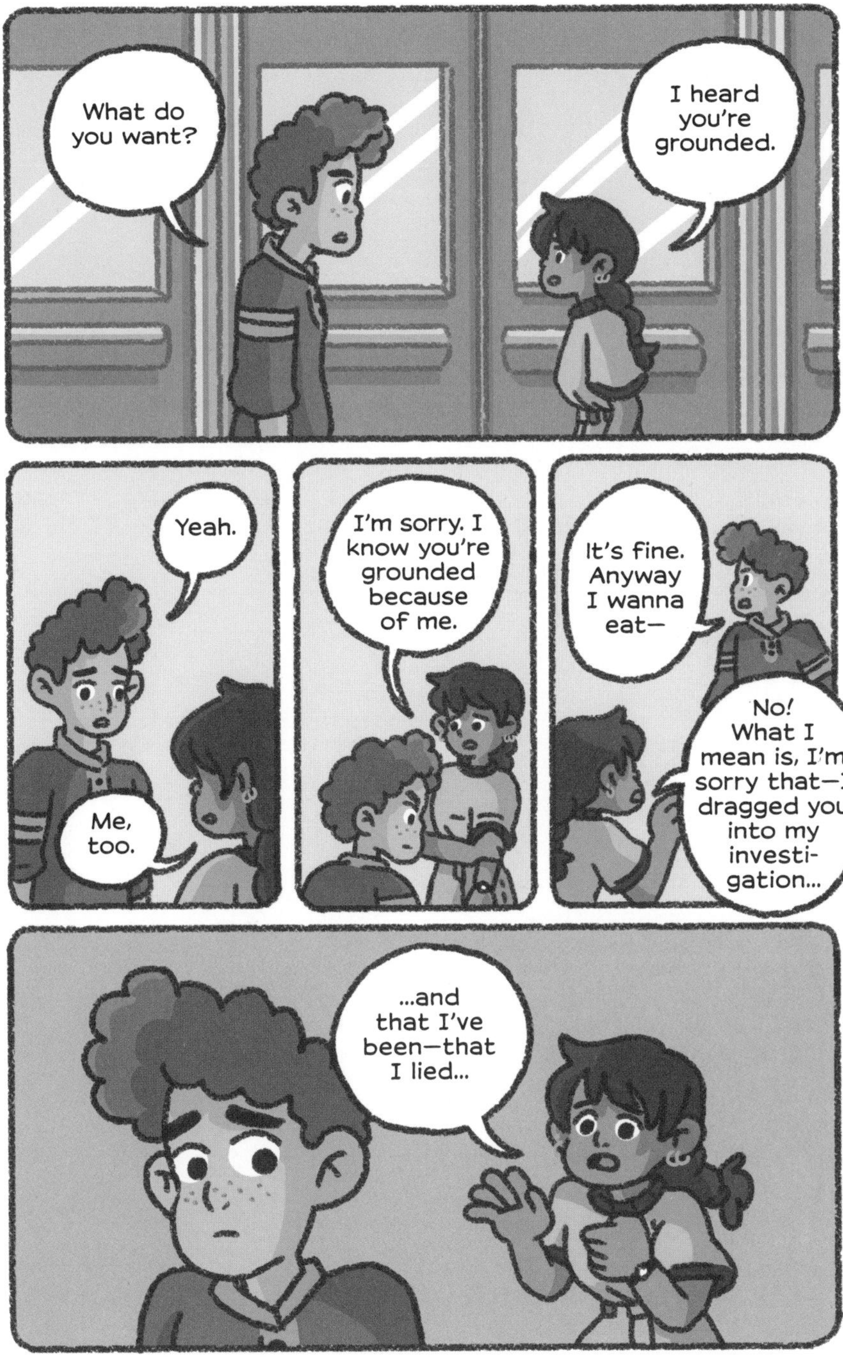
What do you want?
I heard you're grounded.
Yeah.
Me, too.
I'm sorry. I know you're grounded because of me.
It's fine. Anyway I wanna eat—
No! What I mean is, I'm sorry that—I dragged you into my investi-gation...
...and that I've been—that I lied...

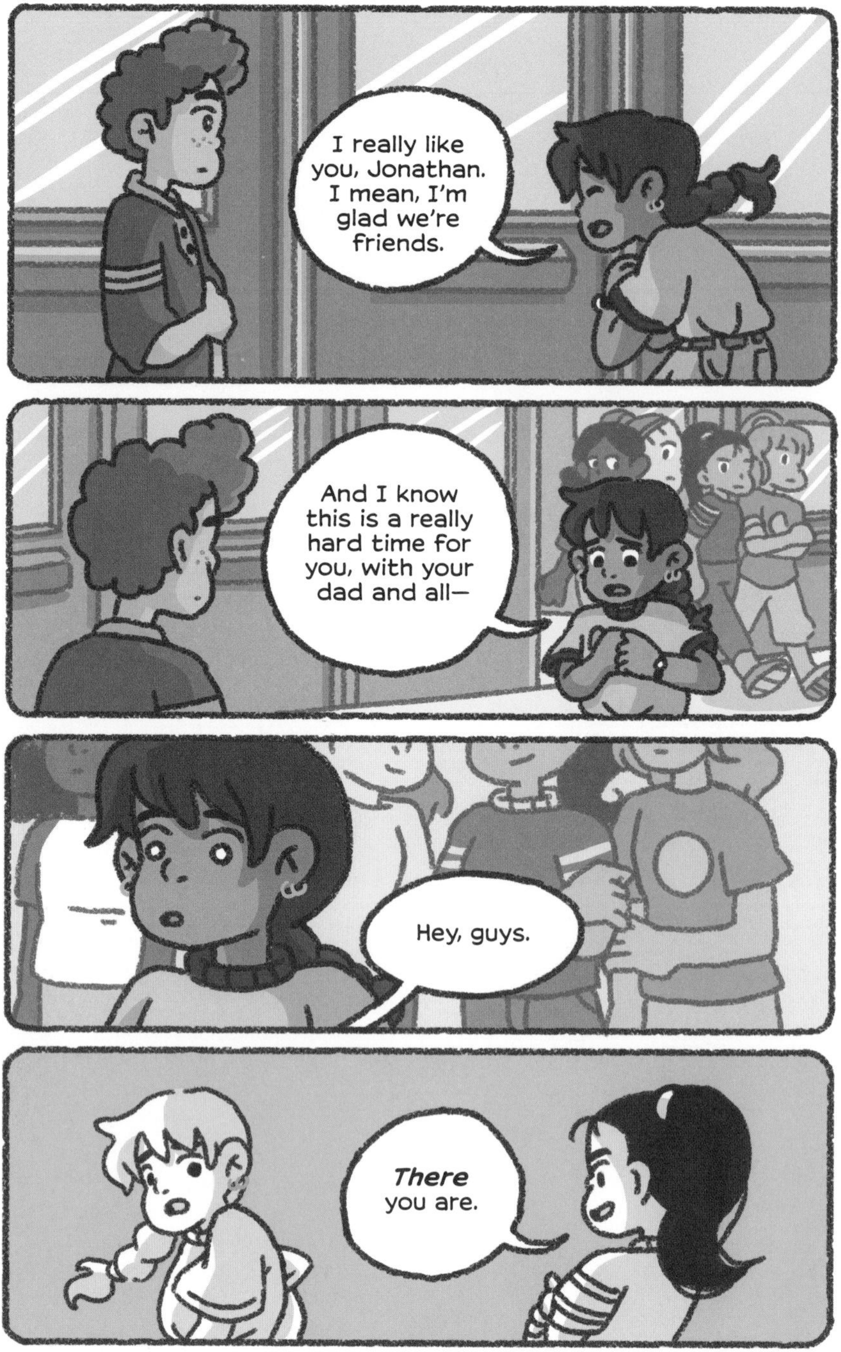
I really like you, Jonathan. I mean, I'm glad we're friends.
And I know this is a really hard time for you, with your dad and all—
Hey, guys.
There you are.

171

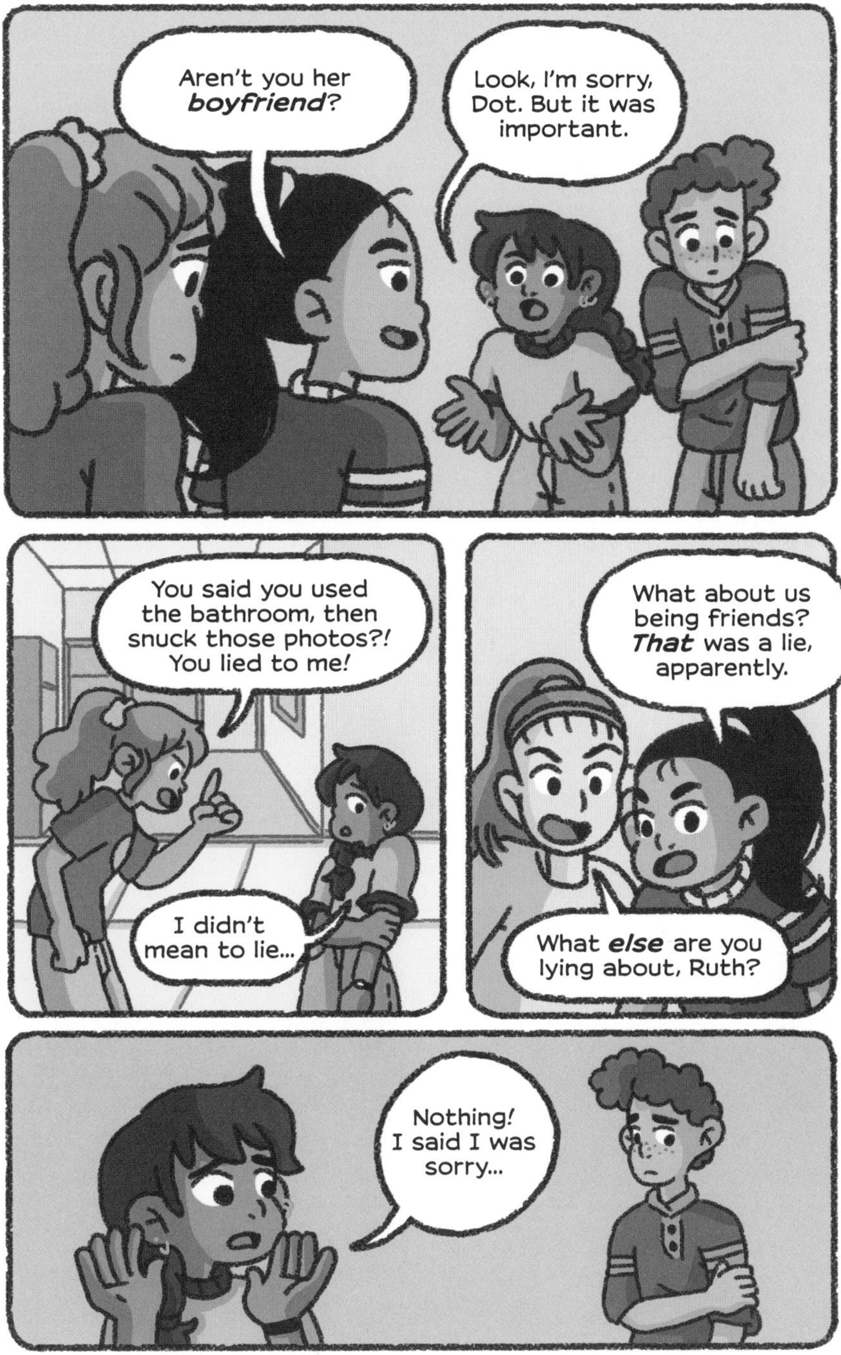

Aren't you her *boyfriend*?
Look, I'm sorry, Dot. But it was important.
You said you used the bathroom, then snuck those photos?! You lied to me!
I didn't mean to lie...
What about us being friends? *That* was a lie, apparently.
What *else* are you lying about, Ruth?
Nothing! I said I was sorry...

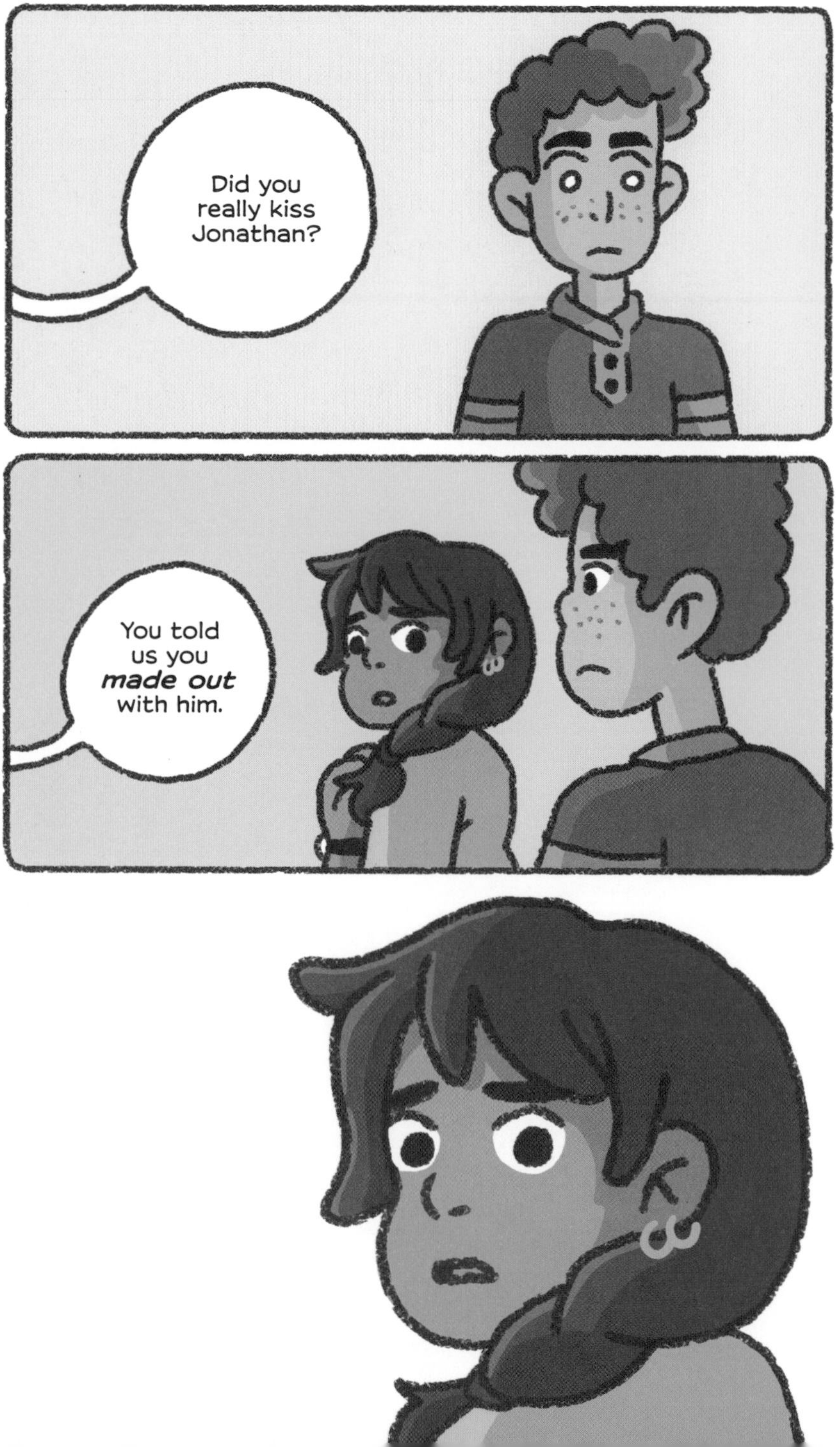
Did you really kiss Jonathan?
You told us you ***made out*** with him.

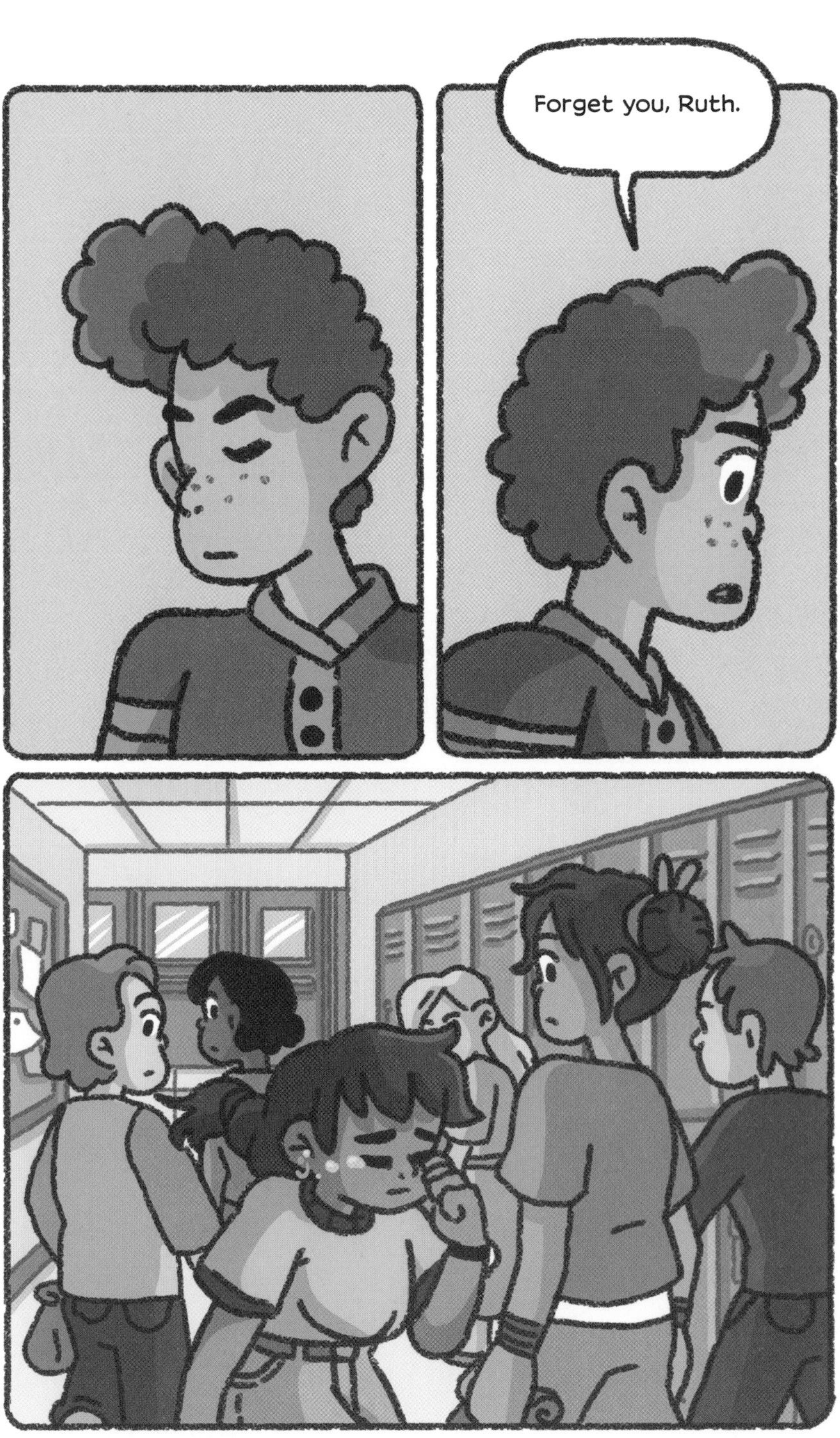
Forget you, Ruth.

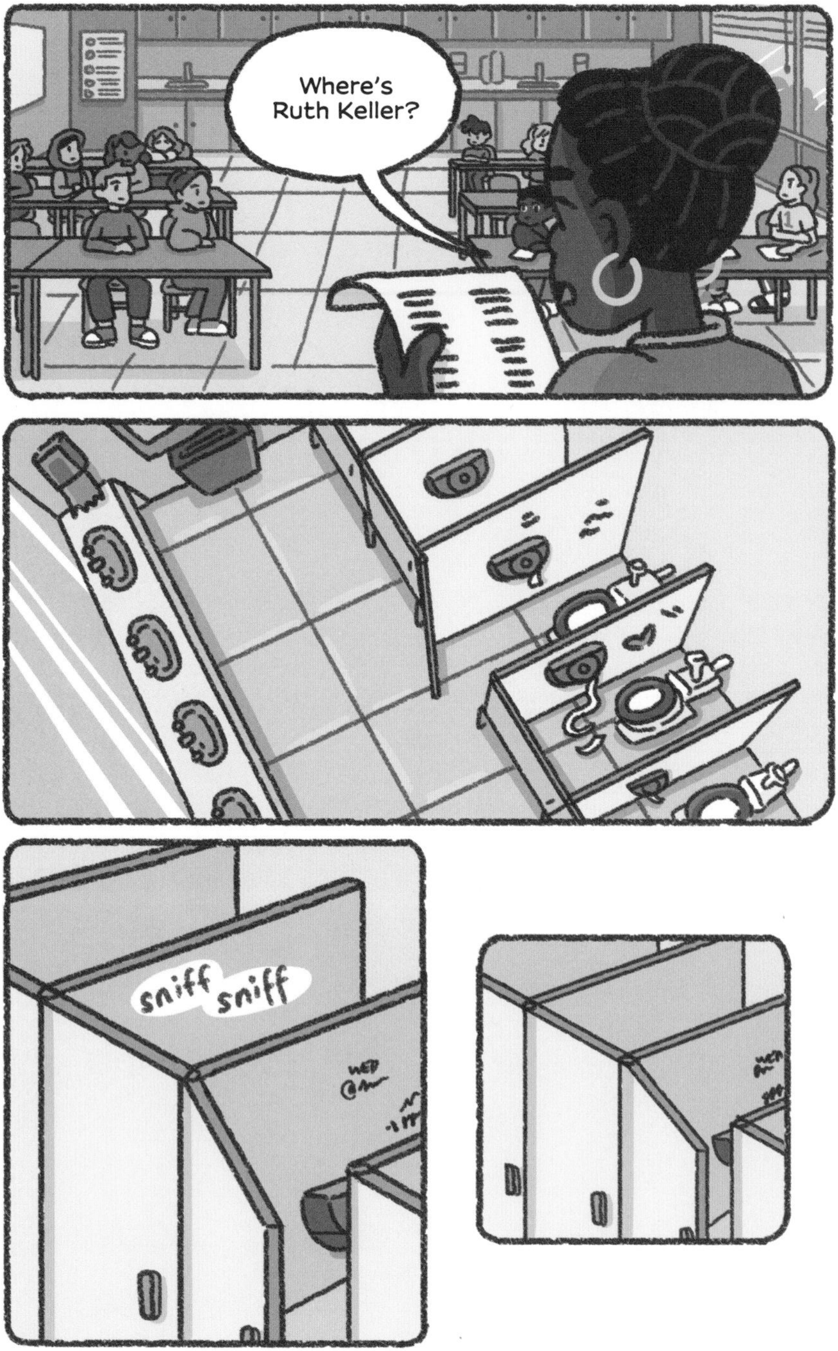
Where's Ruth Keller?
sniff sniff

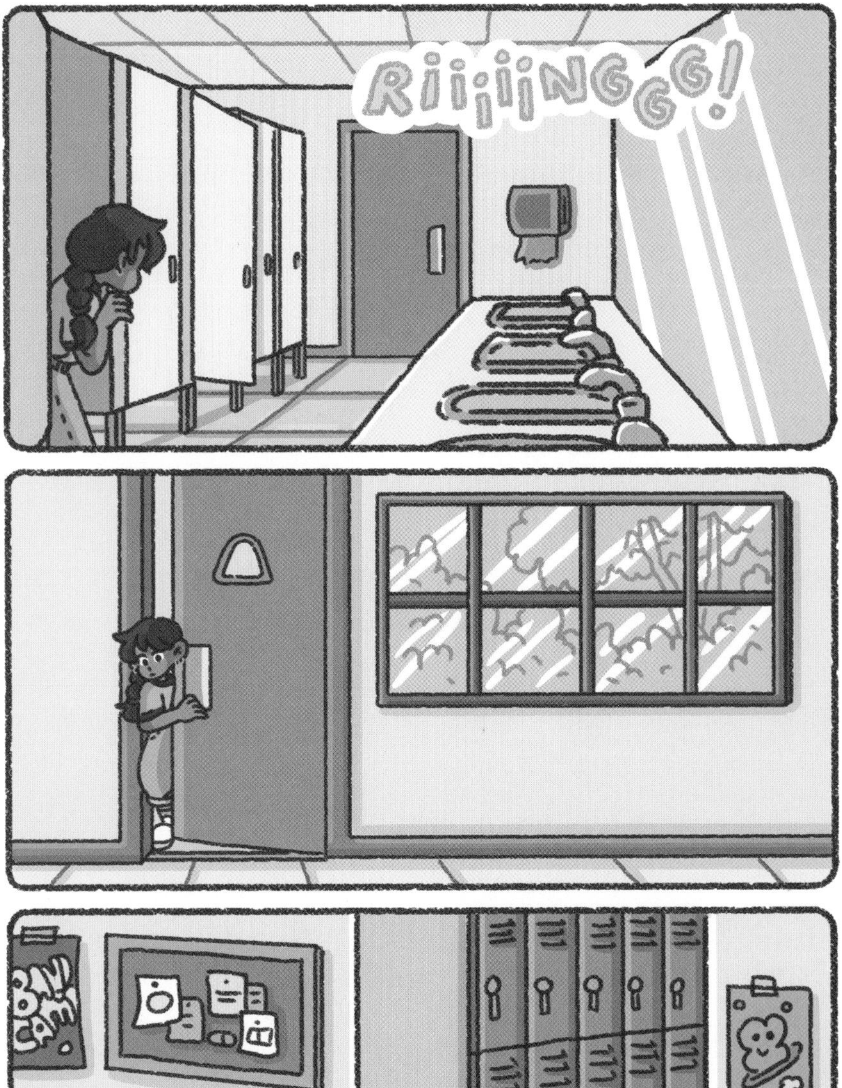
RiiiiiNGGG!

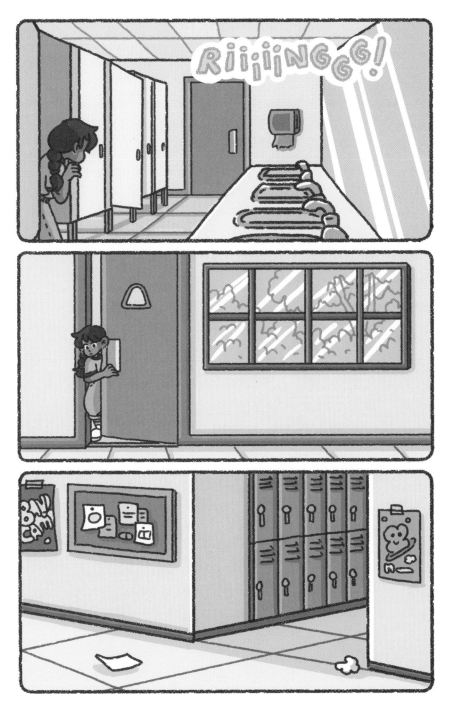

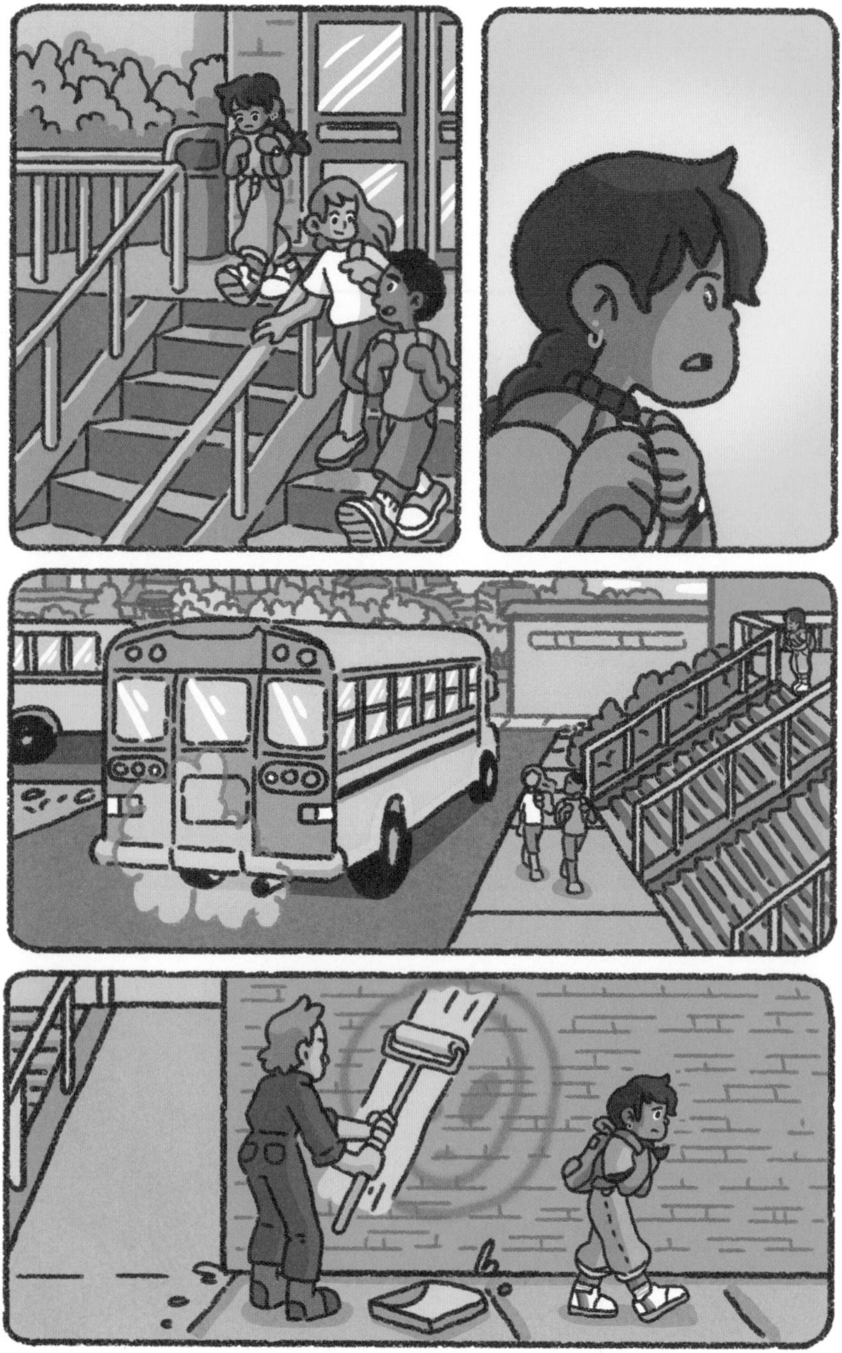

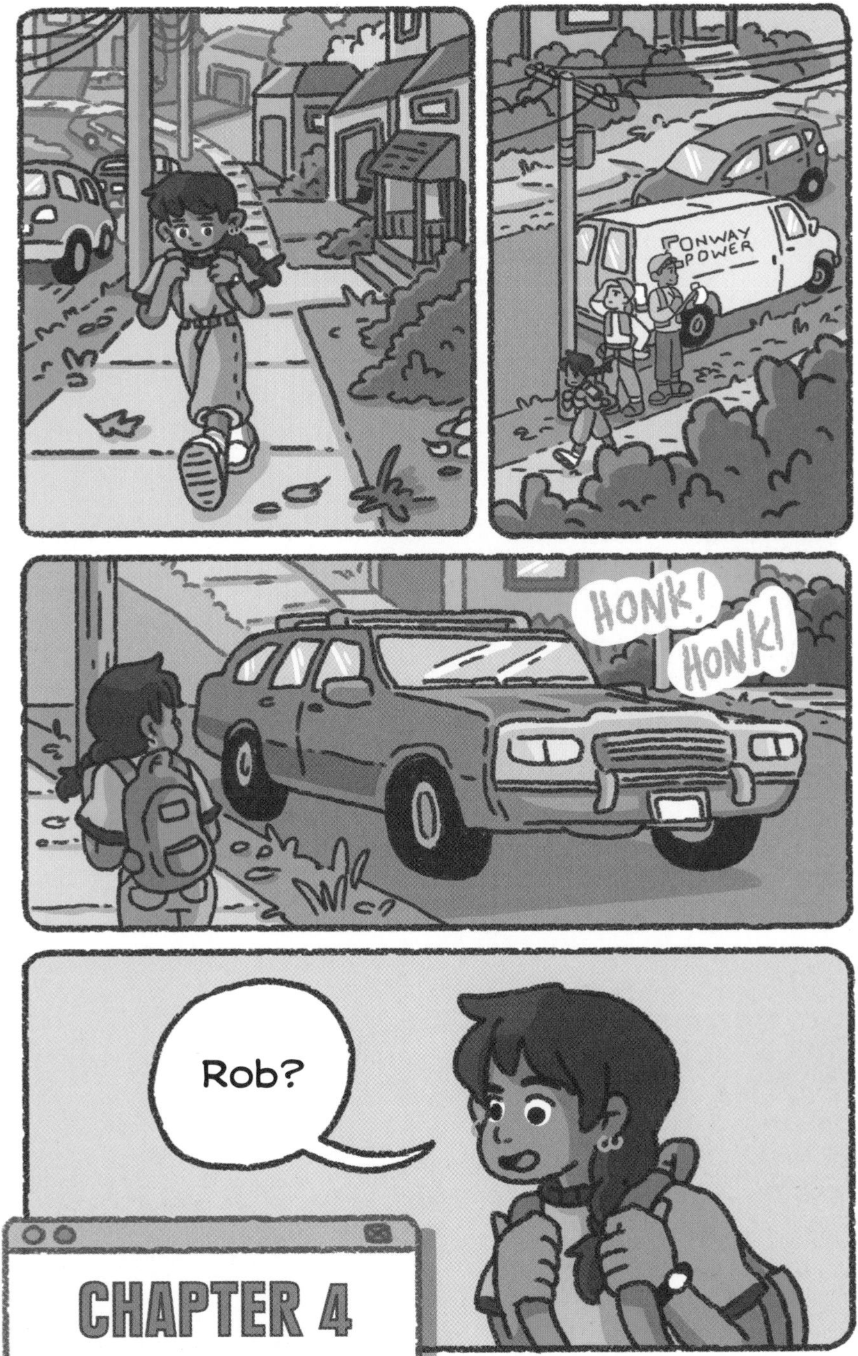
CONWAY
POWER
HONK!
HONK!
Rob?

CHAPTER 4

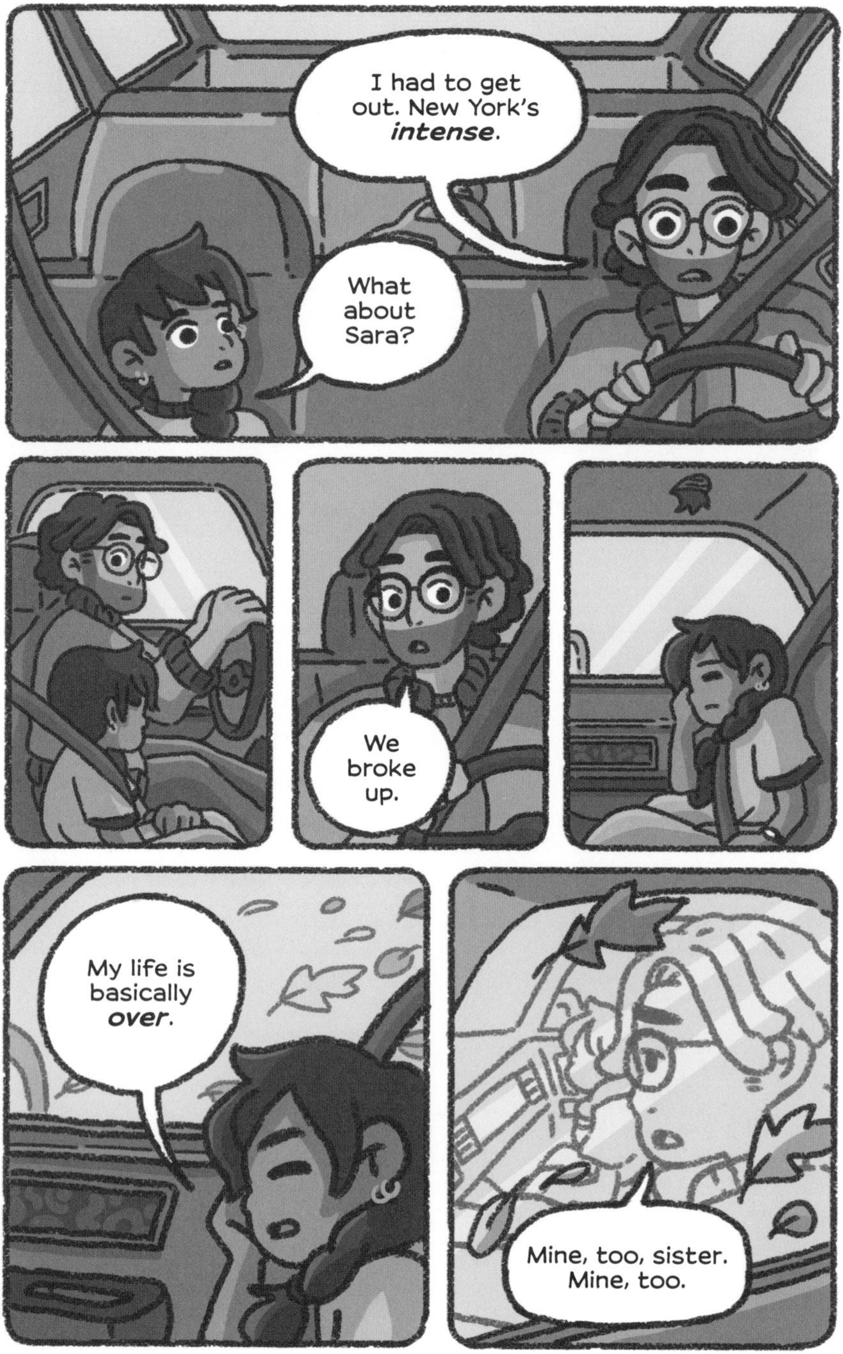
I had to get out. New York's *intense*.
What about Sara?
We broke up.
My life is basically *over*.
Mine, too, sister. Mine, too.

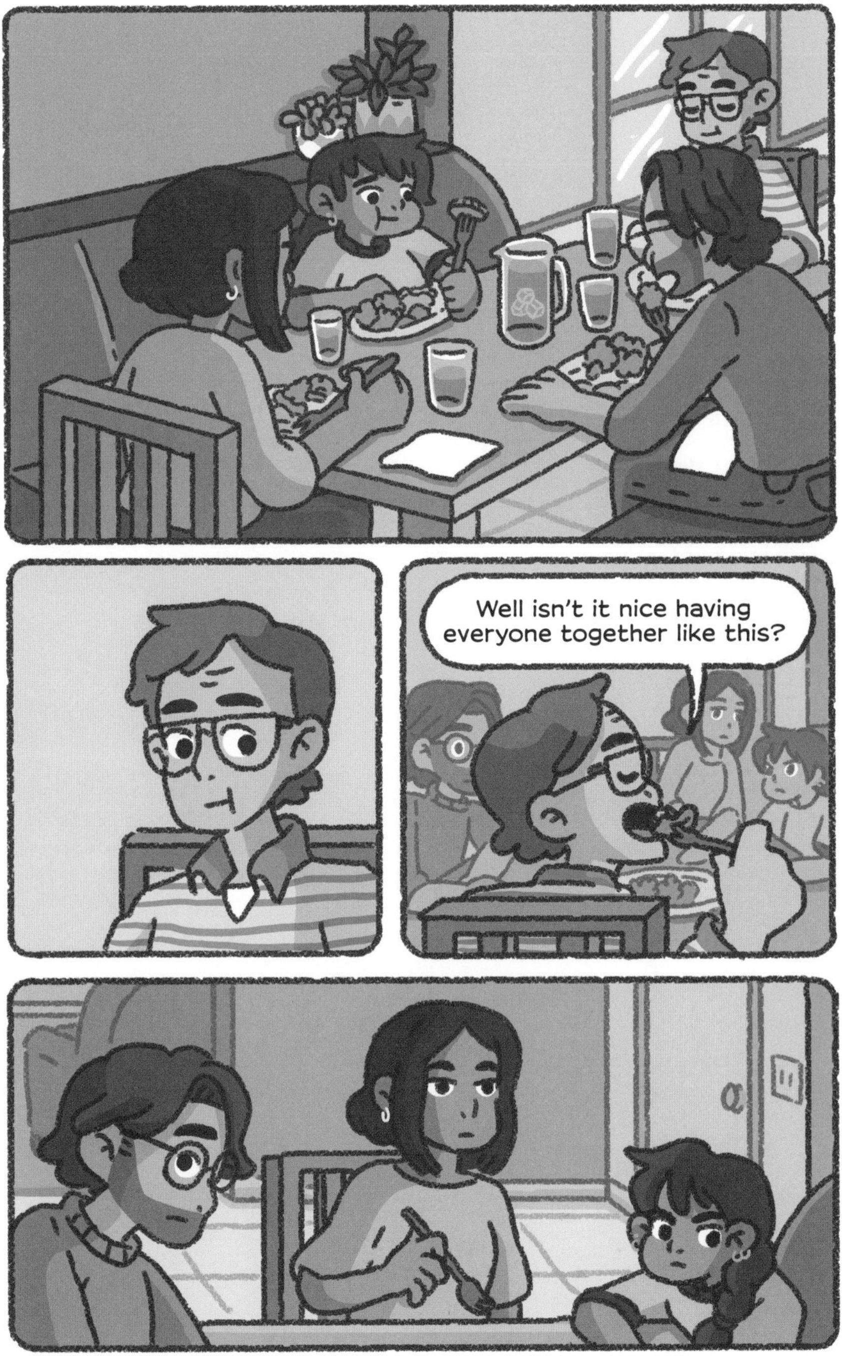
Well isn't it nice having everyone together like this?

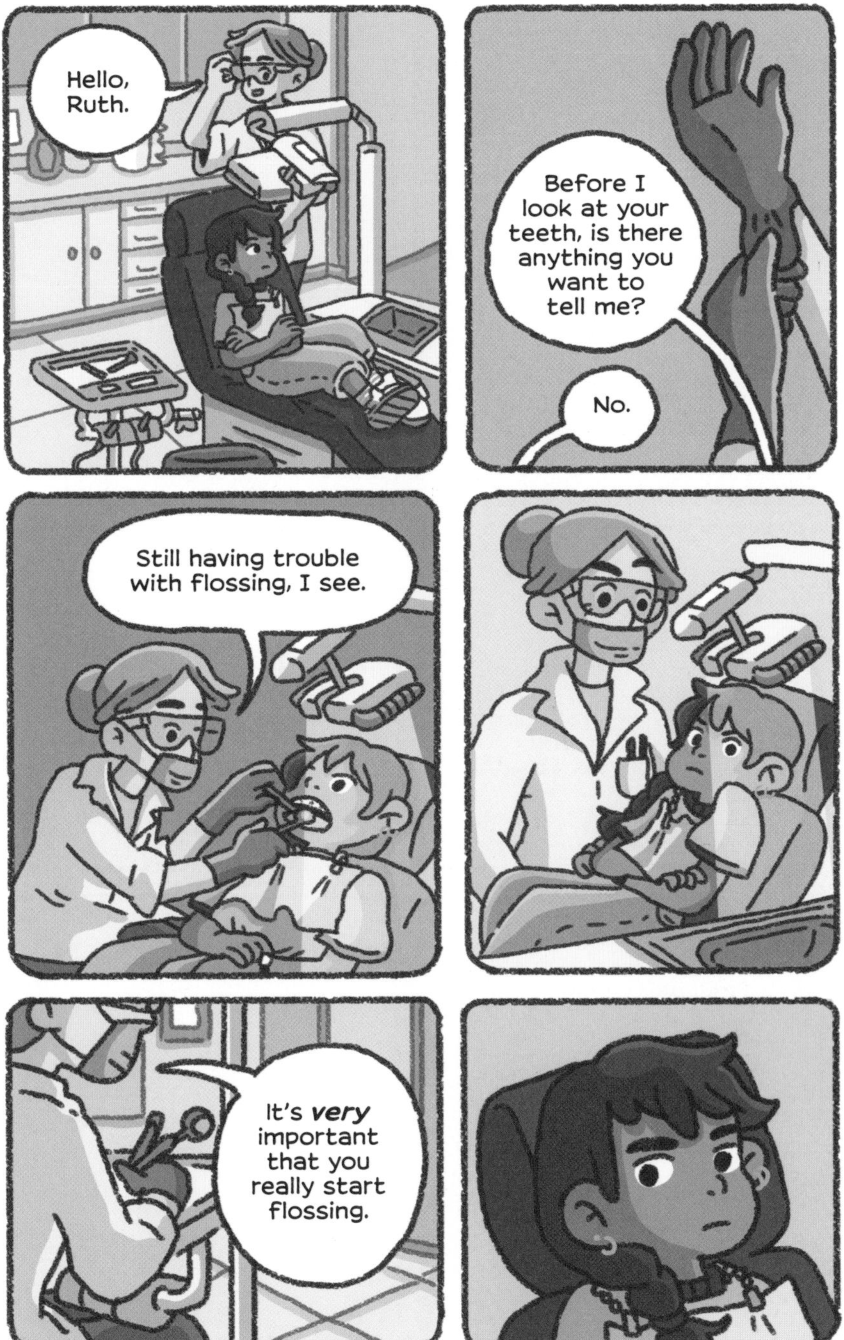
Hello, Ruth.
Before I look at your teeth, is there anything you want to tell me?
No.
Still having trouble with flossing, I see.
It's *very* important that you really start flossing.

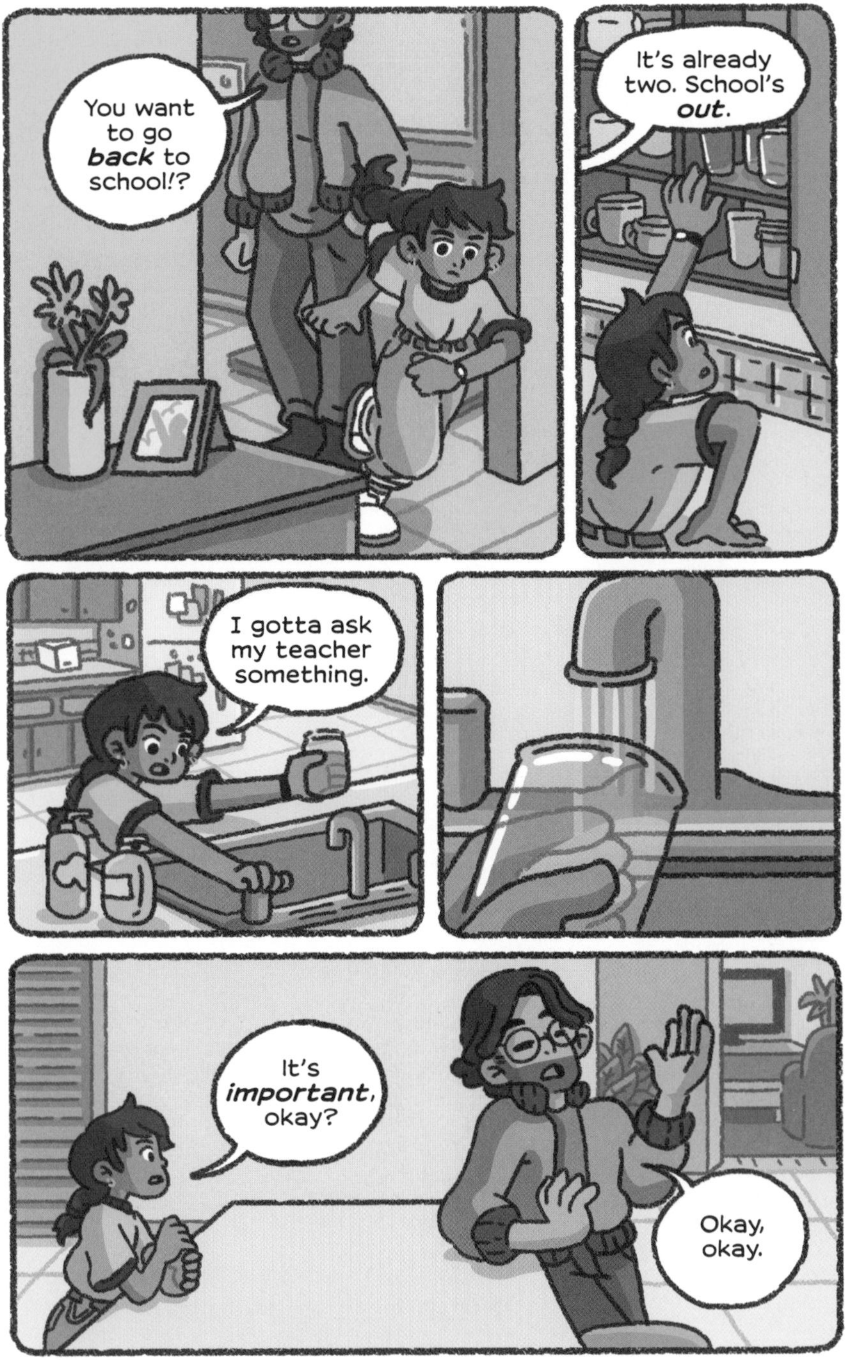
You want to go *back* to school!?
It's already two. School's *out*.
I gotta ask my teacher something.
It's *important*, okay?
Okay, okay.

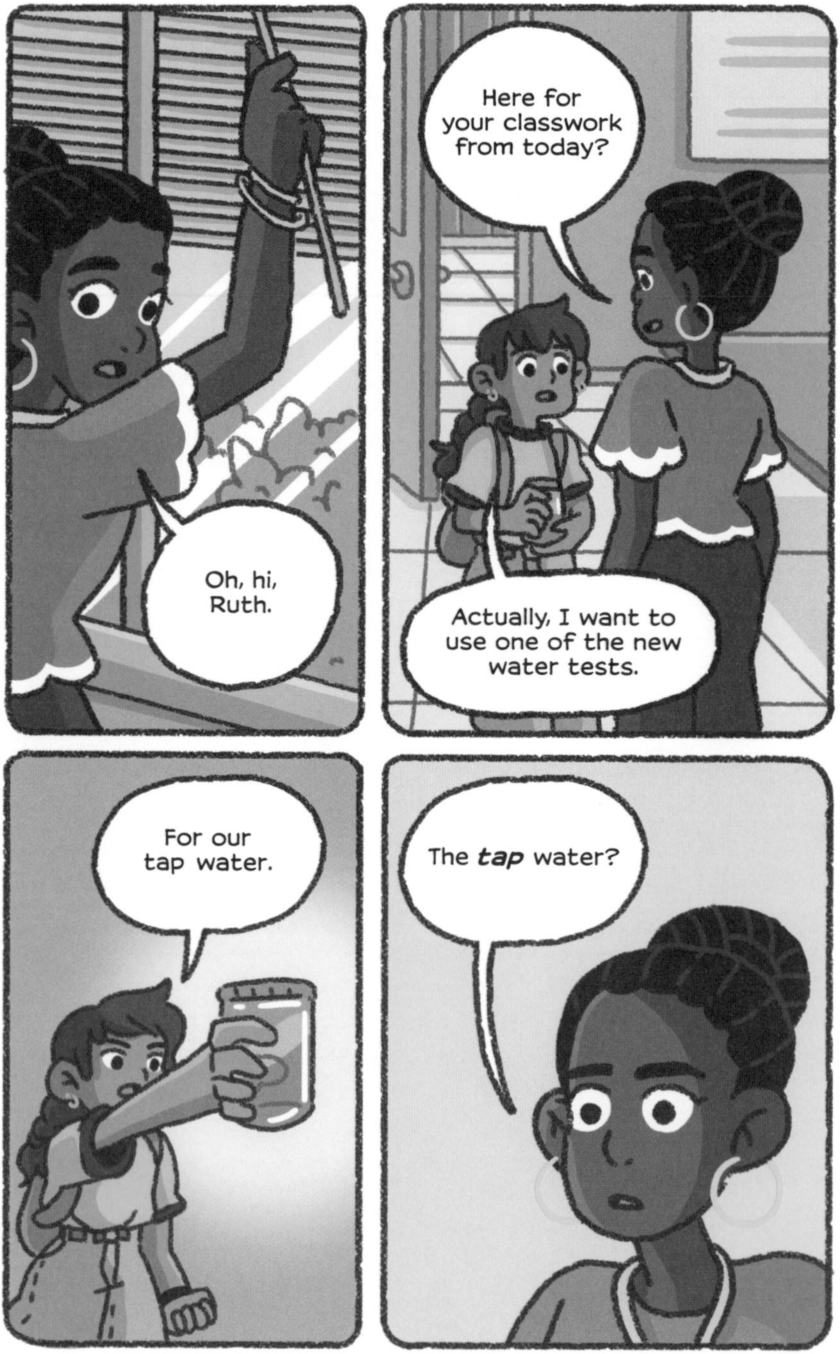

Oh, hi, Ruth.
Here for your classwork from today?
Actually, I want to use one of the new water tests.
For our tap water.
The *tap* water?

189

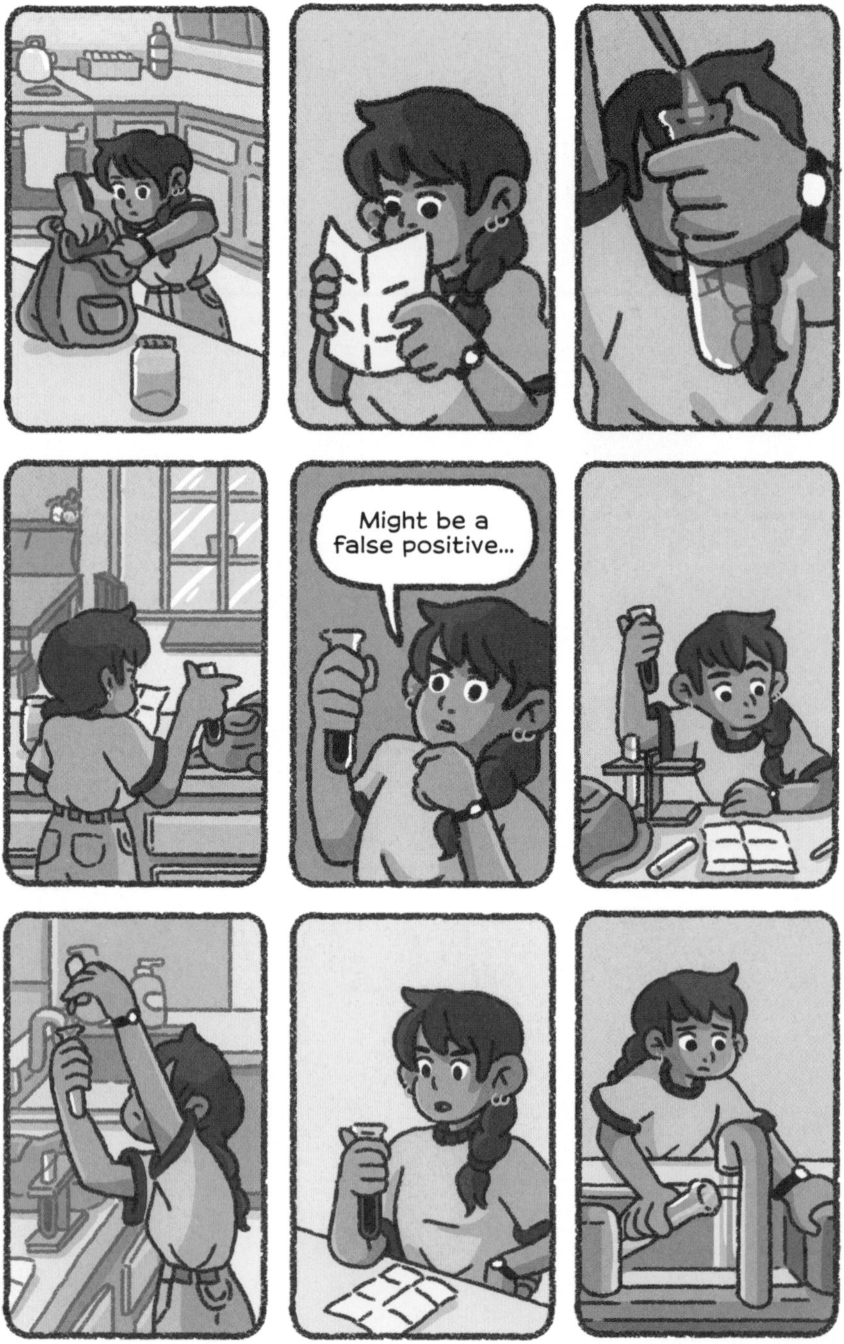
Might be a false positive...

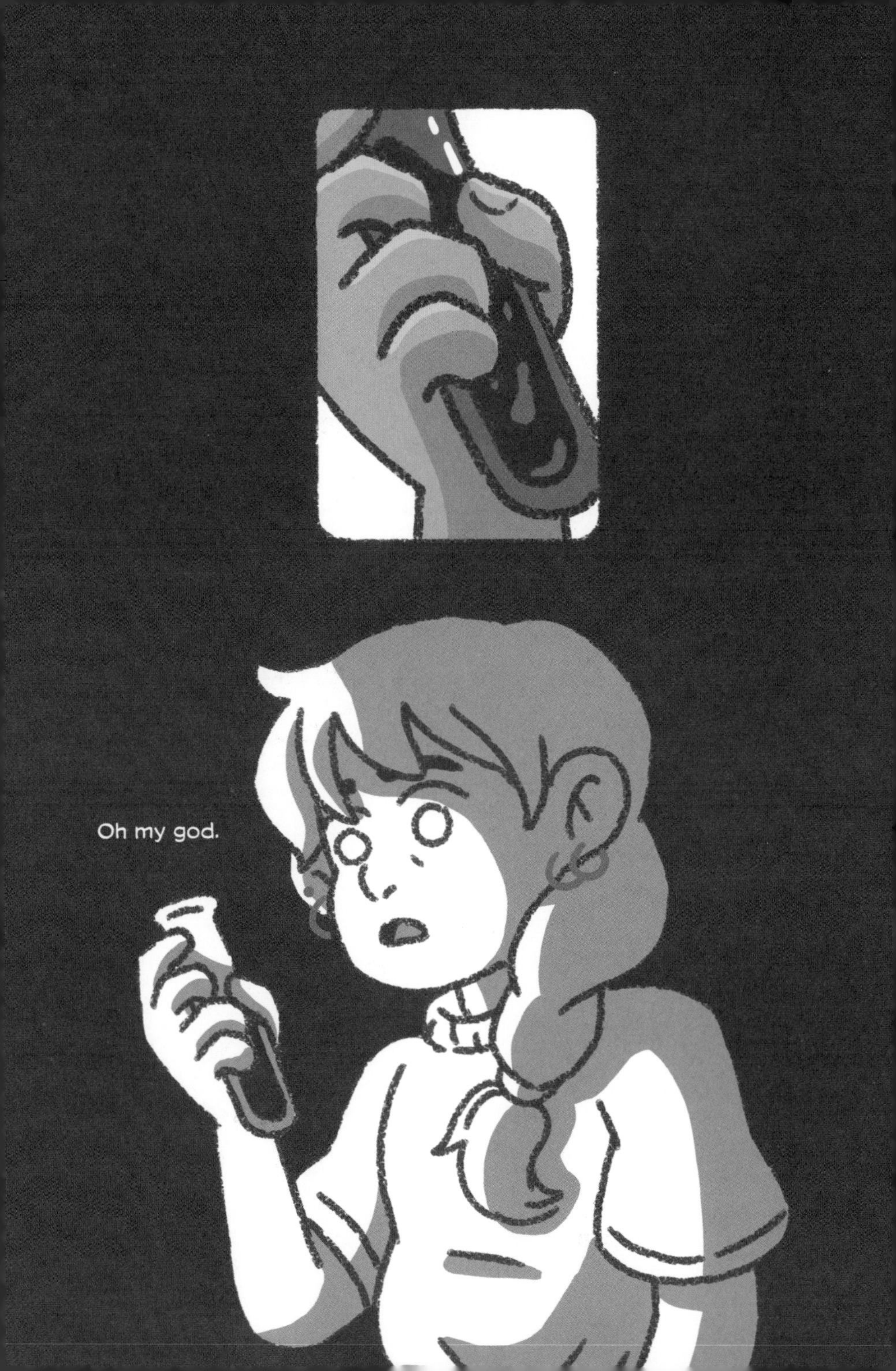
Oh my god.

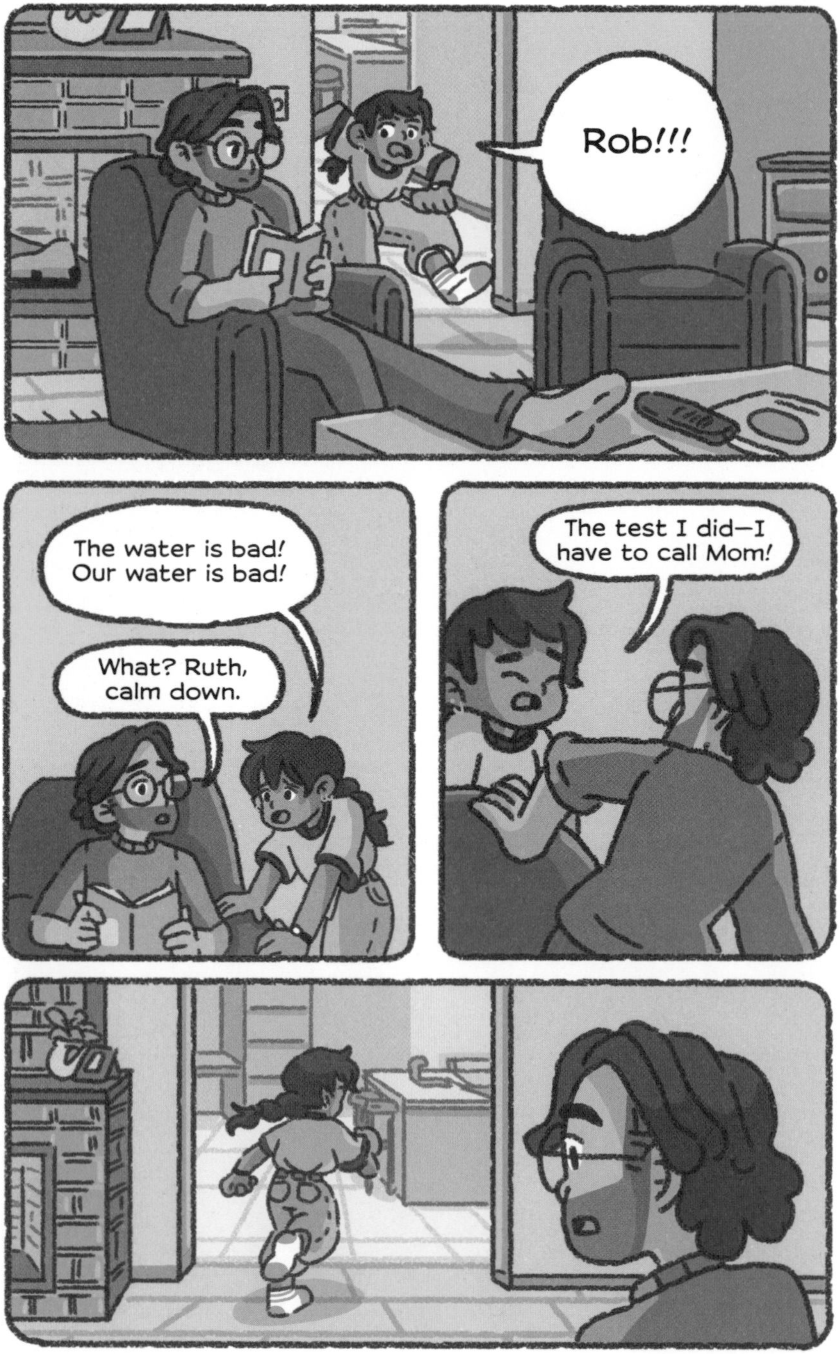
Rob!!!
The water is bad! Our water is bad!
What? Ruth, calm down.
The test I did—I have to call Mom!

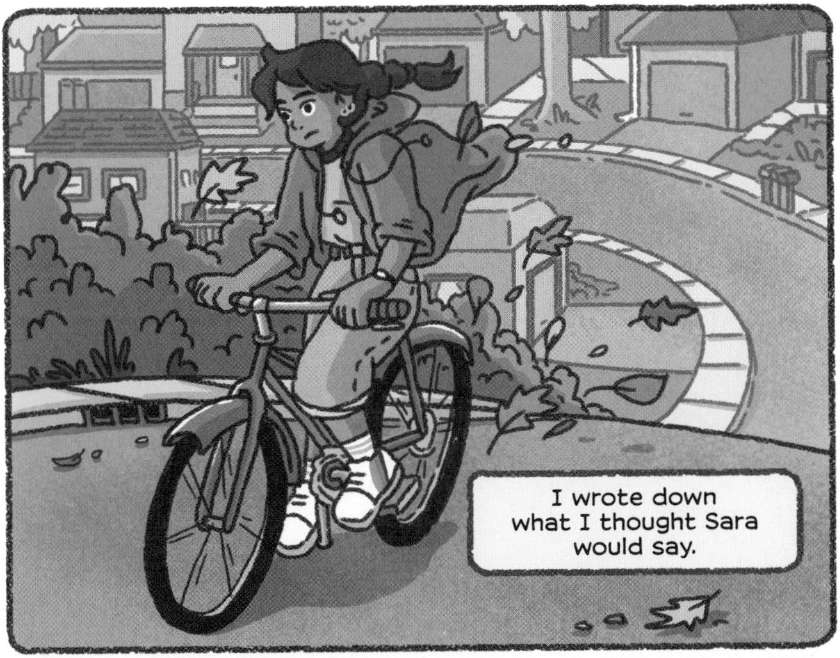
I wrote down what I thought Sara would say.

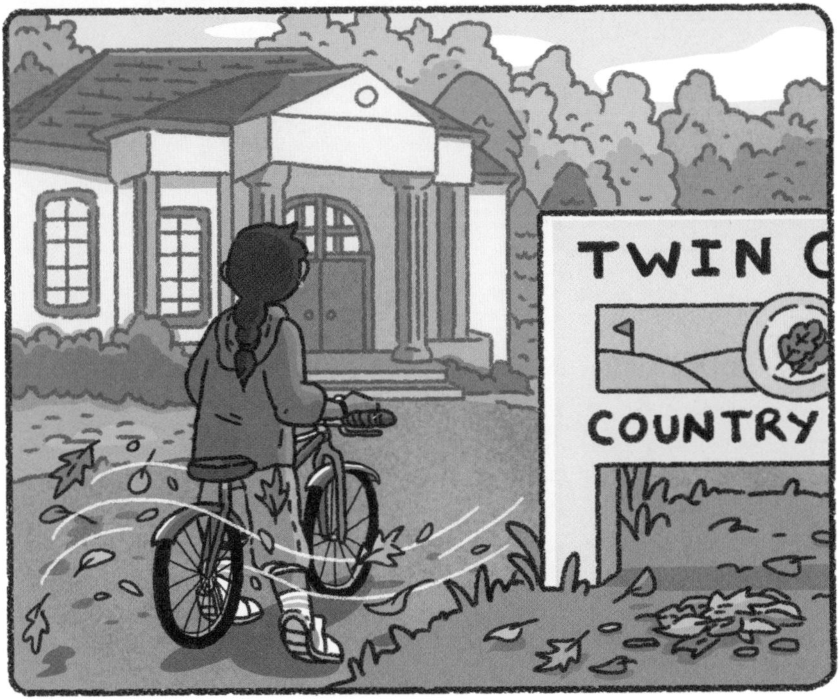
TWIN
COUNTRY

196

CHAPTER 5

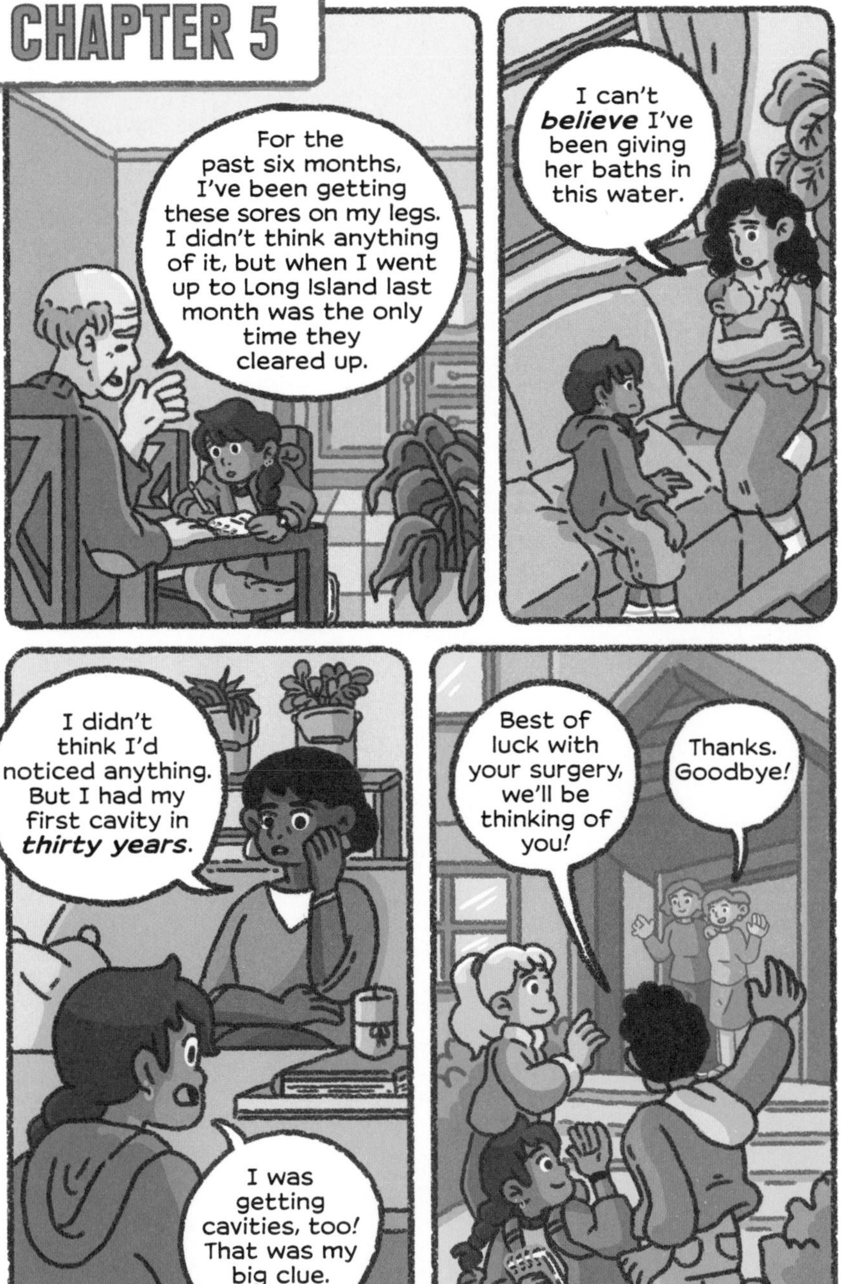
For the past six months, I've been getting these sores on my legs. I didn't think anything of it, but when I went up to Long Island last month was the only time they cleared up.
I can't *believe* I've been giving her baths in this water.
I didn't think I'd noticed anything. But I had my first cavity in *thirty years*.
I was getting cavities, too! That was my big clue.
Best of luck with your surgery, we'll be thinking of you!
Thanks. Goodbye!

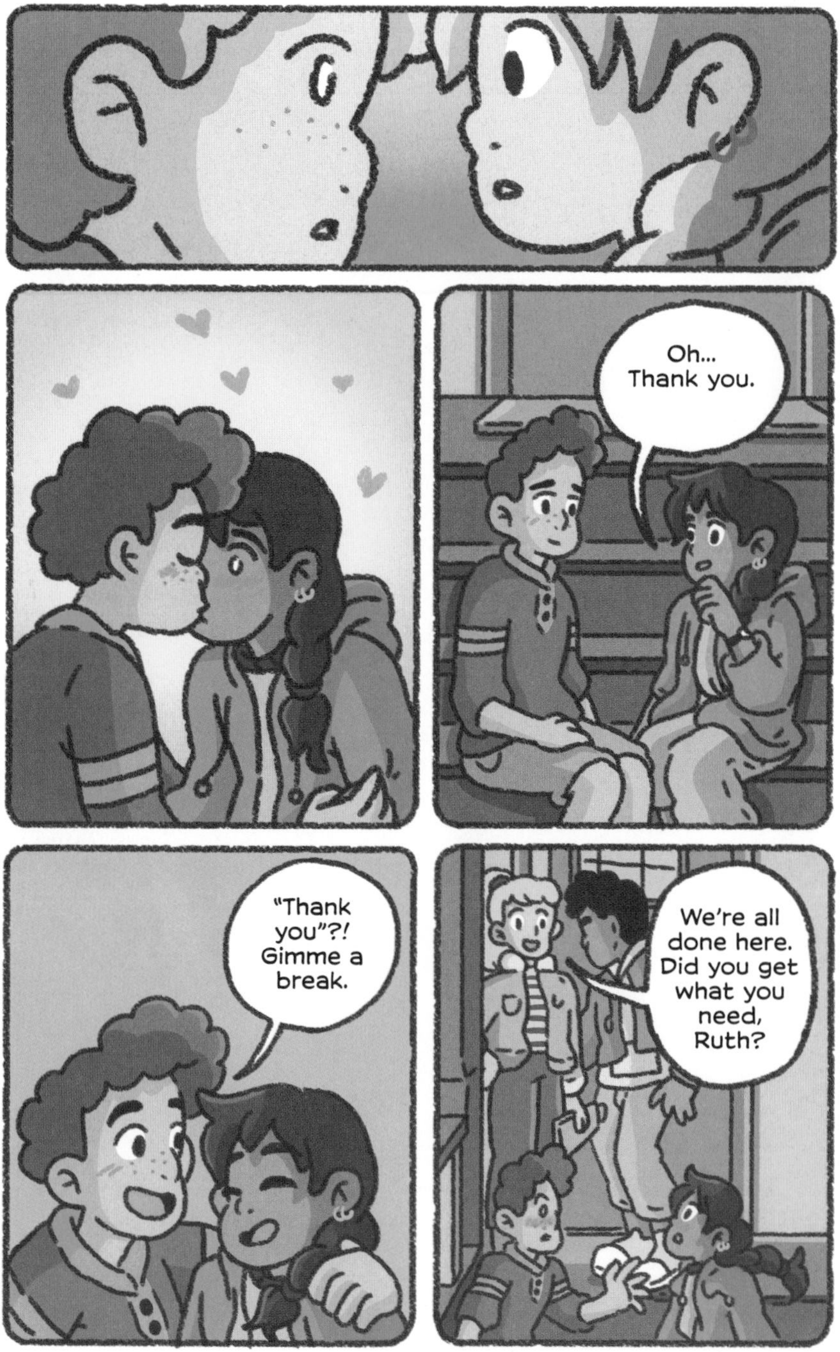
Oh...
Thank you.
"Thank you"?! Gimme a break.
We're all done here. Did you get what you need, Ruth?

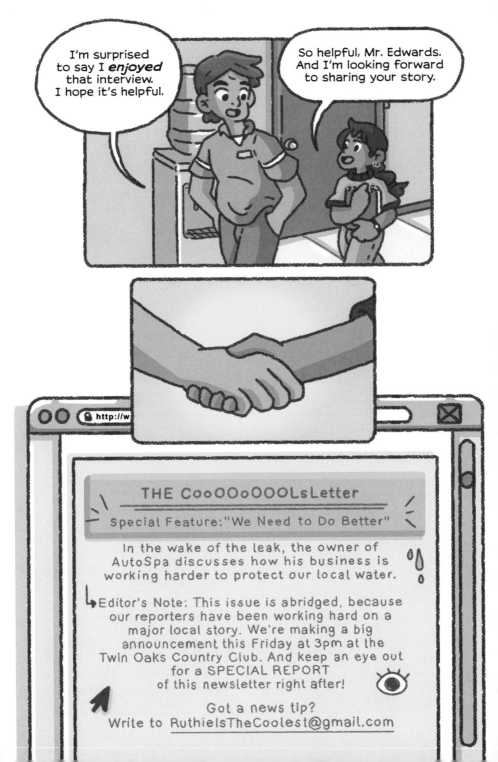

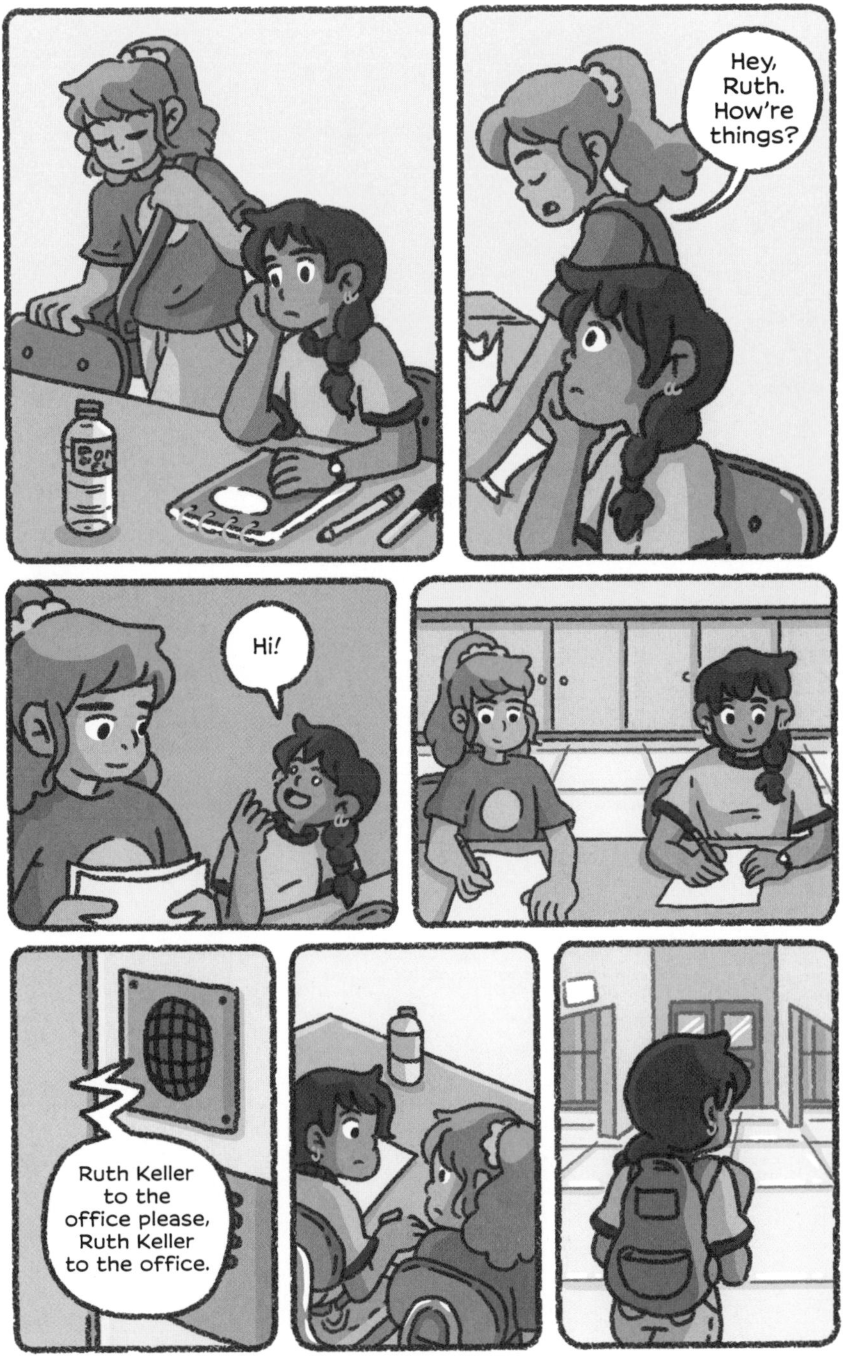
Hey, Ruth. How're things?
Hi!
Ruth Keller to the office please, Ruth Keller to the office.

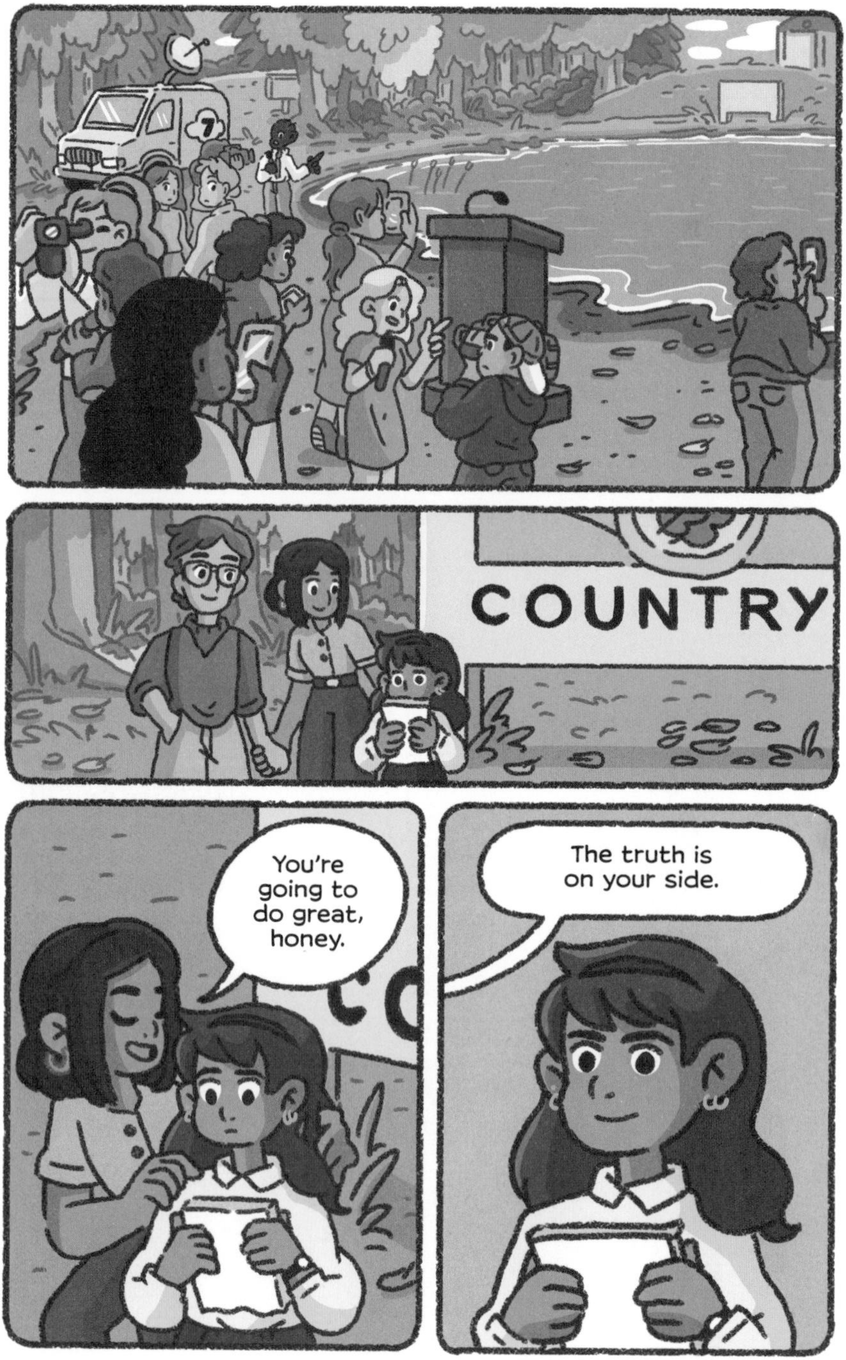
COUNTRY
You're going to do great, honey.
The truth is on your side.

219

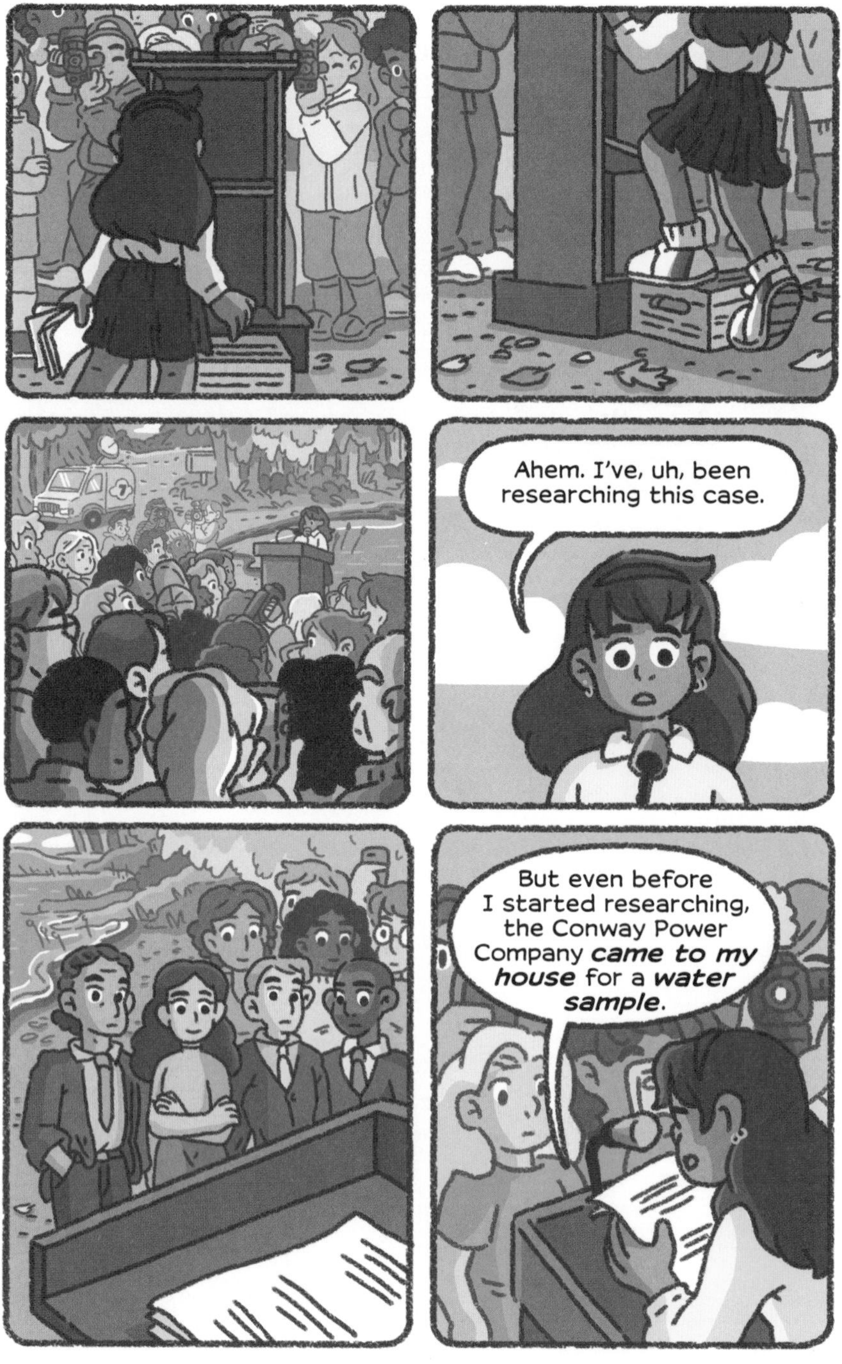
Ahem. I've, uh, been researching this case.
But even before I started researching, the Conway Power Company ***came to my house*** for a ***water sample***.

223

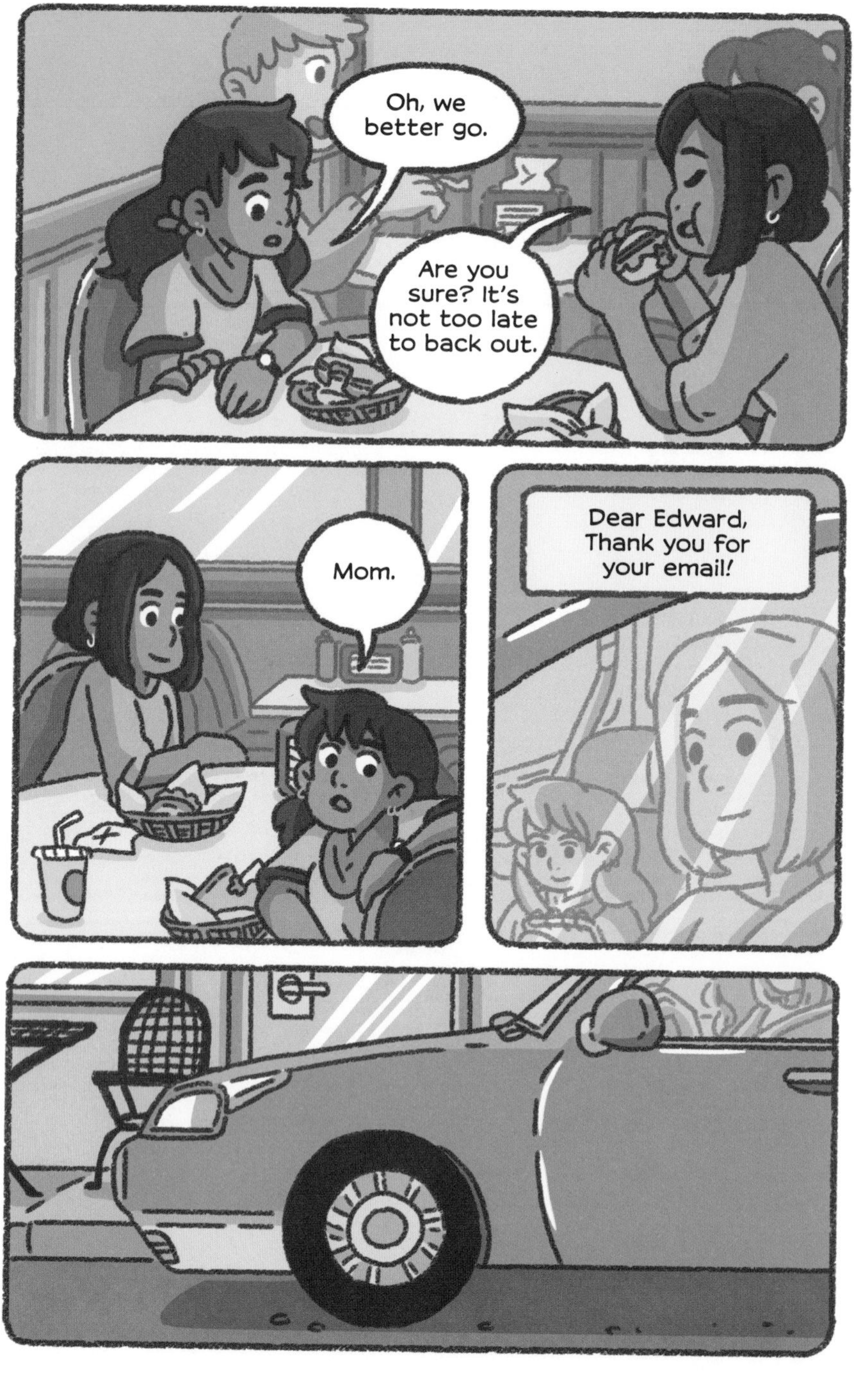
Oh, we better go.
Are you sure? It's not too late to back out.
Mom.
Dear Edward, Thank you for your email!

230

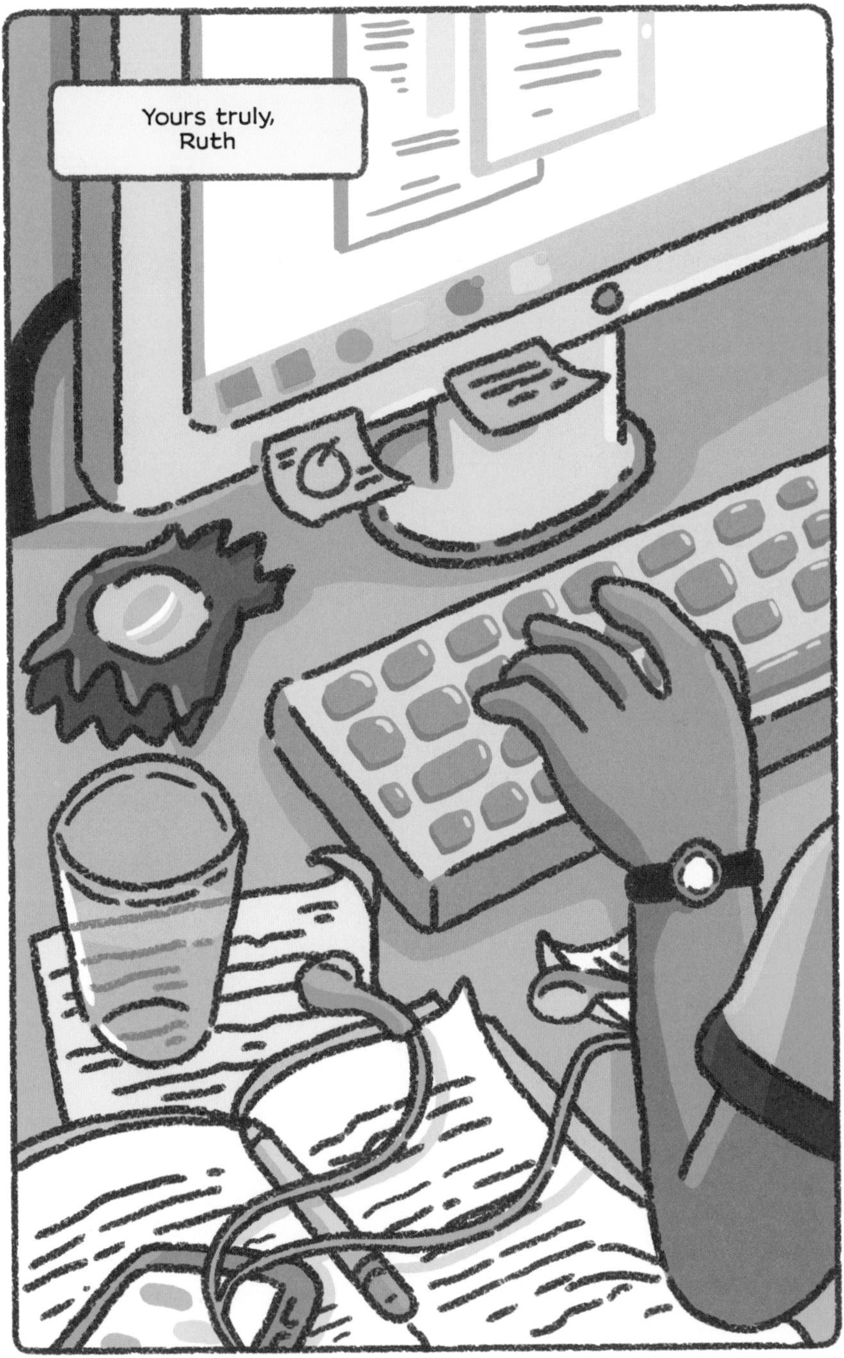
Yours truly,
Ruth

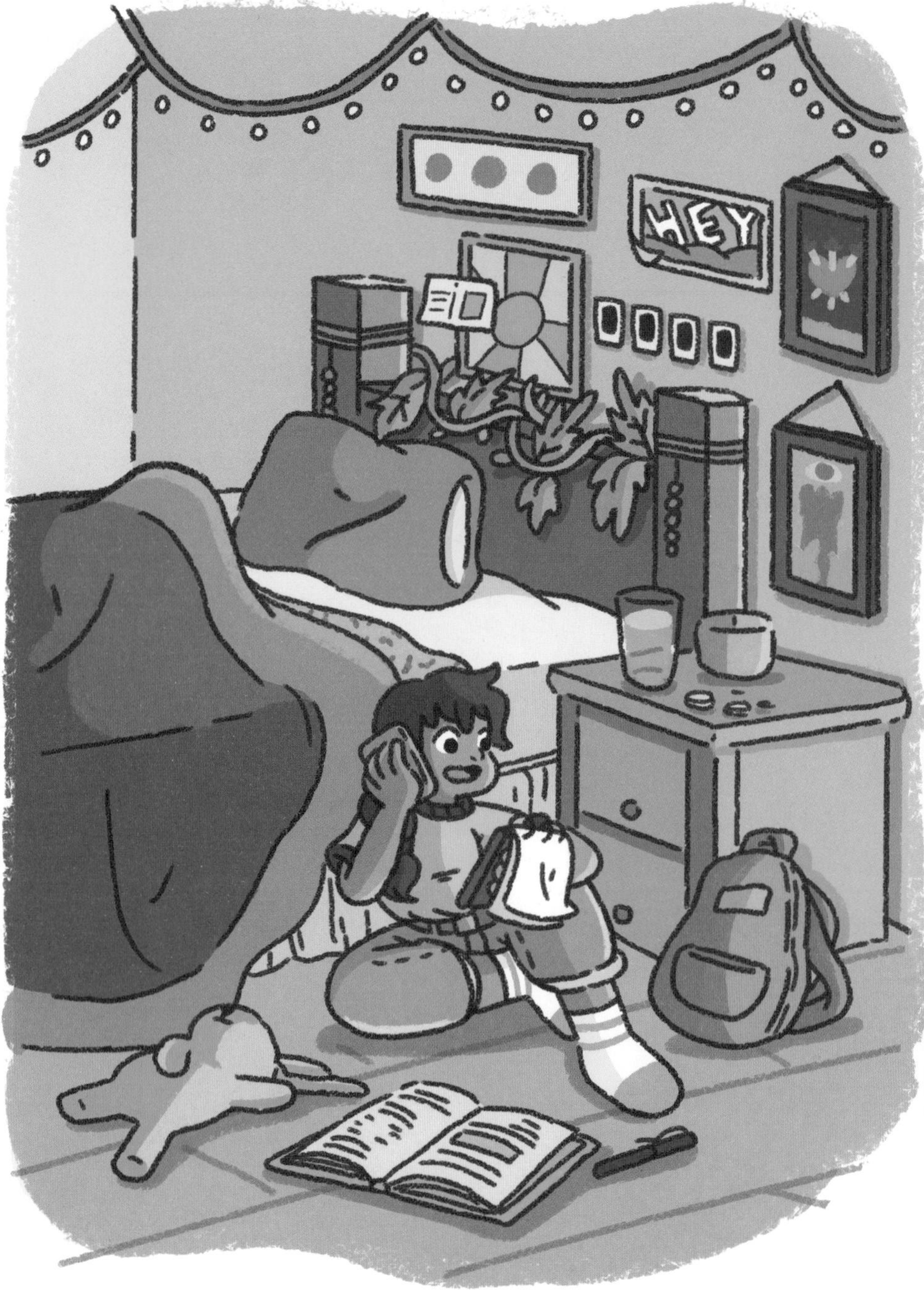
HEY

Afterword

Adults love to talk about how different the world is for young people like you. For example: Did you know that when I was a teenager, our internet connection ran through our telephone line, so I had to disconnect our phone to go online? Because of that, I almost never used the internet. (Because what if my crush called?!)

Actually, you probably knew that already. You, dear reader, know a lot more than I did at your age. Because you have the internet! Knowledge and information are super available to you. (Plus your crush is more likely to text than call.) That is a wonderful thing.

But the bad news is, with so many sources of information available, it is harder to decide which sources deserve your trust. The term "fake news" is a good example of how confusing things can be. Some people say "fake news" to describe falsehoods disguised as journalism. Others use "fake news" to attack real journalism. Although we have millions of ways to get news and knowledge (and messages from our crushes), there are so many divergent opinions, and so many people who seem so sure of opposite things, that it can be hard to sort through them all.

How do we decide what, and whom, to trust?

I was thinking about this question when I decided to write *The Leak*. At its heart, Ruth's is a story about how we decide what is true, and how we share the truth with others. In our society, the discipline of journalism is one of the most powerful means we have to answer these questions—to figure out and honor the truth.

That is why Ruth becomes a journalist. In the beginning, Ruth starts her newsletter because she is curious about the world. She wants to explore, and she wants to share what she learns with her friends. She has good intentions, but she makes mistakes that put her reputation at risk. Ruth becomes a true journalist only once she learns what it means to be objective and fair, to cite her sources, and to admit when she is wrong.

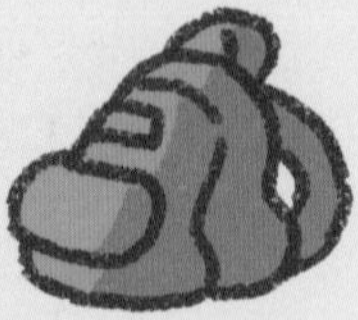

These are the principles that define journalism. Long before "fake news" was a thing, powerful people who wanted to lie, cheat, and steal have tried to manipulate the news so that they didn't get caught. They have published false information, withheld real information, and spread nasty rumors about journalists to prevent their own misdeeds from being exposed. Luckily for us, journalists have stood firm, working according to a code of ethics, and we can always check for ourselves to see if a journalist is sticking to that code, if they merit our trust.

Trustworthy journalists talk to people with firsthand knowledge of and experience with news and events. They cite experts. They describe events objectively, sticking to facts that can be proven, and they are clear about what is unknown. They offer multiple perspectives, not just the most powerful ones. And if they get something wrong, they issue a retraction or a correction (which is a handy rule of thumb: Does your news source issue retractions and corrections? Everyone gets things wrong sometimes—never trust someone who won't admit it.)

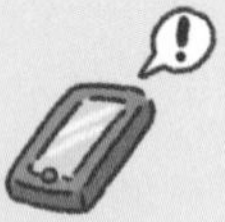
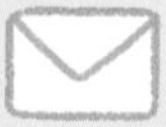
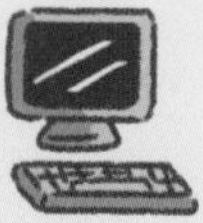

I started this note wanting to tell you that the world has changed. But the truth is, you and I are part of the same human story. That is the story of people doing their best to stand up for the truth—even when the truth is painful or difficult—and to protect others from harm.

That is the story of the water crisis in Flint, Michigan, which Ruth and her friends learn about in Ms. Freeman's science class. In Flint, people could see for themselves that the water coming out of their taps was polluted. But government officials held press conferences and released reports that told everyone not to worry, that the city's water supply was clean and safe. It wasn't until scientists and journalists, working together, established the truth—and made sure everyone knew it—that the city officials were brought to account and the lead-tainted water crisis began to be addressed.

And you are part of that human story, too. You don't have to be a journalist; you could be a scientist, a teacher, an activist, or a doctor. Or you could be a comics artist, telling these stories for future generations in graphic form. What matters is that you honor the truth.

The world is shifting fast—the weather, the oceans, the shape of the landscape, and humankind, too. When you think about it at that global scale, it can seem overwhelming, as if there's nothing you can do.

But you don't have to give up. Because at the local level, in your community, nothing is inevitable. If someone (often a corporation) wants to pollute your water, to ignore people's illnesses, and to generally abuse the earth we share, they will also want you to believe that there is nothing you can do to stop them. And that, dear reader, is just not true.

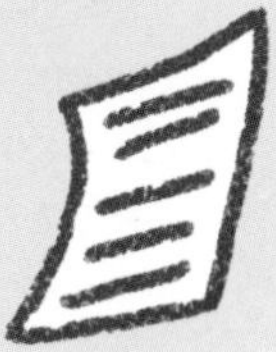

You will always have a voice. It may be hard at first, but if you keep speaking up, eventually people will listen. So be sure you are speaking the truth.

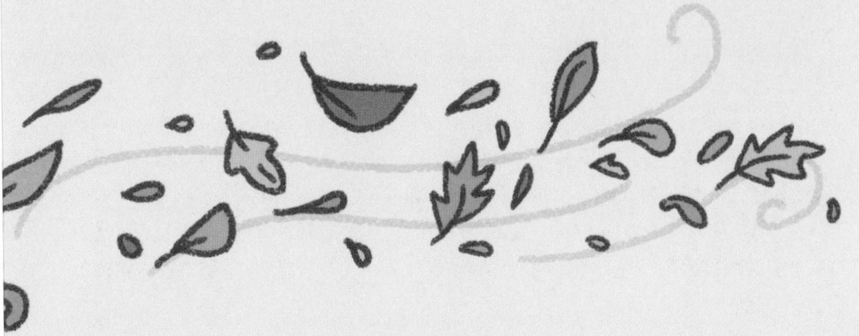

Acknowledgments

So many thanks to Mark Siegel, a wise and wonderful editor, artist, mentor, and friend; you made this book the best it can be. Thank you to Robyn Chapman, Kirk Benshoff, Samia Fakih, Sunny Lee, and everyone at First Second for always being available and encouraging. We are so grateful for the heartfelt work you put into this book!

From Kate:

Thank you to *Detroit Free Press, Michigan Live, The New York Times,* and *NPR* for providing trustworthy journalism about water quality issues in communities around the United States, including Flint, Michigan; your reporting informed this story.

Thank you to Emily Forland, who is the very best. Thank you to JT Petty for reading all the earliest drafts, and to Zoe Brunton for reading the very last. Thank you Lina Brunton and Emily Meredith for reading, too. Thank you Oliver Baranczyk for everything. And thank you thank you *thank you* to Andrea Bell for lending your gorgeous, singular talent to Ruth's story— you brought this book to life.

From Andrea:

Thank you to my favorite dad for your unwavering support and love. Thank you to all the friends who fed me, made sure I was drinking enough water, and let me lean on them during the process of making this book. Y'all really are the best cheerleaders. Lastly, a special thank you to Kate for creating such a poignant story that speaks to all ages, but especially to the precocious young Andrea still in my heart.